THE
LIGHTNING'S
CLAIM

First edition: November 2020

BALIANT PUBLISHING

https://www.kmfahyauthor.com

Cover Design by Maria Spada

https://www.mariaspada.com

Edited by Emma O'Connell

https://emmasedit.com

Formatted by Clare Kae

https://www.clarekae.com

ISBN (paperback): 978-1-7361672-1-2

ISBN (e-book): 978-1-7361672-0-5

ACKNOWLEDGMENTS

To all those who've taken this crazy journey with me.

To Katie, my best friend, who gave me the strength every single day to get up and write again. Your endless encouragement, love, and 4 a.m. reading made this book a reality, and I can never thank you enough.

To Katie A. and Clare, my Skittle Sisters. Your wisdom and support throughout this publishing process made all the difference in my life. You are both so giving, so generous, and two of the most incredible women I have ever met.

To Nicholas, my creative sounding board, filler of plot holes, and constant source of inspiration. You've motivated my writing since the day we met, and gave me the courage I needed to share my work with the world.

To Alicia and Jena, who watched this book grow from its conception and helped me turn those whacky concepts into something beautiful. You taught me so much about writing, and have cheered me on every step of the way.

And, because I always said I would when it came time to publish: To my dear friends at the Old Chicago bar in Greeley, Colorado, where I wrote the vast majority of these words. You've treated me like family, and always kept the Blue Moon and laughter flowing.

Thank you.

CONTENTS

CHAPTER 1

Kitieri chose her steps wisely. The cobblestones along the dilapidated street jutted up at odd angles, waiting to trip the next person foolish enough to lift their gaze, and the last thing she needed was a sprained ankle to put her out of work.

Especially when I'm this close.

Slipping her hand into the pocket of her leather jacket, her fingers brushed the small pebbles that had congregated in the deepest corner of the lining. Every day of hard labor, every bit earned, brought her closer to freedom.

Kitieri blew a stream of air through pursed lips, shaking her hand free of the pocket's confines to wrap both arms tightly around her aching body. Across the street, a fire element lit the lantern hanging outside his rickety front door with a snap of his fingers before returning to his work, and Kitieri squinted against the setting sun to catch a glimpse of the day's project—a small doll, it seemed.

She smiled wistfully. Though they'd never spoken, she always admired the process and artistry of the fire's woodworking, burning away tiny pieces with his red-hot fingertips to create art. Every day, as she passed his house on her way home from the mines, she longed for such a useful element. Hells, *anything* other than the curse with which she'd been saddled would be an improvement.

Fire glanced up to catch her stare, and Kitieri shot her gaze back down to the cobblestones, ashamed. Wishing didn't put food on the table. Her shovel did.

With her next breath, Kitieri tasted the hint of tangy electricity on the air, and she froze in the middle of the street. Someone rammed into her shoulder from behind, knocking her forward.

"Watch it!" the man shouted, throwing his dirty, calloused hands into the air. Kitieri ignored him, lifting her eyes to the sky. Spattered with the vivid golds, pinks, and purples of the setting sun, it betrayed no hint of the terror that roiled above the clouds. As she lifted one hand into the breeze, the familiar tingling sensation touched her fingers.

A Strike was close.

Kitieri quickened her pace, slipping past the man who'd run into her and others in the oblivious crowd. Most were weary miners, like her, coming home from work, but none could smell the mounting charge... and this one was coming fast. She didn't need to look to know that there was not a life-saving Gadget among the crowd. Not in *this* part of town. Here, those who could not afford to buy the protection simply died, and the Blue Killer did not give second chances.

The first warning sent a hot pulse through Kitieri's body, jarring her insides and stealing her breath away. Screams erupted from the crowd as people fled for shelter, and Fire abandoned the unfinished doll on his chair to rush inside and slam the door behind him. Kitieri kicked into a full sprint, cobblestones be damned, even as cold dread churned in her stomach.

It's too far.

She'd never make it home before the three warnings were up and one poor soul lost their life. To step outside was to dance with death, and the Blue Killer always claimed a victim.

The second warning hit, stronger than the first, eliciting a gasp from Kitieri as she stumbled. Windows and doors slammed shut all along the street; it was every man for himself when the warnings started, and no one took risks on a stranger.

Kitieri swore, glancing around for her best chance at survival.

Find a shelter. Any shelter.

The Strike's range usually only spanned about one neighborhood, and once or twice she'd managed to escape its clutches by simply running, but the best chance always rested with a roof and walls.

The third and final warning knocked Kitieri to her knees; her palms hit the cold, damp cobblestones as electricity pulsed through her body in sickening waves. Shaking, she forced a deep breath into her lungs.

The atmosphere shifted, and Kitieri felt the eye of the Strike appear. Its energy called to hers, an unholy screech only she could hear, and its burning gaze swiveled. The invisible demon skittered above the clouds, hungry for death as it swept over the remaining panicked stragglers in the street to fix its eye on her. It had made its choice, and it was ready to kill.

Kitieri launched to her feet, sprinting down the treacherous road as the Strike followed, gathering its hateful energy. No matter how fast she ran, she would be reduced to a pile of ashes in mere seconds if she didn't find shelter.

Turning, she spied a squat structure nestled back between two houses with a low-lying window, and ran for her life as the Strike readied itself.

"I don't think so," she growled.

Her muscles screamed as she pushed her body at full speed, running on adrenaline alone. She kicked off the ground onto a square bale that had fallen from its pile beneath the window and launched herself through the glass, elbows first. It shattered under the impact, flying all around her as she hit the floor, and a flash of blue split the sky with a deafening crack.

Kitieri lay frozen, body trembling, with her arms still poised over her head. The light outside returned to the muted shades of dusk, and she let out a long, shaky breath.

"Holy shit," she whispered.

Thousands of tiny glass shards clinked and fell to the floor as she lowered her arms and rolled onto her side. When she looked up, several pairs of beady, glinting eyes were watching her from across the dim room, and she jumped back against the wall.

One of the creatures stepped from the shadow.

Goats.

Kitieri's hand flew to her chest with a relieved sigh, and she tilted her head back with a dark laugh.

"Thank you, nonexistent gods, for sparing my insignificant life," she declared with a mock bow as she regained her feet. "I am not worthy of your grand punishment."

She brushed the dirt off her black pants and jacket and shook the remaining pieces of glass out of her long, pale hair. Minor cuts laced the backs of her hands and similar pricks of pain dotted her face, but it was nothing that wouldn't heal in a day or two.

"Gods, my ass," she muttered. The nearest goat ducked its head, brown eyes still fixated on her with those weird, horizontal pupils, and she frowned. "What do *you* want?"

The goat twitched its ears and sauntered back to its companions, who had already lost interest in their unexpected visitor. Kitieri walked to the window, where jagged pieces stuck out all around the edges, and chewed the inside of her lip. Though glass was fairly inexpensive in Shirasette, even the smallest of setbacks could put a family under in this district.

She plunged her hand into her jacket pocket and fished out the four little chips of black stone — her day's pay. So little for such exhausting labor. But if she worked even harder over the next few days, maybe she could—

The loud bleat of a goat startled her out of her thoughts, and she jumped. With a soft sigh, Kitieri set two of the bits down on the windowsill amidst the glass shards.

"Sorry about your window," she said to the goat, and let herself out the stable door.

She had not taken three steps before she spotted the corpse, charred and smoking in the grass. It looked to be a large bird, perhaps a raven or hawk. The smell of burning feathers and flesh filled her nose, and she turned her head away. Though the lightning sought out human blood whenever possible, there was always a victim. She'd been a split second away from that bird's fate, she knew, and suddenly the price of two bits for a window *and* her life didn't seem so steep.

Kitieri returned to the main street, now utterly abandoned. A few window shutters opened up, but the day was effectively over for these working folk. A chill settled in the air as the sky grew darker, and Kitieri set a brisk pace toward home.

At the sight of the little hut, she released the breath she'd been holding and covered the rest of the distance at a jog. As the door swung open into the dark interior, a high-pitched shriek greeted her ears.

"Kitieri!"

Two small forms bolted from the shadows, and she dropped to one knee to welcome her younger siblings into her arms.

"We were so afraid the lightning got you!" Jera cried.

"We felt the warnings here," Taff added.

Kitieri pulled back, smoothing the straight blonde hair on both heads. Taff was the middle sibling, five years older than Jera but seven years Kitieri's junior.

"Not even close," she lied. "Jera, why don't you light the lantern?"

"Really?" Jera's innocent face broke into a wide smile, and Kitieri grinned back. She could afford to relax the rules for just one night. A bit of light and warmth might do them all some good.

"Really," she confirmed. "Taff, bring out the rest of the meat and cheese, and we can have a proper feast tonight. How about that?"

Beaming, Jera ran for the matches. Taff stayed put, folding his arms across his narrow chest.

"'Not even close,' huh?" He raised one eyebrow, but kept his voice down. "What's with all the cuts on your face, then?"

Kitieri raised a hand to touch her cheek, where the cool night air had numbed the sting during her walk home. She sighed, standing up from her kneeling position, and suppressed a grimace at the protest of her stiff muscles. Taff's brow twitched in concern, and she laid a hand on his shoulder.

"I'm fine, Taff," she said. "There's no reason to get Jera worked up over something that didn't happen."

Taff studied her for a moment, but let the subject drop.

"Can we afford that?" he asked, jerking a thumb over his shoulder to where Jera was dragging the heavy metal lantern onto the kitchen table.

"It's all right," she assured him. "I'll go to the market tomorrow after work. We can't live our entire lives starving in the dark."

"I wish you'd let *me* go to the market for you," Taff sighed.

"No," Kitieri said. "Until I can afford the Gadget, you and Jera are only safe here."

He dropped his gaze to his feet, and Kitieri gave his shoulder a light shake.

"Hey," she whispered. "I know this is hard on you, but we're close."

Taff looked up at her, surprise flashing in his eyes.

"*How* close?"

Before Kitieri could answer, Jera came rushing back with the big lantern grasped in both hands, lighting up their faces in the warm glow.

"Thank you, Jera!" Kitieri took the lantern and hung it from its hook in the wall. "Now how about that feast, Taff?"

With a defeated grin, her brother walked to the pantry, Jera bouncing after him.

As their good-natured squabbling commenced, Kitieri slipped into her and Jera's shared bedroom to pull off her leather jacket. It had been an unusually expensive gift from her father to her mother many years ago, and Kitieri cherished its strong, yet supple material. She wondered from time to time if her mother would be proud or disappointed that she wore it in the cintra mines for its protection against the harsh wind. Disappointed was the most likely of the two, she imagined. She'd always fit into that category when compared to her talented elemental siblings.

Kitieri hung the jacket on the rack, dragging her fingers down one of the soft sleeves.

"I wish you worked against Strikes like you do against wind," she mumbled. But only the cintra-laden Gadgets worked against those. The idiotic-looking, *impossibly* expensive backpacks were the ultimate sign of wealth throughout Shirasette, and miners were never supposed to be able to afford them.

Pulling the remainder of her day's pay from the jacket's pocket, Kitieri crossed to the wide, squat dresser and pulled out the box in which her mother had kept their family keepsakes. Kitieri had long ago sold anything of value, and it now held her savings from the past three years.

She opened the lid and stared at the collection of shiny black stones. Pushing the small bits aside with her finger, she pulled out the two caps at the bottom of the box. The flat, polished stones almost took up her entire palm.

Kitieri still remembered holding her first cap after exchanging a thousand bits at the Church of Enahris. She recalled the man's annoyed look as he'd counted one thousand rocks out onto the table, but that was how the mines paid her, and she'd made it a point to avoid both Churches when possible. Nothing good happened in those places, as her father used to say.

But after almost three years, her little box held two caps, nine rounds, and ninety-two bits. Examining the two remaining bits after the window disaster, Kitieri reluctantly set them aside. She'd told Taff she'd go to the market tomorrow, and putting money promised to other things into her savings felt like a lie. If she could get some good bargains and save all of her pay for the next two days, she would finally have enough to buy a Gadget.

Two more days.

She closed the box, daring to let the grin cross her face. She had worked herself to the bone for this, and her eighteen-year-old body felt closer to forty from the constant digging and hauling. Still, she had to admit, she was luckier than some. The mines were protected from Strikes with all the cintra buried in the hills, leaving her vulnerable only on her way to and from work. Everyone knew it was a trap, keeping miners in the never-ending cycle of labor for pitiful wages, but it had been her only option when their parents had died. *Someone* had to provide for Taff and Jera.

Kitieri closed the drawer and walked back to the main room, where Taff was arranging the meats and cheeses on a wooden platter. Kitieri leaned against the doorframe, watching him swat playfully at Jera as she reached for bits of food before he was done.

"Kitieri!" Jera noticed her reappearance and ran to her. "Look what I learned today!"

Kitieri pushed off the frame with her elbow, squinting down at Jera's outstretched palms in the soft lamplight. Her sister's face was screwed up in concentration, and her hands trembled with the effort. Kitieri frowned. Was Jera really trying to…?

A sheen covered Jera's palms, and Kitieri's eyes widened.

"Jera!"

"Keep watching!" the girl ordered, keeping her focus on her hands. The sheen of moisture condensed into bigger droplets that rolled down her fingers to pool in her palms, and she looked up at Kitieri with big gray eyes full of pride.

Kitieri barked a short laugh. "Jera, that's incredible! I've never heard of anyone creating their element from nothing at your age before!"

Jera flicked her hands up, sending the tiny pools of water into an evaporated puff between them.

"I know water is one of the easiest to learn because our bodies and the air already have so much of it," she said with a shrug.

"Oh yeah?" Kitieri asked. "How did you hear that?"

"Mama's books," Jera replied, pointing to the wide bookcase along the wall near the door. Kitieri's gaze followed her finger, surprised. She'd all but forgotten that bookcase existed after she'd been laughed out of the marketplace for trying to sell them. No one had the money or time for books in this part of town.

Another memory bubbled to the surface, unbidden, and she saw her mother holding the thick instructional book on wielding the elements in an attempt to teach her eldest daughter. Shame wriggled into Kitieri's gut at the memory of her failure, and she turned back to her sister.

"Well, you have a talent, Jera," she said. "With a real education, you could become one of the best water elements I've ever seen."

"Really?" Jera squeaked. Kitieri nodded, smiling down at her sister's beaming face.

"And you, Taff?" She looked up at her brother. "How is your practice coming?"

Taff raised his head, as if he hadn't been paying attention to the rest of the conversation. He lifted his right hand in a fist, snapping the fingers open with a burst of fire. Flipping his hand over, he shaped his element into a perfect fiery sphere like a bouncy ball, and threw a mischievous look at his little sister.

"Ready, Jera?"

Jera straightened, putting out both hands as Taff tossed the fireball to her. The flame extinguished in her wet palms with a hiss, and she broke into a fit of giggles.

"Very impressive," Kitieri said, clapping. "How long have you two been practicing that?"

"Just today!" Jera jumped up and down. "*Please* show us yours, Kitieri!"

Kitieri put a hand on Jera's head, smoothing her hair.

"Jera, you know I don't practice my element," she said, moving past her to the table. "Come eat, now."

"Why not?" Jera whined, coming to her seat across from Kitieri.

"You know why."

"But you could be really good, and not even know it!"

"We are not discussing it, all right?"

Kitieri picked up Jera's plate, and from the corner of her eye, caught a silent exchange between her siblings.

"Something you want to say?" She raised an eyebrow at Taff, who dropped his gaze.

"We — I — think you should practice again," he mumbled.

Kitieri set the plate down, leaning her full body weight on both hands.

"What is it with all this tonight? You both know why I don't practice. It's *way* too dangerous. We're lucky I locked it when I did, or we'd be worse off than we are now." She turned her attention back to the plates. "And besides, I spend all day making sure we have something to eat every once in a while. I don't have time for any of that now, unless it's in Gadget form."

Taff and Jera looked back to each other, but held their silence.

"Hey." Kitieri tilted her head. "Don't make me the villain, here. You both understand why I do what I do, right?"

Her siblings kept their eyes on the table.

"*Right?*"

They nodded in unison, and Kitieri sighed. "Come on, let's just have a nice dinner. This is a happy night. We're celebrating!"

"Celebrating what?" Jera's head snapped up.

"Your breakthrough, of course!" Kitieri raised her clay water cup. "To Jera!"

"To Jera!" Taff echoed, bringing a wide smile to her little face.

"To *me*!" she cried, kneeling on her chair to lean over the table and clink cups. Taff and Jera sat back as Kitieri finished filling her sister's plate.

"On your butt, please, Jera," she said, passing the plate to her. Jera grinned sheepishly, pulling her feet out from under her.

"There's nobody here but us," she mumbled.

"I know," Kitieri replied, "but we won't always be so isolated, and I don't want you growing up feral because I never taught you manners."

"Feral?" Jera cocked her head.

"Like a wild cat," Taff said. "You know, the ones that hiss and spit at you in the alleyways."

Jera turned wide, inquisitive eyes on him, and Kitieri felt a pang of guilt. The lightning had been a threat for Jera's entire life, and she'd spent very little time away from the safety of their house in her six years. Was it better to have known a world of freedom and lost it, she wondered, or to not know any different?

Her gaze drifted to Taff, who was miming a hissing cat, hunching his back and clawing the air with curved fingers. Taff had only been a baby when the lightning started, but he'd been able to see Shirasette on errands with their father as he got older. Back then, the Strikes had come only once or twice a week. Now their increasing violence and frequency made it harder and harder to leave the house without a Gadget, and that only made the damned things more expensive. Before long, a simple trip to the market would mean certain death for anyone outside the elite circles of the two Churches.

"Kitieri says we are close to getting a Gadget," Taff said to Jera, leaning over the table. Jera's face lit up brighter than the lantern.

"Then you'll be safe, Kitieri!" she cried.

"I'm not going to wear it," Kitieri said. "Taff will take it so he can help with the errands and go to work, and we can save even faster for one of your very own. How does that sound?"

"A Gadget... for *me*? So I can meet the alleycats?" Jera's hands smacked flat on the table, her jaw dropping open. Kitieri laughed.

"Yes. Then I will take you to meet the alleycats."

In the back of her mind, Kitieri hoped there were some cats left to show her. She had seen precious few street animals in the past year, now that she considered it. But, that aside, Jera deserved a life outside these walls.

"But if I go to work, Jera," Taff said, "you'll be spending a lot more time alone here."

Jera looked at him, uncertain. "Alone?"

"Come on, Taff," Kitieri said, nudging him with her elbow. "Jera's a big girl now."

"Yeah!" Jera's shout filled the small room. "I can take care of my*self*."

"That's right." Kitieri smiled, extending one hand to Taff and the other across the table to Jera. Her siblings placed their hands in hers, soft and smooth in her callused palms. "Remember what Dad always said," she told them. "'The Manons will always survive.'"

CHAPTER 2

Kitieri forced the shovel into the steep hillside, ignoring the pain in her blistered hands. The thin black gloves did little against the metal handle, and she'd pushed herself harder than normal over the past two days in hopes of that small bonus a productive worker sometimes received. The mines' operators made so much money that the piddly bits felt more like an insult, but money was money. If she had to walk straight through the hells of Enahris and Histan, she would be free of this place someday.

Kitieri pulled her shovel back, tossing its contents into the trough beside her. The dark soil filtered through a fine metal mesh over the top, and Kitieri sifted through the dirt with her hand.

A pale purple glint in the late afternoon sun caught her eye, and Kitieri pulled out one of the largest pieces of cintra she'd ever seen in her three years of work. She brushed away the excess soil, staring in awe at the plum-sized rock in her palm. The clean, perfect lines of the crystal caught the sun in flashes as she tilted her palm this way and that, admiring its natural beauty.

How many meals this could provide, she thought. Even the raw stuff sold for so much these days that a crystal of *this* size could probably buy an entire Gadget.

Kitieri shook her head, refusing to so much as entertain the thought of stealing. Even if it were feasible to smuggle it out, only the black market vendors would consider such a transaction, and she'd still incur unnecessary risk. If she was imprisoned for theft, Taff and Jera would be left alone with no care, no source of income, and no protection.

Her best chance with this rock was earning that bonus.

"Hey."

Kitieri jumped at the gruff voice behind her, reflexively closing her hand around the cintra as she spun around to face a black horse. Dressed in fine clothes and shining leather boots, its rider glared down at her.

"You seem mighty interested there," the man said. "Getting some big ideas?"

"No! No, I—" Kitieri stammered, falling over her words. Heat rushed to her face and neck, and the suspicion on the man's face deepened. He spurred the horse forward, holding out his open hand, and she braced herself for the fall of the riding crop across her shoulders as she dropped the cintra into his palm.

"I'm sorry," she stammered, "I've just never seen one that size before."

The overseer grunted, and Kitieri dared to glance up at him. His scowl bored into her, erasing any hope she'd still harbored for the bonus. She was lucky he hadn't laid into her with the crop yet or called for one of those full-body searches, but still her heart rebelled as she lowered her eyes back to her feet.

The leather saddle creaked, and hooves crunched on the gravel as the overseer turned his horse away.

"Get back to work," he barked over his shoulder. Kitieri reached for her shovel with a silent sigh, hoisting it to slam it into the rocky soil once more as several small objects pelted the arm of her jacket. Her eyes snapped open wide to see four bits hit the gravel at her feet.

Kitieri dropped to the ground so fast her head spun, scooping up the little black pebbles.

A full day's pay!

Tears sprang to her eyes as she cupped the bits in her hands. The overseer never looked back, riding away down the busy line of miners.

This was it. These four stones brought her total to three caps, and enough for a Gadget.

HOME WAS in sight when the first warning struck, vibrating through Kitieri's body in hot waves. Cries of shock and fear echoed off the buildings, and she felt the shift as electricity moved in the atmosphere. She'd felt the air thicken and had noticed the charge on the breeze a while back, but she'd thought she would make it before the warning. Eyes on her front door, she broke into a jog.

The piercing cry of a baby gripped her with icy fingers, and Kitieri stopped to look behind her. Across the street, a young, dark-haired woman bounced the child, muttering unintelligibly, hands shaking so badly it was a wonder she kept the baby in her arms. The woman cast about in panic and terror as people fled around her.

"Shit," Kitieri muttered under her breath. Taking in strangers just wasn't something people did when the Strikes came. The risks of being slowed down and killed, being robbed, or simply making a friend and becoming attached were all too great.

But as the child wailed in its mother's arms, the woman turned her wide, panicked eyes on Kitieri. Tear-tracks marked her dirty face as hopelessness set into the frail, gaunt features, and Kitieri growled in the back of her throat before running to her.

"Come on, follow me," she said, resting a hand on her arm. "I live right there. Take shelter with us."

The woman remained frozen, enormous dark eyes fixated on her. Kitieri tugged on her arm, nodding in encouragement as the second warning hit. The baby's cries doubled in urgency as they both ducked down against the shock, and Kitieri dragged them toward home. After the first few steps, the woman seemed to comprehend Kitieri's intention and started moving her feet, her sobs mingling with her child's screams.

Kitieri's hand was almost on the door when the third warning struck, knocking both of them to their knees; Kitieri threw her arms around the woman to keep the little one from hitting the ground.

"*Taff!*" she screamed. The door flew open. "Get the baby!"

Hands shot out to take the child, and Kitieri pushed the woman into the house in front of her. The door slammed shut behind them, wooden bolt falling into place as the deafening *crack* came outside and the garish blue light filled their home.

With the Strike passed, Kitieri turned to the woman.

"Are you all right?"

"My baby!" the woman cried, clambering to her feet. "Where's my baby?"

"Right here." Taff stepped forward, cradling the screaming bundle of blankets. The woman snatched the child from Taff's arms, pressing her lips against the wispy dark hair on its head. Sobs shook her body as she held the infant tight, rocking side to side.

"You saved us," she finally managed, lifting her head.

"Just glad I could help," Kitieri said. "This is Taff and Jera, and I'm Kitieri."

The woman nodded, a faint smile coming to her tear-stained face. On second glance, without the lines of terror marring her features, Kitieri realized she was younger than she'd thought—maybe twenty or twenty-one years old.

"W-well, Kitieri…" The woman sniffed, brushing a hand over her wet cheek. "Thank you… for what you did. I'm Noia, and this is my daughter, Vina."

Jera stepped forward, eyes wide and curious.

"Hi, Vina," she said, standing on her tiptoes to peek at the baby. "Aw, she has a little beauty mark on her cheek. See, I have one, too!"

Calming slowly from the ordeal, Vina fixed her huge eyes on Jera's face. Noia bent forward.

"Would you like to hold her?" she asked. Jera nodded, and held out her arms. As Noia passed the baby over, showing Jera how to hold her properly, Kitieri cleared her throat.

"So, home is a ways away, I take it?" she asked. Though she didn't look up, Noia's expression went flat and unreadable. "I just mean, because you couldn't make it there with the Strike. I mean, you weren't running…"

Noia met her eyes, and Kitieri snapped her mouth shut.

"We have no home," Noia said.

"What? How?" Kitieri asked. "How have you…"

The last thing she wanted was to appear insensitive, but she could not fathom how this woman had managed to live homeless with her baby amidst the lightning. Hells, even the cats were disappearing.

"It's our first night on the street," Noia said softly. "My husband, Histan bless him, was killed by the lightning two months ago, and we had very little saved. We lived off his pay from the mines."

"That's where Kitieri works!" Jera piped up.

Noia gave her a tight smile. "I can tell," she replied, looking back to Kitieri. "Your hands look just like his, covered in calluses and blisters."

Kitieri glanced down at her palms, which looked nothing like the soft hands of her element-wielding siblings; that was a life she had long ago left behind.

"What happened to your house?" Kitieri redirected the conversation.

Noia hung her head. "Without Beran's income, Vina and I were starving. You're supporting three on a miner's wages, too. Tell me, how long do you think your family would last if something happened to you?"

Kitieri glanced at Taff and swallowed, but let Noia continue.

"I sold everything we had. I tried to get work, but... my education was poor and the mines are no place for a baby. They wouldn't allow her even if I tried. When we used up our meager savings and ran out of food, I knew we had to leave. My only other option was to beg on the streets, exposing us both to the lightning."

Noia took a shuddering breath, just as Vina started fussing in Jera's arms. Taking the child back, Noia rocked her gently, gazing into her daughter's eyes.

"So," she continued, "I sold our house to a rich man for three caps."

"Oh." Kitieri needed no more explanation to understand this woman's plan. The idea of trading her home for a Gadget twisted Kitieri's stomach into a knot.

"We were heading for the Church of Histan when that Strike came," Noia went on. "They'll sell us the Gadget we need."

Kitieri swallowed, searching for the right words. Any words. The thought of this young mother and her child out on the streets, begging for bits and scraps of food from the cruel upper class with only a Gadget for protection, made her sick. She'd seen the men in red coats murder the poor like dogs in the street at a first warning when the Gadget-less begged for protection. She'd seen people beaten and robbed for the prized possessions. While she knew the Churches were the only place to acquire the Gadgets, Kitieri abhorred the thought of adding to their rich coffers. They wouldn't take Noia in, wouldn't offer her shelter... they'd simply take her money and turn her out to die.

They were nothing but heartless monsters running a monopoly on survival.

"I'll go with you, then," Kitieri said. "You can eat dinner here with us, and then we can walk to the Church of Histan together. We should be safe enough, since a Strike just passed."

"Oh, no." Noia shook her head. "You don't have to come with us. We'll be all right."

"Well, it just so happens that I'm also in the market for a Gadget tonight," Kitieri said.

Taff's head swiveled on his shoulders. "What? *Tonight*?"

Kitieri nodded, smiling as her brother's mouth fell open and the warmth of his joy spread through her tired body.

"So if you'll have me," she said to Noia, "I would love to accompany you after dinner."

Noia's eyes darted between the siblings, but her head bobbed in a slow nod.

"All right," she said. "I can't deny that we could use the meal and some company."

Kitieri smiled, and gestured to her brother. "Taff, light the lantern and grab an extra chair. Jera, will you set the table, please?"

As they sprang into action, Kitieri's heart felt fuller than it had in years. Not only was she finally in a position to help her own family, she had the means to help someone else, too. For the first time in three years, she thought, everything was going to be all right.

CHAPTER 3

The two made their way up the cobblestone street by moonlight, and Kitieri breathed in the crisp, clean air.

"It's a nice evening," she commented idly, looking over at Noia. The young woman looked nervous and uncomfortable. "What's the matter?"

"I just…" Noia looked down at Vina.

"What?" Kitieri prompted.

"We've never been out this late before, unprotected. I know we just had a Strike, but that doesn't mean anything. The lightning could come at any time."

Kitieri lifted her hand, feeling the soft breeze on her fingertips.

"What are you doing?" Noia asked, one cheek scrunching up in confusion.

"Testing the air," Kitieri replied, dropping her hand. "We're safe for now."

"How could you possibly know that?"

Kitieri avoided her gaze.

"I can feel it," she said. "The air gets thick and heavy before a strike, and it smells like metal. It's easy to breathe right now, which means we've got some time."

Noia continued to stare, looking at Kitieri like she was insane.

"Are you an electric element or something?" she asked.

"No," Kitieri said. "I can just feel it."

Silence fell between them, and Kitieri felt the heat flushing her cheeks.

"So." She cleared her throat. "You're a member of the Church of Histan, then?"

"Yes," Noia replied. "I was born into it."

Kitieri considered her next words. She had no wish to offend, but it was difficult to understand why anyone would go along with either of the Churches' tyrannical system of government, and the red officers that patrolled their district left a particularly bad taste in her mouth for Histan's Church.

"I'll be honest," she said, "I haven't heard much good about the Church of Histan. They seem a little..."

"Strict?"

"I was going to say brutal, but sure."

Noia shrugged. "I guess it could be called that. But they're the lawmakers. If they weren't like that, people would just do whatever they wanted."

"I guess," Kitieri said, brows furrowing. "Have you thought about going to the Church of Enahris? I heard another miner talking about how they'll sometimes help with food now."

"Yes," Noia replied, "I've heard their current Baliant is fairly generous, but they wouldn't help a member of the Church of Histan."

"I see."

"What about you?" Noia asked. "I've never seen you at services before, but it seems like you must belong to the Church of Histan as well."

Kitieri snorted. "Why, do I look the part?"

"No." Noia smiled with a soft blush. "You just live in their district and you're going to buy a Gadget from them, so I assumed. People only buy Gadgets from their own Church."

"Oh." Kitieri's grin faded. "No, my family doesn't belong to a Church."

Noia stopped in her tracks, and Kitieri turned back to her.

"What?"

"You're illegals?"

Kitieri laughed nervously, glancing over her shoulder. "Illegals? What are you talking about?"

"Everyone has to choose a Church," Noia said. "Most people stay with their Church of birth, but a child can choose to move when they come of age at fifteen. You didn't know this?"

Kitieri shook her head.

"My parents never told me that. They didn't agree with how the Churches ran the city, and never took us to any services or events. When they died, we just… kept living the same way. I took up my father's job in the mines, and we focused on survival. With no Gadgets in the family, we've stayed secluded from the rest of the city. But that's finally about to change." Kitieri shifted the bag that hung over her shoulder, reassuring herself that all the money was still there.

"What happened to them?" Noia asked.

"My parents?"

"If you don't mind me asking."

Kitieri watched her feet as they continued on their way, grappling with the deep emotions that lived beneath the surface.

"We assume it was the lightning," she said. "They went out to run an errand one day, and just… never came back. There was a Strike that afternoon, so we think that must be what happened."

"I'm so sorry," Noia whispered. "But—the Blue Killer only takes one. You think it took them both?"

"I always figured they held each other when they realized they couldn't escape it. It's the only thing that makes sense."

"That's so awful," Noia said. "I know how it felt when Beran didn't come home—I still cry every day. I can't imagine losing both parents in one Strike at that age."

Kitieri tried to swallow the lump in her throat.

"Everyone's lost someone," she said. "So many dead, and still nobody knows why it's happening."

"The Church says it's a punishment," Noia said.

"Yeah, yeah, I've heard that. It just doesn't make any sense to me."

"Why not?"

Kitieri scoffed. "It's just not how the lightning behaves. It's hungry for anyone—anything it can get. Hells, I've been targeted over and over, and I'm still here. So if it's a punishment and the gods are after me, they're doing a piss-poor job of it."

Noia stared at her. "Targeted?"

"Yeah," Kitieri said. "It fixates on you, and it's like you can look it right in the eye. Have you never felt that?"

"I… can't say that I have," Noia replied, frowning. "But punishment is what the Churches say."

"So according to them, your husband deserved to die. Do you believe that?"

Noia winced, and held Vina a little tighter to her chest. The baby made a soft cooing sound before slipping back into her slumber.

"I'm sorry," Kitieri muttered. "That was—"

"No, you're right," Noia said. Her eyes were sad, but the hurt was leaving their depths.Kitieri held her tongue as Noia processed her thoughts, walking in silence.

"We're taught that the lightning is meant to keep people in line," Noia continued, "but everyone I've known who's been killed was never anything but kind and good."

Kitieri's chest tightened as the faces of her parents flashed across her mind.

"I don't know," Noia continued, "maybe the Church is wrong. I was taught to never question their teachings, but why doesn't the lightning ever take the wicked?"

"Because they buy their security," Kitieri said, her voice coming out low and gravelly.

"That's true," Noia conceded. "Then, if not the divine, what do you think causes it?"

"I don't know." Kitieri sighed. "None of it makes any sense. My parents were two of the most loving, devoted people I have ever known. All the pieces of shit that deserve the lightning have Gadgets, so I guess they're immune to judgement. *Those* are the people that need a culling. The rest of us are out here working ourselves to death for pebbles, and they make absurd amounts of money off our labor. The entire system makes me sick."

Running out of breath, she sucked cool air into her lungs. She glanced at Noia, whom she expected to be looking at her like she was crazy again. Instead, she found knowing eyes and deep understanding.

"All I know," Kitieri continued, "is that the Churches don't care about the people. They're happy to let the poor die out here if it means they're safe. Even if the gods do exist, why would they create a world just to rip it apart with this kind of terror? The only explanation I can come up with is that we're some sick, twisted game for them. I can't find anything to worship in that."

Noia nodded solemnly. "I don't think our gods are evil, but it does feel some days as if maybe they've abandoned us."

"Are abandonment and lack of existence really all that different?"

Noia grinned. "I guess not."

Turning a corner, they came into view of the towering Church of Histan, set across from an open courtyard. Its light, smooth façade looked like the formidable wall of a great fortress, broken only by tall, narrow windows and the shadow of a balcony protruding above the main doors.

Apprehension clawed at Kitieri's heart; the mere sight of it made her want to turn around and go straight back home. She knew she had no choice, but she wished there was another way.

Noia noticed her slowed pace, and turned back to her. "Are you all right?"

Kitieri blinked. "Yeah, I'm fine. I just…" Something about the intimidating Church prompted her to speak the words that had been on her mind since dinner. "Noia, you and Vina don't have to live on the streets."

Noia's dark brows came together, and Kitieri continued before she could flat out reject the idea.

"That's your plan, right? You're going to buy a Gadget and take to the streets to beg for survival."

"Well…" Noia looked away, rocking Vina. "I just can't see any other way."

"I know." Kitieri stepped close to her. "But I've seen what happens to those people, Noia. You don't have to live like that."

"What do you mean? What happens to them?"

Kitieri swallowed. Her nerves were on edge as the Church of Histan loomed above them, stark and foreboding in the moonlight.

"I'm just worried about you both," she said. "I'm afraid they'll see a target, and your Gadget will be stolen. I'm afraid you'll be robbed, or hurt. These people"—Kitieri gestured to the Church before them —"will do whatever they can to raise themselves up and beat us down. At the very least, without further protection you could be bombarded by those looking for safety during a Strike. That's why all these elites carry weapons, and I've seen them used."

"What do you suggest?" Noia asked. "We have nothing. We can't even—"

"Come live with us."

Noia's eyes widened. "What?"

"Yes. The three of us can share a room, and you two can have Taff's room. We'll have two Gadgets in the house then, and you'll have someone to watch Vina while you work. She'll be safe, and you can save up for a better life for you both."

"Oh," Noia breathed, "I couldn't possibly—"

"What other choice do you have?" Kitieri raised her palms. "The streets are no place for a baby, and you know that. Together, we can give our families a chance at a real life. Don't you want that?"

Noia's eyes were glistening, but it was dark enough that Kitieri could not quite make out her full expression.

"I... I don't know what to say," she choked.

"Say 'yes.' We can take care of each other. This life is hard, but it's a little less hard with friends."

A broad smile spread across Noia's face. Before Kitieri could react, a thin, bony arm pulled her into a hug, with the baby cradled between them.

"Thank you. Thank you so much," Noia whispered into her ear.

Kitieri hugged her back, closing her eyes. "Everything's going to be all right," she said.

Noia pulled away, but her hand lingered on Kitieri's arm. "Somehow, I believe you."

Relief washed over Kitieri. She knew better than to make friends, but this would be different. They'd have Gadgets, and the lightning couldn't just take them on a whim. She'd been raised to protect what little she had in this world, but there was still room to care for others. If she hoarded what she had and locked someone out when she could have helped, how was she any better than the rich elites she hated?

Noia looked back to the Church. "Shall we?"

Kitieri nodded. "Let's go."

They walked across the Church Square, its colored stones arranged in great circles centered around a tall, thin pillar. Kitieri's eyes lingered on the pillar as they passed, traveling up and down its gleaming surface. Its placement seemed strange, jutting up from the circular stones as if it was some kind of monument. A statue of Histan felt the more obvious choice, but she guessed the pillar had its own meaning.

Noia followed her gaze but quickly averted her eyes, training them back on their destination.

"What?" Kitieri asked, glancing back to the pillar to see if she'd missed something that might have offended Noia.

"I don't like that thing," she said.

"What is it?"

"It's terrible, is what it is."

Kitieri waited for an explanation, but Noia remained silent as they walked. She considered pushing the subject, but let it drop. She'd ask again later.

The pair came to the wide stone stairs leading up to the great double doors of the Church, each stair wide enough to require multiple steps before reaching the next. Gaining the top, Kitieri paused as two men in red uniforms moved to block the door.

"What business have you with the Church of Histan?" one asked.

"We're here to purchase two Gad— uh, PCRs."

The red officers exchanged a chuckle, and Kitieri blushed. Everyone she knew called them Gadgets, and she always forgot they had that fancy acronym that stood for 'Personal Cintra Reactor.'

"Uh-huh, sure," the other officer folded his arms. "Let's see the money."

Kitieri pulled her bag in front of her, clutching the flap hard to keep her trembling hands still, and showed the man the contents. He leaned forward, scrutinizing the dark interior before jerking his chin toward Noia. "You?"

Noia shifted Vina to one arm, fishing a purse from her skirt pocket.

"Wait here." The officer opened one of the great double doors, disappearing into the Church and leaving Kitieri and Noia standing awkwardly before the remaining officer.

"Nice night." Noia smiled at the man, who shot her an annoyed look as he shifted his Gadget on his shoulders, ignoring her comment. Kitieri tapped her toes in her boots, looking anywhere but at the pissy officer.

Mercifully, the doors swung open quickly and they were greeted by the sight of a tall man in long black robes, silhouetted against a soft interior glow. A tiny gasp from Noia made Kitieri jump.

"Chief Advisor," she mumbled, bowing her head, "we're so sorry to bother you."

Kitieri glanced between the two, ducking her own head as Noia threw her a stern look.

"The money?" He lifted a dark eyebrow.

"C-can we see the Gadgets first?" Kitieri asked, fighting the urge to take a step back. The man pursed his lips, but turned with a dramatic flare of his long robes to walk back into the Church. Kitieri blinked, watching him walk away until one of the officers waved.

"Well?" he snapped. "Go."

Kitieri hurried through the doors beside Noia and the heavy door swung closed behind them, latching with a *clang* that echoed off the high, vaulted ceilings. Soft firelight illuminated the chamber from two lines of sconces in the walls, and a red runner down the grand center aisle quieted their footfalls. At the far end stood a giant, shining sculpture of a god.

Histan's image was striking in the lamplight. The statue stood taller than five men on each other's shoulders, looking down on them with consternation as one fist hefted a great, jeweled sword into the air. Nothing about the sculpture's presence was kind and welcoming, and Kitieri suppressed a shudder.

"This way," the Chief Advisor said, turning toward a side door. A narrow set of stairs took them up two floors before they reached a dim hallway, passing a series of doors.

Finally, the man stopped, knocking on one such door. He looked at them for the first time since they'd entered the church, and Kitieri noted his squinty, narrow eyes and pockmarked skin. His dark gray hair, pulled back into a low ponytail, made his long face appear even more pointy and angular.

When the door creaked open, a short, rotund man peered out at them.

"What's all this, Stil?" he demanded.

"These women wish to purchase two PCRs."

"At *this* hour?"

Stil rolled his eyes. "It's not that late, Coff."

Coff poked his head further out the door, glaring at Kitieri and Noia. He looked them up and down, appraising them one at a time, until Stil leaned forward.

"They have the money."

Coff cut his eyes up to the tall man, then disappeared into the room with a grumble. Stil gestured for them to enter before him.

A few candles burned, but Kitieri still had to strain her eyes to see. Grunting noises came from where Coff appeared to be struggling with something heavy in a dark closet, and Kitieri stole a glance at Stil, who had his arms folded impatiently.

The man turned, dragging two square packs behind him, and the dulled scraping sound of the metal through the black leather casing filled the room. With a dramatic huff, Coff dropped the packs to his sides.

"Payment," he barked, holding out an open hand. Kitieri pulled the flap of her shoulder bag open and grasped the little sack of black stones, relishing the weight of three brutal years leaving her palm as she dropped the sack into Coff's hand. He ripped the bag open, counting out the caps and rounds. He shot her a sour look at the mess of bits that she hadn't gotten the chance to exchange, but she watched him count every single pebble. It was all there.

"Yours." Coff beckoned to Noia as he pocketed Kitieri's money. The old man felt the three caps in his hand, peeking into the purse just to be sure before shoving it into his pocket.

"Your names?" he grumbled.

"Kitieri Manon."

"Noia Kisson."

Coff scribbled the names into a booklet on the side table, then gestured to the Gadgets on the floor.

"That's it?" Noia asked.

"What else would there be?" Stil asked. The condescension in his tone set Kitieri's temper on edge, but she remained silent. "Take your purchases and be gone."

Kitieri knelt beside the square pack, undoing the double buckles of the front flap, and pulled out the backboard that gave the Gadget its structure. Embedded into the wooden board, a thick metal plate spiked out to five equidistant points, like those of an invisible star. At the tip of each point rested thin, flat shards of translucent purple cintra nestled into the metal. The things were bulky, but the space was necessary to activate the cintra's electricity-nullifying properties as they vibrated against the metal and each other in reaction to the charge.

Kitieri's hands shook as she ran her fingertips over the crystals, and she fought back the tears that sprang to her eyes.

This is real. This is happening, she told herself. How many times had she awoken from this exact dream right at this moment, just as she went to pick it up…?

With Stil and Coff's eyes boring into her, she slid the backboard back into the leather casing and slipped her arms through the backpack straps. The weight felt good and real against her back. She truly wasn't dreaming, this time. This was reality, and she was finally wearing a *real* Gadget.

She looked to Noia, who was struggling with Vina and her Gadget at the same time.

"Here." Kitieri held out her arms for the child, holding her while her mother situated the leather case on her back.

"I'll see you out," Stil said, opening the door to the hallway.

"Thank you, sir," Kitieri said to Coff, and the man waved her away with a grumble.

Stil led them back down the stairs and into the main chamber. The bright lamplight felt like a shock after the dim hallways, but the glow was welcome.

As soon as Kitieri and Noia entered the Sanctuary, Stil slammed the door behind them. A key clicked in the lock from the other side, and Kitieri glanced at Noia.

"Let's get out of here," she said, pulling Noia down the red runner. As they stepped out into the night, Kitieri smelled the building charge in the air and grinned. For the first time in ten years, she could walk home without fear.

The officers' eyes followed her down the stairs and Kitieri set a brisk pace across the Square, slowing only once they'd turned the corner.

"Whew," Kitieri muttered with a quick shudder. "That was weird, right?"

"Definitely weird," Noia agreed with a chuckle, but her smile was far brighter now. Her joy and relief was infectious, and Kitieri smiled back as she watched Noia coo to Vina, bouncing her gently. The moonlight on her dark curls was stunning, and Kitieri felt a momentary flutter in her stomach.

Noia glanced at her, grin widening. "What?"

Kitieri looked away, hoping Noia couldn't see the pink she felt burning in her cheeks.

"Nothing," she replied. "It's just... good to see you happy. It's good to *feel* happy."

Noia took a deep breath, lifting her face to the starry sky. "It is, isn't it?"

Kitieri stole another glance, eyes tracing the fine, delicate line of her jaw as the charge in the air jumped. She stopped short, hands flying to the straps of her Gadget, and Noia turned with a concerned expression.

"What's wrong?"

Kitieri remained silent, standing perfectly still as the metallic taste of electricity almost burned her tongue. Was she supposed to still be this sensitive to the — ?

The first warning sent the familiar hot pulse through her system, and Kitieri gasped as she staggered back a step.

Vina's coos turned to a high-pitched scream, and Noia's eyes flew wide open.

"Kitieri," she whispered, "I thought the Gadgets protected against the warnings."

Kitieri ground her teeth, heart racing. "They do."

Damn it!

Kitieri whipped around, grabbing Noia's hand as she bolted back for the Church.

"Run!"

CHAPTER 4

Kitieri sprinted between buildings, just reaching the Square as the second warning struck. She'd been ready for it, feeling it coil in the air, but Noia fell behind with a gasp.

"Don't slow down!" she shouted. "We can make it!"

Though Vina screamed with all her might, Kitieri pulled Noia to her feet, forcing her onward.

"The Church?" Noia asked, breathless and wheezing under the weight of the Gadget and her baby. Kitieri didn't answer, eyes glued to the double doors. "They won't let us back in!"

"The hells they won't."

As Kitieri charged toward the central pillar, an echoing cry from across the Square caught her attention. At the corner of the stairs, two red uniforms fought back a man and woman with two small, crying children clinging to their mother's legs.

"Let us in, Histan damn you!" the man shouted, swinging at one of the officers.

"You know the law!" one officer yelled back as the other brandished a long black bat. "Get back!"

"There are *children* out here!"

"You shouldn't have your family out without protection. Get *back*!"

The children's screams doubled as the third warning struck, and the man lunged at the officer with the bat. Kitieri kept the red officers in the corner of her eye as she launched up the awkwardly spaced stairs, dragging Noia behind her, but their attention remained glued to the desperate man and his sobbing wife as she held her children.

Though Kitieri's heart broke for the family, she pushed ahead for the top of the stairs. She grasped the shining bronze handle with both hands and wrenched the door open, pushing Noia inside before her. The blue flash cracked outside just as the door slammed closed, and Kitieri heard the gut-wrenching scream only a mother could give.

"*My baby!*"

Kitieri collapsed on the cold stone floor, paralyzed other than her hard, fast breathing. She could hear Vina nearby, her cries muffled in layers of cloth, and she pushed herself up on her hands.

"Noia, are you all right?"

"That baby..." Noia choked.

"I know." Kitieri moved closer. "I know. Is Vina okay?"

Noia sniffled, allowing Vina's face out of the folds of her shirt so she could breathe. "Yes. I—I just don't understand... Why didn't the Gadgets work?"

Kitieri pushed out a loud burst of air. "I have a suspicion."

"You do?"

"Come with me."

Kitieri got to her feet with the heavy Gadget, taking Noia's hand to pull her up before marching down the red runner toward Histan's statue. Movement behind the statue caught Kitieri's eye, and a door creaked as a man stepped out.

"Wait—halt!" he called. "Who's there?"

Kitieri continued her fast pace down the aisle, heading straight for the man. A flicker of uncertainty registered in his eyes, and he called over his shoulder before descending the sculpture's dais to meet her.

"I said *halt!*" he commanded. "What business have you in the Church of Histan at this hour? We do not welcome the homeless—"

Hot anger flowed in Kitieri's veins, warming her body and flushing her cheeks. She ripped the leather straps off her shoulders and tossed the Gadget to the ground between them. It hit with a loud thud, cutting off the man's pompous bullshit.

"I was just here purchasing a G—a PCR from a man named Coff," she said. The man looked between her and the Gadget on the red carpet, a frown wrinkling his features.

"And?"

"And there was a Strike just now, and neither of these so-called PCRs worked. You sold us *junk*! You took our money and sent us out there to die."

Kitieri registered more movement behind the statue, but kept her eyes locked on this man as he lifted his chin, indignant.

"Where are your licenses for these PCRs?" he asked.

Kitieri felt her jaw drop. "What in the two hells are you talking about?"

"All operators of a PCR must be able to produce a license on demand. I need to see your licenses, now."

"Are you kidding me? I just told you they were trash! These are not real! We have been *robbed*!"

"Licenses!" the man boomed. Kitieri's hands closed into tight fists, and as she considered just punching the man straight in his ugly nose, Noia's soft voice piped up beside her.

"A man named Stil witnessed our transaction. Could you fetch him, perhaps?"

Kitieri's eyes focused on the newcomer, who had stepped out from behind Histan's sculpture with a group of men in red uniforms in tow.

"You!" She pointed a finger at Stil as he came to stand beside the man. "You sold us fakes!"

"Kitieri," Noia muttered, resting a hand on her arm. "He might be able to help us."

As much as Kitieri wanted to lunge at the man, she kept still to let Noia speak.

"Chief Advisor," Noia said, her voice soft and sweet, "would you mind telling this man that my friend and I did, in fact, purchase two PCRs from Coff tonight?"

Stil shifted his weight to one leg, crossing his arms and raising an eyebrow in that infuriating manner that Kitieri had already come to hate. "I don't recall any such event."

Kitieri's heart fell to the floor.

Noia blinked, but maintained her smooth composure. "Surely you do."

Stil turned to the short man beside him.

"Beso, I swear to you that I have never seen either of these women in my life. They are clearly a couple of beggars that picked up some fake PCRs on the black market, and are now trying to claim we owe some sort of refund for their garbage."

The heat in Kitieri's face was starting to make her sweat. She gaped at the man's boldfaced lies, her mind spinning in an attempt to find a way back out of this disaster.

Beso mimicked Stil's stern posture.

"Did you acquire these mock PCRs on the black market?" he asked. "Tell the truth now, and we *may* not arrest you."

Kitieri's lungs constricted. "You've got this wrong," she said. "We want nothing more than what we paid our hard-earned money for."

Stil gestured at the leather pack that Kitieri had tossed to the floor.

"Yet you said that these do not work. Therefore, they could not have possibly been from us. The Church of Histan is not the black market, child. We deal only in the highest-quality cintra, and thus PCRs. How do you expect to demand some alleged payment back for property for which you have no proof of sale, nor a license to carry?"

Beso scoffed. "You stand in violation of *several* laws. In the name of our Lord Histan, you are under arrest."

The men in the red uniforms sprang forward, seeming to materialize out of the red carpet. Two of them grabbed Kitieri's arms, but her attention was pulled to Noia as Vina let out a deafening shriek.

"*No!* Not my baby!" Noia cried as one man wrenched the infant from her arms. "Please, don't take my baby!"

The desperation in her voice moved Kitieri to action. She dropped down into a sudden crouch, twisting her body to break the officers' hold on her arms. Her fist smashed into one man's face with a spray of blood before she turned and kicked the other square in the stomach, knocking him to the floor.

Before they could swarm her, she plucked Vina from the officer's awkward hold and kicked Noia's captor hard in the shin.

"Noia, let's *go!*"

Vina held tight to her chest, Kitieri sprinted down the red runner. While running for her life was nothing new, the fate of two dependents hanging on her every action gave her a new edge.

"Bar the door, bar the door!"

Kitieri heard the call behind her and caught a glimpse of more officers running down the side walls. She pushed harder, vision shaking as her boots pounded the floor. Noia's panting assured Kitieri she was close on her heels.

She reached the doors before the officers, slamming through with her shoulders hunched and twisted into the form of a human battering ram. The door flung open as a blinding pain stopped her cold.

Kitieri's knees buckled as the pain overwhelmed her senses, and she toppled toward the unforgiving stone stairs.

Don't land on the baby...

She tried to twist midair, but couldn't tell if her seizing body complied. The back of her head hit a sharp stone edge, and a flash of white engulfed the world around her.

CHAPTER 5

K itieri opened her eyes to a dark stone ceiling and immediately closed them again. Agony racked her body, and the pounding in her head sent waves of nausea rolling through her.

"Kitieri?"

The soft voice came from above, and she dared to open her eyes to just a slit. Through the hazy blur, she could just make out a pale, heart-shaped face.

"Noia." Her voice came out raspy and hoarse. A shift in position told Kitieri that her head was resting in Noia's lap.

"Shh. Don't talk." Kitieri became aware of a hand stroking her hair.

"What... what happened?"

The gentle puff of air from Noia's sigh brushed Kitieri's cheek. "An electric element caught you," she said. "I saw the bolt shoot from his fingers."

Kitieri moved to push herself up on her elbow, but cried out as sharp pain blossomed across her shoulder and back.

"Stay still," Noia said. "You fell pretty hard on the stairs. Your right shoulder is probably dislocated, and your head was bleeding badly for a while."

Images from her last conscious moments started to flicker through her mind. She remembered the fall now. She remembered...

"Vina?" Noia's hand stroked her hair again. "Where's Vina? Did I fall on her?"

"No," Noia said. "I don't know how you managed it, but she wasn't hurt."

Kitieri sighed in relief, wincing at the pain in her ribs.

"You fell on your back and hit your head. I was able to hold Vina again before they caught up, and…" Kitieri heard the catch in her voice. "…They took her."

Kitieri let her eyes close again.

"I'm so sorry."

The hand resumed stroking her hair.

"You have nothing to apologize for," Noia replied. "This wasn't your fault. We were swindled, and now they can't let us leave for fear that we'd spread it. I guess they assumed we'd either die by lightning or be arrested for not having the licenses they didn't tell us about, and all evidence would be erased before we even knew the Gadgets were fake."

"Fucking monsters," Kitieri mumbled, eyes still closed. "Where are we? What happens now?"

Another soft sigh. Kitieri opened one eye to see Noia's face turned toward a faint light source.

"Nothing good," Noia replied, her voice sad and distant.

"Meaning?"

The kind touch of Noia's hand stroking her hair repeatedly felt good, but Kitieri's mind was starting to lose its fog. "Noia?"

"We've been accused of slander and attempted robbery of the Church of Histan."

"That's ridiculous."

"You and I know that, but it doesn't matter. We're a pet case for them."

Kitieri watched Noia's face in the soft, blueish light—moonlight, she realized, coming in from a small window. Around her neck, a glinting silver band caught Kitieri's eye.

"What's that?" she asked.

"What's what?"

"That thing on your neck. I don't remember you wearing any jewelry."

"The oran collar?" Noia asked, reaching up to touch the band around her throat. "All prisoners get them. You have one, too. The oran crystals around the inside prevent us from using our elements against the officers — not that it matters much for me."

"Why not?"

"I'm just a weak air element. The most I could ever do was snuff candles from across the room. Handy enough for sweeping, though, I guess. My mother was a powerful arbor element, and we had the most beautiful gardens when I was growing up. She could make a sprout grow and produce fruit in one day, so we were never hungry." Noia looked back to the window. "If I'd taken after her, I'd still have Vina and our home."

Kitieri looked away, letting her gaze drift aimlessly around the dark room, contemplating the different paths her life might've taken if she'd been born with the power to produce fresh food on a whim. Instead, she'd developed every parent's nightmare.

"I'm sorry, Noia."

"For what?"

"I know you trusted the Church. I'm sorry they would do this to one of their own."

Noia snorted, still looking toward the window.

"At services, they pretend to care about the city and its people. They talk about a future where everyone will have protection from the lightning, but I've never actually seen them help a soul. I just didn't realize they were *trying* to kill us. Stil is the Baliant's Chief Advisor, so this corruption goes up at *least* that far." She shook her head. "Your parents were right to keep you away from all of this. When you first told me you were illegal, I thought you were crazy. After all, people are put to death every day for far lesser crimes. Your family must have known something mine didn't."

Kitieri stared up at Noia, her gaze tracing the reflective oran collar in the faint light. Church membership wasn't a frequent topic of conversation around the mines, and she'd learned long ago not to make friends. No one had asked her Church, and she hadn't asked theirs... until Noia.

"I don't know," she said finally. "Whatever their motives, they died before they could tell me."

"Yes," Noia said. "A bit strange, isn't it?"

Kitieri narrowed her eyes. "Strange?"

"You told me your parents left to run an errand. What was that errand?"

"What? I don't—"

"Had they been saving money?"

Kitieri pushed herself up on one hand, avoiding the use of her throbbing right side.

"Yeah," she said. "Is there something you want to tell me?"

Noia turned her head back from the window, and Kitieri was taken aback by the defiance in her dark eyes. She held little resemblance to that starving, terrified woman Kitieri had pulled off the street.

"You're smart, Kitieri," Noia said. "That leads me to believe that your parents were smart, too. The lightning has been our reality for ten years, now, and I don't know any couple with three children that would not ensure the survival of one parent if they were caught in a Strike. They wouldn't hold each other in their final goodbyes. They would make sure one of them made it back home."

Kitieri blinked, trying to process Noia's words, but already her heart was beginning to race.

"It has a familiar ring, doesn't it?" Noia continued. "A miner and his wife, saving money to help their family, left on an errand and never came back."

Kitieri's lungs felt as if a great hand was squeezing them, and her face broke into a cold sweat. She could see Taff and Jera sitting at the table, awaiting her return. What would they think when the dawn arrived without her?

She leaned into the stone wall, welcoming its steadfast support as realization sank in.

"They tried to buy a Gadget for us," she whispered, "and the Church found out their illegal status." Trembling against the wall, Kitieri raised her head. "The Church of Histan murdered my parents."

Noia pressed her lips into a thin line with a solemn nod.

"They don't see it that way, though," she said. "According to them, Histan himself condemned them for their crimes."

"What are you talking about?"

"Do you remember the pillar?"

"The one in the courtyard that you said was terrible?"

"It is," Noia said. "It's how they try accused criminals. They chain them to the pillar for a full day to await Histan's judgment. If they survive, they are declared innocent and set free. If they are killed by a Strike, then Histan has condemned them, and their souls go to Histan's hell."

Kitieri's jaw went slack as she gaped at the woman.

"That's a sick joke," she said, drawing back.

"I wish I was joking."

Kitieri scoffed. "I can't even remember the last time we've gone a full day without a Strike. Normally there's two or three now."

"That's the point." Noia tilted her head, studying her hands in her lap. "The accused always die, and the Church can claim their hands are clean."

Kitieri slumped back against the wall, turning her face to the darkness of their cell. Sickening horror and dread coursed through her, fighting for control.

"It's what happened to your parents," Noia said, "and it's what will happen to us. They can't let us go now that we've seen their corruption and lies."

Kitieri pressed her eyes closed, trying to still her rapid breathing. Panic and dizziness threatened to take over, and she shook her head violently.

"What about our families?" she asked, the words coming out in a rush despite her attempts at calming herself. A quiet sniffle beside her drew Kitieri out of her own vortex of emotion, and she leaned forward. Moonlight reflected off the tears that streaked Noia's face, and a perfect droplet fell from her chin.

"Vina is already theirs," she choked out. "I'll never see her again. She'll be raised as a servant to one of the elites if she's lucky, just like all the other children who've lost their parents to the lightning. I've seen it too many times, even after offering to take my nephew in when we lost my sister."

"Hells, Noia," Kitieri breathed, little more than a whisper. "I—"

"But they don't know about your siblings." Noia took Kitieri's hand in her own. "If they never came looking for you, that means they didn't know you were out there. Your parents must have lied to keep you safe."

Noia's final word cracked, and her shoulders hunched forward as the sobs overtook her frail body. Kitieri leaned in, pulling her close with her good arm as tears blurred her own vision. A hundred phrases ran through her head, all lies and empty promises. There was nothing she could say to make this better, to turn back the hands of time and erase this evil. Even if she could, it would only put them back to barely surviving. They'd hit a dead end. There was no 'better life' for people like them.

Warm tears fell on Kitieri's white shirt where her jacket had been pushed aside, turning the fabric cold against her skin. She tightened her arm around Noia, resting her chin on top of her head as she took in the warm scent of her curls. That familiar feeling came creeping back, slithering through the recesses of her mind and chilling her core as she closed her eyes.

Despair. Hopelessness. Defeat.

They had been her constant companions since the death of her parents, lurking around every corner, waiting for something to go wrong. She'd defied them time and time again, somehow finding the strength to provide for the family she had left, but they had never truly gone.

Still, letting her demons win had never been much of an option.

"Hey," she whispered into Noia's hair. "We aren't dead yet."

"We might as well be."

"Don't say that. We can still get out of this."

"How?"

Kitieri took in a deep breath, measuring its slow release as her mind raced. *Taff was right. I should have practiced.*

"Let's just agree on something," she said.

"What?"

"If anything happens to one of us, we will take care of the other's family."

Noia's hitching breaths had calmed, and her head now rested quietly on Kitieri's shoulder. When she didn't respond, Kitieri gave her a gentle shake.

"Promise me," she prompted.

"All right," Noia mumbled. "I promise."

The cell's heavy door jumped and sprang to life on its hinges, and

Kitieri pushed off the wall with a start. Noia leapt to her feet, but the pain shooting down her right side kept Kitieri trapped in a defensive half-crouch against the wall.

Four red officers entered the cell, placing a torch in each sconce on either side of the door. Behind them walked a tall man in sleek black and gold robes, with a golden sash tied about the waist.

Kitieri's lip curled in a hateful snarl, and Stil smiled back at her.

"Ah, good. You're awake for processing," he said. As he came to stand directly in front of her, Kitieri noticed a thin leather-bound book tucked under his arm. "State your name."

Kitieri raised her eyes from the book to Stil's long, pockmarked face, and spat. "Go to Histan's hell."

The officers jumped forward, one grabbing Kitieri by her injured arm while another hit her in the stomach with a leather-wrapped bat. She doubled over, crumpling to the floor as her shoulder screamed in pain, and bit down on her lip to keep quiet.

Stil crouched beside her, returning a kerchief to his pocket.

"You really are a violent one, aren't you?" He shook his head, clicking his tongue in disapproval. "You just can't do anything the easy way."

"Why should I make my murder easier on you?" she growled. Stil placed a hand on his chest, as if hurt by the remark.

"Murder? Oh, no, my girl, you are mistaken. What happens now is in Our Lord Histan's hands. Only He can truly judge the innocent and the evil."

"Right." Kitieri nodded. "Whatever helps you sleep at night, pig."

The bat came down on her hunched spine, laying her out flat with a shocked cry. Pain blossomed across her body, Kitieri writhing on the stones with a hoarse moan. She gasped for air as the worst of it washed over her, grinding her forehead against the floor to arch her back until the air could return to her lungs.

"Are you ready to have a civil conversation, Ms. Manon?"

Kitieri froze, even in the grip of the pain, and a nausea unrelated to the abuse gripped her. "I never told you my name."

"Oh, you told us. Don't you remember?" Stil smiled again.

"The fake Gadgets," Noia breathed. "You asked for our names."

Kitieri closed her eyes, fighting the urge to vomit.

"*Kitieri* Manon, was it?" Stil frowned as if he was unsure, flipping through his book for reference. "Ah, there it is."

"Why did you even ask?" Kitieri's lips were so close to the ground, her voice sounded strange in her own ears.

"To see if you were feeling cooperative," Stil replied. "The answer is apparently, 'no.' But don't worry, I'll give you another chance."

Kitieri opened her eyes, cutting them to the side to glare at the man. He was so smug and proud of himself, it made her blood boil with hatred.

"Do you have any family, Kitieri?" The dreaded question rolled from his lips like a thick syrup.

"No."

"Really? None at all?"

"None at all."

"See, I find that very interesting."

Stil stood from his crouch, turning back pages in his book as he paced the length of the narrow cell, and Kitieri struggled to regain a sitting position. Noia dropped down beside her, pushing her up to lean against the wall again.

"Are you okay?" she whispered, brushing strands of hair from Kitieri's face. Kitieri nodded through her grimace, settling to where she could keep her own body upright. Stil's voice from across the cell turned their heads.

"Here it is," he announced, tapping a page of his book with his finger. "You see, when I heard your name, it caught my attention. Manon is a rather uncommon name in Shirasette, but I knew I'd heard it before. So, I did a little research while you were napping."

Stil crossed back from the far end of the cell, his heels clicking on the floor beneath the swishing robes. He snapped the book closed with a sharp pop.

"As it turns out, your parents denied *your* existence before they died, as well."

Kitieri's throat closed up, and something about the man's smug grin sent a hot spike of adrenaline through her body. Her pain disappeared as she launched herself to her feet, throwing her hardest punch. Her fist met the man's face as if in slow motion, and she felt the crunch of bone as his nose shattered.

Stil's shout echoed through the cell, second only to the screaming Kitieri faintly recognized as her own. She saw the blood in the air before the bats brought her down, beating her into a defensive huddle with her bloodied hand over her head.

"*Stop it!*" Noia cried behind her. A sudden weight pressed Kitieri to the ground, shielding her from the blows as Noia's yelp rang in her ear.

"Noia!" Kitieri croaked. "Get off, they'll kill you!"

"No," Noia said, teeth clenched. "I won't let them beat you to death."

"This isn't your fight!"

But the room had quieted, and Kitieri could no longer feel the thud of the bats coming down. They lay in a heap, panting.

"Charming." Stil's voice had lost its drawl, and now carried a dangerous edge. "Get this one out of my way."

The weight lifted as Noia was pulled off Kitieri's back, kicking and screaming.

"Don't hurt her!" Kitieri yelled, pushing herself up. She watched two of the officers deposit Noia against the far wall before the heel of Stil's shoe dug into her spine, slamming her back to the ground. He pressed harder, leaning forward on his knee, and she could feel his eyes boring into the back of her head.

"I am done playing nice," he said, his soft voice dripping with a deadly intensity. Kitieri gasped for air, unable to breathe under his full, crushing weight. She bucked, trying to get enough space for her lungs to expand, but he stomped her back to the floor.

"I have given you every chance to cooperate with me," he continued, "and you have refused. I believe you *do* have family in this city — two siblings, to be exact. I asked around after hearing your name, and it turns out that a midwife who now works for the Church remembers delivering *three* healthy children for the Manons, and admitted she was paid to leave without filing a form of membership to either Church. You and your siblings are *illegal* here."

The lack of oxygen sent shooting stars across Kitieri's vision, and her body was trying to gasp involuntarily. She felt like a fish out of water, pinned to a board by a cruel child to die a slow, painful death.

"So." Stil's weight lifted abruptly, and Kitieri arched her back, coughing and sputtering as air flooded her lungs. "Here's what you need to know. Unregistered children are illegal in Shirasette. Every person must be part of one of the two Churches from birth. I can appreciate that perhaps your criminal parents did not teach you this law, as they spent their lives in avoidance of divine worship—until they wanted access to a PCR, of course—but that does not make you or your siblings any less illegal."

Stil crouched beside her again, cupping her chin forcefully in his hand. When her eyes met his, she saw the smeared blood all over his face and mouth where he had attempted to clean himself up. His nose was flatter in a grotesque way, and blood still trickled down in a thin stream.

"Here is my proposition," he said. "You will tell me where they are, and I will graciously allow them entry into our Church. They will be absolved of their illegal status, and given a home here with soft beds and plenty to eat. Isn't that what you want for them?"

"To be your slaves?"

Stil gripped her chin harder, twisting her head until her expression registered the pain.

"Of course, I can't force you to tell me, can I?" His smug smiled returned, showing bloodstained teeth. "But consider this. If you do not tell me, I will have to launch a search, and I have *never* left a search empty-handed. I will find your siblings, and when I do, they will die painful, bloody deaths. You, alone, can choose their fates, Kitieri. What'll it be?"

Kitieri stared into Stil's cold, dark eyes. It horrified her to think of Taff and Jera in the hands of this monster, but she did not for a moment believe he'd let them live either way.

"I have no siblings."

Stil's gaunt cheek twitched. "Understood."

He released his grip, letting her collapse back to the floor, and turned to the officers.

"It's nearly dawn," he said. "Prepare this one for her Judgement at the pillar."

Kitieri braced herself for rough handling, starting at Noia's cry.

"No, not her," Kitieri gasped, reaching out a hand. Noia's skirt brushed her fingertips as they hauled her out.

"Kitieri!"

The desperate call raked across Kitieri's heart as Noia was dragged from the cell.

"And mount a city-wide search for the remaining illegal Manon siblings," Stil commanded, following the officers out the door. Turning to her, he finished, "May we find them in time for them to see their sister die."

CHAPTER 6

The room was deathly silent and still, as if all the air had been sucked out. Kitieri remained in the middle of the floor where Stil had left her, shaking. Her body felt broken, unusable, and pain consumed her thoughts. She was of no use to anyone anymore.

Muffled through the glass of the cell's window, a familiar cry grabbed her attention, and she cracked one eye open to see new sunlight creeping along the gray stone walls.

The shouts from outside carried on, broken by bouts of sobbing, and she made a monumental effort to shake off the pain-ridden fog.

Noia.

Kitieri rolled over, fighting to gain a kneeling position with her right arm tucked to her side to protect her shoulder, and closed her eyes in a tight grimace. As badly as she hurt, she was still sure that the worst of her injuries had happened on the stairs outside. The bats, she hoped, would only leave bruises.

She pulled herself to the window in a limping crawl, dragging herself up the wall to peer through the glass.

The cell's window sat just above ground, putting Kitieri at eye-level with the red and beige stones that paved the Square. In the center, the pillar's stark silhouette pierced the yellow-pink sky. At its base a lone figure stood in chains, dark curls caught on a gentle breeze.

Kitieri lifted her fingertips to the glass as a tear slid down her face.

"Noia, I'm so sorry," she whispered. Pushing herself up on her toes, Kitieri almost touched her nose to the glass to test the draft coming in. So far, the air was still clean of charge.

She turned away, resting against the wall.

Think. Make a plan. Do something.

The first step had to be fixing this damned shoulder. She could not afford just one functioning arm right now. Kitieri braced her back against the wall, steeling herself. She'd seen it done at the mines once after an accident, but there had been others around to help.

"Just pop it back in. That's all it is," she told herself. Grabbing her right wrist, Kitieri pulled the arm straight out in front of her. She gritted her teeth against the pain, and yelped at the sharp *pop* as the joint snapped back into place. With a loud exhale, she blinked her watering eyes and tucked the arm in close to her body.

Breathe. In. Out. In. Out.

When the worst of the pain had passed, Kitieri turned back to the window. No red officers stood in sight, but civilians wandered across the Square, tossing furtive glances toward the pillar.

She tapped on the glass, gauging its density; it was far too thick for her to punch out. If she could manage the leverage for a kick, it might be possible, but—

Hinges creaked behind her, and Kitieri whirled to face the cell door.

Good, she thought. *I'll kill you this time, or die trying.*

But no one entered. The scrape of thin, flimsy metal on stone met her ears, and Kitieri jumped as a tray of food shot across the room. She looked up from the tray to see the door swinging closed, and lurched forward.

"Wait!" she cried, throwing out a hand.

Kitieri grabbed the door's edge by her fingertips and yanked it back open. A woman in a long skirt and apron screamed, jumping back behind a red officer.

"Hands off!" the man shouted, whipping his bat out from its loop on his belt. Kitieri ducked into a defensive crouch, but held firm to the door. "Get back!"

The weapon came up over his shoulder, and Kitieri darted past him before the bat could fall. The woman wailed beside her meal cart, hands waving up by her face as if a diseased rat had just been set loose.

Kitieri fled down a long hallway lined with identical doors. Her injured hip protested with shooting bursts of pain every time her foot hit the floor, and she cursed the limp's encumbrance as the officer bellowed after her.

This is insane, she thought. *You're an idiot for even trying this.*

But she'd had no choice. What more could they possibly do to her?

A break ahead in the monotonous hall of doors sparked a glimmer of hope in Kitieri's breast, and she pushed her aching body faster. If she could lose this officer in a maze of hallways, she *might* stand a chance.

As she took the corner at full speed, her feet lost purchase and flew out from under her. She hit the floor and slid straight into the wall of the adjoining hallway like she'd stepped in a pool of oil.

Shaking her head to clear her vision, Kitieri spotted two red officers marching toward her, one pulling his hand back to his side.

Oh, an ice element. *Perfect.*

The first officer caught her, stepping carefully on the ice before he stomped his foot down on her hair. The sheet of ice disappeared, and the other two came to stand over her.

"I've been advised that this prisoner is violent," the first officer told them. "She goes to the pillar tomorrow. Thank you for your help in apprehending her."

With her head pinned to the floor by the shiny black boot, Kitieri contemplated the force she could get behind a punch to the man's shin, and how far she could get before…

The ice element glowered down at her as if reading her thoughts, and shook his head in disgust.

"Little more than animals," he scoffed. "I look forward to the day that the lightning finally takes them all. They're a blight on our city."

"Then who would mine your cintra and do all the work for you lazy sadists?" Kitieri spat. A booted kick to her back made her hiss and Ice knelt beside her, leaning in close.

"Stupid little bitch," he sneered. "What do you think slaves are for? The fact that they pay those heathen miners *anything* is a joke. When the Church of Enahris falls to us—and they will—this city will finally become what it was meant to be."

Kitieri stared at the man, struck dumb.

"We aren't supposed to talk about that," Ice's companion growled.

Ice stood with a dark chuckle.

"This one's dead, anyways. Another menace off the streets. You want help getting it back to its cell?"

Kitieri's captor knelt beside her, snapping a thin cable to the oran collar around her neck.

"Nah, I've got it."

He hauled Kitieri to her feet as the other two went on their way, and gave the cable a hard jerk. Kitieri stumbled forward, and the officer laughed.

"After you, my *lady*," he mocked, gesturing for her to walk first. That nixed strangling him from behind, she thought bitterly, dragging her feet down the hall.

The officer shoved Kitieri back into her cell with a strike of his bat and she fell forward, knocking the tray and its contents against the far wall. The door slammed closed with such force that it vibrated the stone floor.

Kitieri brushed the splattered grits off her face and jacket, and caught a glimpse of the cable still swinging from her collar. She grabbed it, holding up its looped end.

Like a dog, she thought. *'Little more than animals.'*

She dropped the cable with a snort, letting it trail behind her as she moved back to the window. Noia was still there, head hung low, and Kitieri dropped her forehead to the cold window ledge as her hands balled into fists. Ice's words rattled in her mind, joining the unrelenting sense of despair already lodged there.

Noia would die. Taff and Jera would die. She herself would die, and there would be nothing she could do against the horrors of this place.

A cool draft from the window touched her skin, and Kitieri's eyes flew open as the electric scent burned in her nose.

"No," she whispered, looking out at Noia again. "No, no, no."

She touched the window, trying to gauge the charge with her fingertips. Though the glass dulled its sting, the sensation was unmistakable. Kitieri's heart raced, and her hands went clammy.

I'm not ready.

I don't have a choice.

Kitieri looked down at her trembling palms and closed her eyes. It had been so long since she'd opened the gates. Would it be there?

A deafening moment of silence passed before the burn in her fingertips answered her question. Kitieri threw her head back as the power coursed through her for the first time in years, seething inside her with a wild, untamable fire.

"That's right!" She laughed. "It takes more oran than that to stop a Strike!"

Sparks danced between her fingers like little white fairies, connecting to one another in miniature, crackling bolts. Two of the bolts collided, exploding into a full lightning strike between the ceiling and floor, and Kitieri reeled backwards in the face of the raw, unbridled energy. As her backside hit the stone, the dancing sparks disappeared.

She growled, regaining her feet.

Dangerous. Unstable. Uncontrollable.

Kitieri knew the reasons lightning elements had been banned from practicing. Even the strongest couldn't keep their element in check during a Strike. An inexperienced electric element might struggle in the charged atmosphere, but it was the lightnings that accidentally killed their friends and family when the Strike pulled their abilities out of control.

Electricity shocked. Lightning killed.

Kitieri limped back to the window, the sparks lively on her fingers as the Strike's energy called to her own. She'd opened the floodgates now, and it would not be suppressed so easily a second time. It yearned to be free, to lash out from her body… to kill.

"Not today," she whispered. "Today, we save."

She felt the first warning pulse through the glass. Noia lurched as the shock hit her, and Kitieri heard her anguished cry ring out across the Square.

"Hang on, Noia," she mumbled. A bolt flashed between her palms, arching through the air in a beautiful flash of white. She'd never tried to intercept a Strike before, but she had to try.

The second warning came, and Noia sobbed openly at the pillar. Kitieri glanced up at the morning sky, clear and blue; there were never any visual warnings. It was as if the lightning materialized out of nowhere, powerful enough to destroy anything it touched.

The third warning shocked Kitieri through the window, and her element snapped back at the glass with a sizzling pop. The power within her writhed and twisted, begging to be set free.

"Almost," Kitieri said, jaw clenched. She timed the pause after the third warning, always the shortest interval, ready and waiting for that first hint of blinding blue malice.

The surge of electricity pulled on Kitieri's element, and her white lightning struck upwards from the ground on the other side of the glass to collide with the blue bolt in a brilliant fountain of sparks. They locked onto each other, forming a column of sheer, blinding energy, each fighting to overpower the other. Kitieri ground her teeth, shaking under the effort of holding the Strike, and blinked sweat out of her eyes. The blue lightning was far stronger than her own, but if she could just... guide it...

Inches away from diffusing into the ground, the Blue Killer broke the connection. Kitieri's bolt exploded into a million tiny sparks, and the blue bolt flashed to the side, burning an L shape into Kitieri's retinas. The Strike hit Noia with a deafening *crack*, and her ashen corpse fell to the ground, free from the destroyed chains.

A scream ripped from Kitieri's throat, so violent that her vision blurred and her lightning crackled around her, arching to the floor and blackening the walls. Her legs refused to hold her weight and she sank to the floor, one hand dragging along the wall.

She had failed. And Noia had paid the price.

Heaving sobs racked her body, and the minimal contents of her stomach were spewed to the floor. She coughed and gagged, running a hand back through her hair. Her breaths came in ragged gulps, and the bright L glowed behind her closed eyelids. She barely heard the door open.

"Ah. Lovely view, isn't it?" Stil's voice stabbed like a dagger of ice.

Kitieri kept her eyes down, sapped of any energy she'd had left.

"Have you finally learned to behave?" he drawled, the smirk evident in his tone as he crossed the cell. He was trying to goad her into another outburst.

Kitieri sat back on her heels, eyes still trained on the floor. Her tear-stained face felt stiff and swollen, but she wouldn't give this man the satisfaction of watching her wipe the tears away. She turned her palms upward on her knees, curling her fingers.

One more bolt.

But the air was clean again, and the oran collar kept what sparks she might have produced on her own at bay. Kitieri lifted her gaze to Stil, whose brows twitched at her curved fingers.

"Take her to the pillar," he snapped.

Two red officers reached for her arms, but she stood on her own before they could jostle her shoulder. The men exchanged glances; one picked up the cable attached to her collar, but said nothing as they followed Stil from the cell.

"I thought my Judgement was set for tomorrow morning," Kitieri said. Stil cast an annoyed glance over his shoulder.

"You are not privy to the Church's decisions. Our Lord Histan wants you judged and gone as soon as possible."

"Oh, really?" Kitieri barked a laugh. "Did Histan come down from wherever the hells it is he hides and demand my death himself?"

Stil spun on his heel, and slapped Kitieri across the face.

"You *will* show respect here," he commanded.

The sting in her cheek paled in comparison to the rest of her pain, and Kitieri whipped her head back around with a steely glare. A tug on the cable pulled her back, but she held eye contact for a long, tense moment until Stil turned away, continuing their procession down the hallway of doors.

As they ascended several flights of stairs, Kitieri noticed an increase in population in the Church. Some were officers in their red uniforms, one or two wore black robes like Stil's with varying degrees of golden accessories, some were women in skirts and aprons like the one who'd attempted to deliver Kitieri's breakfast, and some wore dark brown cloaks that hooded their features entirely.

Kitieri frowned, watching as one such hooded figure swished past her. Their head was lowered, creating an even deeper shadow that made it appear as if no face existed at all. She recognized that brown cloak from somewhere, she was sure, but the memory felt hazy.

The mines. A clear image of two brown-cloaked people sprang into her mind, standing at the back of the wagon that came to take the cintra loads into the city every week. But that was strange... She'd never seen these cloaked people anywhere else in the city. Did that mean all of the cintra came straight here?

A nearby officer opened a door for Stil with a low bow, and Kitieri found herself back in the Church Sanctuary. Her eyes darted to the red runner where she'd thrown the fake Gadget at that man's feet. Two others in black robes stood there now, and they nodded to Stil as he passed.

Kitieri's stomach clenched. Noia was gone, and she would soon follow. It seemed impossible that a life could go so wrong so quickly.

Stil threw open the main double doors, scattering birds and frightening two children who appeared to be begging on the steps.

"Get out of here, you little shits!" Stil shouted, kicking at one of them. The child yelped, dropping the few bits he'd managed to collect. The other pulled on his arm, and they scampered down the stairs. "And you'd better be glad I'm busy right now, or you'd be *much* sorrier!"

Kitieri looked away. That could so easily be Taff and Jera in a week —*if* they managed to avoid Stil's search.

They made their way down the awkward, widely spaced stairs, and the shining pillar loomed closer. As they reached the foot of the stairs, a pair of red officers passed by carrying something between them on a long board. Kitieri squinted, straining to discern the board's contents.

Her eyes flew open wide and she stumbled back, gagging as the leashed collar choked her. Her scream came out hoarse and airy as she threw a hand over her face, but the image was burned permanently into her mind — Noia's charred, blackened body, reduced almost entirely to ash except for the twisted, grotesque skeletal core. The breeze shifted, and the smell of burned flesh hit her full in the face.

Kitieri retched again, her body heaving on the smooth stone, but there was nothing in her stomach to lose. She spit the phlegm and bitter bile from her mouth, choking and sputtering.

"Get her up," Stil barked, his tone thick with disgust. Kitieri barely registered the pain as the officers forced her to her feet, steering her back toward the pillar. Her feet moved without her conscious permission, obeying the pressure of the bat pressed against her back, and she climbed the three steps to the pillar's dais like a walking corpse. Her wrists and ankles were snapped into shackles connected around the back of the pillar by long chains, while she stared up at the sky. Was it still morning? Was it midday? Did it matter?

As the officers stepped back, Stil came to stand at the foot of the dais, reading words from a book. She didn't care what he was saying. His words rolled over her, a meaningless wash of sound.

"Hey!" A sharp jab in the side forced her out of her haze, and she glared at the man standing beside her with the bat. "He asked if you had any last words."

Kitieri cut her eyes from the officer to Stil, her head slowly turning to follow.

"Yeah, I do," she said, spitting the remaining bile to the stones at her feet. "Fuck you, fuck your Church, and fuck your god."

The officer stumbled down a step, looking shocked. Stil met her glare, and slammed his book closed.

"May His Lord Histan judge you well."

With a dramatic flare of his robes, Stil turned and disappeared back into the Church.

CHAPTER 7

Kitieri rested her head back against the pillar, watching the white clouds roll across the sky. The sun climbed directly overhead, then began to inch into the afternoon.

She'd long ago quit paying attention to the people that passed through the square. The bustling center of activity was crowded with tradesmen, beggars, and folks taking the diagonal shortcut to another side of town. Some of them jeered at her, while others looked on with pity. Most, though, simply ignored her.

Her throat burned with thirst, and she realized it had been nearly twenty-four hours since her last sip of water. As the sun beat down on her, she willed the fluffy white clouds to come together, turn dark, and give her rain, but they remained resolute in their dry, useless frivolity.

As her thoughts wandered, Taff and Jera's faces drifted across her mind. She saw gray eyes full of worry, felt the pressing silence as they waited for any sound of her return—the same heaviness she'd felt as they had awaited the return of their parents. Now she would abandon them, too.

She rocked her head against the pillar, fighting the raw anguish that ate at her insides. Gods, she wished she could speak to them one last time. If only they could hear her from across the city, she would tell them...

Kitieri's deep sigh caught in her lungs. Her throat burned with the air's charge.

Even as her pulse spiked, Kitieri closed her eyes. The rational response was fear, she knew, but something about the mounting electricity felt soothing to her. It called to her in some strange way, as if beckoning her home.

"Kitieri?"

Her heart leapt into her throat and her eyes flew open, searching for the source of her name. Taff came into her vision, trotting up the stairs to the pillar's dais.

"No!" she hissed. "Taff, you can't be here!"

He ignored her, throwing his arms around her and the pillar as one. Kitieri glanced around the Square, sure she was going to see a red officer marching toward them. There were no uniforms in sight, but that didn't mean they weren't coming.

"You never came home!" Taff said, head buried in her shoulder. "The Strikes... we were so scared for you."

"I know. I'm so sorry. But you have to listen to me."

"What's going on, Kitieri? Why are you chained here?"

"Taff, *listen* to me!"

He looked up at her, gray eyes wide. Most days, Taff seemed like a miniature adult to Kitieri, taking the burdens of the world on his shoulders. Sometimes, though, he was just her little brother, as scared and confused as anyone else.

"You can't be here, Taff," she repeated, her voice soft but intense. "There is a Strike coming, and the Church is after you. Get out of here, run home, and get Jera."

"The Church is after us? What do you mean?"

"It means when they find you, they'll kill you. I don't have time to tell you everything, but Jera is counting on you now, all right?"

"Where do we go?" His voice was shaking. Kitieri hated herself for it, but she said the only solution that had come to her mind just now — the one thing she'd wished she could tell them before she died.

"You have to go to the Church of Enahris. They are the only ones Histan's Church can't touch. Tell them you are fifteen, and you want to join them with Jera as your dependent."

"You want us to join a *Church*?"

"It's the only way."

"They'll never believe I'm fifteen."

"You have to try. Now get out of here!"

"No, I'm not going to leave you here!"

"You don't have a choice, Taff. If we both die, Jera will have nothing."

"Hey! Hey, kid, get down from there!"

The red officer approached from across the courtyard, brandishing his bat, and Kitieri felt the blood drain from her face.

"Taff, *run!*" she screamed. He took a reluctant step back, looking desperately between Kitieri and the officer. "GO!"

Taff stumbled down the steps, backing away. Kitieri screamed at him again as the officer passed her. He slammed his bat into her stomach, cutting off her cry as she lurched forward.

"Don't touch her!" Taff shouted, running for the officer. Kitieri watched in abject horror as her brother rushed the man, and the bat lifted for a blow to the boy's head.

The first warning struck, stopping Taff in his tracks. The officer froze, bat still lifted over his head. Secure in his proximity to the Church, the man had come out without a Gadget; with a malicious snarl, he turned and ran for the doors. The Square emptied with a chorus of cries and shouts as people hurried for home.

"Kitieri," Taff whimpered, standing at the foot of the dais.

"You have to run as fast and as far as you can," she told him. "Try to get out of range or find shelter before the Strike."

"But—you'll die."

Kitieri bit her lip, nodding her tilted head. "Yeah."

Tears welled up in Taff's eyes, like windows to a stormy ocean. Before Kitieri could stop him, he bounded up the stairs of the dais and threw his arms around her again. The second warning shocked them both.

"Taff, you have to let go. You're running out of time."

Taff shook his head. "I can't leave you to die."

"This isn't about just you and me. You have Jera to think about— she's *your* responsibility now."

The conflict in Taff's eyes shattered Kitieri's heart. No boy should ever be forced to choose between his sisters, she knew, but Kitieri was already a lost cause. Taff and Jera might still have a chance if they managed to escape to the Church of Enahris.

The final warning hit, and their bodies seized in tandem as the voltage arrested all thought and movement. The lightning element within her reacted, bursting free in shooting arcs of deadly white light.

Taff lifted his head from her shoulder, his tear-stained face a picture of terrified awe.

"Kitieri, your lightning! It's working again!"

Kitieri looked down at him.

"It always worked," she said. "I could just never control it enough for it to be safe."

She felt the Strike lock in, turning its burning eye on its victims. Her own lightning flashed around them, striking out at random.

It was too late for running now. He'd never escape the range, and he'd be just as exposed as her to the whims of the Blue Killer. Kitieri gritted her teeth, bowing her head to bring it closer to Taff's.

There was only one option left.

"Stay close, now, Taff," she whispered. His thin body trembled against hers, arms tight around her. Kitieri closed her eyes as the Strike came for them. She felt its pulse, like a hungry monster. She could smell it moving. The white flashes around her ceased as the blue bolt split the sky.

Kitieri screamed, throwing all of her power upwards before the blackness enveloped her.

"KITIERI? KITIERI!"

Something was shaking her. Light filtered in through the darkness, pricking at her eyes.

No, leave me alone. I'm tired…

"Wake up!"

Pain sliced through her consciousness as her shoulder was moved. She tried to swat the annoyance away, but something caught her hand.

"Kitieri, please, you have to wake up!"

She recognized that voice. Taff. He sounded scared.

Protective instincts took over, and Kitieri opened her eyes further to the blinding light. Taff's familiar face leaned in close, like he was searching for something. When his eyes met hers, a smile graced his drawn features.

"Are you all right?" he asked.

"No."

Taff's smile widened. "Can you move?"

Kitieri experimented with a finger. When that didn't hurt, she tried her wrist and elbow, then her whole upper body. Her body was stiff and bruised, but it still functioned.

Taff helped pull her into a sitting position, steadying her with both hands.

"I don't know how, but your chains broke in the Strike," he said. "We have to go!"

Kitieri looked down, blinking the dazed bleariness from her vision. The shackles remained clamped to her wrists and ankles, and the severed lengths of their chains pooled around her on the dais.

How...?

"What happened?" she asked.

"I don't know, but I think your lightning saved us from the Strike."

Memories were flooding back to her now. The pillar. The lightning. Stil. *Noia.*

Kitieri's mind and body snapped fully awake, and she threw a glance around the Square. No one was in sight.

"How long was I out?" she asked.

"Twenty seconds?"

"That's it?"

Taff nodded.

The doors to the Church swung open, and Kitieri caught a glimpse of the red uniforms. She launched to her feet, pushing Taff off the dais before her.

"Whoa! Stop!" an officer called.

"Run!" she yelled to Taff, who was already going full tilt. Kitieri followed close on his heels to the edge of the Square, gathering up the trailing chains as best she could. As soon as the Church fell out of view past the tall buildings that lined the Square, she grabbed Taff's arm and pulled him into a dark alleyway.

"What are we doing?" he hissed. "If we stop, they'll catch us!"

"We can't lead them straight home," Kitieri replied. "Stay back."

Taff plastered himself against the wall of the house, and Kitieri leaned forward just enough to keep an eye on the main street.

The sounds of booted feet and shouting echoed down the alley, and Kitieri pressed a hand to Taff's chest to keep him still. His heart raced under her palm, and her hand moved with his rapid breathing. She wanted to comfort him, but remained silent, eyes trained on the sliver of road she could see from her position.

The voices grew louder, and the din of boots hitting the cobblestones passed their hiding place. She watched the red uniforms run straight by, calling for the capture of the Manons. As the sounds faded, Taff's heart rate began to even out.

"What's happening, Kitieri?" he demanded. "Why are they saying that? Why do they want us dead?"

Kitieri sighed, tearing her eyes away from the road. She moved her hand from Taff's chest to his skinny shoulder. "It's a lot to explain."

"The short version, then."

Kitieri nodded. She owed him that much.

"The Church of Histan is full of some very corrupt people. They stole our Gadget money and accused us of attempted robbery. They found out that our family was never registered with a Church, which is apparently very illegal. We're criminals for avoiding Church membership, and they want us dead. That, and I've seen their corruption. They don't want that getting out, so they tried to kill me like they did Noia."

"Noia's dead?" Taff gasped. "What about Vina?"

Kitieri bit her bottom lip hard. "They have her, and I'm going to get her back."

"*Now?*"

"No." Kitieri peeked back out toward the street. "We have to take care of ourselves first, or there will be no one to help Vina... or anyone else in this city."

"What do you mean?"

"I'll tell you more once we get Jera. Come on."

Kitieri trotted to the alley entrance, peering out onto the bright street. People were moving about again after the Strike, and she saw no red officers in the mix.

She shoved the chains up her jacket sleeves and into her boots, eliminating as much of their clinking and swaying as possible. How the Strike had managed to break the chains without leaving the tiniest burn on either Taff or herself was beyond her comprehension, but all that mattered now was that it *had*. She pulled Taff out of the alleyway, setting their pace at a brisk walk.

"Keep your head down and act normal," she muttered. "Stay just one step behind me and follow my every move."

She hugged the walls of the houses to her left, clinging to the shadows cast by the afternoon sun. Taff echoed her every footstep, walking so close that his shoulder brushed her arm.

A pair of red officers emerged from the alleyway in front of them, engaged in a quiet discussion. Taff bumped her arm, but Kitieri pressed on, watching them through her hanging hair. Without even a glance her way, they moved on to the next alley across the street. They were searching for a frantic escapee, not some poor girl walking home from work.

Beside her, Taff's tension was palpable.

"Relax," she whispered. "If you look scared, it will draw attention."

A few more turns on small side roads brought them to their neighborhood, and despite her advice to Taff, Kitieri had a hard time keeping her pace steady. If they were lucky, they'd be able to make the Church of Enahris by nightfall. Her skin crawled at the thought of entering any Church ever again, but it was their only chance.

When home came into sight, Kitieri allowed herself a small breath of relief at finding it unguarded. She reached for the door, trying its handle, but it didn't budge.

"I told her to lock it after me," Taff said.

"Jera." Kitieri spoke to the door, rapping on the wood. "It's us. Let us in."

Silence followed by muffled sounds reached Kitieri's ears. She glanced down at Taff, brows drawing together, before they heard the clunk of the bolt lifting. The door opened with a loud creak, swinging into what appeared to be an empty house.

Alarms sounded in Kitieri's mind, screaming for her to turn and run. She caught the creaking door with one hand, staying Taff's advance with the other.

"Jera?"

She leaned forward to peek around the door, and felt the cold, sharp blade of a knife under her chin.

Kitieri froze, her blood running cold. She could see only the gloved hand that held the blade, its owner hidden in the shadow of the door. A movement to the right drew her eyes, and her composure crumbled.

"No." The word broke on her lips as tears sprang to her eyes. From the shadows of the doorway leading to her and Jera's room, a red officer emerged. In one hand he held Jera by the shoulder in a firm grip, a knife to her throat in the other.

"Kitieri." Tears streamed down Jera's face, and her breathing hitched as the officer jerked her shoulder.

"Silence," he commanded.

"Please don't hurt her." Kitieri knew that begging would get her nowhere, but she couldn't stop the words. "I'll do whatever you want."

A third officer stepped out from Taff's room, swinging his bat. "How kind of you to show, Ms. Manon. Will your brother be joining us?"

Kitieri heard a scuffle behind her, but the knife at her throat pushed upwards to keep her stationary.

"Get off me!" She heard Taff's voice on the street, and her heart sank. Another officer pushed past Kitieri, shoving Taff into the house with a knife at his back.

"That's better," said the ranking officer. "Now, let's get down to business. I am Gall, commander of Division Three, officer of the Church of Histan. You are accused of illegal status in this city without registration to a Church."

Kitieri turned to face the officer, even as the cold blade cut across the skin of her throat. The smoldering embers of her rage lit anew, and their heat flushed her cheeks. Though her heart pounded, her words came slowly, heavy with the hatred that coursed through her veins.

"I endured your beatings. I stood at your pillar. I faced your Judgement, and I survived. According to the laws of your own Church, I am innocent."

Gall's confidence faltered, and he shot one of his officers a flustered glance before drawing himself up to his full height.

"Our orders stand," he said. "The Manons are still illegal in —"

"So you admit it." Kitieri's ire cut across his explanation.

"Admit?" he scoffed.

"The Judgement is a *lie*. Your holy pillar was never about inno-cence or guilt. It's about murdering those who oppose you." Kitieri leaned into the knife at her throat, her venomous glare locked on Gall. "And I refused to die."

Gall's expression grew dark, and he crossed the room to jab a shaking finger in her face.

"That lightning was *meant* for you," he said. "I don't know what trick you used to escape, but you are no more innocent than the scum that fried before you. The Church of Histan does not tolerate criminals, especially illegals like you and your siblings."

"We're not illegal," Kitieri snapped. The blatant lie would never stand under scrutiny, but she needed to buy time.

Gall cocked a thick eyebrow, twirling his bat. "Is that so?"

"Yes. We belong to the Church of Enahris."

"That is not in our records."

"Perhaps your records are outdated."

Gall's brows furrowed. "Be advised, Ms. Manon, that lying about one's Church registration is an offense equal to illegal status. It would be a shame to pile further crimes onto your remarkably tainted record, would you not agree?"

Kitieri held the man's gaze as the bat swung menacingly in and out of her peripheral vision. "Since you hand out death sentences like candy, I don't see what difference it makes."

Gall sneered, gripping his bat tighter.

"But I'm not lying," Kitieri said. "We're members of the Church of Enahris, and that means you can't touch us."

Gall's bat quivered in anticipation as he glowered down at her. She could see the wheels turning in his mind, and suppressed the shudder that threatened to give her away as she met his glare. She nearly flinched as the bat snapped into resting position against the length of his forearm.

"Prove it."

Panic writhed in Kitieri's gut. Not only could she prove nothing, she hadn't even the faintest clue how to lie about it. Was she supposed to have papers or something?

"Come on, Gall," the officer holding Jera said. "You know whatever she has is as fake as that PCR she used to frame the Church. She's a liar."

Gall did not look back at his officer, but folded his arms across his chest.

"A fair point," he said. "Well, Ms Manon, what do you say we pay a little visit to the Church of Enahris together?"

Kitieri's jaw clenched, but there was no choice in Gall's question.

The officer behind the door reached out, forcefully turning her back out into the street.

This time, she could not keep her hands from shaking as only one thought sounded repeatedly in her head.

We're fucked.

CHAPTER 8

The Church of Enahris towered over its sprawling Square, the setting sun reflecting off the tall, narrow windows that dominated its front. Though Kitieri wanted nothing more than to turn and run, she found herself fascinated by the staggering differences between this place and its brother Church.

Bordered by a row of trees, the Square extended a warm invitation with benches and flowering hedges along the smooth stone walkways, all centered around a twisted flowering tree. Kitieri marveled as they passed, admiring the intricacy of the many slender trunks woven into one, their branches fanning out into a vibrant array of colorful leaves and flowers. The pressure of the knife against her back cut her admiration short, pushing her forward.

They climbed the stairs to the arched front doors, and Gall pounded three times. One of the doors opened almost immediately, and a short woman in a gray dress greeted them with a ready smile.

"My, what have we here?" she squeaked, resting a hand on her ample bosom.

"We wish to speak to your Baliant," Gall announced.

"Oh, well… ah… the Baliant may be a bit busy—"

"It's urgent."

"A-all right. Just one moment. Do come in, will you?"

The woman turned, and the officer behind Kitieri shoved her

through the door. She tripped on the threshold, boot slapping down hard on the polished stone floor as she caught herself.

"No need for that, good officer!" the woman said, waving back at them. "Just wait right here."

As she bounced away, Kitieri's gaze wandered the Sanctuary. It was similar enough to Histan's, with high arched ceilings and stone pillars running down both sides. Lamps hung from the walls, and candelabras stood chest-height to Kitieri. At the far end stood the expected statue of Enahris, depicted in modest robes with a rose in one hand, while the other seemed to be reaching down as if to offer someone help. Her posture was bent toward the imaginary recipient of what Kitieri guessed was supposed to be grace or mercy, and she rolled her eyes.

She didn't have time for sight-seeing. In a few minutes, Enahris' Baliant would come in and tell the truth. This was just an elaborate field trip on the way to their inevitable deaths.

Kitieri glanced at Taff and Jera, who were looking around the Church. Taff caught her eye, and she gave him what she hoped was a reassuring smile.

She couldn't save them. She knew that. But neither would she go down without a fight.

Kitieri eyed the nearest candelabra stand, gauging its viability as a weapon. It stood about three big steps away, but the officer behind her had not lost his attentiveness. If there was some sort of distraction…

Four officers in gray uniforms entered the Sanctuary, snapping to attention as another figure came through the door, white robes billowing behind her. Kitieri squinted as she strode down the center aisle toward them.

This was the Baliant? Leader of the Church of Enahris?

As she drew closer, Kitieri realized it was not a trick of the light. Strikingly tall and lithe, the woman before her could not have been older than twenty-two. Her face registered no emotion, smooth dark skin standing in stark contrast to her white garb, high cheekbones accentuated in the soft lamplight. Above all, Kitieri found herself entirely captivated by bright amber eyes, glowing against the woman's dark skin and cropped black hair.

"To what do we owe this visit from our brother Church?" The

woman spoke in a cool, measured tone, coming to a stop before them. Gall bent forward in a begrudging bow.

"Thank you for meeting us, Baliant Catarva," he said, disdain clear in his voice. "These three stand accused of illegal status in the city of Shirasette. We do not have them on record as belonging to either Church, and yet Ms. Manon claims they have joined the Church of Enahris. With a history of fraud, neither her word nor her documents could be trusted, and we have strong reason to believe that she is lying to escape consequences. The only way to confirm her claim was to speak with you directly."

One perfectly shaped dark eyebrow twitched as Catarva turned her piercing gaze on Kitieri. Though her heart pounded, Kitieri kept her head up to meet the woman's eyes even as her insides withered under the scrutiny. Her borrowed time was up.

She pictured the nearby candelabra as Catarva stared her down. It was a desperate move, but the door was just behind them. If she could get to it in one bound, she could—

"Yes, Officer. The Manons are members of my Church."

Kitieri's thoughts ground to a halt, and her body froze. She dared not even look at the officer when Gall snapped his head around to glare at her.

"Are you absolutely certain, Baliant?"

"Are you questioning whether or not I know my own people?"

"I—this is—she—"

"Officer, I'm quite sure you have more important business requiring your attention than harassing members of a Church not your own. I will have their documents sent to you first thing tomorrow."

Gall broke into a sputtering fit, and Kitieri turned her head just enough to see his face turn as red as his uniform jacket. Catarva cracked a cold smile.

"Good night, Officers."

Gall turned on his heel and stormed out of the Church with his men in tow, muttering a string of curses under his breath. When the doors slammed shut, the plump woman let out a loud huff.

"I just can't stand those Histan officers," she declared. "It's always violence first with them!"

Kitieri stared at the door in disbelief. Taut nerves vibrated her body as she waited for it to fly open again, and she jumped as Jera flung her arms around her waist, crying against her jacket. Kitieri looked back to Catarva, and found herself fixed in an unreadable stare.

"Thank you," she managed, holding Jera's head. With a thoughtful nod, Catarva turned to the short woman.

"Minna, our guests look hungry and tired. Would you be so kind as to prepare a room and ask the staff to set my table for four this evening?"

"Yes, Baliant!" Minna bowed before bouncing off to carry out her tasks.

"Uh, that's not necessary." Kitieri shook her head. "We don't want to put you out any further."

"Nonsense." Catarva cut her off, stepping on her last word. "You are members of our Church now, are you not? I would see you fed and cared for. Inra, would you be so kind?"

Kitieri blinked. The words coming from the woman's lips were pleasant, but a discomfort swelled in her chest. The red-haired officer behind Catarva stepped up close to her, reaching out for her neck, and Kitieri flinched, instinctively knocking the officer's hand away with a swing of her fist.

"Easy!" Inra said, leaning back with her hands up. "I'm just going to take that collar off. Can I do that?"

Kitieri touched the metal band around her neck, surprised. She'd forgotten it was there.

"Sorry," she muttered. Inra stepped in again, slower this time.

"It's all right," she said quietly. "It looks like you've been through the hells, but you're safe here."

Kitieri watched the officer's kind, freckled face as she slid one finger up under the collar, momentarily tightening the band around her throat. Her hazel eyes closed, and the pressure around Kitieri's neck dissipated. When Inra stepped back, she held a blob of melted silver and brownish-red crystals in her palm, and Kitieri grinned. Metal elements were rare in Shirasette; she'd never seen one work before.

"Better get these, too," Inra said, gesturing to the chains tucked up into her jacket. In less than a minute, Kitieri's wrists and ankles were free from their shackles.

"Haldin." Catarva addressed another of her officers with an almost calculating drawl, and a tall man with light brown hair and a strong jaw stepped up beside her. "Please escort the Manons to the bath chambers so they may refresh themselves before dinner. I will have Minna bring fresh clothes."

Haldin bowed before turning away, and Kitieri followed with Jera clinging to her leg, Taff close behind. The Baliant's eyes bored into her back until Haldin led them out of view through a side door, and Kitieri breathed a silent sigh of relief.

"What happened, Kitieri?" Jera asked, tugging on her jacket. "Why didn't you come home?"

Kitieri glanced at Haldin's back as they walked, trying to swallow the fear that swelled in her throat. Were they really going to the... baths? Why would the Baliant do this? What kind of trap were they walking into?

"Kitieri?" Jera tugged harder.

"I'll tell you everything later, okay?"

"We thought something happened to you."

"I know. I'm sorry."

"Why did those men come to our house? Why did they want to hurt us?"

"Jera, not now."

"What is going *on*?"

"Hey." Kitieri squeezed her sister's shoulder. "Let's play a game. What do you think is going to be for dinner?"

Jera's eyes brightened, and her wide smile showed her first missing tooth. "Cheese?"

"I'm sure there will be cheese." Kitieri smiled. "And maybe even roasted meat."

"Roasted meat?" Taff piped up behind them.

"I'd bet on it," Kitieri said over her shoulder.

"What if it's a *ham*?" Jera said, wide eyes sparkling.

"Chicken is more likely," Taff countered.

"How do *you* know?"

"Pfft. No one is wasting a ham on us."

Kitieri listened to her siblings squabble as Haldin led them through the maze of hallways. With the oran collar gone, she tested her element. It buzzed beneath her skin in response, skittering to her fingertips to await her command, and she looked back up at the man in front of her.

I swear, you try one thing, and I will kill you, she thought.

"Here we are." Haldin came to an abrupt stop, gesturing to two doors standing opposite one another. "Women's here, men's there."

Kitieri inspected the doors suspiciously, pulling Jera in closer to her, and the man ducked his head a little.

"Everything all right?" he asked.

Kitieri sucked in a quick breath, meeting his pale blue eyes. Where she'd expected disdain, malice, bemusement... *anything*... she saw only earnest concern.

"Yeah," she replied quickly. "Uh, thank you."

Haldin nodded once, taking his leave, and Kitieri watched him go. He was just going to walk away? No guards...?

"Hey." Taff's voice pulled her back. "I'll be waiting out here when you two are done."

Kitieri nodded, steering Jera to the other door, and hot steam hit her face as they entered. A long line of pools set into the stone floor ran the length of the dim chamber, curtain rods separating each one. Kitieri jumped back as a young woman appeared through the haze.

"Sorry to frighten you." The woman smiled. "May I help you?"

"Uh," Kitieri said, "no. No, thanks. We can help ourselves."

"It's all right," she assured them. "It's my job. Can I take your clothes?"

Kitieri looked down at the state of her garments. Ripped pants revealed a scabbed knee, and she was covered in dirt and ash. Her mother's jacket had been torn, and the lining showed through beneath the leather.

"No, thanks," she said, more apologetically this time. "If it's all the same, we'll just take care of ourselves."

"Of course," the woman said. "You may prefer the end bath down there. Soap is provided."

Kitieri nodded her thanks, and walked hand in hand with Jera to the last pool in the room, where the lamplight hardly reached. She yanked the curtains closed around them, further deepening the shadows.

"Can you tell me what's happening now?" Jera whispered. She looked up at the ceiling, surprised to hear her voice echoing back at her so loudly. Kitieri grinned.

"Arms up."

Jera rolled her big gray eyes, but followed Kitieri's directions before sliding into the pool as Kitieri grabbed the soap bar on the ledge.

"It's so warm!" Jera exclaimed. Kitieri laughed as the echoes carried her sister's voice all the way to the other end of the bath chamber. "And it smells like *flowers*!"

Kitieri poured water over Jera's head, working the soap into her hair, and felt a pang of guilt as her hands came away brown with built-up grime. Baths had been a rare luxury her entire life, requiring a trip to the public bathhouse. The last time she'd taken Taff and Jera, a Strike had sent them sprinting for the tall building, and the risk had hardly seemed worth it since. That, coupled with her long work days in the mines…

Shit, the mines, Kitieri thought with a fresh wave of anxiety. Her overseer would be furious that she hadn't shown up today. She'd been late only once in the past three years, because Taff had gotten sick, and she'd almost lost her job over it. *If* she was able to get back tomorrow, Kitieri hoped they might let her return to work with some hard begging and a beating. Her aching body groaned at the thought.

"Kitieri?" Jera's soft voice interrupted her panicked spiral. "Are you okay?"

Kitieri forced a smile, dipping the soap back into the water. "Yeah. Yeah, I'm okay."

Jera lifted her hand with a little splash to rest it on Kitieri's. "Everything is going to be fine now."

Kitieri pushed back a piece of wet hair clinging to Jera's forehead. "What makes you say that?"

"Good things are happening. Baths and *food*! These are nice people."

Kitieri sighed, turning her hand over to hold Jera's tight.

"I hope you're right," she said. *Because I will raze this place to the ground before I let them hurt you.*

"I'm right." Jera grinned. "You always say that the Manons will survive."

Kitieri gave a soft laugh. "That's what Dad always said. And don't forget it."

Jera pulled her hand back into the pool, dunking her head to get the soap out of her hair.

"Aren't you getting in?" she asked.

Kitieri sat back on her heels. "Yeah."

Scooting back from the pool, she pulled off her dusty, scuffed-up boots and set them aside. As she tried to remove her jacket, her shoulder erupted into agonizing pain, and Kitieri ground her teeth.

"Jera, turn around."

Her sister giggled. "Why?"

"Because I asked you."

Jera turned with a shrug, moving to play with the soap bubbles on the other side of the pool. Kitieri shrugged her good shoulder, trying to shimmy out of the jacket without too much pain, but the lining clung to the sweat and dirt on her skin.

"Come on," she muttered, closing her eyes to rest for a moment. The gentle sound of dripping water on stone reached her ears, and Kitieri opened her eyes to an empty pool. With a start, she turned to find Jera standing behind her, wrapping herself in one of the gray towels.

"I'll help you," she said, taking the jacket collar in both hands. She slid it off Kitieri's shoulders, folded it neatly, and set it on top of her own clothes. "What happened to your arm?"

Kitieri shook her head, biting down on her lip as Jera pulled off her sleeveless black shirt.

"I fell on some stairs," she said evasively. Jera dropped the garment on top of the pile and crouched down beside her, huge eyes full of concern.

"Is that how you got the rest of these, too?" she asked, tracing a long bruise, and Kitieri looked down at the angry welts and purple splotches that covered her body.

"Kind of," she replied, pulling off the rest of her clothes. "They're just bruises, Jera. I'll be all right."

As she sank into the warm water, her stiff muscles heaved a sigh of relief and her aches started to melt away. Goosebumps ran across her arms and shoulders, and Kitieri welcomed the sensation with a long exhale.

"Who did that to you?" Jera came to sit on the edge of the pool, dipping her feet into the water. Kitieri opened her eyes.

"The same kind of men who came to our house."

"In the red jackets?"

"Yes." Kitieri turned, resting a hand on Jera's knee. "Now, listen to me, Jera. This is very important. When you see a red jacket like that, always go the other way. Don't draw attention to yourself, just quietly get away from them as fast as you can."

"Why?"

"Just to be safe."

"Aren't we safe here?"

Kitieri glanced at the closed curtain around their pool, wondering who might be listening on the other side.

"I don't know," she whispered. "Just stay close to me while we're here, and do everything I say, all right?"

Jera nodded, picking up the chunk of soap on the ledge. As she worked the suds into Kitieri's tangled hair, pleasurable goosebumps ran down Kitieri's arms again.

"Thank you, Jera," she mumbled.

"You take care of us," Jera said. "And now you're hurt, so I can take care of *you*."

Kitieri smiled. "When did you grow up so much?"

"Mmm…" Jera hummed a high pitch, as if contemplating the answer to a difficult question. "I think yesterday, maybe."

Kitieri laughed, grabbing Jera's ankle under the water. Jera shrieked, kicking and laughing, and Kitieri didn't care that her voice carried across the chamber.

"Excuse me, ladies?"

Kitieri jumped off the pool wall at the voice, heart leaping into her throat. She exhaled in a rush as the short, plump woman from the Sanctuary stepped in, holding a basket of clothes.

"Apologies!" Minna said, stepping through the curtain. "I brought a fresh change for you. I'll just take these old things—"

Kitieri flung her arm out of the pool as she reached for the old pile, spraying water everywhere. "No!"

Minna jumped back.

"I'm sorry." Kitieri drew her hand back. "Just—leave the jacket."

"This old thing?" Minna picked up the torn leather garment, looking it up and down as if it might give her some kind of disease.

"Yeah."

"As you wish, Ms. Manon." Minna set the basket of new clothes on the floor, leaving the existing pile untouched. "I will be waiting outside when you're done."

Minna bowed, and the curtain fluttered back into place.

"Thank you," Kitieri called after her. Jera nudged her with her foot under the water once the door to the bath chamber closed.

"I think you scared her," she whispered with a giggle.

Kitieri grinned, turning back to the pool. "She scared me first."

Jera's giggles doubled in volume as Kitieri dipped under the water, rinsing the soap from her hair and scrubbing her entire body. Jera handed her one of the gray towels as she stepped out, and they dressed in the loose-fitting clothing. Kitieri combed through Jera's hair with her fingers, braiding it down her back before they gathered their old clothes and left.

Taff was leaning against the wall beside Minna when they emerged from the steamy chamber, dressed in the same light gray pants and loose-fitting top.

"Oh, don't you three look so much better!" Minna piped, beaming. "And you *smell* better, too."

She bounced away, and they followed her back through the twisting hallways.

As they ascended into the upper levels of the Church, the stair landings became increasingly dominated by tall, arched windows looking out over the Square. Stars twinkled in the velvet sky around the last hints of orange on the horizon, and Kitieri paused. Just one day ago, she and Noia had set out for the Church of Histan in hopes of a better life. One day—and an entire lifetime, it seemed.

Kitieri stopped at one of the windows, touching the glass with tentative fingertips, and felt the clean, light draft seeping in.

I'm sorry you never got that life, Noia.

A gentle hand on her arm turned Kitieri from the window, and she looked down at Taff.

"Are you all right?" he asked. Behind him, Minna was halfway up the next set of stairs, carrying on a cheerful conversation with Jera. Kitieri pressed her lips together with a soft sigh through her nose, and nodded.

They climbed floor after floor, each window looking out higher above the city. Their pace slowed, and Minna's huffing and puffing became audible up ahead until she finally paused on a landing.

"Honestly," she panted, "you'd think I'd be better at this by now! It just never gets any easier."

Kitieri smiled. She was in no rush.

"I was wondering..." she started, taking advantage of the break. Minna's brows rose in interest, eager for the extended rest.

"Yes, my dear?"

Kitieri gave her an innocent look. "You seem to work closely with the Baliant. Do you know her well?"

"Oh yes, I practically raised her!" Minna laughed. "Well, not 'practically.' I *did* raise her."

"Oh." Kitieri hadn't expected that answer.

Minna lifted her skirts to continue up the next flight of stairs. "She's a fine Baliant, wise beyond her years. I'm sure you'll love her— everybody does. Well, *almost* everybody."

"Almost?" Kitieri raised an eyebrow.

Minna giggled nervously. "The Board doesn't count, as I see it. They don't like *anybody*."

"What's the Board?" Kitieri asked.

"The Board of Advisors? You've never...?" Mina took in a quick breath. "Ah, well, each Church has a Board of Advisors that serve the Baliant. They aid in decisions of government, law, spending... you know, all the boring stuff." Minna smiled warmly. "They're set up to be checks and balances so no one person has too much control, but this particular Board is just..."

Minna shook her head with a gargled sound of frustration before turning her focus back to saving breath for the ascent. Kitieri pictured Stil's black robes and gold sash and suppressed a shudder. If she hadn't used up all her luck accidentally repelling that Strike at the pillar, she'd be able to get Taff and Jera out of here before she ever saw another black robe.

"How long has she been Baliant?" she asked, changing the subject. "She seems so..."

"Yes, she is quite young for such a prestigious role," Minna said. "But that is probably a story better left for her to tell. Here we are!"

They reached what *had* to be the top floor of the Church, and Minna knocked on a double set of ornate mahogany doors. One opened, and Kitieri was surprised to see Catarva herself.

"Thank you, Minna," she said, smiling wide enough to show bright white teeth. "Please, come in."

Catarva left the door, and Minna ushered Kitieri and her siblings into a spacious room dominated by a large oblong table lined with eight plush, high-backed chairs. Kitieri expected Catarva to take her seat, but the Baliant skirted the table to enter the chamber beyond, and they followed into a bright dining room.

Settings were laid out at the far end of another long table, and Minna rushed ahead to pull out the cushioned chairs. While Catarva took her place at the head, Kitieri motioned for Taff and Jera to go around the left side as she took the right, choosing the chair to the Baliant's left. Kitieri held insistent eye contact with Jera as they took Catarva's invitation to sit, planting her feet on the floor and hands in her lap. Jera mimicked her proper movements with a grin.

Servants entered, filling water goblets and pouring wine from a carafe into small crystal chalices. Kitieri eyed the water as the servant moved around the table, the burning thirst pricking at her throat. As soon as Catarva lifted her own glass, Kitieri brought the cold liquid to her lips; despite her attempts at propriety, the chalice returned to the table nearly empty.

"Well," Catarva said, commanding the attention of the room, "welcome to the Church of Enahris. You all know my name, but I do not know yours."

Kitieri gestured to her siblings. "This is Taff, that's Jera, and I'm Kitieri."

Catarva nodded at each in turn while a servant set cups of soup before them. Jera's eyes widened as she leaned over the cup and Kitieri cleared her throat, sending her back into a polite position.

"It is a pleasure to have you here," Catarva said, taking a sip of the soup. On her cue, Taff and Jera began scooping up the thick, creamy broth, slurping it loudly from their spoons while Kitieri kept her eyes on the Baliant.

"Why did you do it?"

Catarva's eyes lifted from her spoon, and Kitieri was again struck by their bright amber color.

"Their intentions, should I deny you, were clear," the Baliant replied. "While I do not condone the brutal ways of our brother Church, I am seldom in a position to intervene. Today, however, presented a rare opportunity for me."

"So you scored a point in some kind of game?" Kitieri's eyes narrowed.

Catarva smiled, taking another sip of her soup. "All politics are a game, Ms. Kitieri. To assume otherwise is to fool yourself into believing this world to be a fair, righteous place. But no, it runs deeper than that." The Baliant shifted in her seat. "News of what happened in Histan's Square preceded your arrival."

Kitieri looked down at her soup. News traveled fast.

Catarva's eyes lingered on her, assessing her every movement.

"I am correct, then," she continued. "You are the young woman that survived the Judgement."

The words rolled off her tongue like cold honey, slow and smooth. Kitieri kept her head down, but noticed Taff and Jera go still across the table. Despite her gnawing hunger, all appetite fled as her mouth went dry. She licked her lips, summoning just enough moisture to speak.

"I know... I know that I should have submitted to the gods for my crimes..." Kitieri choked on the last word, and cleared her throat. "And I know that my element is banned in the city. But my brother was there. *I* was the one being judged, not him, and I couldn't let him die for me."

The words came faster and faster as she spoke, and Catarva extended a hand toward her on the table.

"You are not on trial here, Kitieri."

A servant collected the soup cups, and Kitieri's left its place untouched.

"I'm not?"

Catarva lowered her chin, raising an eyebrow. "Any human to stand at that pillar would stop the lightning if they could."

Kitieri fiddled with one of the silver forks to her left. "Last I heard, lightnings were banned from practicing because they were too dangerous."

Catarva folded her hands, intertwining her long, slender fingers. "That's an old law."

Kitieri's brows twitched into a faint frown. "Does it not exist anymore?"

"It does." Catarva spoke slowly, deliberately. "But there's not been much cause to enforce it of late."

The main course arrived, and Jera elbowed Taff as a large beef roast was set before them, surrounded by potatoes and mounds of steaming vegetables. Kitieri leaned out of the way to let the servant distribute her portion, pondering Catarva's words. As the rich aromas filled her nose, a loud grumble tore from Kitieri's stomach. Her hand flew to her abdomen and she cast a sideways glance to see if Catarva had noticed, but the woman was smiling at Jera's awestruck expression.

"Please, eat," Catarva laughed.

Jera looked up at Kitieri, her fork and knife poised at the ready, and Kitieri nodded. Taff and Jera dug into the roast like they were in an eating contest with free food for life as the prize.

"Why don't you enforce the lightning ban anymore?" Kitieri asked, taking a bite of her own dinner. Though she tried to keep her expression neutral, the burst of flavors and hot juices in her mouth made her eyes water. She had never tasted anything so delicious in her entire life.

"Because until today, lightnings were thought to no longer exist."

Kitieri's head snapped up, and her chewing slowed.

"So you can see, perhaps," Catarva continued, "why your arrival here presented such a unique opportunity."

Kitieri set her fork on the edge of her plate. "I'm not sure I understand."

"You have a rare talent in a dangerous world, Kitieri," the Baliant said. "That you managed to survive your own element into adulthood, alone, is phenomenal. But what's more, you can *wield* it."

"I — I don't know about that."

"You walked away from that pillar unscathed." Catarva leaned in, bright eyes intense. "Even before the lightnings died, no one has *ever* managed such a feat. How did you do it?"

Kitieri looked to Taff, who was watching her with wide eyes.

"I'm not sure," she muttered. "It just… happened."

"I see." Catarva straightened, poking daintily at the food on her plate with her upside down fork. "I'm curious. What sort of training did you receive as a child?"

The image of their mother in her chair, holding her book on elements, flashed through Kitieri's mind.

"Not much," she said. "The lightning was dangerous even before the Strikes started, when I was eight. One day, I accidentally killed the hog my dad had saved up for, so… I never used it again."

"You *locked* it?" Catarva's hard eyes were intent on Kitieri. "That is exceptional control for such a young age. I knew many adults who could not lock their lightning once the Strikes started."

"I don't have control." Kitieri frowned. "That was the whole problem. I was going to hurt my family if I didn't do something, so I had to lock it."

The Baliant gave her a patronizing smile, and Kitieri felt her temper ignite. "While I understand your reservations, Kitieri, control can be taught. It's nothing that training can't fix."

"Training? What training?"

"Through the Church of Enahris, of course."

An incredulous laugh escaped before Kitieri could stop it.

"Hold on," she said. "You're telling me that the Church of Enahris just wants to give me free elemental training?"

"Well." Catarva dipped her head, dabbing at her lips with a linen napkin. "It's a fair bit more complicated than that."

Of course it is.

The uneasy feeling that had settled in her stomach the moment she'd stepped foot in the Sanctuary reared its head. This woman was far too interested in her element; it was, beyond a doubt, the only reason she'd claimed them as members of her Church when she could have told the truth.

Kitieri looked across the table at her siblings, who were scraping their plates clean. She'd barely kept them one step ahead of death since she'd left to buy that damned Gadget. Every move made, every word spoken, had removed one danger only to threaten with something more insidious. Catarva had not spoken the words yet, but Kitieri felt the walls of entrapment closing in around her. Taking them in had been a calculated move, and the Baliant would seek her repayment.

Servants whisked the dinner plates away, and miniature porcelain cups filled with a fluffy brown substance appeared on the table. Taff poked at his skeptically, while Jera leaned so close she almost dipped her nose in it.

"What is it?" she asked, scrunching her face.

Catarva laughed. "Try it. I think you'll like it."

Jera dipped her spoon into the spongy dessert, bringing it to her mouth, and her eyes shot open wide. "It's so *good*!"

She dove into the rest of the cup and Taff joined, emboldened by his sister's proclamation. Catarva's expression became serious again as she turned back to Kitieri.

"I have an offer for you," she said.

Kitieri met her gaze, jaw clenched. The word "offer" made it sound like she had the option to turn it down, but Kitieri held to no such hope.

"What." She forced the word out.

"I have made it no secret that your particular skillset is of great interest to the Church of Enahris," Catarva said. "You hold a unique advantage over any man in this city, and for that reason, I would very much like for you to consider joining us as an officer of the Church."

Kitieri remained still in her seat, repeating the words twice in her mind.

"I'm sorry," she said after a long pause. "Was that a *job* offer?"

"It was."

"As an *officer*?"

"Yes." Catarva suppressed the amusement that pulled at the corners of her lips. "Starting pay is a round per week, with housing, clothing, and meals provided here."

Kitieri blew out a fast puff of air. That was more money than she could make in a whole month at the mines. She shook her head. It didn't matter.

"As generous as that is," she said, "I can't leave my family. They need me at home."

"Oh, your siblings can stay with you as dependents, and you will be allotted one of our family suites in the north wing. We have fantastic educational programs for the families of our officers and staff, where they can pursue academics, weaponry, elemental training, or just about any trade they desire, and PCR's are available upon request. You, of course, will go through specialized combat and elemental training in our officers' program."

Kitieri looked down at her hands, picking at one of her nails. Of all the things she'd expected Catarva to say, this had been last on the list. She was already in the Baliant's debt for putting the Church of Histan off their heels, and now she was offering safety, food, beds, education, training, and more money than Kitieri could even fathom. Every item

Catarva threw in to sweeten the pot felt like another nail in some hidden coffin, and it made Kitieri's skin crawl.

A drop of blood sprang up on her finger where she'd picked the skin raw, and she quickly folded her hands in her lap.

"And may I ask," she said, "what is expected in return for all of this generosity?"

"You would work for the Church," Catarva replied.

"What does the Church want with my lightning?"

Kitieri met the hard amber eyes, and Catarva's expression softened into a demure smile. "A chat for another time, perhaps."

Shocking.

"What if I say no?"

Catarva pushed her chair back from the table. "It's a job offer, Kitieri, not enslavement. You are always free to leave."

She stood, coming to her full height in the long, impressive robes, and servants moved for the double doors leading deeper into the Baliant's chambers.

"Sleep on it," she said, turning for the doors.

"Wait." Before she realized what she was doing, Kitieri found herself on her feet. Catarva looked back over her shoulder, calm and neutral.

"Yes?"

"I'll do it."

Catarva bowed her head with a slow smile.

"Very good," she said. "Your training begins tomorrow."

———

MINNA UNLOCKED one of the hallway's many doors, pushing it open into a candlelit room.

"Your accommodations for the evening," she announced, inviting them in with a sweep of her hand. "I took the liberty of lighting the candles before dinner so it would be nice and cozy for you."

As she moved across the room toward another door, keys jangling, Kitieri glanced around the small quarters. Two beds stood against the far wall with one nightstand between them, and a mirror and washbasin rested on a short chest of drawers.

"I know it's small for the three of you," Minna said over her shoulder, "but it's only for tonight. Tomorrow, I'll get one of the officers' suites ready for you, and you'll all have much more room. For now, you can use this room, too."

She opened the second door to an adjoining chamber, identical to the first, and turned with a smile. "I thought the little gentleman might prefer his own space."

"Oh, you're a *gentleman*," Kitieri whispered down to him, nudging him with her elbow. Taff nudged her back, grinning.

Minna went on. "Check the drawers; you should have everything you need. I guessed on sizes, but I am hardly ever wrong anymore. Lots of practice! Oh, except for you, my dear." She beckoned for Kitieri to come closer. "I will need precise measurements from you before I leave, as you will need a uniform first thing tomorrow morning. We normally have much more time for these types of arrangements, but it seems Baliant Catarva is anxious to get you started! Hopefully Meral can make a few quick alterations to one of the uniforms in her stock…"

The woman trailed off, fumbling with a roll of measuring tape. She instructed Kitieri through the necessary movements, lifting her arms and turning her around, while Jera giggled. Satisfied, she rolled the tape up and shoved it back in her apron pocket.

"That should do it!" she chirped. "I'll leave you be now. Do sleep well, and I will see you bright and early tomorrow for your first day."

The door latched with a gentle click, and Kitieri let out a long, slow sigh. After a moment of silence, Taff turned to Kitieri with a quizzical look.

"Do we live here now?"

Kitieri sank down onto the edge of the nearest bed, rubbing her face with both hands. "I guess so."

Jera hopped onto the bed beside her, bouncing on the soft mattress. "What about home?"

Kitieri ran a hand over her sister's clean hair, smoothing the little strands that stuck out of her braid. "It will still be there."

Taff sat down on her other side, his eyes serious in the flickering candlelight.

"Do you really want to work for them?" he asked.

"No," Kitieri answered, looking down. "But I had to accept."

"Why?"

"Did you hear what she said? She's offering you two a life that I would *never* be able to afford working in the mines. And that's *if* I could get that job back, which I doubt. I didn't show up today, and they'd be looking for any excuse to lay into me. Histan's Church stole every bit I'd saved, so we'd be starting over from scratch." She turned her head to meet her brother's stare. "I *had* to accept."

"I thought Churches were bad," Jera said, swinging her legs over the side of the bed.

"We're just going to have to wait and see," Kitieri replied. "We can't control what others do, we can only control ourselves. Right?"

Jera nodded. "And all we can do is our best."

"That's right." Kitieri squeezed her shoulder. "But I need you both to be very careful here. It sounds like I'm going to be busy, and I won't be able to be with you during the day. I need you to look out for each other, okay? And... I need you to promise me something."

"What?" Jera leaned in, like she was eager to learn a secret.

"If you don't feel safe, or anything happens that makes you uncomfortable, I need you to tell me as soon as you can. We are going to have to be honest with each other through every step of this, all right? We stick together."

A tight grin curved Taff's lips. "The Manons survive."

"No matter what," Jera added.

Kitieri smiled, pulling them both in close to her. "No matter what."

CHAPTER 9

"**B**reakfast, breakfast, breakfast!" Jera chanted, jumping up and down at the door to their room. "Come *on*, Taff, hurry up!"

Taff emerged from the adjoining room, pulling a dark gray shirt over his head.

"Cool off, will you?" he said through the shirt's fabric. As his head popped out of the hole, his hair a staticky mess, he stopped in his tracks. "Whoa, *Kitieri*."

Kitieri held out her arms, looking down at the officer's uniform Minna had delivered earlier. The gray pants tucked neatly into tall black boots, and the matching gray jacket fit her form perfectly. The stretchy material allowed for a large range of motion without constriction, and breathed much better than she'd expected.

"Pretty sharp, huh?" she asked. Taff nodded, jutting out his lower lip in approval.

"Breakfast," Jera whined, hanging dramatically on the door handle.

"All right, we're going, Jera," Kitieri laughed, pulling her sister off the door.

Minna awaited them outside. "Oh my, don't you look wonderful!" she said, taking in Kitieri's appearance. "It fits beautifully. That Meral is a master, she really is. Let's get you fed, then!"

She led the way down to the dining hall; they could smell the aromas long before they reached the open archway.

The sheer size of the hall stole Kitieri's breath. One long table ran down the middle, piled with a variety of dishes, and dining tables lined both walls. Jera's hands flew to her cheeks as her mouth fell open.

"I can take whatever I want?" she asked.

"Yes," Minna laughed, walking them to the end of the line that ran the length of the center table. "We take most of our meals in this style. The coursed meal you saw last night is by invitation only. You are fortunate that Baliant Catarva has taken such a liking to you."

"Why's that?" Kitieri asked.

"Well, not many get to dine in her private quarters. Not even new officers."

"Ah."

They reached the end of the table, and Jera grabbed one of the big plates off its stack.

"Only take what you're sure you can eat," Kitieri told her.

"Mmhmm." Jera dove for the tongs as soon as the officer ahead of her set them down. A burst of laughter behind her made Kitieri turn to look at a group of officers at one of the tables. In mid-laugh, one of them made eye contact with her and nudged his friend. As the second turned to look at her, Kitieri spun back to the serving table, cheeks burning. She could feel their eyes on her back as she moved down the line.

Scooping up a serving of eggs, she peered over Jera's shoulder at her plate. "Jera, there's no way you can eat all that!"

Jera snatched her plate out of Kitieri's reach. "Yes, I can!"

Kitieri fixed her with a stern look. "There had better not be one crumb left."

"Don't underestimate her," Taff said, clicking a pair of metal tongs before grabbing a piece of sliced ham. "That girl's a bottomless pit."

Minna giggled, touching a hand to her dimpled cheek. "You children are so funny!"

"Yeah, they're hilarious," Kitieri muttered, catching Jera's eye once more as she went for a biscuit. Jera looked away, but set the biscuit back in its heated metal tin.

They followed Minna to one of the smaller tables against the windowless wall of the dining hall, and Kitieri threw Jera a scathing look as she sat down with her mouth already full.

"Well, Officer, are you excited?" Minna asked, leaning over her plate. Kitieri paused with the fork halfway to her mouth.

"I guess so."

Minna squeaked a half laugh. "You *guess*? Do you know what an honor it is to be an officer of the Church of Enahris?"

"Uhh…"

"This Church turns away *hundreds* of people a day who come asking to train as an officer."

"Hundreds, huh?"

"Something like that. Anyways, the Baliant is very picky about who she chooses. Our force may not match Histan's for size, but we certainly beat them out for quality."

All the more reason to hire a random kid off the street, Kitieri thought. She shoved her loaded fork into her mouth to avoid answering out loud, and looked over at Jera. The colossal plate she'd built was already half empty. *But as long as they're fed and happy…*

"So what happens after breakfast?" Taff asked Minna.

"Your sister will go with Officer Haldin to start her training, and you two will come with me to sign up for lessons. Have you thought about what interests you?"

Jera's head popped up. "Do you have horses?"

"We do! The stable is behind the Church. Do you want to learn to ride?"

"Yes!"

"You've never even seen a horse before," Taff said.

"I saw pictures in Mom's books," Jera replied, scraping her plate clean.

"What about you, then?" Minna asked Taff.

"I'll need to see what the choices are," Taff said, leaning against the back of his chair. "But I think I'd like to look at weaponry or combat."

"Going for officer like your sister?"

"I don't know." Taff shrugged. "I'd just like to be able to defend the people I care about."

Kitieri's heart melted. She'd always assumed her serious, calculating little brother would use his brains over his non-existent braun. *Maybe one day.* She heaved a sigh, and stood from the table.

"Where can we take our plates?"

"Don't worry about them, dear, the servants will pick them up."

Jera jumped off her chair. "This place is awesome!"

"Don't get used to it," Kitieri muttered.

"Oh, there's Officer Haldin," Minna said. "Looks like he's about to leave. Let's catch him."

The man was just standing from his bench, talking to one of the other officers at the table, and looked up as Minna approached.

"Good morning, Minna." Haldin smiled, and his eyes settled on Kitieri. "Ms.—Manon, was it?"

"Kitieri."

Minna backed away, pulling Taff and Jera with her. "Come, let's leave the officers to it."

As the woman steered them away, Kitieri watched her siblings go, wishing she could stay with them. Jera turned to give her a little wave as Minna ushered her from the hall, and Kitieri wiggled her fingers back at her.

"Maybe she's older than she looks."

Kitieri heard the murmur behind her, and turned back to the officers still seated at the end of the long table. Several snickered into their plates, and Kitieri felt her neck grow hot.

"What was that?" she asked, looking over the group to pinpoint who'd spoken.

"They're yours, right?" another officer said—a woman seated at the end.

"They're my siblings, yes."

"See, I told you," came the first voice. "She's just a kid herself."

Kitieri looked to the speaker, a dark-haired man with a finely trimmed beard. He'd already gone back to his breakfast, stabbing potatoes, eggs, and ham onto his fork all at once. The heat in Kitieri's cheeks traveled down her neck, and she knew her face was red. Her hands tingled as she glared at the man.

"Do we have some sort of problem?"

The officer paused his stabbing, looking up at her with a raised eyebrow. "I don't know. Do we?"

"Jorid," Haldin warned. Jorid straightened, leaning away from his plate.

"Do you know how many good, experienced men and women are ahead of you for this position?"

Kitieri crossed her arms. "I hear there are hundreds."

"And you think you're better than them?"

"I couldn't say." Kitieri matched Jorid's glare. "But if you're so mad, maybe you should confront your Baliant on her choices."

Jorid stood, throwing his chair back on two legs. "You *dare* question Catarva?"

"I didn't question her—you did."

A flare caught Kitieri's eye, and she glanced down to see a flicker of fire in Jorid's palm.

"Not here!" Haldin shot a hand out to Jorid, whose stare stayed locked on Kitieri. She stood firm, hand curled into summoning position. The sparks itched in her fingers, ready to lash out.

Jorid flicked his eyes to her palm, twitching a brow in invitation. "Come on, little girl. If you're tough enough to make officer, show me what you've got."

"Jorid!" Haldin barked. "I said, *not here!*"

Jorid held the controlled flame in his hand, smirking as Haldin's words rang between them. A single white spark popped from Kitieri's fingertip, unbidden, and she snapped her hand closed in a tight fist. The charge burned inside, and she swallowed its will to strike. Murdering a fellow officer over a pissing contest on her first day probably wasn't a great idea.

"If you'll excuse us, we have a training schedule to follow," Haldin said, throwing Jorid a smoldering glare as he left the table.

"You've sure got your work cut out for you, Haldin," Jorid called after them. Ignoring him, Haldin set a brisk pace to the exit, and Kitieri was forced to lengthen her strides uncomfortably to avoid trotting after him like a puppy.

Once clear of the dining hall, Haldin slowed his pace and allowed Kitieri to walk beside him.

"You'll have to ignore Jorid," he said. "He doesn't take well to any of the new recruits, and the fact that you're a special case makes it worse."

Kitieri unclenched her fist with a silent exhalation. She'd been sure Haldin was going to lay into her for the confrontation, and something told her she did not want to get on this man's bad side.

"But he does have a point," Haldin continued, taking such an abrupt turn that Kitieri had to scamper after him.

"What point is that?" she asked, defensive.

"We have a list of qualified candidates just waiting to train. As far as our fellow officers are concerned, it makes no sense for the Baliant to ignore protocol in your favor. But I know what you are."

Haldin stopped in the narrow, deserted hallway, turning to face Kitieri.

"I saw the spark on your finger back there," he said. "I know what you are, but anyone except a well-trained electric would assume that's the element they saw. I think it's best that we keep it that way for now, don't you?"

Kitieri blinked. "Sure."

Haldin's pale blue eyes searched her face, and their proximity in the tight hallway started to make Kitieri uneasy.

"How good is your control?" he asked in a hushed tone.

Kitieri looked down at her boots. "I don't know."

"How do you not know? How many have you killed?"

Kitieri snapped her head up, offended. "*None*, thank y—"

"So control is one hundred percent?"

"Well…" Kitieri averted her gaze. "If you count the ten years it was locked."

"Shit." Haldin dropped his head, rubbing his temple. "This is worse than I thought. When did you come out of lock?"

"Yesterday."

"No mishaps since then?"

"No?"

Haldin put a closed fist to his mouth, breathing out through his nose. "All right," he said. "We don't have much time. Follow me."

His long strides swept him down the hall, and Kitieri jogged after him.

"Time for what?" she asked.

"If you've just come out of lock, you have a tight window to get this thing under control."

"Or?"

Haldin stopped at a door at the end of the hall, resting his hand on the knob. When he turned back, the raw grief on his face was palpable.

"There's a reason even the strongest lightnings are dead," he said. "The longer it's out of lock, the stronger your element will grow. Either it will run wild, killing at random, or it will burn you up from the inside out. Probably both."

Kitieri stood frozen, horrified by the man's words and the anguished expression on his face that told her he knew these things all too well.

"You knew a lightning?" she whispered.

"My wife," he said, his voice flat and cold. "Seven years ago. Our son died with her the day it finally overcame her. You are lucky you locked it so young, because once the Strikes started…" His knuckles went white on the doorknob. "There was nothing we could do."

He wrenched the door open and stepped into the dark room, reemerging with a Gadget in each hand.

"Haldin," she started, voice and hands trembling. "I —"

"Don't be sorry," he said, shoving one of the Gadgets into her arms. "Just *don't* let it happen to you, too. Do you hear me?"

She nodded, fingers closing around the stiff black leather.

"Catarva had one hell of a time convincing me to take you on as a trainee last night," he said, "but I'm the only one in her command who has trained lightnings and knows how they work. She was right about one thing, and it's that without me, you *and* those kids will be dead in two weeks."

Kitieri's hands went numb on the Gadget's casing, and she felt the blood drain from her face.

"So." Haldin's commanding tone reverberated off the stone walls as he shouldered the pack. "Ready to train?"

He started back down the hall and Kitieri followed, head spinning.

"Remember that room," he said over his shoulder. "It's where all the PCR's are kept, and it's protocol for officers to wear one any time they exit the Church. Not that it will do *you* much good."

"Why? Do the Gadgets not work for lightnings?"

Haldin wiggled his hand with a tilt of his head. "Eh, not really. It will feel different for a while, but as your element grows, the PCR will become meaningless. The Strikes are an unnatural force that have been shown to overcome both oran and cintra when pulled to a lightning's element. Even while locked, I'm sure you've had more than your fair share of close calls with the Blue Killer."

"Yeah," Kitieri muttered, remembering the goats. "If I'm out, it usually finds me."

Haldin nodded. "It can smell you. It's drawn to you, just like your element is drawn to it. They are different, and yet the same, feeding off each other in a vicious cycle."

He stopped at another door to slip his arm through his Gadget's second strap, and Kitieri realized she was still clutching hers in her hands. As the case settled against her back, a cooling sensation washed over her. The nagging burn that had been biting at her fingertips since breakfast vanished as her lightning retreated deep within her.

"Feels different, right?" Haldin asked, watching her.

"It's weird," Kitieri conceded. "Kind of... numb."

"Enjoy that while it lasts," he said, pushing the door open. Bright morning light flooded the hallway, and Haldin led her out into a packed dirt yard surrounded by a high wall. On the far side, near the metal gate, a few men in gray uniforms sparred with long, pointed staffs.

"This is our training yard, where I would normally hand you a spear and put you through a brutal workout." Haldin turned with a wry grin. "But we have more pressing issues."

To put it lightly, Kitieri thought, shifting the heavy Gadget on her back. The protective cintra dropped a haze over her senses, muffling her perception of her surroundings, and she shook her head in an attempt to clear her thoughts.

"So you're going to tell me how I repelled that Strike?" she asked.

"Excuse me?"

Kitieri frowned. "At Histan's pillar. Baliant Catarva didn't tell you?"

"She told me you survived the Judgement," he replied, brows furrowed, "but I think you're mistaken on the terminology. No one *repels* a Strike. The Blue Killer always takes a victim."

"Mmm, no." Kitieri shifted again. "Not this time. It came for me, and I repelled it. There was no victim."

"That's impossible."

"I'm telling you what happened."

"Kitieri, no lightning produced by human hands will ever over-power a Strike. It's out of the question."

Kitieri saw the blue L shape again, burned forever into her mind as a memory of her failure. A shudder ran over her as she watched Noia's black corpse fall to the stone in her mind's eye, reliving the gravity of her misjudgment.

Haldin was right. Her lightning would never be as strong as the Blue Killer.

But that wasn't what happened the second time...

"I didn't overpower the Strike," she said. "I used it. Like a water controls rain."

Haldin huffed a short, dry laugh. "A Strike is not rain. It doesn't —"

"I'm sure of it," Kitieri said, gaining confidence. "My own lightning disappeared at the last second, and I told the Strike what to do. I sent it back up, where it came from... and that's where it went."

Haldin studied her, blue eyes intense.

"All right," he said, cocking his head as he turned to head for the middle of the yard. "Whatever happened yesterday, we have no time to waste here."

Kitieri frowned after him, biting back the ready retort on her lips. If he refused to believe her, she'd just have to prove it.

"Can you summon your lightning at all through the PCR?" he asked, turning back.

She turned her attention inward, closing her eyes. Her element's subtle purr hummed deep within her, sleepy, distant, and... unresponsive. She closed her eyes tighter, urging the lightning to her fingers, but it remained still and cool beneath the Gadget's weight.

With a sigh, Kitieri dropped her hands and opened her eyes.

"No," she admitted. Proving her lightning's potential was off to a solid start.

Haldin nodded. "We'll have to train without the Gadgets for now. It's not ideal, but we'll keep a close eye on your control. Hey, Amond!"

One of the officers across the yard disengaged immediately from his sparring match.

"Yes, sir?"

Kitieri raised an eyebrow. Apparently Haldin held some kind of rank, though a cursory glance at his uniform displayed no embroidery or marks to set him apart.

"Give us a bit, will you?" Haldin asked. The training officers nodded quickly, leaning their spears against the wall. She waited for the inevitable jibes, but the men left silently through the gate, with only intrigued glances back at Kitieri.

Haldin was definitely a man she wanted on her side.

"Right." He clapped once, turning back to her. "Gadget off."

Hot energy rushed through Kitieri's body as the straps slid from her shoulders. White sparks sizzled on her fingertips and she slammed her hands into tight fists, pulling them in close to her body.

"First lesson." Haldin grinned. "Don't rely on physical means to control your element."

Kitieri squinted. "Huh?"

Haldin gestured to her clenched fists. "I know it's natural to try to close it off, but that method won't work for long. Your mind holds the power, not your body."

Kitieri slowly unfurled her clenched fingers, and the sparks resumed their little dance. Her mind? That made no sense. Never in her life had her lightning felt like an extension of her mind as it burned in her chest, arms, and hands. Her lightning had always been nothing but physical... until the day she'd locked it, at least.

"What you have to understand," Haldin said, "is that our elements work mostly as defense mechanisms. That's true for everyone, but lightnings were by far the most volatile even before the Strikes started. Our elements respond to our emotions and reflexes, just like—"

He shot his hand towards her and snapped his fingers in her face. Kitieri flinched at the sudden pop, and felt her lightning zing down her arms with her small adrenaline spike. Haldin pulled his hand back, grin widening.

"Just like that," he finished. "And managing that will take far more mental training than physical. Now, let's see what we're working with." He scanned the yard and pointed. "See that pebble there?"

Kitieri followed his finger until her gaze landed on a little rock near the wall, and she nodded.

"Strike it," he said.

Kitieri took in a breath, and her palms broke into a sweat.

"Okay." Her voice came out small and high.

It's just a rock.

She called her lightning to her hands and sparks popped from her fingers, neither painful nor pleasant. Just... strange. A foreign feeling that still felt so familiar, like a memory from a dream.

She focused on the pebble, resisting the overwhelming urge to clench her fists. She'd never used her lightning on purpose outside of a Strike before.

Closing her eyes, Kitieri held out her hand and summoned all of the energy into her palm.

Please just hit this rock.

The lightning released with a powerful kick, and an icy chill gripped her hand for a fleeting moment. She opened one eye to find the rock untouched.

Opening her other eye revealed the charred, black mark on the stone wall, and she clicked her tongue against the roof of her mouth. "That's embarrassing."

"It's all right," Haldin assured her. "You've never done this before. But learning to use your element like this could save your life when the time comes to exercise control during a Strike. Try it again, but be more deliberate this time."

"More deliberate?" Kitieri asked, lowering her brows.

"Tell me that last one wasn't a shot in the dark," Haldin chuckled, tilting his head. "You let go too soon, and had no real visual of your target. Bring your next one straight down."

"From... from the sky?"

"Yes. It doesn't have to come from your hand. Use your element's natural tendency and strike from above for a much higher chance of hitting your target."

Kitieri clenched her jaw, remembering her spectacular failure to stop Noia's Strike in Histan's Square. The blaze of her lightning meeting the Blue Killer would forever burn in her mind, but Haldin was right. It hadn't come from her hand, then, but the ground.

"All right," she whispered, refocusing on the rock. This time when she closed her eyes, she did not lose sight of her target. It lingered in her consciousness, perfectly framed in her mind's eye. The only thing in the yard that mattered.

Her lightning reacted differently this time. While its buzz remained constant in her curled fingers, its power felt lighter. Easier to wield, somehow.

All thoughts bent on the pebble, Kitieri lifted her arm, waiting for the lightning's burn to reach its peak, and ripped it down to her side. A violent crack split the yard, shaking the ground beneath her feet.

She didn't peek reluctantly this time. She didn't need to. She lifted her gaze to find the pebble utterly destroyed, in a spray of tiny blackened pieces.

"Yes!" Haldin's cheer startled her. "A truly impressive second attempt."

Kitieri's cheeks flushed against her will. "Thanks," she mumbled.

"Now." Haldin put out a hand. As he took a breath to give his next instruction, a call rang across the training yard.

"Officer Haldin!"

Kitieri turned to see a young gray officer leaning out of the Church's doorway.

"One moment," Haldin said to her, dipping his head in a quick apology. He strode toward the Church, meeting the young man halfway, and Kitieri found herself following him. Only once their hushed tones reached her ears did she realize the conversation wasn't meant for her, and she turned to awkwardly examine the yard's far wall.

"They can't do that!" Haldin exclaimed, his vehemence raising the hairs on Kitieri's neck. More whispers. She strained her hearing this time, catching only tiny snippets.

"—Histan—district dispute, and our officers... Catarva—negotiations for release, but—refused."

"Damn it!" Haldin swore.

The crunch of his boots turning on dirt alerted Kitieri to his shift in attention before he spoke her name.

"Kitieri, I apologize," he said. She spun on her heel, lifting her brows in feigned surprise. "I have to go; something has come up. You are dismissed, but be prepared for early training tomorrow."

Kitieri nodded, an affirmative response dying on her lips as Haldin turned and rushed from the training yard with the officer; she snapped her mouth closed.

That was weird.

Now alone in the training yard, she heaved a loud sigh. Dismissed? For the day...?

She glanced up at the sky to gauge the sun's position, and noted the dark storm clouds coalescing on the horizon. Lightning—real, natural lightning—flashed against the clouds' dark underbelly, and she let out another sigh, softer this time.

I did harness that Strike.

Haldin didn't believe her, but that didn't make her wrong.

She glanced toward the yard's gate, and a strange tingle ignited in her breast. Taff and Jera in lessons, learning more than she could've ever hoped to provide, and her with an entire afternoon to do with as she pleased. She had no desire to wander the Church hallways all day, but the grounds piqued her interest.

She couldn't help grinning as she made for the metal gate, pulling it open to a manicured stone pathway between two walls. She followed the walkway through an inner network of courtyards and outbuildings until an arched gateway opened out into Enahris' Square.

"Ah, there she is."

Kitieri whirled around at the familiar voice, and found the speaker at the top of the Church stairs. Jorid leaned on his spear, sneering down at her.

"Is Haldin sick of you already?" he called. "Can't say I blame him."

Two officers beside him snickered, and Kitieri rolled her eyes. This guy was starting to get on her last nerve.

"Hey!" he shouted after her. She heard his boots on the stairs, and turned to face him as he stalked toward her. "I'm talking to you."

"I have nothing to say to you," she replied.

"Oh-ho-ho," Jorid chortled, batting his friend's shoulder with the back of his hand. "Not so tough now that the boss isn't here to protect you, huh?"

Kitieri's eyes narrowed. "I don't need protection."

"Ha!" Jorid slapped his leg. "Listen to that. She's got this all figured out."

The men on either side of him joined in the laughter.

"Come on then, little girl." Jorid took a step toward her. "Let's finish what we started."

The flame ignited in his palm, dancing at the edge of Kitieri's vision as she kept her eyes trained on his face.

"I'm not going to fight you," she said.

Jorid smirked. "Don't have what it takes?"

Kitieri shook her head with a dismissive snort, and turned to walk away. As she took her second step, something gripped her ankle.

What the —

Looking down, she saw a thin vine sprouting from between two stones in the walkway, twisting around her calf and squeezing her boot hard enough to cause pain. Stepping in front of his arbor friend, Jorid towered over her, the humor gone from his expression.

"What do you want from me?" Kitieri snapped, trying to pull free of the painful vine as it worked its way up to her knee. Jorid bent forward, bringing his face close to hers.

"I want you to leave," he growled. "You don't belong here, and you disgrace our title. I don't know what kind of lies you told to get this far, but you are far from worthy of this position."

As the man leaned menacingly over her, Kitieri's lightning reacted. It zipped through her body, growing angry and defensive as the vine held her in place, and she squeezed her hands closed.

Shit! The Gadget's back in the yard.

"You need to back off," she warned.

Jorid raised his eyebrow. "Prove yourself an officer, then, and make me."

He jabbed a flaming fingertip into her shoulder, singeing the gray jacket down to her skin. Kitieri batted his hand away with a sharp hiss. The lightning roared inside her, ready to protect its wielder. It raced up and down her arms, burning in her chest and biting at her hands, screaming for a chance to strike.

"I said, back the fuck up!" she shouted. Jorid jerked his head back, but recovered with a deadly grin.

"I'm serious," she continued, pulling desperately against the vine around her leg. "I don't want to kill you."

Jorid laughed. "Big words for a girl who can't even produce an element in self-defense."

He jammed his fiery finger into the hole in her jacket, searing her skin, and Kitieri yelped as the lightning tore free from her hands.

The world flashed white around her, and a deafening crack nearly ruptured her ear drums. Her scream lingered in the air, slicing into the deathly silence that followed.

Oh, fuck.

She stood paralyzed, eyes closed tight.

I killed him. He's dead. I murdered him. I —

"What... in the *gods'* names..."

Kitieri's eyes flew open to see the three officers writhing on the Church steps. Jorid struggled up to a sitting position, his face twisted into a horrified snarl.

"You," he thundered, lifting a shaking finger. Kitieri moved to back away and found her ankle free from the vine, its burned remains scattered on the stones. Without another moment's hesitation, she turned and ran.

"That's right!" Jorid called after her. "You'd *better* run! I will see you jailed for attempted murder by an illegal practice!"

Kitieri did not look back, letting adrenaline and panic carry her deep into the city.

CHAPTER 10

Kitieri's pace finally slowed as her lungs burned, begging for respite. A cold rain soaked her uniform, chilling her flushed skin as it ran down her back and legs into her boots, and she stopped to catch her breath under the overhang of a ramshackle house.

Her body trembled uncontrollably as she slid down the wall, and she let her tears mix with the rain and sweat that drenched her cheeks.

Dangerous. Unstable. Uncontrollable.

One tiny moment of victory in the training yard didn't change the truth of those words.

Shuddering breaths rattled in her throat as she fought for air through the sobs. She rocked back and forth, knees pulled to her chest, until the tears started to run out and her energy waned.

"I'm sorry," she whispered into the thrum of the rain. What for, she wasn't sure at first, but remorse overtook her emotions, flooding her thoughts.

It wasn't Jorid; he could choke, for all she cared. This was bigger than some courtyard bully.

I'm sorry, Jera, that I can't give you a life you deserve. I'm sorry, Taff, that I can't protect you. I'm sorry that every moment I'm with you, you're in danger.

She bent forward as another sob racked her body.

"I'm sorry for what I am," she choked.

A steady stream of rainwater poured from the house's gutter into the street, and Kitieri stared at the splatter on the stones until the lines blurred. As her vision hazed to gray dots, anxious thoughts fluttering through her mind, a small movement in her peripheral vision caught her attention and she became acutely aware of the sensation of being watched.

Kitieri whipped her head around and spied a corner of dark fabric disappearing into an alleyway two houses down. Senses jumping to high alert, she pushed to her feet and jogged out into the rain to peer around the corner.

"Hey," she called, moving warily toward the alley. It was probably nothing. A curious kid, maybe. But the hairs on the back of her neck still stood on end from the feeling of those eyes boring into her, and her brows furrowed as she prepared to lean around the corner of the house.

The door just beside her gave a loud creak as it swung open, and Kitieri jumped back.

"Officer!" A stout, jolly woman in a faded blue dress and soiled apron stood framed in the doorway. "My, it is *pouring*. You'll catch your death out here! Can I offer you some hot tea and a dry place to wait out this storm?"

Kitieri blinked rain from her eyes, stunned.

"Uh…" She glanced back to the corner of the house, peering through the driving sheets for another glimpse at the stranger, but found nothing.

"Come, come." The woman beckoned. "You must be freezing. I've already got the water on."

"I'm… I'm all right," Kitieri replied, forcing a smile.

"It's a long walk back to the Church in all this mess."

Kitieri looked back the way she'd come, realizing that her hair was plastered to her face and neck, and a chill racked her body. Of that, the woman was correct—it was quite the trek back, and the strange figure had long disappeared by now.

She sighed. "Okay. If you're sure."

The woman beamed, holding the door open wide for Kitieri to pass through. "Have a seat!" She pulled out a chair from the modest table, and hurried over to the fireplace to grab the kettle. "I'm Tira."

"Nice to meet you, Tira. I'm Kitieri."

Tira returned to the table with the kettle and an extra cup, and draped a wool blanket over Kitieri's shoulders.

"You are just soaked through," she muttered. "Where's your partner?"

Kitieri looked up. "My partner?"

"Well, yes, gray officers always patrol in pairs."

"Oh." Kitieri gave her a feeble smile. "Just me today."

"I see." Tira nudged the teacup. "Drink up, while it's hot."

Kitieri took the cup in her hands, letting it warm her palms as she scrutinized the woman.

"It was kind of you to invite me in," she said, sipping at her tea. Expecting the bitter taste of the root tea her mother had always made, the sweet, fruity flavors caught Kitieri by surprise, and she pulled her head back to sniff at the cup's rising steam.

"Oh, we always invite our kind officers in." Tira waved her hand. "In fact, I'm surprised I've never seen you before. Do you normally patrol a different sector, or are you new?"

"Pretty new." Kitieri took another sip, shivering as the hot liquid warmed her from the inside, and glanced around the small room. Nothing about the place showed any signs of wealth or luxury, but sweet berry teas like this were always twice the price of root teas at the market.

"We just love our officers," Tira was saying. "Baliant Catarva has been doing extraordinary things since she took over seven years ago."

Kitieri's eyes widened before she could remind herself to keep her expression neutral. *Seven years*? Hells, she couldn't have been older than fifteen when she'd become Baliant.

"Wouldn't you agree?" Tira prompted, tipping her cup to her lips.

"Oh, yeah." Kitieri nodded. "She's great."

Catarva's intent amber eyes flashed in her mind, and Kitieri shifted uncomfortably in her seat.

"Far better than her predecessor, I must say," Tira muttered, then snapped her head up with her lips pinned closed as Kitieri leaned forward.

"Why do you say that?"

"I meant no offense," Tira said with a shake of her head.

"None taken." Kitieri smiled reassuringly. "I'm just curious why you think that."

"Well…" Tira set her cup gingerly on the table. "As an officer of the Church, *you* would know better than I. But Baliant Catarva is changing things. It's a slow process, sure, but she's trying, despite the… difficulties."

Kitieri's brow twitched. "I don't follow."

Tira laughed, shrill and nervous. "My, you really *are* new, aren't you?"

Kitieri's face flushed, and she dropped her gaze to the table. *Just shut up while you're ahead.*

"Suffice it to say," Tira went on, "that since our current Baliant took the seat, the company of the gray officers that patrol our sector has become much more pleasant. You can really see their loyalty to her, and it's always more fulfilling to help people than to punish them, wouldn't you say?"

Kitieri nodded with a thin smile. Though she hadn't a clue about what most of Tira's rambling meant, she found reassurance that the gray uniforms were looked upon differently than the red ones, and the tiniest sliver of guilt fell away from her acceptance of her new position. But even so, the list of kind, *decent* uses a leader might have for a lightning element in her debt was a short one.

"Though I must say I'm surprised," Tira said. "I've never seen an officer out and about without a Gad—ah, PCR since the Strikes started."

"Yeah," Kitieri muttered. "I, uh, didn't mean to get this far out…" She trailed off, hearing Jorid's words ringing in her head.

"Oh, no need to explain yourself to *me*." Tira laughed. "I've been saving for one for years so my son can get out of those mines and get a better paying job. He's thirteen now, and I want him to start saving for a family and a house of his own someday. But the mines are just…"

"A trap," Kitieri finished. "I know. Grueling labor for insulting pay, all in exchange for protection until it's time to walk home."

Surprise crossed Tira's face before she drank from her cup.

"You almost sound like you've experienced it," she said with a chuckle. "But no miner *ever* makes officer. You know what they say: 'once a miner, always a miner.'"

Kitieri nodded, biting down hard on the inside of her lip.

"They do say that," she murmured. "Will you do me a favor, Tira?"

The woman's face brightened. "Anything, Officer!"

"When it's time to buy that Gadget, ask for me specifically. Kitieri Manon. All right?"

Tira tilted her head with a bemused squint. "I didn't think officers had anything to do with the Gadgets. That's all the Board of Advisors, from what I've heard."

"I don't care who's in charge of it," Kitieri said. "You ask for *me*. I'll make sure you get what you need for a fair price."

Tira nodded. "Okay. I'll do that."

"Good." Kitieri leaned back in her chair with a sigh, and felt a twinge in her hand. Her body stiffened, and she turned her head to the window, where the first hint of a charge wafted in on the cool draft.

Oh, shit.

Her element reacted to the charged air, burning her palms beneath the skin, and Kitieri snapped her hands into tight fists as she bolted from her chair.

"I have to go."

Tira stood, bewildered. "Is everything all right, Officer?"

"Yes—" Kitieri tripped over her chair. "Yes, I'm fine, I just…" She risked opening her hand to grab the door handle. "…Have to go. Thank you for the tea."

She rushed out into the street, where the rain had let up to a slow drizzle and people were resuming their work.

No, no, stay inside, she thought frantically. Tira trotted after her.

"Officer, what's wrong?"

"Tira, go back inside!" she snapped. Whirling around to the rest of the street, she shouted, "All of you, get inside!"

Members of the crowd threw her strange glances, ranging from indignant to fearful, but none heeded her warning. Panic rose in Kitieri's throat. No one *ever* listened.

The first warning struck just then, ripping an arc of white lightning from Kitieri's hand to strike the ground as people screamed and fled every which way. Those nearest to her stumbled back in surprise and fear, skirting around to give her a wide berth. Kitieri held her hand closed with the other, buried in her stomach.

"Officer!" Tira cried. "You don't have a Gadget—you *must* come inside!"

"I can't." Kitieri shook her head and backed away, grappling with the seething lightning as it beat against its bodily cage. *If I do, I'll kill you.*

Her lightning flared as the second warning threatened to pull it out of control, and Kitieri doubled over, gasping at the unbearable burn in her arms and chest.

She looked up, horrified to find so many still out on the street searching desperately for shelter. Too many people too far from their homes… and they were all in so much more danger than they realized. The Strike took only one, but she could kill them *all* if she lost control.

But I won't.

Kitieri closed her eyes, envisioning the crooked cobblestone right in front of her, where no one stood.

You want to strike something?

She raised her fist, and as the third warning electrified the air, she brought her hand down with a blinding bolt of white lightning. It obliterated the cobblestone, shooting rubble and debris everywhere. Chunks of stone pelted her face and neck, clinging to her still-wet hair, and Kitieri grinned as the element coiled in her hand. Despite the surrounding panic, she felt many pairs of eyes swivel to watch her.

"Ready to work now?" she muttered to her hand. The lightning responded with a pain-free buzz on her fingers.

The Strike's hateful eye locked on her from above, confident in its kill. She felt its attraction to her element, drawn to her element like a powerful magnet, and she remembered Haldin's words.

"It's drawn to you, just like your element is drawn to it. They are different, and yet the same, feeding off each other in a vicious cycle."

"Different, yet the same," Kitieri whispered. The Strike gathered its energy, hungry for death. "You can't have me. I *own* you!"

The blue bolt roared down, engulfing her in a vortex of pure, unadulterated energy and heat. Even with her eyes shut tight, the brilliance was painful. Her hands shook at her sides, fingers curved to channel the power, and she pushed back against the force pressing down on her.

In an instant, a dark coolness washed over her sweat-drenched body. No sound reached her ears, and she felt as if she was floating on a cloud of black nothing.

I passed out again.

A whisper and the crunch of shoes on rubble filtered through the barrier.

No...

She peeked from one eye, and her senses flooded back to her. She still stood, hunched and panting as a circle of bewildered onlookers stared, unabashed. She forced her back to straighten, uncurling her clenched fingers and releasing the tension in her arms and shoulders as more people emerged from their homes to survey the aftermath. It was a sick habit, but people always looked for the charred body in the wake of a Strike.

Sorry to disappoint.

She turned and caught a glimpse of Tira huddling in her door-frame, one hand clamped over her mouth.

"Remember what I said," Kitieri told her. "Ask for me."

Tira nodded vigorously, and Kitieri started back for the Church with a sigh. She couldn't avoid the place forever. As long as Taff and Jera were there, it was her only home.

The surrounding circle of gawkers parted to make way as hundreds of eyes followed her retreat, their murmurs rising into the chilled air to mingle with the gentle sounds of the rain.

KITIERI PAUSED at the circle of trees that lined Enahris' Square as her eyes fell on the blackened stones at the foot of the stairs. Her fingers moved unconsciously to the singed hole in the shoulder of her jacket, bared skin still smarting from Jorid's fiery jab.

"You're lucky I didn't fry you," she muttered. "'Attempted murder,' my ass."

She kicked the crispy remains of the vine as she passed, sending them up in little puffs of ash on the wind. The new guard shift paid her no mind as she crossed the Square to the arched gateway leading into the network of the Church's yards and outbuildings to retrieve the Gadget she'd left in the training yard.

As she followed the walkway between the high walls, one of the tall metal gates swung open into her path. High-pitched laughter and shouts met her ears, and Kitieri watched a young woman lead a group of children across the path and through another gate. One of the last children in line stopped and turned toward her, and her face lit up.

"Kitieri!" Jera shouted, running for her.

"Hi!" Kitieri dropped down on one knee, scooping her sister into a tight hug. The sweet, familiar scent of her hair as it hit her face pushed the worries from Kitieri's mind, melting away her anxiety.

"You came to see me!" Jera said, smiling from ear to ear. Kitieri beamed back.

"I just couldn't stand being away from you." She tickled her sister's sides and Jera shrieked, her infectious giggle bouncing off the surrounding walls. "How are the classes?"

Jera's eyes widened. "I *love* this place!" she declared. "I got to meet *horses* today! There's a gray one named Ashes that really likes me because I fed her carrots. I learned how to brush her, and comb her mane, and—"

"Officer."

Kitieri snapped her head up, smile fading. Haldin stood in the middle of the walkway, and Jorid lurked behind him with a smug grin.

"Okay, Jera," Kitieri whispered, resting a hand on her shoulder, "why don't you go ahead and catch up with your class? I don't want you to miss anything."

Jera smiled and threw her arms around Kitieri's neck. Kitieri held her tight, closing her eyes as she breathed in her scent one more time, before her sister turned and ran after her classmates.

Standing from her kneeling position, Kitieri met Haldin's stern gaze.

"Come with me," he said, turning.

Jorid sneered as he turned to follow, and Kitieri glared at the back of his head as Haldin led them through the Church and up the seemingly endless stairs. This kind of climb, she realized, could only mean one thing.

Catarva opened the carved wooden doors at the first knock, and Haldin pulled them closed again as they all moved to stand around the central oblong meeting table. Catarva walked around the far side, bracing both hands on the back of a tall, cushioned chair.

"Welcome, officers," she said. "You are all here because disturbing news has been brought to my attention."

"Yes, Baliant." Jorid bowed before shooting Kitieri a scathing glance. "This girl tried to kill me and two fellow officers—"

"I did *not* try to kill you!" Kitieri interrupted, but he raised his voice to speak over her.

"—on Church grounds, with an *illegal* element. She summoned a bolt of lightning with the intent to murder."

"Intent?" Kitieri spat. "If I wanted you dead, you'd be dead."

"Kitieri." Haldin shot a hand out toward her, silencing any further rebuttal.

"I have injuries proving this occurrence," Jorid continued. "Her bolt threw me back against the Church stairs, causing severe lacerations to the head, and there are two witnesses to the scene."

Kitieri glanced at Haldin before firing back. "Are you going to mention the part where you and your buddies cornered me, held me with an arbor element, and *burned* me so that I would fight back?"

Jorid glowered at Kitieri.

"*You* are the one using an illegal element," he said. "Your kind is far too dangerous to—"

"Jorid, would you please excuse us?"

Catarva's voice cut through the man's blustery condemnation like a thread of fine silk, and he fumbled over his last words.

"But, Baliant, I—"

"You will be compensated for your hardships today," she said.

"I don't want compensation," Jorid sputtered. "I want her *jailed* for this monstrous—"

"Please excuse us."

Haldin opened the door, leaving Jorid little choice but to storm out in a raging huff. As he closed the door behind him, Haldin put his back to the ornate wood with a long sigh.

"Hells," he whispered, pinching the bridge of his nose.

"I didn't try to kill him," Kitieri repeated, looking between the officer and Catarva.

"We know," Catarva replied, walking around the table to rest against its edge. "That's not our greatest concern."

"It's not?"

Haldin walked to stand beside the Baliant.

"Why did you leave your PCR in the training yard?" he asked, and Kitieri looked down.

"I didn't mean to," she mumbled. "I'm not used to wearing them, and I'm sorry. But I *was* right about what I said... before my training started."

Haldin's brow furrowed. "Kitieri, I told you—"

"I've done it *twice* now," she said. "I can harness the Strikes, and there is no victim."

"People could have been *killed*," Haldin said. "Leaving your PCR was utterly irresponsible, especially without having the faintest idea how your element will respond to a Strike."

"I know," Kitieri snapped. "But I *can* control it."

"For *now*."

The gravity in Haldin's tone gave Kitieri pause.

"I told you earlier," he continued, "your element will only grow more uncontrollable the longer it is out of lock. It is already reacting to your emotions when you're cornered or stressed, like what happened with Jorid, and it will continue to get worse. Next time, it will kill someone. This is not a game, Kitieri."

"I know that." Kitieri looked up. "But today, I *saved* a life. Someone's mother or son is still alive because I was there. Shouldn't we be focusing on that?"

Haldin exchanged a glance with Catarva. "We don't have that luxury right now," he said.

"What do you mean?"

Catarva took a step toward her, bringing her palms together and intertwining her long fingers.

"Jorid went to the Board of Advisors before he came to me," she said. "They are livid that I went around them to bring you on as an officer."

Haldin rolled his eyes. "Amadora's just mad she didn't get to bully you," he muttered. Catarva threw him a tight side smile before turning a solemn expression on Kitieri.

"But you're the Baliant," Kitieri said. "Can't you do whatever you want?"

"I wish." Catarva cocked an eyebrow. "My power here is only so absolute. The Board of Advisors has long been in place to keep balance and objectivity in matters of government, and I am often outvoted. Of course, I don't *need* permission to hire an officer, but you are a special case. They feel I have undermined their authority in keeping your true nature a secret but, as we know, we did not have days to spare in this matter. Your training had to begin immediately if you were to survive."

"But now that they know what you are," Haldin said, "the Board's attention is focused on you. Jorid made a strong case for your imprisonment today, and they were inclined to agree with him."

Fear rose in Kitieri's throat.

"Lightning *is* a banned practice, after all," Catarva added.

"But I didn't hurt anyone," Kitieri said, glancing between the two.

"And therein lies your saving grace," Catarva replied. "I was able to talk the Board down from their motion for imprisonment, but you will be under extreme scrutiny now. They are convinced that it is only a matter of time before people start dying at your hands. Any Strike can be your undoing."

Kitieri winced as the words struck like an open palm across her face. Even as she rebelled inwardly, their truth stung.

With a sharp inhalation, Catarva looked to Haldin with a curt nod. The officer walked to a wide, sturdy chest of drawers under a window, and turned back with five metal hoops dangling from his fingers. The light filtering in through the window's sheer curtains caught the reddish glint of the bands' inner linings, and Kitieri stumbled back against the wall.

"No," she whimpered. Panic coursed through her body as her breathing went fast and shallow, and she glanced to the door handle. Haldin moved to stop her escape, but Catarva put out a hand.

"Wait, Haldin."

Kitieri turned her head from the door to stare at the Baliant, eyes flicking to Haldin to be sure he stayed back.

"Kitieri, I know what this must feel like," Catarva started.

"No, you *don't*," Kitieri hissed. "You have no idea what happened last time. I won't wear one of those again."

"You don't have many other options," Haldin said. His voice was gentle, but his eyes left little room for negotiation. "Oran bands were the only way the Advisors would agree to let you walk free."

Kitieri watched the metal circles swing from his fingers, taunting her. She saw the silver around Noia's neck as she cried, and felt the squeeze of the collar around her own throat as the cable pulled it tight.

A silent droplet splashed on her jacket, and she realized she was crying.

"I can't," she whispered. "I can't do that."

Catarva shook her head. "Haldin is right. You must."

Kitieri's temper flared, and she turned on the woman. "I didn't want this. I didn't want to come here, or work for you, or do *any* of this. You wanted me here for some reason, and I said yes because you promised my brother and sister a life!"

"They can still have that life," Catarva said, lifting her head. Kitieri's breathing hitched, and she swiped at the tears now streaming down her cheeks.

"You said I could leave whenever I wanted," she ground out.

"You can." Catarva's voice lowered as she stepped forward, resting a hand on Kitieri's arm. "But is that what you want?"

Though tears obscured her vision, Kitieri glanced again to the oran bands on Haldin's fingers. One was bigger than the others; the collar, no doubt. The other four looked the right size for ankles or wrists, and Kitieri tore her eyes away as Catarva's soft voice called her attention back.

"I understand that you went through something truly traumatic at the Church of Histan," she said. "And for that I am deeply sorry. I know it is difficult to see now, but Haldin and I want the opposite for you. We want your freedom as much as you do, but in order for that to happen we need to buy enough time for you to get your element under control. The oran bands can do that."

"They won't work." Kitieri shook her head. "It didn't work at Histan's Church, and it won't work now."

"They're not meant to completely suppress your lightning," Haldin explained. "They are just to keep it manageable until you can get a handle on it and recreate that suppression naturally. The bands will minimize… accidents."

"They will keep you *and* your family safer," Catarva added.

Kitieri frowned, turning a skeptical eye on her. "Let me ask this, then," she said. "Why are you suddenly so concerned about my safety when you didn't even know I existed until last night?"

Catarva and Haldin exchanged an unreadable look, and Kitieri's frown deepened.

"If you want to put those things on me, I have a right to know what's going on."

Catarva sighed. "You're right. I didn't know you existed yesterday because you were still locked until your experience at the pillar. I told you at dinner that your appearance here presented quite the opportunity—one that goes both ways."

Kitieri narrowed her eyes. "Are you going to make me solve a riddle?"

Catarva pursed her lips.

"We need each other," she said. "You need my protection and Haldin's training to survive, and I need a way to harness the lightning."

"For what?" Kitieri snapped. "You have everything you could ever need here. You don't have to walk home from work every day without protection, waiting for your turn to die. You never even have to step foot outside, so what would you need with my lightning?"

Catarva stared, unprovoked, even as something sparked behind her amber eyes.

"There is much you do not yet understand, Kitieri," she said quietly. "The Church of Enahris is under attack from all sides."

"*All* sides?" Kitieri asked. "Isn't it just the Church of Histan?"

Curiosity flashed across the Baliant's fine features as she tilted her head. "You are aware of our brother Church's transgressions against us?"

"I heard the red officers talking," she replied. "They mentioned the fall of the Church of Enahris so that Shirasette could reach its full glory."

Catarva took in a long breath. "Unfortunately, that is only one of the fights we face, and the lesser one at that."

"What else, then?"

"I know you've felt it," Catarva said. "Even with your element locked, you can't tell me that you haven't felt the lightning growing stronger."

Kitieri paused, then nodded.

"And more frequent," she admitted.

"Yes." Catarva circled the table, slow and regal in the flowing white robes. "My experts give us two years."

"Until what?"

"Until the lightning takes over." Catarva stopped on the far side of the table, leaning on it with both hands. "It will override our PCRs, and people will no longer be able to step foot outside without being struck down."

Kitieri blinked.

"People will starve in their homes," Catarva went on. "Farmers, miners, builders... all of them will die, and the chain of supply will dry up. If we do nothing, it will mean extinction."

"Th-they're sure?" Kitieri croaked.

"Yes."

Kitieri ran a hand through her hair with a shuddering exhalation. "Fuck," she whispered. "But... what does that have to do with me?"

Catarva straightened. "It depends on how well you can learn to control your element."

"What?" A short laugh burst from Kitieri's chest. "You can't possibly think I can somehow save *everyone*. I mean, that's... it's just..."

Her laugh petered out as Catarva's grim expression brought her to silence.

"As I said, there is much you do not understand, Kitieri," the Baliant said. "For now, trust that your survival means as much to me as it does to you and your siblings."

Kitieri looked down, and Catarva leaned forward to catch her eye again.

"Let us help you," she said. "Wear the bands, stay out of trouble with the Advisors, and maybe we can get through this alive."

Though Kitieri's eyes met the Baliant's gaze, her mind raced. What was Catarva hiding? How could she possibly save so many people? The lightning would override the Gadgets, and...

"Kitieri." Haldin's soft voice cut through her thoughts, and she turned to him. "Can I put these on you?"

She looked again to the bands he held, and fought the squeamish reaction in her stomach. Her hands tingled as her lightning responded, and she clenched her jaw with a stiff nod.

Her lightning's subtle burn subsided as the crystals touched her skin, and Kitieri closed her eyes. *Don't think about it. Just don't think about it.* The cold metal clicked into place around her neck first, then her wrists, and then came a tap on the toe of her boot.

"I need your ankles, too," Haldin said, kneeling before her. Kitieri braced her back on the wall to pull off her boots, and Haldin snapped the bands closed just above her joints. With each snap, the warm buzzing within her quieted further until all she felt was cold.

"Feel any different?" he asked, standing.

"Yeah," Kitieri said flatly, adjusting one of the wristbands. "How do they come off?"

"I have the key," Haldin said, holding up a tiny pin on a crowded keyring. Kitieri glanced at it before leaning down to pull her boots back on. "As your training progresses, we will remove them one by one."

"Thank you, Kitieri." Catarva came around the table again, coming to stand right in front of her. "I know this is difficult, given what you've been through, but it is the only way forward."

Kitieri swallowed the painful lump in her throat as she stood up straight. "Am I dismissed?"

Catarva dipped her head.

"Dismissed."

CHAPTER 11

By the time Kitieri reached the final landing above the ground floor, tears had soaked the high neckline of her uniform jacket. She stopped at the arched window, looking out over the network of walls and pathways that connected the Church grounds.

The faint, metallic scent of a coming Strike tickled in her nose as she approached, and she reached out a hand.

Let me still feel it.

Her fingertips brushed the glass, and felt nothing but the cold, smooth surface. No burn stirred in her chest or rushed down her arms, and Kitieri pulled her hand back.

It was dangerous. She knew that. Any misstep could spell disaster, and every Strike risked the lives of those she held most dear. Without control, she was a monster.

She *knew* that.

But the lightning was still a part of her. Even in lock, its presence had been there, purring inside her ever since she could remember, and its sudden absence felt like a piece of her soul had been taken.

Only until I learn control.

The window fogged under Kitieri's long sigh, and she turned away, descending the final set of stairs. As she turned the corner, a heavy force checked her sore right shoulder, and she staggered back.

"*Ow*, what the — ?"

Her hand flew to the throbbing joint, and she looked up to see a tall, stocky officer smirking down at her.

"Oh, sorry, did that hurt?" he sneered. As Kitieri stared, bewildered, five more gray officers appeared behind him.

"Look, Corte, it's the chosen one," one of them drawled.

"We've been waiting for you," Corte said. "And what's this?" The man hooked his finger under the exposed band around Kitieri's wrist, and she jerked back.

"Don't fucking touch me!" she spat.

"Or what?" Corte advanced as Kitieri backed away. "You thought you could threaten an officer and get away with it? That's not how things work around here, girl. You should rot in prison for what you did."

"I didn't touch your scummy friend," Kitieri seethed. Her back hit a wall, and Corte's malicious grin widened as he pinned her there.

"See, that's not how he tells it." Corte looked over his shoulder. "I don't know, guys, who do you think we should believe?"

The five officers' laughs echoed through the wide hall, and Corte turned back to Kitieri with a deadly grin.

"And now… you have no element."

He lifted his hand to reach for her collar, and Kitieri's reflexes engaged. She knocked his hand away and swung her closed fist at his face. Corte blocked the punch, and slammed her back into the wall so hard that stars burst across Kitieri's vision.

Even as her head swam, she hooked her leg around the back of Corte's knee, sweeping him to the ground with a loud thud. Intent on escape, she jumped over him only to be knocked back by a fist she hadn't seen coming. She fell over Corte as he tried to stand, tumbling to the floor with a sharp cry. A booted foot lifted in preparation to kick her, and she curled into a tight ball to brace herself.

"*Hey!*"

Haldin's deep voice reverberated off the stone walls, and Kitieri peeked one eye open to see the coming kick freeze in mid-air as Haldin reached the bottom step.

"You are all on immediate suspension," he thundered, "and you will report first thing tomorrow morning to the Board of Advisors. I will have *all* of your asses for this kind of behavior!"

A mumbling chorus of apologies reached Kitieri's ears, and she pushed herself up on one elbow.

"Get out of my sight."

The six officers scuffled away under Haldin's murderous glare, and Kitieri watched his tense shoulders fall with a sigh. She looked away as he turned to her. Expecting admonishment, she frowned when Haldin's outstretched hand appeared in her vision.

"Let me help you," he said. Kitieri ignored the officer, getting to her feet alone.

"I'm fine," she said.

"Are you sure?" Haldin gestured to her face. "That looks like it hurts."

As the adrenaline drained from her system, Kitieri became aware of the warm, metallic taste in her mouth, and lifted two fingers to her lower lip that came away bright red.

"That's great," she mumbled. Haldin offered her a clean white square of linen from his pocket.

"No, thanks," she said, turning away.

"Looking forward to answering questions from two curious kids, huh?"

Kitieri narrowed her eyes at the officer, and grabbed the kerchief with an exasperated huff. "*Fine.*"

The cloth soaked up more than she had expected, and she looked up at Haldin with her eyebrows raised. He tapped the side of his own chin, and she scrubbed at that spot with a clean corner of the linen.

"Better," Haldin confirmed. "Would you accompany me to dinner?"

"I'm not hungry."

"Understandable. But I'm sure your brother and sister would like to see you. They are escorted to the hall by their final teacher of the day."

Kitieri rolled her eyes. "All right. But you're going to have to stop using my siblings against me."

Haldin grinned and turned toward the wafting scents making their way from the dining hall. As she walked beside him, Kitieri folded the bloodied rag and shoved it into her pocket.

"Thank you," she muttered.

"Don't mention it, I have plenty."

"I mean, for…" Kitieri waved a hand over her shoulder in the direction the six officers had fled. "…That."

"Oh." Haldin bowed his head. "I'm sorry about them. They're good men, but they don't understand. I will *never* condone violence against a fellow officer, and the repercussions of their actions will be severe. As I'm sure you know, the right combination of fear and misunderstanding can wreak havoc on an otherwise sound mind."

"Yeah, I get it," Kitieri said, keeping her eyes on the floor. "They think I stole something from them. That I don't belong here."

Haldin dipped his head to the side. "They'll get over it. What you and I need to focus on is your training."

"Right." Kitieri touched the band on her wrist. "I don't suppose you're interested in telling me what Catarva meant by all that back there."

Haldin's expression tensed, fine lines forming around his mouth. "It's not my place," he said. "The Baliant will disclose more as she sees fit, and it's our job as officers to respect her decisions and follow her orders."

"Mm." Kitieri nodded. "But you seem to know more than any of the others."

Haldin cut her a dark look. "I'm her Commander. I *should* know more."

"Oh." Kitieri scratched her forehead to hide her blush. His high rank had been clear since the training yard, but *Commander*? Of the entire Church?

The warm glow of the dining hall illuminated the hallway as they approached, and Kitieri's stomach rumbled at the sweet and savory aromas in the air.

I guess I was *hungry*, she thought. The anticipation of her awaiting siblings put a spring in her step, and she was almost to the beckoning doorway when Haldin grabbed her wrist.

"What?" She spun, pulling her hand back. The man's solemn expression quelled her momentary excitement, and Kitieri shrank back. "What's wrong?"

"There is one thing that I need to be honest with you about," Haldin said quietly. Kitieri searched his face, reading every line and wrinkle.

"All right?"

Haldin checked over his shoulder before leaning in close. "Catarva didn't want me to share this with you yet, but I think you should know," he said. "We don't have as much time to get your element under control as I'd hoped, so your training is going to have to be expedited. It's bad enough we've already lost a full day."

Kitieri's brows furrowed. "Why, what's—"

"Just know that we're going to need you soon."

Kitieri's eyes widened. "I thought she said two years."

"Not for that," Haldin said. "Not yet, anyways. This is something different."

The fine lines of worry marking his face reminded Kitieri of his expression in the training yard that morning.

"Does this have to do with why you left today?" she asked.

"Yes." Haldin's tone was short and clipped. "I'm doing what I can to buy time, but when this thing comes to a head, I'm going to need you."

Before Kitieri could respond, two officers passed and Haldin broke the tension.

"Hi, Haldin." The woman waved.

"Evening, officers," Haldin replied with a warm smile, leaning away from Kitieri. Though their curious stares shifted to her, Kitieri kept her eyes on him.

"Shall we, then?" he asked, still wearing his friendly façade as he followed the other two.

"Haldin, wait—"

"Tomorrow," he said. "Meet me in the training yard at dawn." As they stepped through the arched doorway, he paused again. "Eat well, and get your rest tonight. The coming days will be nothing short of brutal."

Across the room, two voices called her name, and she turned to see Taff and Jera waving her over. She returned the wave with an enthusiastic nod, and looked back to find Haldin walking away.

"Tell them as little as possible," he said over his shoulder. "I'll see you at dawn."

Kitieri sighed as the man struck up jovial conversation with another officer, leaving no room for her questions.

Nothing short of brutal? She blew a puff of air through her nose. *You've never worked in the mines.*

"Kitieri!" Jera flailed her arms, and Taff held up the third plate of food that was saving her spot. With a wide grin, she trotted over to them.

"Hey!" she cried, throwing her arms around them both as they rushed to her. "It's so good to see you again!"

"It's only been a day," Taff said, pulling back.

"A very *long* day," Kitieri corrected. "What are you looking at?"

Taff's narrowed eyes were fixated on her face. "What happened to your mouth?"

Kitieri touched the sore spot on her lower lip and felt the heat and swelling there.

"Just a training accident," she said. "Let's eat before dinner gets cold."

Jera nestled close to her on the bench, shoveling carrots and beans into her mouth at an alarming rate, while Taff circled to his own side of the table. His eyes lingered on her as he took his seat.

"It's rude to stare," Kitieri said, stabbing roasted potatoes onto her fork.

"What's that on your neck?"

Kitieri huffed, looking up from her plate. She'd already known Taff was too observant to fool, but that did not make the coming conversation any more enticing.

Jera poked at the band around her wrist. "This one, too. They look like the one that lady melted."

"They're a lot like that," Kitieri said, putting her hand over her sister's, "but kind of different."

"Different how?" Taff asked. "What do they do?"

Kitieri pressed her lips together, meeting Taff's hard gray eyes. "They're to help me control my element," she said quietly. "So it's not as dangerous for all of us."

Jera laughed. "It's not dangerous for *us*, though."

"It is." A lump lodged in Kitieri's throat, choking off her explanation, so she squeezed Jera's hand.

"Is it like they said, then?" Taff's voice was small as he looked down at his plate.

"Like who said?" Kitieri asked.

Taff shrugged, swinging his feet under the bench. "I overheard two of the instructors talking as they walked us here. They said Catarva was crazy for letting a lightning walk free, because…" He trailed off.

"Because what, Taff?"

"Because you're going to kill us all."

Kitieri bit hard into her swollen lip, and Jera jerked beside her.

"What?" she whispered. "You are?"

"Of *course* not," Kitieri said, squeezing Jera's hand harder. "You know that I love you both more than anything, right? And that I would never, *ever* hurt you?"

Jera nodded, but Taff kept his head down. Kitieri tapped the table. "Taff?"

Reluctantly, he looked up.

"That's why I'm wearing these bands," she said. "To protect you. To protect *all* of us. Yes, the lightning is dangerous, but I can learn to control it… and I will. I promise."

"But you were wearing the same thing at the pillar and it didn't stop you then," Taff said.

"Well, now I have five instead of one," Kitieri said. She forced a smile, holding up her wrists to Jera. "See, I can't possibly hurt anyone with *five!*"

Jera broke into a ready grin, while Taff stared at her from across the table.

"I just have to be careful," Kitieri sighed, meeting her brother's gaze. "When I learn to control it better on my own, I can take the bands off. Everything will be fine."

Taff sniffed once, dropping his eyes to his lap.

"Believe me," she whispered, reaching out to him. "I would do anything… *anything*… to keep you two safe. Do you hear me?"

Taff took her hand. "Can you promise the same for yourself?"

"I'm going to do my best."

"Again."

Haldin threw out his hands, releasing his electric element for what Kitieri was sure had to be the four-hundredth time. Its charge tickled her lightning, pulling just enough through the blockage of the oran crystals for her to intercept it and ground it before she could be electrocuted.

"Again."

Kitieri strained to keep her power coming through the bands. Sweat ran down her face and neck, soaking her uniform and the strands of hair that clung to her skin.

"Again."

Her hands shook, and her chest heaved with rapid breaths.

"Again."

The lightning didn't come this time.

"Shit," she whispered, just before Haldin's electricity jolted her back against the wall of the training yard and she hit the ground. The powerful shock dissipated quickly, but her head still spun.

"Son of a *bitch*," she muttered, rubbing the back of her head.

Haldin's boots crunched on the dirt, and he offered her a hand. "Excellent work, Kitieri," he said, pulling her to her feet.

As she dusted off her pants and jacket, Kitieri shot him a baleful look. "Didn't *feel* excellent."

Haldin grinned. "It's only been four days. Do you remember day one?"

Kitieri groaned. She'd spent more time on her ass getting shocked on that first full day of training than doing any real work.

"You're learning to make the lightning do something it doesn't want to do," he continued, walking back to his spot across the yard. "Right now, the bands are in its way. But when we remove them, it will be your mind. It's just like lifting weights."

"I know, I know," Kitieri sighed. "But lifting weights is easier."

Haldin smirked. "Much easier. Again."

Kitieri barely caught the electricity, throwing it to the ground.

"Again."

The lightning whined as she forced it to move, raking down her arms like jagged claws. As it reached her fingertips to meet Haldin's element, it surged with a sudden, intense burn.

Kitieri yelped, pulling her hands back, and the electricity threw her against the wall again. Haldin jogged to her, bending down on one knee.

"What happened that time?" he asked.

Kitieri lifted her hands to examine them, before lifting her face to the breeze. "There's a Strike coming," she said, pushing to her feet. "Soon. *Really* soon."

With a curt nod, Haldin walked to where his Gadget rested against the Church wall.

"Remember what I said yesterday," he called to her.

Kitieri nodded, turning at the sound of Haldin's boots coming closer. "No, you shouldn't—"

"Give me your hand," he ordered.

"Haldin, I told you there's a Strike coming any second. You shouldn't be this close to me."

"Your *hand*."

With a deep frown, she complied. Haldin pulled his keys from his belt, sorting through them until he held the tiny pin between his fingers.

Kitieri ripped her arm away. "No, Haldin. I'm not ready for that."

"You are."

"No, I'm *not*. I could kill you!"

"You won't. Look at me." He grasped both of her shoulders so tight that she winced in pain. "Look at me."

His pale eyes reflected her panicked expression, and he loosened his grip.

"It's time to take the next step," he said. "I told you this would have to be fast."

Kitieri trembled as the bands fell away from both her wrists, leaving damp rings of sweat that cooled in the wind. Haldin backed away, returning the keys to his belt.

"Just remember what we talked about," he said. "You are the one in charge. Show it no fear."

The first warning pulled a hoarse gasp from Kitieri's throat as her lightning thrashed. Even with the other three bands still at work, the element raced up and down her arms, throwing itself against her closed fists.

"Good." Haldin nodded, circling her with a wide berth. "No sparks."

Kitieri closed her eyes, releasing a long breath through pursed lips. The familiar pain thrummed in her chest, wailing to be set free.

Another deep breath. The second warning was coming, and it would try her control.

"No fear. No emotion," Haldin coached. "You are a stone pillar, cold and empty. Give it nothing to consume."

Just as Haldin had made her practice relentlessly over the past four days, Kitieri schooled her mind to emptiness. Her thoughts slowed along with her heart rate, and she felt the inner burn begin to cool.

The second warning stoked the fire, and her lightning screamed anew. Kitieri doubled over, gritting her teeth and pressing her fists into her chest to stop the sparks from flying.

"Not with your body," Haldin called. "With your mind. Take the control!"

Kitieri sucked in a gulp of cool air, forcing herself to stand up straight. It hurt so badly… did he have any idea how much this hurt?

Eyes squeezed closed, she wrestled with the lightning. She pushed against it with her mind, squashing it down with the heavy weight of nothingness.

No fear. No emotion.

"Yes! That's it," Haldin said, but she barely heard him anymore. Her mind felt a thousand miles away, drifting in an endless black sea. Here, nothing burned.

The third warning shattered her illusion, fanning the flames to a roaring height. Even as the lightning threatened to burn her alive, Kitieri stood steadfast.

You are mine. I control you.

"Fantastic!" Haldin's voice echoed through the abyss of her thoughts. Though her lightning bucked and seethed, its attention turned to her instead of the looming Strike. Her element quivered and hummed, awaiting her direction as the eye of the Strike locked onto her.

The Blue Killer roared down from the sky, jaws open and fangs poised to kill, and Kitieri's element connected with the unimaginable power as she lifted her hand to the sky.

Go back!

Before it could envelop her in its hateful vortex, the Strike was gone.

A welcome chill rushed through her, soothing the worst of the burn, and her element returned contentedly to its docile state. A sharp pop made her jump, and she turned to find Haldin clapping.

"Absolutely incredible," he said, shaking his head as he approached. "You were right, Kitieri. You *do* repel it. I've never seen anything like it in my life—and not one spark out of you! How'd it feel?"

Kitieri laughed, wiping the sweat from her brow with her sleeve. "Terrible," she replied. "It hurts like a bitch."

"That part will get better, I promise," Haldin said. "The more efficient you get at controlling its reaction to the Strikes, the more your element will learn to rely on your commands instead of its natural instinct."

"I hope it gets better fast, because that sucks."

Haldin chuckled and clapped her on the back. "You need water."

As he made for the Church door, Kitieri called after him. "Aren't you going to put the bands back on?"

Haldin turned with a crooked grin. "No. You've graduated."

CHAPTER 12

The nagging, persistent tingle dragged Kitieri from the depths of sleep, and she rolled onto her back with a groan.

"Seriously?" she grumbled, staring up at the ceiling. Ever since Haldin had removed her wristbands two days ago, the lightning had been testing the remaining three, finding the most inopportune times to prod her. Its burn nibbled at her fingertips, restless and anxious.

Kitieri closed her eyes again. She wouldn't be able to sleep through a Strike. She needed to get up and find a safe place in case her control slipped, but her eyelids felt so heavy…

"Kitieri?"

She bolted upright in bed to find Jera standing in her loose white nightgown at the door.

"Hey," she breathed, "what are you doing awake?"

"I couldn't sleep," Jera mumbled, wrapping her arms about herself. Kitieri smiled and patted the edge of the mattress.

"What's wrong?" She smoothed Jera's wild, tangled hair as she climbed onto the bed and snuggled into Kitieri's shoulder.

"I had a bad dream," she said into the thick quilt.

"About what?"

"The lightning came, and then you were gone."

Jera nestled closer, and Kitieri put her arm around her. "Hey, it's

124

okay," she whispered. "The lightning's not going to get me, *or* you. I promise."

"And Ashes was gone, too."

"Who's Ashes?"

Jera rolled over to shoot Kitieri an annoyed glare. "My *horse*, remember?"

"Right." Kitieri grinned. "I remember. Nothing is going to happen to me or Ashes, okay?" Jera shifted back, cuddling closer to her with a yawn.

"I just feel like something really *bad* is going to happen," she whispered.

Kitieri pressed her lips into a line, stroking Jera's hair until her breathing evened. As her quiet snores filled the dark room, Kitieri gritted her teeth against the rising pain in her hands, creeping down her arms as the charge intensified in the air.

Carefully, she inched her arm out from under Jera's head, settling her on the pillow as she pulled free. As much as she wished to stay, drifting back to sleep with her sister nestled against her, she had to leave. The lightning called.

Kitieri slipped from the bed and padded to the dresser, pulling out one of the soft black shirts the officers wore under their jackets and her uniform pants. She left the jacket hanging on its rack; she didn't plan on running into anyone except maybe the sentries on guard tonight.

Hand on the doorframe to her room, Kitieri turned back to watch Jera's sleeping form.

"I love you," she whispered. The girl stirred, but did not open her eyes, and Kitieri left with a melancholy grin.

She crossed the common room of their apartment, skirting the plush chair and its little round table on the way to the door. The bolt slammed back with a loud click and Kitieri froze, face twisting. Snores still emanated from both rooms, and accompanied by the door's soft whine, Kitieri slipped out into the hallway. The burn in her arms now welled in her chest, writhing impatiently.

I'm working on it, okay?

Dark stairs led her down toward the main floor, lit by the faint blue light of the moon streaming through the arched windows at every landing. Halfway down one flight of steps, a sharp clink met her ears, and Kitieri turned to peer through the shadows. She ducked her head, leaning sideways, but caught no further movement around the corner.

She remembered the flap of the dark cloak through the driving rain one week ago, and her brows furrowed. The same feeling tingled along her skin now—the feeling that she was being watched. Not just watched... followed.

Kitieri backed down the stairs with deliberate steps that rang off the stone walls, hoping to catch a glimpse of her pursuer. But upon her final step onto the landing, her sole companion remained the heavy silence of the fortress around her. The lightning flared in her chest again, and Kitieri turned to continue on with a low growl.

Two more flights of stairs brought her to the spacious Sanctuary, and Kitieri's eyes rested on the place she'd stood eight days ago, plotting murder by candelabra with the red officer's knife at her back. She felt the ghost of her old life lingering there in the shadows—a starving, terrified, broken girl facing death with no way to save the ones she loved. That girl had died that day, Kitieri realized... and she had no idea who'd taken her place.

She clung to the outer wall of the Sanctuary, running her knuckles along the backs of the long wooden benches as she hid in the lamps' shadows. Their light was dim in the late hour, battling the blue of the moonlight filtering in through the tall frosted windows that lined the cavernous chamber.

Kitieri glanced down at her clenched fists, fighting her element for control. Though she would have laughed at the thought six days ago, she missed the security of the oran bands around her wrists. Haldin had been right—the longer she was out of lock, the more deadly her lightning became, and that scared her. The training was helping her control, but the element was still so unpredictable. So *powerful*.

Kitieri's lightning pulsed, exploding through her body with the first warning, and she winced, ducking down behind one of the benches.

"Not with your body. With your mind."

As she forced herself to stand, one of the Church doors creaked open, and she dropped back down behind the bench. What a great time for a guard change.

A single pair of footsteps echoed through the Sanctuary, and Kitieri frowned. Where was the other officer on duty? Where was their relief?

She peeked over the bench, squinting through the hazy moonlight. The young man's clean-shaven face looked unfamiliar, and his black clothing masked his movements in the dim light. The only feature that stood out was the Gadget on his back.

He wasn't one of theirs, Kitieri was sure: where his lack of familiarity did not damn him, his movements finished the job. He cast about the Sanctuary as if ghosts lurked in every shadow, ready to drag him to the hells, and Kitieri dipped lower in her hiding place.

This is wrong.

The heat and pain flared again with the second warning, thrashing against its bodily cage, and she bit back an anguished groan as her insides burned. Her thoughts tumbled through her mind, bouncing off each other in chaos as her lightning ran rampant.

Control. No fear. No emotion.

A bead of sweat ran down her nose, dripping onto the polished stone floor as she huddled in a tense crouch. In a moment, it would all be over...

Just as she braced against the third warning, a loud creak split the silence and Kitieri twisted on her boot heels to face the source of the noise—the side door through which she'd come. Sneaking from the shadows, appearing tiny in the large doorframe, was a little girl in a soft white nightgown.

Jera.

Heat rushed to Kitieri's face, and the lightning fled from her mind as the stranger pulled a wicked dagger from his belt. He was almost at the door, almost on top of her, and Kitieri was too far away.

"Jera, get *back*!" she called, vaulting over the bench. Jera's eyes flew open wide as she spotted the curved blade glinting in the moonlight, and the man turned a horrified look on Kitieri.

Even as she sprinted for him, running hard down the center aisle, the man's eyes flicked to Jera's crouched, trembling form. He lunged, reaching for the girl's wrist as she screamed, and Kitieri threw her hand out.

"Don't touch her!"

Just as her arm reached full extension, the Blue Killer struck outside and ripped the lightning from Kitieri's hand.

The blue flash through the windows mingled with the blinding white bolt as it tore through the Sanctuary. As the searing heat left Kitieri's body, its hollow void filled with a cold, black dread.

It was gone. She couldn't call it back.

Pitch black fell around her, thick and heavy in the aftermath of the lightning. Silence roared in her ears, and the only evidence of her consciousness came as the smell of charred flesh.

No. Oh gods, no.

"Jera?" she called, frozen in place. She blinked repeatedly, trying to force her vision's return to no avail. A soft whimper reached her ears, and Kitieri broke her paralysis to stumble forward. Her sister's faint outline came into view, shaking violently.

"Kitieri."

The small voice shattered Kitieri's heart, and she lurched forward to pull the girl's thin, quivering frame against her.

"I'm so sorry," she sobbed into her sister's hair, rocking back and forth. Jera's arms snaked around her neck, returning the embrace.

"Is he gone?" Jera whispered. With a shaking breath, Kitieri turned her head to the figure on the floor, vaguely recognizable as a human being, and squeezed her eyes closed.

"Yeah," she whispered back. "Are you okay? Are you hurt?"

Jera pulled away, examining her hands and body. "I don't think so."

"Thank the gods," Kitieri muttered, holding Jera tight to her once more.

Both Church doors flew open, and the sound of boots on the stone floor filled the Sanctuary. Kitieri glanced over her shoulder, and registered the gray uniforms in the low light.

Great, now *the sentries show.*

"Gods, it stinks in here," came a female voice as the lighter pair of footsteps slowed. The heavier pair of boots approached behind her, and Kitieri released Jera with a sigh, standing to face the officer. As she turned, her entire body tensed.

"Well," Jorid drawled, emerging into a patch of moonlight. "I told them you'd kill someone sooner or later."

Kitieri squared her shoulders.

"And where have *you* been?" she asked, not bothering to soften the steely edge in her tone. "If you'd done your job, I wouldn't have had to do it for you."

Jorid's expression went thunderously dark, and his shoulders hunched forward.

"I *was* doing my job," he growled, "investigating a disturbance at the south gate. Not that it's any of your business."

"Who's this?" The woman poked the blackened remains with the end of her spear, knocking off flakes of charred flesh, and Kitieri looked away.

"He was one of Histan's," she said. Bile rose in her throat, and she fought the hard gag reflex that threatened to choke her.

"Where's your proof?" Jorid asked. Kitieri cut him a hard glare.

"Because from what I can see," he went on, "you made sure to destroy any hope of identification by burning this poor soul to a crisp."

A myriad of thoughts and possible responses flitted to Kitieri's lips before she banished each and every one, and her blood started to run cold. She couldn't prove anything, and this man would twist anything that came out of her mouth. Since Corte and his buddies had been suspended on her account, she'd faced a large-scale silent treatment from many of her fellow officers, and Jorid had been increasingly hateful with every passing interaction. This was the chance he'd been lying in wait to catch—his chance to push her down like he'd wanted to the first day they'd met.

The woman's spear clanged as it hit metal, and she gasped.

"A PCR?" she muttered. "How…?"

Cold realization slithered into Kitieri's gut. "It's fake."

"What was that?" The woman turned to her.

"Check the cintra," Kitieri said more clearly. "It isn't real."

"That's enough of your bullshit, Manon," Jorid said, his gruff voice cutting across Kitieri's. "I'm putting you under a hold to await the Board's judgement."

A chill raked through Kitieri at his last word. "You're *arresting* me?" she asked. "You can't do that—"

"I can." Jorid cut her off, grabbing her arms. "You're a known danger to the community. The Board will thank me."

As he forced her around to snap Oran cuffs on her wrists behind her back, Kitieri came face to face with Jera.

"What's going on?" the girl whimpered.

"It's okay." Kitieri tried to force a smile even as Jera's eyes brimmed with tears, lip trembling.

"Don't go away," she begged. Kitieri bit into her lip hard enough to taste blood, and she blinked away the tears that clouded her vision.

"I love you," she whispered.

Jera cried out as Jorid pushed Kitieri toward the door, clinging to the tail of her shirt. The woman pulled her back, prying her fingers from the fabric as Jera's wails echoed through the Sanctuary.

"Don't *leave!*" Jera's words broke over heaving sobs as Jorid steered Kitieri through the door, slamming it behind them.

CHAPTER 13

Kitieri leaned her head back against the wall in the corner of her cell. Vivid nightmares plagued every second of her sleep on the rare chance that she dozed off, snapping her back to consciousness and brutal reality.

Awake or asleep, it didn't matter. Horror and guilt tore at her either way, as the sickening smell of death hung in her nose and her sister's screams ricocheted through her mind.

She'd protected her sister. She'd protected the Church. She'd done the right thing, and she'd do it again if she had to. The man had been a dangerous threat. She wasn't a murderer. She... she...

Kitieri dropped her head, letting her loose hair fall over her face.

Over the hours of repetition, her words had begun to crumble under the weight of objective scrutiny. Did she really believe that? Would *anyone* believe it?

She'd saved her sister, but the root of her horror dug much deeper. She'd had no control. None. The lightning had acted on its own, taking the man's life instead of Jera's in a bout of sheer happenstance.

A violent shudder passed through Kitieri's body. If the heap of ashes on the Sanctuary floor had been Jera... if her lightning had been off by one inch... would she be able to declare herself innocent of murder?

No.

A single drop traced the wet tracks down her cheeks from tears long spent. She'd been foolish to believe she'd be any different than all the lightnings that had died at the dawn of the Strikes. *No* one could control something like this. A power so strong, so hateful, so angry could only kill. She was every bit the monster Jorid feared. Left free and unchecked, she would end up just like the rest of her kind, taking her loved ones down with her like Haldin's wife.

A fresh wave of guilt slammed into Kitieri. For some reason, against all odds, Haldin had believed in her. He'd fought for her, and poured all of his energy and willpower into the hope that she would somehow become the officer the Church of Enahris needed. Haldin had been the closest thing she'd ever had to a friend, and she'd let him down... just like everyone else who'd depended on her to be something she could never be.

Light flooded the small chamber, and Kitieri's eyes closed reflexively against the pain. A film of moisture gathered as she forced them open, spilling over to follow the well-worn tear tracks down her face.

"You've been summoned by the Baliant and her Board of Advisors," a man said. Kitieri squinted up at his blurry silhouette, but did not recognize his voice.

Here we go.

The officer pulled her to her feet, his touch neither gentle nor cruel, and guided her from the cell into a torchlit hallway. Kitieri counted the stairs, marking every landing in the back of her mind. They'd climbed five floors before a window appeared, frosted with dew as the sun's first rays just grazed its glass.

Another nine flights brought Kitieri before the rich double doors, where Haldin stood waiting. She dropped her eyes as the officer marched her before the man.

"Thank you, Raden," Haldin said. "I'm putting you on post while I'm in there."

"Yes, Commander."

"Kitieri."

She jumped at the sound of her name, glancing up at Haldin's pale eyes. The shadows around them seemed darker, the fine lines in his skin more pronounced as he looked down at her.

"Haldin," she started, fighting her dry throat, "I'm so—"

"Listen to me." He leaned forward, the weight of his hands falling on both her shoulders. "Say as little as you can in there. Do *not* speak unless spoken to. Do you understand?"

Kitieri responded with a tight nod.

"These people can and will turn anything you say against you," he continued. "I've seen them do it time and time again. They will demean you, they will call you a liar, they will go for your throat, and if you let them, they will win. They make a job out of winning." His hands tightened on her shoulders. "And they're out for your blood now."

Kitieri stared into Haldin's eyes, speechless. *Winning?* What could they win against her that she didn't deserve?

As Haldin turned for the door, the oran cuffs stopped Kitieri from reaching out. "Wait."

Haldin looked over his shoulder.

"I just want you to know that I'm sorry," she said. "For letting you down."

Haldin went still, studying her face. "What makes you think you let me down?"

"You trusted me enough to take the bands off and I failed. I can't control it. I never could, and this whole thing is just—"

Haldin stepped forward, jabbing a finger in her face, and Kitieri drew back as his fingertip almost prodded her nose.

"You *can*," he whispered. "And I don't want to hear any more talk like that from you. If I have anything to say about it, we'll be back in the training yard this afternoon." Haldin lowered his pointing finger, and his expression softened. "I know that what happened scared you, Kitieri," he continued. "It would scare any sane person. But do you remember what you told me the day I gave you those oran bands?"

Kitieri swallowed, dreading the echo of the ignorant shit she'd said that day. She'd been upset, and what was worse, she'd truly thought then that she could control her element. She'd believed that—

"You can save lives," Haldin said.

Voice trembling, Kitieri forced herself to hold his gaze. "I don't think that anymore."

Haldin sighed through his nose. "*I* believe it. In time, you will again, too."

Turning, he pushed the door open, and Kitieri followed him into the room. Six faces situated around the oblong table turned to stare as she entered, their eyes locking on her like vultures.

"About time, Commander," an elderly woman barked, shaking the loose skin about her jowls. A single silver ringlet escaped the tight bun atop her head to rest on the shoulder of her black robes, adorned with the same golden sash Stil had worn. Kitieri looked away, stomach turning at the unwelcome memories.

"Sorry to keep you waiting, Chief Advisor." Tension laced Haldin's polite words, and the woman rolled her eyes behind her half-moon spectacles.

Haldin positioned Kitieri at the end of the long table with no chair, leaving her to stand on display as the Advisors gawked.

"Those *are* oran cuffs, now?" asked the large man with the dark, bushy eyebrows. He gestured at Kitieri's midsection, as if they could all see straight through her to the cuffs behind her back.

"Of course," Haldin replied.

Attention shifted to the door opposite the chamber's entrance from the hall, and Kitieri blew out a silent breath as the six Advisors turned to watch the servant reenter.

"The Baliant of Enahris," he announced with a low bow. The Advisors stood as Catarva swept into the room with a commanding air in the regal white robes, taking her place at the far end of the table from Kitieri. Their eyes met, and through her neutral expression, Kitieri caught a glimpse of a kind smile.

"This meeting of the Board of Advisors is in session," she said. "Thank you, Chief Advisor Amadora, Advisors Ghentrin, Farr, Rulka, Darrow, Emerit, and Commander Haldin for your time and service this morning."

"Ugh, he's *staying*?" Amadora peered around the one other woman present, whom Kitieri assumed to be Rulka, to glare at Haldin.

"Yes," Catarva replied. "This is a matter involving multiple officers under his command, and he is Officer Kitieri's instructor. He is staying. Please, take your seats."

All at the table sank into the high-backed chairs, except Kitieri. She stood awkwardly, resisting the temptation to fidget as the Advisors resumed their staring. A few of their gazes were curious, though most held a mixture of fear and contempt—especially those of Amadora and Eyebrows.

The Chief Advisor cleared her throat.

"Officer Kitieri Manon, you stand on trial here today for murder by use of an illegal element. How do you respond?"

Kitieri's palms broke into a clammy sweat as she scanned the expectant faces at the table. How was she expected to answer that? "I—"

"It wasn't murder."

Haldin's voice to her left startled Kitieri, and she snapped her head around to stare at him. Eyebrows scoffed, slapping an open hand on the table.

"Not murder?" he boomed. "We've got a body burned beyond recognition here, so I am quite interested to hear how you plan to twist *this* one."

"Ghentrin." Catarva's cool tone covered the man's rumbling.

"Officer Kitieri acted as any of my trained officers would in such a circumstance," Haldin said. "As you heard in their accounts earlier, Officers Jorid and Kinu were pulled away from their posts, and this man slipped through. Kitieri protected our Church from invasion with lethal use of her element—a skill in which *all* of my officers are trained."

He cut his eyes to Amadora with his last words, and Kitieri sensed a history between them on the topic. The woman sniffed, lifting her chin.

"Well," she huffed, jowls shaking again, "most of your officers wield legal elements and exhibit full control. This one does *not*."

"You are not qualified to determine her level of control," Haldin spat. "*I* am. Officer Kitieri has trained relentlessly since her arrival here, and she has made great progress—"

"Progress is not proficiency," said the tall, thin man beside Ghentrin. "She still presents a very real danger to society."

"Precisely, Darrow," Amadora said. "Lightnings were outlawed for a reason. There is no such thing as true control with an element like that."

"That is *not* true," Haldin countered. "I have seen her work, and I can tell you right now that Officer Kitieri has the capacity for full control. Her training, in addition to the oran bands—"

"Ah, yes," Darrow drawled, lifting a long finger to his chin, "the oran bands that you removed from her wrists without our permission, if I recall."

Haldin's expression darkened, and Kitieri watched him with mounting apprehension. What was he doing? What was he *thinking*? Why in the hells would he jeopardize his position and rank to go against the Board like this on her behalf?

She could not deny the validity of the Board's points on the dangers of her existence, and the last thing she wanted was for Haldin to go down with her.

Stop, Haldin. Please, stop.

"We agreed that *I* had the right to determine the path of her training," the Commander said, smashing his finger into the tabletop. "It is my job to determine when she is—"

"It was *your* job to keep her from murdering people," Amadora said, almost shouting over Haldin's words. "And you failed miserably. Frankly, I've half a mind to hold you responsible as an accomplice in this murder."

"No." The word slipped from Kitieri's lips before she could stop it, and every eye in the room came to rest on her. Though her throat closed up, she forced a quick breath into her lungs. "He's not responsible for this. I am."

"Kitieri." Haldin's low warning reached her ears. "Don't say anything else. Let me handle this."

She did not dare look at him before pressing on. "I went down to the Sanctuary last night because I knew there was a Strike coming," she said, ignoring Haldin's sigh. "My element can feel them, and I wanted to be outside and away from everyone when it hit. Before I could get there, an agent of the Church of Histan walked right through our front doors. I don't know why, but I *do* know that he meant harm. He was skittish and he threatened my sister, who'd followed me. So yes, you're right to say that I killed a man and that I'm dangerous. I won't disagree with you on that. But what I'm wondering is why none of you seem concerned about *who* I killed and what he was doing here."

Ghentrin made a phlegmy sound of disgust in his throat, swatting the air.

"You can't prove who you murdered," he said. "All we have to go on is your word, and you'll excuse me if I'm not the first in line to believe it. You could claim *anything* right now, and this fool would lie through his teeth to confirm it." The man flung a meaty hand in Haldin's direction, and Kitieri's temper flared in her breast.

Fuck you, you pompous piece of shit.

"Does the Church of Enahris make fake PCRs?" she asked.

"Excuse me?" Amadora pulled her head back, bearing a strong resemblance to an indignant turtle.

"Do we make and sell fake PCRs?" Kitieri repeated herself with a forced air of innocent curiosity.

"Of course not!" Ghentrin bellowed.

"Then there's your proof." Kitieri dropped her high, innocent pitch to a growl, and watched Ghentrin blink in confusion. "The man was wearing a fake PCR, which is why my lightning could touch him in the first place. So unless you are willing to collectively admit that you steal from the people of this city and send them out into the lightning to die, you don't have a choice but to recognize this man as being of the Church of Histan."

"Well," Amadora said, squinting over her spectacles, "agent of Histan or not, he should have been taken *alive*. It is not your call to execute on a whim, Officer."

Kitieri's face grew hot with simultaneous anger and embarrassment as all possible replies eluded her. Information *would* have been more valuable than his death…

"Are you serious, Amadora?" Haldin said, leaning around Rulka. "You *know* what the Church of Histan is doing right this very second, holding our own officers hostage, and you have the gall to defend them?"

"I am defending no one," Amadora spat back. "The Church of Histan has committed an act of war, and we will respond accordingly."

Haldin's eyes grew wide and his face turned pale. "You're saying…" He paused, breath catching in his throat. "You mean to declare war… on the Church of Histan?"

"Yes." Amadora lifted her head, squaring her shoulders. "We cannot let their actions go unanswered."

Kitieri's gaze darted between the two as her mind scrambled to keep up with the exchange. Officers held hostage…?

"I have *told* you there is a better way!" Haldin's fist on the table startled her.

"Oh yes—your little pet project here?" Amadora lifted a hand toward Kitieri, eyebrows raised. "That's your better way?"

Her shrill laughter filled the room, followed by Ghentrin's deep guffaw and quiet, nervous chuckles from the rest of the Board. Darrow and one of the other men wore a smirk, but the last man and Rulka did not smile at all. Rulka glanced to Kitieri, dark waves cascading over her shoulder as their eyes met for a fleeting moment.

"You truly think some half-trained little girl can turn the tides?" Amadora asked, still shaking with bursts of laughter. "She's liable to kill our own officers *and* herself in the process. Trust me, Haldin, her sentence will be a kindness."

Kitieri's blood chilled as she considered for the first time the kind of sentence this woman might mean.

"So let me get this straight," Haldin said in a low voice, seething just below the surface. "Because of your fear of one officer's power, you would send all of my officers against a superior force into a war that you know we can't win —"

"They are not your officers, Commander," Amadora barked. "They work for the Church of Enahris, and they will follow my ord —"

"They are *my* officers, not the Board's." Catarva cut across her Chief Advisor, her velvety tone blacker than night. "And I will not send good, loyal men and women to slaughter. Officer Kitieri can help us buy the time we need."

Amadora swiveled in her chair, turning a scathing glare on the Baliant. "You only have so much power here," she hissed. "And a unanimous Board outweighs the wishes of the Baliant."

Haldin clenched his fist, elbow resting on the table. "You would let them die," he said quietly. "You would let them all die for the sake of a power struggle you know we can never win."

Amadora tossed her head. "We don't keep a ready force of officers just for show, Commander. Occasionally, they must earn their keep."

Haldin's jaw dropped open, and Kitieri felt her renewed rage bubble to the surface. *Pawns. We're just pawns to them. Not even people.*

The ghost of the red officer's words brushed her thoughts, and she saw the ice element standing over her with his malicious sneer. *Little more than animals.*

Her stomach turned as she looked around the table. Power would always beget greed for more power, until all beneath them were quelled into submission or death. For all their talk of war, the Boards of Enahris and Histan were not so different after all.

Amadora stood abruptly, pushing her chair back with surprising force.

"This discussion is over," she announced. "The Board is in agreement that this young woman is a danger to herself and others due to her lack of elemental control."

"In *agreement*?" Haldin lurched forward, palms turned upwards. "Half of them never even —"

"We must stick to our laws," Amadora screeched over Haldin. "A lightning is *far* too dangerous to allow free rein in this climate. As Chief Advisor, I am bringing this matter to a final vote. I propose the indefinite imprisonment of Officer Kitieri Manon, pending release upon her proven ability to return her illegal element to a locked status, never to be used again. In addition, I propose that Commander Haldin Arnod be placed under an order of zero contact with the prisoner, as he is far too emotionally involved in this matter to act in the best interests of our Church community."

"*What*?" Haldin vaulted from his chair. "That is absurd! If I can't train her, there's no possible way —"

"All in favor, say 'aye!'" Amadora cried over Haldin's objections. A hesitant chorus of vague vowel sounds lifted from the table, and Kitieri could swear the bitch blew smoke from her nostrils. "All in favor," she repeated more slowly, "say '*aye*.'"

As the vowel chorus came back stronger this time, the shimmer of Rulka's dark waves caught Kitieri's eye. She was shaking her head, Kitieri realized.

"Amadora," the woman started, "I don't…"

Before Kitieri's eyes, the Chief Advisor appeared to grow exponentially in height as she towered over Rulka.

"I agree to the imprisonment," Rulka assured her quickly, "but… I think her training should continue."

"It's all or nothing, Rulka, and you've heard the other votes."

Rulka deliberated a moment longer under Amadora's dark glare.

"Aye, then," she muttered.

"That's a unanimous Board," Amadora announced triumphantly, "leaving no reason for the Baliant's vote."

"Amadora." Catarva stood abruptly. "I will not tolerate this tyranny. I wish to hear a *sound* reasoning from every one of my Advisors on this decision."

The old woman spun on the Baliant, baring her yellowing teeth. "You dare question me, girl?" she hissed.

Kitieri jerked her head back, astounded at the demeaning nature of the Chief Advisor's address. *Girl?*

Amadora stepped closer to Catarva, lowering her voice so that Kitieri could hardly hear her words. "*I* built this Church," she seethed in a rasping whisper. "I dedicated my life to this institution to make it what it is, and believe me, Catarva, I can take it all back. I can ruin everything you so proudly stand on. The Board stands behind *me*, and I will keep this position until the day I die. So is this really the battle you want to choose?"

Catarva's nostrils flared and her eyes flashed as she glanced to Kitieri, but she did not respond.

"Kitieri Manon." Amadora twisted back to her. "You are sentenced to imprisonment until your lightning is no longer a threat."

Kitieri's pounding heart thrummed in her ears as the room threatened to spin. Until she went back into lock? But that was... she couldn't just...

"This is completely unethical, and all of you know it," Haldin shouted. "She did nothing wrong except cross paths with you."

"Save it, Commander," Amadora snapped. "The Board's decision is final, and you're lucky you're not going with her for your poor judgement. Now, call in the posted officer and have the prisoner escorted to her new quarters on the lowest floor. I want her wristbands replaced, and the servants instructed not to open her door for meals. No visitors. Is that clear?"

"Indefinite solitary?" Haldin asked, hoarse. "That's cruel even by *your* standards."

"Those measures are completely unnecessary, Amadora," Catarva added.

Kitieri looked between the three of them as the Chief Advisor hissed and spat like a cat, screeching about the reaches of her power. The ringing in Kitieri's ears drowned out her words.

This couldn't be happening. It wasn't real. She was going to wake up any second, and Jera would still be curled against her in a deep sleep. No one would be dead, her life wouldn't be over...

"Get her out of here." Amadora flipped a hand in Kitieri's direction before gathering up her long black robes to storm out. Haldin released a long breath and rested a hand on Kitieri's arm, nodding for her to move for the door.

"Haldin?" Her voice came out a whimper, and she tried to clear her throat.

"I am going to do everything in my power to overturn this," he said in her ear.

Kitieri's hands started to shake as the implications of Amadora's sentence sank in, and questions flooded her mind. "How do I prove it to them if I manage to lock my lightning again?"

Haldin looked at her as he reached for the door handle, and Kitieri withered under the profound pain and sorrow in his eyes. "You don't."

"But—"

"I promise I will not rest until you see daylight again, but I need you to promise something, too."

"What?"

"That you'll hang on down there."

Kitieri blinked as he pulled the door open, and Officer Raden turned with a nod to Haldin. Just as the Commander started to speak, Kitieri felt a heavy presence behind her and looked over her shoulder to see Ghentrin hovering over them.

"Just making sure the Commander gives *all* the instructions," he said with a wide grin. Leaning closer, his face came inches from hers even as Kitieri pulled back in disgust. "Thought you were untouchable with the Baliant on your side, didn't you?" he sneered. "This is what happens when you cross us. I hope you like the dark."

"Back off, Ghentrin," Haldin growled, pulling Kitieri out into the hall by her elbow. He slammed the door closed in the Advisor's face, and Kitieri heard a muffled grunt from the other side. "Raden, you have your orders," he said, releasing Kitieri's arm.

As the officer moved to steer her toward the stairs, Haldin turned his back, touching his forehead.

"Wait," Kitieri said. "Wait, *please.*" She resisted Raden's guiding hand, and his grip tightened.

"You heard the Commander," he said, raising his eyebrows in warning.

"Haldin," she called. The man remained still, shoulders hunched. "What will happen to Taff and Jera?"

Haldin broke the tension in his stance and looked back at her.

"They still have a home here," he said. "I'll make sure they're taken care of."

A sob burst from Kitieri's throat, unexpected, as Raden pushed her closer to the stairs. "Tell them I love them."

Haldin shut his eyes. "I will."

Raden forced her down the first step, and Kitieri tore her eyes from the Commander to watch her feet.

"I'm sorry." Haldin's voice, raw and trembling, followed her down the stairwell. When she looked back, he was gone.

CHAPTER 14

The flickering lamplight danced on the dark walls of the cell, casting long shadows across the room that played tricks on Kitieri's eyes. She shifted on the hard mattress, relieving pressure on her numb, tingling arm, and rolled onto her back to watch the warm glow twitch across the ceiling.

You should save the oil if you're not using it.

"I know," she whispered back to herself. Yet she did not move. Shapes appeared in the flame's exaggerated shadows, displayed across the stone ceiling, and she let her mind wander through the twisted story they told. "I *am* using it, though."

Staring at shadows doesn't count.

Kitieri released a deep sigh, turning her head to stare directly into the lamp's flame. It wasn't her love of the light itself that kept the wick burning. It was that cold, dreaded emptiness that came when the light went out; the fear that threatened to consume her when the black silence pressed in around her. When the oil ran dry, the demons of her darkest thoughts came out to play.

A metallic click rang off the walls, and Kitieri jumped as light spilled across the floor through a narrow opening in the bottom of the cell's door. A thin metal tray slid into the room and the flap slammed closed, leaving the small space lit only by the flickering flame once more.

Kitieri stared at the tray, contemplating her hunger in proportion to the expenditure of effort required to retrieve the thing. Her stomach reacted with a gurgle as the scent reached her nose, and she pushed off the bed apathetically. A hunger strike wasn't going to get her anywhere down here. No one cared if she lived or died anymore. It was all the same to them.

She crouched next to the tray, examining its contents. A biscuit, two pieces of ham, a slice of cheese, and a cup of chopped fruit.

Breakfast.

It was morning, then—not that the time of day meant anything anymore. How many breakfasts had it been now? Seven? Eight?

Kitieri picked up the tray and walked it to the desk where the lamp rested, pushing a pile of crumpled papers onto the floor to make room. The metal feet of the chair screeched against stone as she dragged it from its place, sitting hard on its cold, unforgiving seat. As usual, no cutlery graced the tray.

Because think of all the damage I might do with a stray knife, she thought. *I might carve my name into the wall or something.*

She swallowed the dry biscuit, chasing it with a juicy apple slice while pointedly ignoring the imagery of what she might truly do with a knife if they gave her one.

"I need you to promise something, too." Haldin's voice rang in her memory as she picked up a piece of the ham, dangling it in the flickering light. *"Hang on down there…"*

Kitieri's appetite fled, and she dropped the ham back to the tray.

"Well, you're going to need to get me more oil if I'm going to have any chance of that," she mumbled with a sour glance at the lamp. She pushed the tray aside, revealing the wide, clothbound book she'd found in one of the desk's drawers upon her imprisonment. Its pages were empty, except those she'd torn out that now lay scattered on the floor. Kitieri touched the blank paper, wondering if the books were rationed like the oil, or if, when she'd covered its last free corner, it would be gone forever.

Chewing the inside of her cheek, she glanced at the discarded wads at her feet. She'd wasted a lot of good paper already, but maybe some of it was salvageable. She leaned down to grab one of the crumpled balls and stretched it flat on the desk.

Dear Taff and—

Kitieri instantly returned the sheet to its wadded form, clutching it so tightly in her hands that her knuckles turned white.

Not that one. Not ready for that one.

She lobbed the paper ball across the cell to keep from picking it up again by accident, but the damage was done. She turned back to rest her elbows on the desk, cradling her head in her hands.

Though she pulled out every mental defense she had, images of Taff and Jera seeped into her thoughts. She saw Jera piling forkfuls of food into her mouth, laughing at her brother. She saw Taff curled up in the corner chair back at home, reading one of Mother's books—the one about Shirasette's history and the formation of the Churches. He'd been convinced the gods were real for weeks after reading it, and Father had finally taken him out for a walk to discuss the matter. Kitieri had often wondered what Father had said to Taff for him to return home so pale, but he'd never spoken of the gods again…

The pillar, Kitieri realized with a sharp breath. Father had shown him the pillar, and that was how he'd found her so easily.

She squeezed her eyes closed, rocking her head back and forth in an attempt to drown out the thoughts. Every smiling face from her memories had twisted into the expressions of anguish and despair she'd seen when their parents had never come home. So much abandonment and loneliness had they endured, only to face it all over again at her hands.

It's for their own good. It's better this way.

Is it?

You can't hurt them this way.

I already have. Tears stung her eyes, forcing their way out at the corners to trickle down her face.

No. Keep it together.

Why? What's the point?

Her inner dialogue went quiet, and Kitieri leaned back in the chair. What *was* there to hold on to? The hope that Haldin would make good on his promise to get her out of here? She greatly respected the man, but that outcome was far from likely. Amadora had trampled him and everyone else in that room, brushing off every argument like the annoyance of a buzzing fly. Even if Haldin did manage a miracle, it wouldn't come until Amadora died and a new Chief Advisor was appointed. She'd declared that much at the trial.

Kitieri's shoulders drooped, and her soul shriveled at the thought. Even just another eight days seemed insurmountable, *unsurvivable*... let alone years.

"Hang on down there."

Kitieri shook her head. "How?"

Silence answered her, broken only by the soft purring of the burning wick. She stared into the flame again, biting hard on her bottom lip, and pounded both fists on the desk.

"Tell me, damn it, and I would try!"

The remains of the biscuit flipped onto the floor, and the light flickered as the force jostled the lamp. Kitieri pushed back from the desk in a rage, swiping the breakfast tray off its surface with a deafening crash as the metal struck stone. She whirled away, clasping her hands behind her head to keep from upending the entire desk, and her wordless scream filled the cell.

When her lungs emptied and the scream died, lingering only in the echoes still bouncing from wall to wall, Kitieri found herself on her knees. She bent forward, touching her forehead to the cold floor as she wrapped her arms around her body. The loose gray clothing did little against the chill, and a shiver ran down her spine. In the wake of her violent outburst, realization crept in with a deathly calm.

I'm going to die down here. Alone. And forgotten.

Not forgotten, her own thoughts answered. *Taff and Jera won't forget you.*

Kitieri lifted her head, resting back on her heels. *I hope they do.* Another shiver racked her body. *I hope they move on from me, and live the happy lives they both deserve.*

From the dark recesses of the back of her mind, a thought she could hardly bear to put to words crept forward. *I hope they realize how much safer and better off they are without me.*

Stillness weighed heavily on her shoulders, holding her body in its hunched, wilted form. No tears fell as she remained on the floor, unseeing eyes fixed on the cell's metal door in front of her. Her mind went numb, shutting out the voices of both reason and chaos.

Behind her, the lamp sputtered and popped, gasping its final breaths as the oil ran out, and Kitieri closed her eyes. Better to greet the darkness on her own terms...

Voices sounded in the hallway outside, and Kitieri opened her eyes again just as the flame was extinguished completely. Though she could not see her own hands in front of her face, she leaned forward to listen through the thick door. She could just make out the murmur of male voices on the other side, followed by the sharp jingle of keys. The door jerked and its hinges screeched for the first time since it had closed behind her eight days prior, and Kitieri scrambled backwards on her palms.

The light pouring in stabbed at her eyes. She twisted away, throwing her elbow over her face.

"What in the hells is the matter with her?" one voice asked.

"I don't know," another replied. "Maybe she's scared."

"*She's* scared?" the first voice mumbled.

"Come on, let's get this over with. Manon?"

Kitieri blinked furiously, lowering her elbow enough to see two blurry figures standing in the doorway. "Yeah?" she croaked.

"Your presence is required in the Sanctuary."

Kitieri squinted at the bright doorway. "What?"

"You heard me. Now, come on. Commander's orders."

Kitieri wiped a tear from her sensitive eyes and got to her feet.

"Put this on." The second speaker, the man with the deeper voice, shoved a Gadget into Kitieri's arms.

"I thought you said the Sanctu—"

"Just do it," he demanded. "I'm not taking any risks with you."

Kitieri slipped her arms through the leather straps and felt the weight of the Gadget settle against her back. With the five oran bands already in place, the cintra's limited effect only cast its familiar hazy cloud over her senses.

"And these," the first voice said. The smaller figure stepped into the cell, and Kitieri noticed the silvery flash of oran cuffs in the light from the hallway.

Gods—it's buried already. Still, she offered her wrists. She was not about to jeopardize any chance she had of leaving this hole.

Though the hallway was lit only by occasional lamps spaced along the walls, Kitieri basked in their warm glow. The officers walked on either side of her, one guiding her with a hand on her upper arm. Only when the cell door was out of sight did Kitieri dare hazard a question.

"What's going on?"

The officers exchanged a glance over her head, and the bigger one sighed. "Some woman showed up yesterday morning, demanding to see Officer Kitieri Manon," he said. "Won't budge, no matter what we say."

"Since the Sanctuary is technically open to the public, we can't exactly throw her out," the other said.

Kitieri frowned as they took on another set of stairs. Who in the hells…?

"What I don't get," Deep Voice said, "is why the Chief Advisor didn't just tell her the truth up front. 'Sorry, she's in prison forever' probably would have sent her on her way."

"I don't understand most of what that woman does," High Voice conceded, "but I do know that we are in deep shit if she finds out we did this."

"Hey," Deep Voice said with a shrug, "it's our job to follow orders, and the only direct order *I* heard came from the Commander. He's probably right, anyways. If we just give the woman what she wants and get this one back to her cell, no one will ever have to know."

"I still don't like it," High Voice whined. He looked Kitieri up and down, inching as far away from her as the narrow staircase would allow.

On the sixth landing, Kitieri looked up the next flight to see bright morning light streaming through the window. *Sunlight!*

She rushed toward the window, and the officers hurried after her.

"Hey! Where…"

High Voice trailed off as Kitieri stopped at the window, planting her cuffed hands against the glass. The trees greeted her with a gentle wave in the breeze, and a wide smile spread across her face as she soaked up the warmth.

"All right." Deep Voice tugged at her arm, though the coarse edge in his tone had softened. "Come on, now, no dallying."

He pulled her from the window, forcing her away from the beautiful sight, and the shadow of the Church interior cooled her face once more. Around the next corner waited the Sanctuary.

As they approached the door, High Voice stopped them. "Wait. The cuffs."

"Oh, yeah." Deep Voice reached around the back of his belt for his keys, and held them up in front of Kitieri's face. "I'm going to take these off you," he said. "As far as this woman is concerned, you are still an officer who's just not been feeling well—got it?"

Kitieri nodded.

"Try anything, and you will be extremely sorry," High Voice added, lifting a shimmering hand covered with ice. With a flick of his wrist, the ice disappeared, and Deep Voice opened the door.

As Kitieri stepped through, a high-pitched shriek pulled her attention to the main door, where a stout woman came bounding up the center aisle.

"Officer Kitieri!" the voice cried. As the surprise wore off, recognition struck her.

"Tira!" she exclaimed, rushing forward to meet the woman. Tira grabbed her hands in her own as they met, squeezing them with a beaming grin.

"I'm so sorry you're ill," she said. "You're just as pale as a linen sheet. Nothing too serious, I hope?"

Kitieri squeezed her hands in return. "I'm feeling much better now. It is *really* good to see you, Tira."

"Oh, it's wonderful to see you, too!" Tira said. "I was hoping you'd be on patrol in my area again, but I suppose you got a different assignment."

"Something like that, yeah. What are you doing here?"

Tira ducked her head as she released Kitieri's hands, reaching around for the bag slung over her shoulder. "You told me to ask for you, remember? When it was time."

She opened the bag, revealing three caps at the bottom.

"Oh," Kitieri breathed. "Right. Uh…"

She glanced over her shoulder at the officers standing back near the door, watching her every move.

"I hated to be so pushy about it, but it seemed really important to you," Tira said. "I would have just come back when you were feeling better, but it's a bit of a long walk with no protection." She shrugged with a nervous giggle. "Scary enough getting here the first time, you know?"

"Yeah," Kitieri said, staring at the shining black stones. *I'm getting iced for this*. "You know what, Tira?" She reached out, closing the bag in Tira's hands. "Save your money. Put it towards your son's house."

"But I need the—"

"Take mine." Kitieri shrugged off the heavy pack, pressing it into Tira's arms. The woman's jaw dropped as she stared down at the thing, and a shout rang out behind her.

"What do you think you're doing?" High Voice demanded. "That is not yours to—"

Kitieri wheeled around, putting out one hand, and threw her energy against the oran bands. *Just one spark. Come on.*

Her repressed lightning stirred, lifting its groggy head.

One damned spark!

Kitieri pushed hard against the bands, dragging forth every shred of power she could muster, and felt the prick of heat reach her fingertip. A pop of white burst from her skin, fizzling out before it even reached the floor, but High Voice pulled up short with a defensive hand over his face.

"We can make a scene, or you can let her go," Kitieri said.

The officer glanced back at Deep Voice, whose glare might've injured a small child. "All right, wrap it up," he barked. "You got what you came for, woman, now *go*."

Kitieri turned back to Tira, whose wide eyes flitted between the officers. "I can't accept this, Officer, I—"

"You can," Kitieri said. "Take it and go."

"Go on!" Deep Voice shouted, striding toward them. Tira nodded vigorously, and raced out of the Church with the Gadget clutched to her chest.

"What in the two hells was that?" he demanded, grabbing Kitieri's arm with a hard jerk.

"What does it matter to you?" Kitieri snapped. "The Church has more than enough, and no one will ever miss that one. Let the woman have her life."

Deep Voice growled, slapping the oran cuffs back on her wrists so hard that Kitieri winced, and shoved her toward the door.

"Enough of this. Back down there *now*, before you cause any more damage."

The officers pushed her through the door, forcing her into short bursts of jogging to keep up with their long, determined strides. As they turned her for the stairs, facing the last window before eternal darkness, every muscle in Kitieri's body froze. The maw of the staircase yawned, ready to swallow her whole… and this time, there would be no coming back out.

"No dallying!" Deep Voice said, shoving her forward. Kitieri tripped over her own feet at the sudden force, landing on one knee at the top stair.

"Please don't," she begged. On another day, at any other time, she would've hated her weakness, but all that mattered as she stared down the dark stairwell was *not* going back.

"You can go easy, or you can go hard," High Voice said.

He held up his icy hand in warning, and Deep Voice pulled her to her feet. Panic rose in Kitieri's throat and she resisted the man's grip, scrambling back from the edge.

"Hard it is, then," High Voice said. Kitieri jerked her arm, but the bigger officer held her fast as the icy hand reached for her. She turned her head away, closing her eyes as she strained against the firm hold, thinking frantically through any possible means of escape. Her lightning was useless with the five bands *and* the cuffs, and Deep Voice was easily twice her size.

The burning sensation of unbearable cold touched her hand, and she jerked back in a desperate final attempt to free herself. Her eyes flew open as her shoulder hit the floor, skidding backwards with unchecked momentum.

Deep Voice's body collapsed to the floor beside her with a heavy thud, and Kitieri's mouth opened in a silent, airless gasp. At the edge of the stairs, High Voice lay writhing and moaning. Before she could blink, she was hauled to her feet and a roughened hand clamped over her mouth.

"Don't make a sound."

Kitieri whipped around as the newcomer released their hold on her. "*Haldin?*"

That familiar side smile pulled up the corner of his mouth as he unlocked the cuffs binding her wrists. "Let's go."

Haldin turned and set a brisk pace down the hallway, and Kitieri ran to catch up. "What did you do to them?" she asked.

Haldin lifted his hand, bright sparks jumping between his fingers. "They'll be fine," he said. "Just pissed. I gave them enough that they should still be there when I come back. Put this on."

He handed her a long, dark garment he'd had slung over his shoulder, and Kitieri shook it out as she trotted beside him. A cloak.

"Haldin, what are you doing?" she hissed. "We are breaking *every* rule Amadora—"

"You want to go back?" He raised an eyebrow at her.

"N-no!" Kitieri stammered, searching for the proper words. "I just… I mean… If we're caught—"

Haldin took a quick turn down an adjoining hallway, almost running Kitieri into the wall as he strode for the door at the far end. He threw it open, walking out into an empty courtyard, and Kitieri's pace slowed. She blinked in the sudden light and lifted her face to its warmth.

"Your hood," Haldin said. Kitieri snapped out of the blissful moment, rushing after him as she fumbled with the cloak's thick ties. Its deep cowl covered most of her face, blocking out the sunlight once more.

Haldin opened the courtyard's gate, peering out before waving over his shoulder for her to follow. She trailed him through yards, gardens, tool sheds, and a chicken coop before he pulled her through a final gate in the tallest outer wall of the Church grounds. As she stepped through, another presence sent her scrambling sideways along the wall, zapping her taut nerves, before she got a better look.

"That's just Ashes," Haldin said, closing the gate behind him. The gray mare lifted her head, ears pricked forward in interest.

"Ashes?" Kitieri mumbled. She knew that name… Jera's horse.

"She's good with beginners," Haldin said. "Now listen to me, Kitieri. Before I say anything else, it's important that you know one thing."

She tore her gaze from the horse to look Haldin in the eye. The lines of worry and exhaustion on his face had deepened twofold since their last meeting, and she sensed a haggard air of desperation about him.

"If you choose to run and go into hiding, I want you to know that I cannot fault that," he said. "I would not blame you for leaving this place far behind at this point."

Kitieri stared, struck silent by his unexpected words.

"But," he continued, "if there's any part of you still willing to take a risk on this, there is one way you might be able to prove yourself to the Board."

"Prove myself?" Kitieri's voice came out high and shaky, and she cleared her throat. "You *are* referring to the same Board I met a week ago, right?"

Haldin nodded, dropping his eyes to the dirt, and the dappled sunlight through the bordering trees obscured his downcast expression. "I admit it's a long shot," he said, "but it's your only path back to a life you once knew. A life with your brother and sister."

Kitieri's jaw clenched as the weight of his words dropped in her stomach.

"We need each other right now," he added, more quietly.

Kitieri looked away, blinking back her emotion. "What do you need from *me*?" she asked.

Haldin stepped forward, leaning into an urgent stance. "Do you remember what I said about a mission the night before your training started?"

A vague memory of pain in her lip while she stood with the Commander in the shadows outside the dining hall surfaced, and she nodded.

"It's time," he said. "The morning you became my trainee, the Church of Histan arrested and imprisoned six of our officers while they were on patrol. They were accused of crossing the borders of the Church districts, and detained by a much larger force of red officers. No matter what I or Catarva did or said, they refused to release them. Two days after you were imprisoned, they executed the first one at the pillar."

Kitieri clapped a hand over her mouth.

"I thought they couldn't do that," she whispered. "I thought they couldn't touch anyone from the Church of Enahris."

"That's the law," Haldin said. "They've declared they had the right because our officers were in their territory, but we all know they're instigating war."

Kitieri twisted her mouth. No shock there. "And the only winners will be the Advisors," she mumbled.

Haldin sighed. "I know," he said softly. "I can't defend what happened at your trial. The Board is corrupt, but there are those willing to listen. Amadora's beaten them down and given them no choice. She's manipulated and twisted what was supposed to be a fair system of government into one where she holds all the power, but I believe there are members of the Board ready to go against her. Without the unanimous vote she's come to rely on, Amadora loses her power and the Baliant's vote takes precedent."

Kitieri scoffed. "I didn't see the Baliant trying very hard in there."

Haldin frowned. "That isn't fair. You have no idea how hard the Baliant has been working to keep her Church and people safe."

"And yet," Kitieri countered, "her officers are dying at the pillar while the Board tramples her and keeps her silent."

"Do not judge what you don't know," Haldin said, lifting a finger. "Catarva would give her life for this Church if she thought it would help, but right now she needs *us*. The Board has stopped every one of her attempts at communication and peace with the Church of Histan, but I truly believe we can break their unanimous vote. I wouldn't ask this of you if I didn't think it possible."

Kitieri crossed her arms. "So what *are* you asking of me, then?"

"Does that mean you're with me?"

She sighed. "If there's a way for me to take a shot at these people, I'm in."

"All right," Haldin said with a quick nod. "Tiernan's Board has executed five of our six officers now. They've held Inra the longest, trying to use her high rank as one of Catarva's personal guards for leverage, information, and Enahris knows what else. But…" Haldin looked down, clearing his throat. "She went to the pillar at dawn."

"Shit," Kitieri breathed. She remembered so clearly the kind hazel eyes and gentle touch as Inra had melted that collar off her neck. It was always the good ones that suffered the most. "And there's been no Strike since then?"

"No," Haldin replied. "That's why it's urgent. There's still time to save Inra's life. If we can do that, we not only gain insight to what the Church of Histan is doing, but we can also provide the Board with proof that you are an important asset and we need you."

"Haldin…" Kitieri started, shaking her head. The Board would never go for that even if she managed to succeed. But as she looked into Haldin's hopeful eyes and watched his exhaustion and pain lift ever so slightly, she bit back the words on her tongue. "Okay," she said instead. "What's the plan?"

"I need you to intercept the Strike meant for Inra."

Kitieri nodded. "Then what?"

"In accordance with their own law, she will be declared innocent and they'll be forced to release her."

Kitieri bit the corner of her lip. "I'll try, Haldin. I really will. But in my experience, the Church of Histan doesn't exactly honor their own process. They don't take kindly to losing, especially when it comes to their precious pillar."

Haldin regarded her for a moment, contemplating her words. "It's still Inra's best chance," he said at last. "If we do nothing, her death is sealed."

Kitieri held her breath for a moment before letting out a small sigh. She did not harbor the same hopes for any of this plan, but he was right about Inra's chances.

The Commander reached for his key ring, pinching the small pin between his fingers. "You won't need these."

As he reached for her wrist, Kitieri pulled back. "M-maybe you should leave them on."

Haldin paused, lowering the key. "It's time, Kitieri," he said.

She fought the subtle trembling that crept through her body, lifting her gaze from the key to Haldin's eyes. "What if I can't control it?" she whispered. "What if I kill Inra, or —"

"You *can*." Haldin laid a hand on her shoulder, and Kitieri felt her tension melt under his touch. She wanted so badly to believe him... "You know what to do," he said. "I trust you."

Kitieri looked into the man's earnest blue eyes. How could *anyone* trust her?

"Now you need to trust yourself." He gave her shoulder a light squeeze. "I know you have the power to save, and it's time for you to believe it, too. You can't hide from your lightning forever. It's part of you."

"I know," she whispered. Closing her eyes, Kitieri remembered the day she'd chafed against the oran bands for stealing that part away. She'd been angry with Haldin that day. Angry with Catarva. Angry with everyone and everything that had forced her down a path she'd never wanted.

But she'd never wanted her lightning either. From the day she'd discovered her element, from the very moment she'd turned to see the dismay on her parents' faces, she'd known she was cursed where others were blessed. Even before the Strikes, everyone had known that lightning was only good for one thing…

No. Two things.

Kitieri took a deep breath and offered her wrists to Haldin. As the bands fell away, her lightning stirred and buzzed, racing through her and tickling her insides. Despite herself, Kitieri smiled.

If it had to be a part of her, then she would make it the good part, or die trying.

"Thank you, Kitieri," Haldin said, mirroring her smile as the bands swung from his fingers. "Now, we have to be fast; the Strike can come at any time. Take Ashes, she'll get you there."

"Oh… no thanks." Kitieri laughed, glancing nervously at the horse. "I can't ride."

"You'll be too slow on foot." Haldin dropped the bands to the ground, and moved to pat the saddle. "Take the horse. Like I said, she's good with beginners. I'll help you up."

Before Kitieri could protest, Haldin hoisted her into the saddle and pushed her right leg over the other side. Kitieri righted herself, grasping the saddle's hard leather pommel as she gaped at the ground.

"Holy shit, I'm so tall," she breathed.

"Feet in the stirrups," Haldin instructed, tucking her toes into the dangling metal rings. "Weight on the balls of your feet, toes up, heels down, straight back, center yourself—there you go. Here are the reins."

He threw the braided leather loop over Ashes' head, passing it to Kitieri. She clutched the reins in one hand while refusing to release the saddle with the other.

"Lean them on her neck whichever way you want to go," he said. "Ashes is sensitive; it doesn't take much. A nudge with your heels tells her to go, and a tug on the reins will slow her down. She's a smooth ride, so hang on and you'll be fine. When you get off, she ground ties."

"Ground ties?" Kitieri croaked.

"Listen," Haldin said, coming to stand at her knee. "I will be waiting here for you at sundown. If you don't come, I'll know that either something happened, or you chose not to return. Bring Inra home, and I *swear* I will take your place before I see you imprisoned again."

Fighting to control her shallow breaths, Kitieri looked down at the man.

Her Commander. Her teacher. Her friend.

By the grace of whatever gods might be out there, she would *not* let him down again.

CHAPTER 15

Kitieri leaned forward, clinging to the saddle's pommel for dear life as Ashes' hooves clattered on the cobblestones.

Don't slip. Please don't fall down, Kitieri silently begged the horse. But the mare was sure-footed in her brisk canter, slowing just enough at turns and congested areas to allow people to dive out of her way. Kitieri squeezed hard with her knees to keep her balance, holding the reins and Ashes' black mane together in one hand. Though she had no illusion of control over this animal, the horse seemed to choose her own path easily enough, deviating only when the reins touched her neck.

She breathed out in a sharp sigh of relief as the looming fortress came into view. Tall and proud, the Church of Histan stood silhouetted against the late morning sun, its dark shadow settling over everything in the vicinity. As Kitieri pulled up on the reins, the air in her nose and throat carried a sharp metallic twinge.

Good damned thing I took the horse.

"Whoa," she said softly, patting the dappled gray neck as the horse slowed to a stop. She leaned to the side, gauging the distance to the ground, and gritted her teeth. "No instructions on how to get off, Haldin?" she grumbled.

Kicking both feet out of the stirrups, she swung her leg over Ashes' neck and pushed off, landing in a crouch. The impact jarred her body and she braced herself with a hand on the cobblestones, assessing any possible injuries.

"Elegant dismount."

Kitieri stood, spinning toward the voice, and located a hooded figure leaning against a wall in the entrance to a shadowed alley. The husky voice didn't strike her as particularly male or female, but the speaker's frame appeared small and thin under the heavy cloak.

Kitieri narrowed her eyes. "Thanks for noticing."

She turned back to Ashes, pulling the reins over her head, but felt the hairs on the back of her neck stand up as the stranger continued to stare. When she looked back again, the hooded figure was several steps closer.

"Who are you?" she snapped. Taking in the long, dark cloak again, Kitieri's frown deepened. Was this…? It couldn't be the same person that had followed her to Tira's house…

"I was starting to think you'd never show," the stranger said in lilting tones.

"Show?"

"You're here for the last gray officer, I presume. The red-haired girl."

Kitieri's squint turned into a glare. "Why do you say that?"

"No need to play coy." A grin crept into the husky voice. "I know who you are. The girl with the lightning."

"Is that so?" Kitieri jerked her chin up. "Only fair that I know you, too, then."

The hood nodded. "You will."

The electricity humming in the air jumped, and Kitieri's lightning rushed to her fingertips. She grimaced at the sudden flash of pain as her element thrashed, unchecked by oran for the first time since she'd come out of lock. She slammed her fists closed, one clamped around Ashes' reins, as she started to back away.

"Look, I don't know what you want, but I have to go," she said, turning for the Church without awaiting a reply. The warnings were coming any second, and this one was going to *hurt*.

Before she rounded the corner that would bring her into view of Histan's Square, Kitieri tossed a glance behind her to find the hooded stranger gone. Her element flared again, biting at her hands, and she growled. Finally a chance to confront her stalker, and the lightning had to act up. *Damn it.*

She looked back to the Church, and movement along the wall caught her eye. Kitieri craned her neck for a better look, and identified a hooded cloak in the shadow.

How in the hells did you —

Wait, *two* cloaks... brown, not black. Kitieri furrowed her brows, watching the two spindly figures enter the gate. The same cloaks that came to the cintra mines on the wagons, she realized. And the same ones she'd seen all over the inside of the Church, so small and silent.

"The kids," Kitieri breathed, as the cloaks disappeared behind the wall. An image of Noia and Vina came to her mind, and she was transported back to the cell beneath the Church of Histan. Noia's crystalline tear fell in the moonlight as she mourned for her daughter's life of servitude over her own death.

"The child slaves." Kitieri put a fist to her mouth. "*Gods*, I hate this place."

Her lightning surged as the first warning tore through her, and Kitieri sucked in a breath, pain flooding her senses. Ashes snorted, ears up and eyes wide, and Kitieri dropped the reins to the ground to stumble away from the animal.

"Stay, or whatever," she ground out. Ashes' huge brown eyes followed her, but she remained in place.

Kitieri inched around the corner, poking her head just out of the shadows to look across the sun-drenched Square. She pressed her eyes closed instantly, but the image had already been burned into her vision. Inra stood at the pillar, chained at the hands and feet. Though her body quivered, the officer lifted her bruised face to the sky, the red hair Kitieri had only ever seen in a neat bun falling around her shoulders in tangled, matted locks.

"It looks like you've been through the hells."

Kitieri heard Inra's words from their first meeting, and squeezed her eyes closed harder. "Welcome to the hells," she whispered.

The second warning hit and Kitieri pulled back, flattening herself against the cool building. It hurt so *bad.*

Control it. Clear your mind. Don't let it feed off your emotion.

She forced herself to stand straight and tall, tapping into the dark abyss that hovered somewhere beyond her racing thoughts.

Give it nothing to consume.

One by one, like prying off cold, dead fingers, Kitieri shed her doubts and insecurities. Haldin's consequences. Inra's fate. Taff and Jera's broken hearts. Each heavy piece fell away, crashing to the ground until there was… nothing.

Lighter than air, there came a strange sensation of floating.

Kitieri opened her eyes. Her element hummed in her palms, its full attention on her command as she turned to face the pillar once more. A few red officers lingered with their Gadgets far across the open space, glancing nervously between the pillar and the Church doors.

Histan forbid another victim escape your grasp, Kitieri thought bitterly.

The third warning wrenched a cry from Inra, whose proud resolve seemed to buckle under the proximity of death. Her chains scraped against the back of the stone pillar, and Kitieri narrowed her eyes. Even if she called the Strike, Inra would still be chained there. They'd never declare her innocent and set her free.

She gritted her teeth. It was a risky move, but there was only one option. She couldn't repel this one. She'd have to catch it and use it.

The lightning buzzed and whirred in Kitieri's hands as the Strike approached.

I have control. I own you—she squeezed her fists—*and I own YOU*. She looked up to the sky to meet the Blue Killer's angry eye. Its energy filled the air, thick and metallic on her tongue as it gathered its hatred.

Come get me.

The Strike tore downward and Kitieri lifted her open hand. Searing pain threatened her control as the blue bolt met her palm, its hideous screech mingling with her scream in a deafening instant before the push. Twisting in brilliant streaks of blue and white, Kitieri threw the combined energies against the chains that wrapped the pillar.

Silence followed, engulfing her before the familiar rush of coolness that followed a Strike. All except…

Kitieri glanced down at the arm that had caught the Strike. Though her mouth fell open in shock, the cry caught in her throat. She stared in horror at the bloodied, melted flesh as her brain struggled to register its reality.

A sharp sob rang through the Square and Kitieri looked up to see Inra vomiting onto the stairs of the pillar's dais, her bonds broken.

Through the jumbled, hazy mess of horror and urgency in her

mind, Kitieri ran for her. A shout from the other side alerted her to the red officers' approach, and the Church door flew open. She sprinted harder, pushing aside the sickening sensation of the breeze along her mangled arm.

"Inra!" she cried. The woman's head lifted, matted locks blowing across her face as her body heaved. "*Run!*"

She saw her name on Inra's lips in silent disbelief.

"RUN!"

The three red officers rushed for them, closing in on the pillar. Kitieri leaped up onto the dais and grabbed Inra's arm to pull her down the stairs.

"Get on the horse!" she commanded. "Haldin is waiting at the south gate—"

Blinding agony closed Kitieri's throat, turning her voice to a blood-curdling scream. She gripped her elbow below the burned, bubbling flesh of her forearm as her pain skyrocketed as though she'd been set on fire. Her eyes bulged as real flames engulfed her whole arm, and she waved wildly in a panicked attempt to put them out. Just as the scream faltered in her empty lungs, the fire vanished.

Her breaths came in ragged gulps as she collapsed, shaking. A garbled cry told her that Inra was faring no better, and Kitieri curled in on herself.

No.

It was the only thing her shattered mind could muster.

Shining black boots entered her vision, peeking out from under black robes that dragged the ground. Cold metal snapped around her good wrist, and another hoarse cry ripped from her throat as a hand grabbed the bloodied one, wrenching it around to force it into a pair of oran cuffs. Unbearable pain addled her thoughts, clouding her mind.

"Ah, welcome back, Ms. Manon."

A voice. She knew that voice.

A face leaned in close to hers, coming so near that the breath of the next words brushed her ear. "I must say, I thought Amadora had you put away for good," he said. "But you're a slippery one, aren't you?"

With monumental effort, Kitieri turned her head just enough to see the speaker's face.

"Well," he snarled, tangling his fingers in her hair, "I hope you enjoyed your last hurrah."

Kitieri drew in a ragged breath, fighting to clear her mind through the torture. "Sending me back to the pillar, Stil?" she rasped.

The long, pockmarked face twisted into a malicious grin, and a dark laugh resonated in his chest. "Oh, no," he replied. "Though I doubt you'd fare so well without your lightning this time."

He grabbed her uninjured hand, and another blinding, sickening rush of pain sent Kitieri writhing, hoarse screams clawing at her raw throat. She jerked and pulled as his fire element melted her skin, but Stil held her hand tight in his.

"The pillar is too good for you now," he said with a cruel sneer. "Too quick."

When he released her hand, Kitieri pulled it back just as ruined and bloodied as the other. Her body shook uncontrollably, racked with unrelenting agony, and she pressed her forehead into the dais. Movement was impossible. All she could do was lie on the stone as her body seized with tremors, begging inwardly for any possible respite. Unconsciousness, death... it didn't matter.

"And you know what else?" Stil asked, lowering his face to Kitieri's. "That little girl you cared so much about? The one you tried to run with? She's mine."

Kitieri lifted her eyes just enough to see Stil's lips moving.

"I made sure to claim her as my *personal* servant in the future. And when that bitch Catarva finally falls, I'll have your brother and sister, too. Maybe you'll even be around long enough to witness it. In fact, I think I'll make sure of that."

At Stil's demented chuckle, Kitieri let her eyes fall closed again. Through the physical torment, only one concept echoed in her mind.

I've failed them all. Everyone.

Stil pulled away as he got to his feet, and his robes brushed her wounds as he turned to leave the dais. "Bring her," he commanded two nearby officers. "I'm anxious to see how she appreciates her new accommodations." His lips twisted into a mocking grin.

Hands fell on Kitieri, scraping and aggravating her burns as they hauled her to an upright position between them. Her feet dragged on the stone, thumping on each step as they carried her down.

"Chief Advisor," another called. Stil shot an annoyed glance at the man. "What about this one?"

A soft whimper reminded Kitieri of Inra's presence, held only a few paces away. Slowly, shaking violently, she looked over at the bruised and battered gray officer. Tear-tracks left stark lines down her dirtied, bloodied face as her eyes found Kitieri's. Eyes full of fear. Pain. Exhaustion.

Kitieri dropped her unsteady gaze. Just another one she couldn't save.

"Get rid of her," Stil said. With a grin back at Kitieri, he added, "We have something better now."

Kitieri's eyes opened wide just in time to see a red officer run his short sword through Inra's abdomen. The woman gagged and sputtered until thick red blood spilled from her mouth, and she toppled backwards into a heap on the stones of Histan's Square.

What little strength had been left in her arms and legs failed, and Kitieri's full weight sank against the officers' grips as the world faded away. Somewhere nearby, she heard the sound of hooves.

Ashes?

Not Ashes. Horses don't just...

Her thoughts drifted away as the officers dropped her to the ground amidst cries and shouts in a new chaos her broken mind could not comprehend. Finally, the blissful black claimed her as all consciousness fled with her pain.

CHAPTER 16

The murmur of quiet voices flitted in and out of earshot, unintelligible in the short bursts that interrupted Kitieri's sleep. She turned her head away from them, clinging to the bright, happy images of Taff's smile and the sound of Jera's laugh tinkling through her subconscious.

The voices faded again, and Kitieri drifted back into the happy dream.

"Sit on your butt, Jera," she said.

Her sister rolled her eyes with a wide grin. "There's no one here but us."

"I know, but we won't always be this isolated..."

The dream jumped.

Taff was miming the alleycats, clawing at the air while Jera shrieked with delight. As he opened his mouth to laugh with her, dark blood poured from his lips onto the table, and he turned his head to look at Kitieri.

"Why didn't you help us?"

Kitieri jolted, kicking her legs to run, but went nowhere.

"NO!"

Her eyes flew open to find that her voice was real, bouncing off the walls of an unfamiliar room. As she bolted into a sitting position, a pair of hands pushed her back down into a large, soft pillow. Kitieri kicked harder, tangling her legs in the blankets and waving her arms in a wild attempt to ward off the forces that held her down.

"Get off me!" she cried, twisting against the strong hands on her shoulders. Two more hands grabbed her flailing legs.

"Shhhh, Kitieri!"

"Get *off*!" She landed a hard kick to the person at her feet, and was rewarded with the thump of a backside hitting the floor and a loud "*oof.*"

"*Kitieri!*"

Increasingly aware of her pain as her body wore out, Kitieri paused her violent rage at the sound of the husky voice. A tall, slender man hovered over her, hands on her shoulders, and a petite woman stepped up beside him. Wisps of gray at her temples stood out from her brown hair, the wrinkles around her brown eyes heavy with hardship and loss, and on her shoulders rested a familiar dark cloak.

"You're the creep from the alley," Kitieri said. Her voice was damaged and hoarse from the screaming, and clearing her throat only made it hurt worse.

"Creep, huh?" The woman crossed her arms. "Well, I guess I can live with that. The hood might have been dramatic, but it's not like I'm exactly welcome around there."

"You've been following me." Kitieri pushed up against the pillow as the man slowly pulled his hands back.

"Guilty." The woman showed a toothy grin.

"What do you—" Kitieri cut off as a head popped up over the foot of the bed. "*Tira?*"

"That's a strong kick you've got, Officer!" Tira chuckled, rosy cheeks flushed extra red as she pulled herself to her feet.

Kitieri's eyes darted between the three of them. "All right, what is going on?" she demanded.

"Easy." The cloaked woman put out a hand. "You've had a rough day. The salve will be in full effect by now, but try not to move too much."

Kitieri's heart-rate spiked as the memories flooded back, and she looked down at her hands. Thin strips of linen wrapped each arm from the elbow to the tips of her fingers, hindering most movement, but her pain was merely a ghost of its former glory.

"Our doctors did the best they could," the woman said. "It's hard when you're living off the map, but we still have some experts in our midst. Name's Batessa—*former* librarian and historian for the Church of Histan, but you can call me Bat. This exceptionally tall man here is Eriat, our resident genius, and I believe you've met our dear Tira."

"Batessa," Kitieri repeated. She'd never heard the name before.

"Bat." The woman smiled. "Just Bat. Here, drink this. It will help settle your nerves."

She offered a cup of steaming tea, and Kitieri caught a whiff of the fruity berry blend before pushing it away. Only one other time had she smelled that tea… at Tira's house.

"All right, *Bat*," Kitieri snapped. "Care to tell me what the fuck is going on?"

"I knew you had an attitude." Bat's grin widened. "It's perfect."

Kitieri narrowed her eyes to a slitted glare. "Where am I?"

Bat opened her palms to the ceiling.

"Welcome," she said, "to the Church of Shirasette."

A long silence passed between them as Kitieri stared the woman down.

"Look, I'm really not in the mood for bullshit," she said finally.

Bat's cheek twitched, but she maintained her smile as she dragged a wooden chair over from the far side of the room.

"It's true," said the tall man, Eriat, as Bat settled on the edge of the chair with her elbows planted on her knees.

"There's no such thing," Kitieri said.

"There is *now*." Bat pulled out a small book from the inner folds of her cloak. Unwrapping its soft leather strip, she flipped the book open and tossed it onto Kitieri's lap. "See for yourself."

The open pages were filled with ink, words formed into two neat columns, and Kitieri rested her bandaged hands on the edges to better read them.

Names. She brushed her hand over the pages, searching the book. All names.

"What is this?" She tore her eyes from the book to look up into Bat's intent stare.

"Tira tells me you don't have much knowledge of the Churches," Bat said. Kitieri tossed a dark glance at Tira, who looked down at her folded hands with a light blush.

"Yes, Tira's been working with us." Bat cut off her question before Kitieri could ask it. "She's come to us for help a time or two, and in return she agreed to learn what she could about you. I have to admit, I didn't think you'd just run right into one of our people so soon, but there you were."

"I-I didn't lie, though," Tira said, brandishing a defensive hand. "Well… that's not true…I *did* lie the second time I saw you, at the Church. I didn't really need a Gadget; Bat sent me to find out why you'd disappeared, and when I saw you I knew something was wrong. But I was still a member of the Church of Enahris the first time we met, I promise!"

"Tira." Bat laid a gentle hand on the woman's shoulder. "It's all right. You have nothing to feel bad for. You've done excellent work, and don't forget that without you, Kitieri would still be a prisoner. Isn't that right?"

Bat turned expectant eyes on Kitieri, who glanced between the two women. "So, Haldin…?" She cleared her throat. "He was working with you, too, to get me out of there?"

"Oh, no." Bat laughed. "No, Handsome had his own agenda, as it turned out, and apparently made his own plan when Tira showed up demanding to see you. I'd been expecting you at the pillar long before you came, so I sent Tira to check out your mysterious absence and the Commander executed my next phase of action better than I ever could have hoped. He sent you right to me."

Kitieri twisted to find the only window in the room. It was still light out, but without any bearings, she couldn't tell if it was morning or afternoon. "How long was I out?"

Bat tilted her head. "Why, got somewhere to be?"

"Yes. Haldin's waiting for me."

Bat barked a shrill laugh. "You're actually planning on going *back* there?" She slapped her knee. "Girl, you're crazier than I thought."

Kitieri leveled the woman with a smoldering glare as Bat made a dramatic show of wiping a tear from under her eye.

"Oh, fine," she sighed. "You were only out a couple hours, but you're really in no shape to be going anywhere."

"Are you gonna stop me?" Kitieri asked.

The humor fled from Bat's face as they locked eyes.

"Will you listen, first?" Bat asked. "I *did* save your life back there from Supreme Asshole. It's the least you can do."

Kitieri rested her shoulders back against the pillow with a quiet growl.

"All right," she said. "Then what in the hells are all of these names about, and what do they have to do with me?"

Bat's expression lit up again, and she leaned forward on the very edge of her seat. "Do you know how the original Churches came to be?"

Kitieri lowered her eyes, shaking her head, and Bat tapped the book in her lap.

"This is how," she said. "Names. Pledges of loyalty and worship from when the gods once walked among us. Histan, the brave and powerful; and Enahris, the compassionate and nurturing, or so they claimed. The people chose their gods, and took their oath of service by writing their names in the Church's book."

"That's ridiculous," Kitieri scoffed. "Gods aren't real."

Bat flashed a grin. "Looking through history, it's undeniable that two beings named Histan and Enahris existed about a thousand years ago. They're all over the scrolls from hundreds of different accounts. My personal theory is that they were two people who simply capitalized on a tumultuous time in our history to take power and assume leadership. There's never *not* been competition between the two, even from their earliest mentions, but that's human nature for you.

"But the important part," Bat went on, nodding to the book, "is how they went about solving their power issues. In those early days of the Churches, there was instant bickering and fighting. Which side was better, which side more powerful, which side had the right to rule the people. So a new law was written, outlining the bare minimum an organization needed to be considered a Church, thus reserving the right to govern their own members without interference from the other."

Eriat leaned against the bedpost near Kitieri's head.

"A poorly written law, at best," he said. "It would never fly by today's standards. Yet it remains on our city's scrolls, engraved in history."

"To be considered a valid Church," Bat continued, "you need a figurehead—a *head*, not a god, mind you—a Baliant, a Board, and at least two thousand pledges. Go ahead and count them, there, if you want."

Kitieri's eyes followed Bat's gesture to the book.

"You're telling me," Kitieri said, leafing slowly through the pages, "that you somehow got two thousand people to abandon their Church to follow *you*?"

"Two thousand, one hundred, and forty-three, to be exact," Bat said proudly. "I mean, to be fair, two thousand was a lot of people back when the law was introduced, but it's still been damned near impossible to get that kind of gathering without being caught and murdered—"

"*Why*?"

Bat froze, and her open mouth curved into a grin. "Now, Kitieri, you can't tell me you haven't seen it."

"Seen what?"

"People are *dying*." Bat lurched forward, hands on her knees. "The Churches are corrupt. The Boards run those places with iron fists, and they're happy to watch people die. They *need* the people to die."

"Need?"

"Why do you think the Boards are instigating a war between their Churches?"

Kitieri looked away, a sick feeling sinking to the pit of her stomach. As insane as this woman sounded, she was right. Even Stil had mentioned Amadora as if she was an ally.

"I don't know," she answered. "Wouldn't the Churches need their people and their officers alive?"

"Ah." Bat held up one knobby finger. "Only if things were status quo. But you see—"

Kitieri's eyes opened wide as air rushed into her lungs. "The lightning," she breathed. "The extinction point Catarva talked about."

Bat's eyebrows shot up. "Catarva let you in on that one, huh? Surprises me."

"She thinks I can help," Kitieri said.

"Oh!" Bat threw her head back in another fit of laughter, slapping Eriat with the back of her hand. "*She* wants Kitieri's help. Oh, that's rich, isn't it?"

Kitieri's temper flared as she watched their amused exchange. "I *want* to help," she snapped. "I don't know how yet, but if I can save lives—"

Bat snatched the book out of Kitieri's lap and brandished it in her face.

"You want to save lives?" She lowered her voice, suddenly vehement. "Here's two thousand, one hundred and forty-three of them that need you. The Churches *had* their chance. Tiernan disappeared ten years ago and left his to the wolves, and Catarva has proven incapable of managing her own. The Boards have far too much power, and all that matters to *them* is that as many people as possible die before the lightning takes over so they can live in comfort on the meager resources that will be left."

Kitieri stared, open-mouthed, as Bat's tirade put words to her deepest fears.

"There's only so much cintra in the city," Bat went on, more softly this time. "It seems endless, but when the lightning overpowers our structures, it will go fast. You're the expert, Eriat—you tell her."

Eriat nodded solemnly beside her, smoothing his well-trimmed white beard.

"Yes, it will," he confirmed. "Before all of this, I was a cintra engineer. I studied the crystals even before the Strikes started, and I had a hand in designing the first PCRs. I was already involved with the Church of Shirasette when Stil assigned me to a bigger project—*much* bigger. He wanted me to design monstrous, immovable machines that could protect specific areas only. They require more cintra than you can imagine, and their projected range in lightning that severe is... pathetically limited. All that is to say that very few will be protected when the lightning takes over. A few farms outside our walls, the Churches and their grounds, and that's about it."

"And a war would go a long way toward clearing out some of those unnecessary mouths to feed, wouldn't it?" Bat said, twisting the corner of her mouth.

Kitieri released her pent-up air, lifting a bandaged hand to her mouth.

"And *that's* how the Church of Shirasette began," Bat said. "What started as an attempt to offer refuge to the homeless, the parentless, the starving—anyone affected by the lightning with no means to help themselves—grew like crazy. We had to keep it under wraps, or Stil would have had us all killed for hiding children he thinks belong to him, and even the Church of Enahris could no longer be trusted once Amadora started turning refugees over to Stil. But even working in secret, more and more people found their way here every day."

Kitieri nodded slowly. If word of this place had reached her or

Noia before… well… they *all* could have been safe.

"Where is 'here'?" she asked.

"You are currently on the second floor of a converted warehouse Eriat owns," Bat said.

"Cintra engineering had its perks, not the least of which was high pay." Eriat shrugged with a grin.

"You're telling me that over two thousand people live in a secret warehouse?" Kitieri asked.

"No, no." Bat laughed. "Only about three hundred live here, mostly orphans and widows. Many only need partial support, like a hot meal now and then, or to borrow a Gadget here and there, and we provide that. Everyone pools their resources for the betterment of the whole, and we save lives."

"But," Eriat said, "the bigger we grow, the greater the danger."

Bat nodded. "It's only a matter of time before Stil finds us. He's aware of our operations, and he's noticing the reduced numbers of orphans and deaths, despite the Strikes' growing frequency. Eriat and I spent many long, sleepless nights looking for a solution."

"And then *you* showed up," Eriat said. Kitieri frowned.

"You didn't think that stunt at the pillar went unnoticed, did you?" Bat asked. "I've been following you ever since. You did it again outside Tira's house and saved a life, and that's when I knew."

"I don't get it," Kitieri said slowly.

"Kitieri," Bat started, looking down at the book of names. "You don't know who you are. I can see it. I see the doubt and pain in your eyes from being hunted and persecuted at every turn. Two Churches want you dead or locked away, but do you know *why*?"

Kitieri dropped her eyes. "I'm dangerous."

Bat's grin widened to show her teeth.

"You are, but not in the way you think," she said. "Since the Strikes started, the Churches have been finding ways to capitalize on them. Fear is a powerful tool that keeps people ignorant and docile, but *you* walk in defiance of every system they have put in place to take complete control. Where they would have the people on their knees, begging the gods for mercy, you stand untouched. You have seen the Judgement and lived. You can call the Strikes and make them your own. At every turn, you defy what they call the punishment of the gods. You prove them wrong. And that gives *you* the power."

Kitieri stared at Bat as the words rushed over her, their implications tangling in her mind like too many threads unraveling simultaneously. Her mouth moved silently, searching for words that would not come as Bat nodded.

"It is that power that garnered these signatures, Kitieri," she said. "These people didn't abandon their Churches and everything they've ever known for me. They signed for *you*."

Kitieri felt her face go pale. "I thought you said you'd been helping these people for a long time…"

"We have," Bat said. "But there was no way they would have actually abandoned their Churches and risked that illegal status without you — the girl with the lightning. The girl who can defy the gods."

Panic surged through Kitieri, and she shook her head so hard that her hair flew in her eyes as she kicked at the blanket over her legs. "No. No. I'm not — No."

She swung her feet over the edge of the bed, gasping as her burns dragged along the linen sheets. She tried to stand, only for a firm hand to push her back down, and she glared up at Eriat.

"This is insane," she hissed, wrenching her shoulder from Eriat's grasp. "I will *not* be responsible for the murder of two thousand people because *you* made me out to be some hero! I don't know what lies you told them, but *I can't save anybody*! I can't even save myself, let alone my brother and sister, or anyone else I made the mistake of caring about. When Stil finds you — and he will — this will NOT be my fault!"

Kitieri pushed off the mattress, flinging her wrapped arm to knock Bat's hand out of the way as she reached for her. She rushed for the door, bare feet slapping on the coarse wooden boards, and pulled up short as Tira stepped in her path.

"Tira," she gasped, fighting the panicked lump in her throat. "Move."

"I can't do that, Officer." The woman shook her head with an apologetic yet stern expression. Kitieri glanced over her shoulder; no one was coming after her. Bat had stood from her chair, but both she and Eriat waited by the bedside, watching.

"Tira, please," Kitieri whispered. "You must see how ridiculous this is. I'm just one person. I'm not a god, or… or…"

"No, you're not a god," Tira replied. "You're something far more special. You're a young woman who stood up for equality and fairness, even when her lightning could do her no good. I saw the oran bands this morning. I saw what you wore. I saw the way those other officers watched you like a criminal. Despite what you were going through, you gave me that Gadget because you thought I needed it. You put my needs above your own, and you were willing to bear the consequences for it."

Kitieri shook her head, chest heaving with shallow breaths as her mind raced. "I can't…"

Tira rested a gentle hand on her arm, barely touching her to avoid the burns.

"It's not a hero we need," she said. "It's not really even a lightning element we need. It's a woman who cares enough for the people around her that she's willing to put her life on the line for them. *That's* what we need."

The painful lump in Kitieri's throat won out, and her shoulders jumped with a quiet sob.

"I know it's a lot," Tira whispered, moving in closer. "But you have given thousands of people something that they thought they'd lost forever."

Kitieri forced her body to take a deep breath, and met Tira's blue-green gaze.

"You gave us hope."

Kitieri clenched her jaw. Soft footsteps approached behind her, and she turned to face Bat and Eriat.

"Tira's right," Bat said. "It's your heart we need. The lightning just helps."

When Kitieri did not return her grin, Bat sighed.

"I understand what you're saying, Kitieri," she said. "You're right to fear Stil. It's exactly that kind of tyranny that kept me up at night worrying, but there's a big detail you're missing here."

Kitieri sighed through her nose. "What's that?"

"In signing this book," Bat said, "these people have *already* made themselves illegal. Right now, every name in here is Churchless. If Stil finds us now, they're all dead. But there is one name that can fix that."

Kitieri folded her arms. "You're trying to tell me that if I sign that book, they'll somehow all be safe?"

"That's exactly what I'm telling you."

Bat opened the book's front cover, revealing one column of names next to a printed series of titles. Kitieri noticed the name Batessa beside *Chief Advisor*, and Eriat's name under *Advisor*, and her eyes scanned upward to the two empty lines on top.

Head: _____

Baliant: _____

"So which is it?" she asked, still staring at the page.

"Both."

Kitieri lifted her eyes from the page, holding Bat's gaze for a tense moment.

"You're making a mistake," she said, lifting her bandaged arm. "I can't even use my lightning anymore. I have no business signing this page."

"You don't need your lightning to save lives right now," Bat said. "Just your name."

"But these people…" Kitieri glanced down at the book, trying to keep her throat from closing up. "They put their lives on the line because they thought I could do something extraordinary… and I can't."

"You will heal," Bat said. "Your lightning will return in time, but Kitieri, listen to me. You've already done the extraordinary. Like Tira said, you've given hope to thousands. Enough for people to stand against the tyranny of their Churches, to stand against the death sentences handed down by the Boards."

Kitieri met Bat's dark eyes. "And what happens when the lightning takes over?" she asked. "You can't keep them all in a warehouse until the food runs out."

A sly grin crossed Bat's face. "There *is* a plan in place," she said. "But I need to know that you're with us first."

Kitieri raised an eyebrow. "What, are you worried I'll run and tell Stil?"

"Amadora, more likely."

Kitieri scowled. "Fuck her."

"You say that, but anything you tell Catarva will get back to her."

"I'm not so sure." Kitieri shook her head. "Catarva knows her Board is corrupt."

Bat squinted one eye. "Then why isn't she doing anything

about it?"

"She can't. Amadora's got such a hold on the Board that they're afraid to—wait." Kitieri's eyes grew wide as a new thought exploded into her mind.

"What?" Bat asked.

"If I sign this book, I'm a Baliant? A real Baliant?"

"That's right," Bat replied. "Tira's got your crest all ready."

With a wide smile, Tira plunged her hand into her skirt pocket and produced a small package wrapped in soft cloth. Pulling back the corners, she revealed a shining golden ring encircling an open hand. The exact same piece adorned Catarva's white robes.

"My son helped make it," Tira said with pride. "Thanks to the Church of Shirasette, he's out of those mines and studying with one of the best metal elements in the city, and they made this together for you."

Kitieri smiled, touched. "It's exquisite work."

Tira beamed, cupping the brooch in both hands, and Kitieri turned back to Bat with a deep breath.

"This plan you speak of," she said. "Who benefits, exactly?"

"The Church of Shirasette, of course," Bat replied.

"And *only* this Church?"

Bat tossed an uneasy glance back at Eriat. "You have to understand the magnitude of what we're dealing with here, Kitieri," she said. "We will only be able to acquire so much cintra, and these machines Eriat is designing... well, we just can't save everyone."

"What about the war?" Kitieri asked, tilting her head with a frown. "What are you planning to do about that?"

Bat and Eriat exchanged another look.

"There's nothing we can do," Bat said softly, "as much as I wish we could stop it. If we had the power to manipulate the Boards' decisions, things never would have gone this far in the first place."

Kitieri saw Haldin's face in her mind before her thoughts flashed through the thousands of innocents that would be killed in such meaningless slaughter.

"What if," she said to the floor, "we *could* manipulate the Boards?"

Where she'd expected a bark of laughter, Kitieri looked up to find a stony, solemn expression on Bat's face.

"What are you suggesting?" the woman asked.

"I can get to them," Kitieri said, heart beating faster in her chest. "Catarva may be trapped now, but if I go back—"

"No, Kitieri." Bat shook her head. "They won't take another chance with you. Amadora will have you killed this time."

"She can't touch a Baliant," Kitieri said.

"Baliant or not, she'll go for your throat, and your element is out of commission."

"*She* doesn't know that."

"Stil knows it, so she will soon enough."

"Not if I move first."

Bat snorted, folding her arms across her chest.

"I don't like this," she said at length. "It's too risky, and for *what*? To save the same people who would see you imprisoned?"

Kitieri took a step forward. "I will not condemn an entire society to death and destruction because of the actions of their leaders. For what, you ask? For the same reasons you started the Church of Shirasette— to help those who cannot help themselves. A war between the two Churches will take thousands of innocent lives. If we had a chance to spare them and did nothing, how is the Church of Shirasette any better than the Church of Histan or Enahris? How would you sleep at night, knowing that you benefited from the same war they created?"

Bat's eyes snapped with an inner fire. "There's not enough cintra—"

"So we'll *make* it work!" Kitieri's voice rang off the walls, and Tira jumped. "Look." Kitieri lowered her voice, moving forward to stand directly in front of Bat. "If you want me as Baliant, then we save *everyone* we can. I will not wittingly leave anyone behind for the benefit of others."

Bat's lips were pressed into a thin, straight line as she met Kitieri's glare. The tension mounted between them as they tested each other's willpower, eyes locked on one another, until Bat stepped back abruptly.

"All right, then," she said with a curt nod. "I will follow you, Baliant."

She opened the book once more, and Kitieri took the offered pen without hesitation this time.

If people were going to die either way, she was going to do something about it.

CHAPTER 17

Kitieri pulled her hood forward, keeping her face in shadow as the breeze tugged on the thick fabric. Ashes' hooves clacked rhythmically on the stones in long strides, and Kitieri gritted her teeth as the choppy gait bounced her around the saddle. She was sure Haldin would have a few words for her poor riding form if he could see her.

As the shadows ahead grew longer and darker, Kitieri glanced over her shoulder to where the setting sun just brushed the horizon.

I can't be late.

She nudged Ashes into a gentle lope, squeezing with her knees to keep from holding on with her hands. The thin leather gloves she'd pulled over her bandages did nothing to ward off the pain, serving only to hide her broken element. Even wearing the borrowed Gadget was a risky show of ineptitude, but... she needed it right now.

Kitieri twisted her mouth into a tight frown. Even with protection, the next Strike would not be kind.

The golden-pink glow of sunset washed over the city as the buildings around her grew taller, sturdier, and more artfully crafted, and Kitieri pulled up on the reins as the Church of Enahris peeked over its surrounding buildings. Bat was somewhere behind her, she knew, getting ready to take up position outside the Square in case she didn't show by midnight, but that did little to quell her nerves. Maybe she *was* crazy for coming back.

Kitieri closed her eyes, blocking out the images of the black cell.

Not this time. This time, she stood above the Board. This time, it was all or nothing. Success or death. Her gloved fingertips grazed the brooch beneath her cloak, tracing its rigid outline, and she lifted her gaze once more.

She was a Baliant now.

She swallowed, suppressing the anxiety that rose in her throat at that one simple thought. The staggering responsibility of so many lives pressed down on her with a crushing weight, but Kitieri kept her eyes on the Church. She'd have to take this one step at a time, and right now her responsibility was here.

The air cooled as the sunlight faded and Kitieri spurred Ashes forward, guiding the mare around to the south gate. Through the border trees, she spotted a waiting gray uniform and released a silent sigh of relief. Haldin had managed to evade Amadora's wrath, after all.

She dropped to the ground with a grunt, and the gray uniform shifted.

"Who's there?"

Kitieri froze. It was not Haldin's voice, but she recognized the gruff timbre. She quickly shrugged the Gadget from her shoulders, ditching it behind the nearest tree. Jorid was the *last* person she wanted to know about her failure. She watched him approach, rooted to the spot.

Shit. Why him? Of all people, why did *he* have to be on sentry duty at this gate?

Jorid's bushy eyebrows came together as he peered into the shadow of her hood, and furious disgust registered on his face.

"*You*," he spat, lifting his spear.

"Where is Commander Haldin?" Kitieri demanded, forcing her voice as low as possible.

"You've got some nerve, showing your face back here," Jorid growled. "I should—"

"Where is Haldin?" Kitieri spoke over him.

"Nowhere *you're* going to find him," Jorid snapped. "Why he risked his life for a murderous bitch like you is beyond me, but I hope you're happy."

Kitieri's blood turned to ice, though she fought to keep her expression neutral. "Where is he?"

"You thought she wouldn't find out?" Jorid snarled. "Haldin knew the Chief Advisor's reach, and *still* he freed you. Now he's in the hole that should have been your grave." He stepped forward, lifting one hand from his spear to summon a burst of flames. "A hole to which I will gladly see you returned."

Before Jorid could make another move, Kitieri put out a gloved hand. "Who do you think is faster?" she hissed.

Fear danced in the man's eyes as he fixated on her palm. "Gonna kill me?" he spat.

Kitieri smirked. "Isn't that what murderous bitches do?"

Jorid's scowl deepened, and the spear shook in his hand. Kitieri watched the struggle play out across his features, as he debated whether or not he was willing to sacrifice his life for a shot at ending hers. His breathing was labored, and his shoulders tensed and hunched under the weight of such a decision.

Kitieri lifted her chin. "Jorid, I know you hate me," she said, "but I promise you, we want the same things. We are not enemies."

The man narrowed his eyes. "How dare you put us on the same level?"

"You clearly hold the Commander in high regard. You want to see him freed, right?"

Jorid's cheek twitched, but the dangerous glint was slowly bleeding out from his expression.

"Well, he *doesn't* deserve to take your place rotting in a cell, if that's what you're asking," he said.

"I agree." Kitieri nodded. "We can change that, but we're going to need each other."

Jorid scoffed and spat on the ground between them. "I *need* you?"

"No," Kitieri said. "Haldin needs you. And if my plan works, you'll be the officer that made it happen."

Jorid glared daggers at her, but Kitieri could see the wheels grinding. "What plan?" he growled.

"It's a lot to explain, and we don't have much time," she said. "But I will promise you one thing."

Jorid grunted, but the slight lift of his spear invited her to continue.

"If it doesn't work, I will go willingly back to that cell."

"Right." Jorid barked a laugh. "I'm supposed to believe that."

"You have my word."

Jorid curled his lip. "Is the word of a murderer supposed to mean something to me?"

Kitieri bit back the snarky retort that sprang to her lips, clenching her jaw. He was still fighting, but she almost had him. She needed his cooperation, no matter how begrudging.

"You know I'm deadly," she said quietly. Jorid's nostrils flared in reluctant acknowledgement. "Now imagine that on *your* side."

A guttural sound emanated from Jorid's throat, the death throes of his resistance. Kitieri waited, watching the dying flames in his hand flicker in the twilight until he snapped his fist closed.

"Trying to play some kind of hero, then?" he muttered.

Kitieri scrutinized his face in the dying light, weighing her next words carefully. It was a gamble, but if it paid off…

"I want Amadora gone," she said.

His dark eyes studied her, darting back and forth. Suspicious, Kitieri noted, but no longer hostile.

"And my promise still stands," she added. "I will see Haldin freed, or take his place."

Slowly, Jorid lowered the butt of his spear to the ground beside him. "I *will* hold you to that," he said, "lightning be damned."

Kitieri grinned. "Understood."

UNDER THE BLACK, moonless sky, Kitieri and Jorid returned Ashes to the care of the stable hands and made their way up the endless stairs toward the Baliant's chambers. As they walked in tense silence, Kitieri's thoughts raced.

She'd gotten through the doors, but the real challenge was yet to come, and now Haldin's life was on the line with the rest of them. If Catarva didn't go for this…

She clenched her jaw. Enahris' Baliant was not an enemy Kitieri would choose to make, but she *had* to run that risk. For Haldin. For Inra. For Noia and Vina. For Taff and Jera.

They passed the floor of officers' suites, and Kitieri's heart twisted. She paused on the landing, staring down the hall toward the place she'd so briefly called home. She ached to run for that door, ripping it open to see her brother and sister. To hold them again. To see that they were unharmed and safe. To tell them she loved them again.

A gruff sound behind her made her jump, and she looked over her shoulder at Jorid, already two steps up the next flight. With a pain that seemed almost physical, clawing at her heart and soul, Kitieri turned her back on the hallway to follow him.

Just a little longer. I'll be there soon.

Jorid eyed her suspiciously as they continued their climb, and Kitieri pointedly ignored his gaze.

"Do you really think you can help him?"

The soft words caught Kitieri off guard, and she looked up at him. In place of the hard, angry scowl that usually graced the man's face, Kitieri saw only raw, earnest pain.

"I'll get him out, or I'll die trying," she replied.

Jorid slowed his steps, appraising her more carefully, and Kitieri stopped and turned to face him in the silence. Was he backing out? *Shit, I won't be able to get past Catarva's chamber sentries without him…*

"You mean that, don't you?" His quiet voice once again came in stark contrast to his hard features.

Kitieri nodded hesitantly, waiting for the other shoe to drop. "I do."

Jorid resumed the climb with a loud sigh. "Then I'm with you."

"With me?" Kitieri eyed him carefully, keeping her two-step distance behind him.

"I want to help," Jorid told her. "I know you don't have much reason to trust me, and frankly, I don't know if I could ever fully trust a lightning, but…" He cleared his throat. "So much of this is on me, and I feel like I need to make it right."

Kitieri waited for him to continue, not daring to break his trajectory.

"I never got what Haldin saw in you," he went on. "I couldn't understand why he was protecting you so hard, and even risking his life to train you. Everyone knows lightnings can't really be trained."

Kitieri let out a snort, and Jorid tossed her a quick glance.

"Anyways." He cleared his throat. "I thought he'd be better off if you just went away. That's why I turned you over to the Board, but he didn't let you go. He went even harder to protect you, and now he's down there because of it." He took in a deep breath. "And I did that to him. As much as I wanted to blame you for all this... I know that I have a responsibility to set things right."

Kitieri blinked, shocked by the man's honesty, and found herself at a loss for words.

"I owe the Commander for everything I am," Jorid said. "My loyalty is to him and him alone. Any Board that condemns that man is no Board of mine, nor of my fellow officers."

A new edge laced his tone in his last words, and Kitieri's head swiveled around to stare at him.

"Are you saying... that the officers would go against the Board's commands?" she whispered.

Jorid nodded. "Before she locked him up, Haldin told us all what the Chief Advisor said at your trial about the coming war. How Amadora would send us all to our deaths for nothing. He wanted us to be prepared."

"For what?"

"The revolution."

Kitieri's eyes widened, but before she could speak, two gray officers appeared over the top of the steps.

"Jorid," one greeted them in surprise, and the familiar voice stopped Kitieri in her tracks.

"Corte," Jorid replied with a nod. Kitieri looked down, allowing the cloak's hood to obscure her face entirely.

"Who's your, ah, friend?" Corte asked. From under her hood, Kitieri watched Corte's shadow bend forward in the lamplight, trying to catch a glimpse of her face. Jorid waited expectantly, and she released a quiet sigh as she lifted her head to meet Corte's gaze. She was running into *all* her best friends tonight.

Corte squinted, tilting his head to peer through the hood's shadow until recognition struck.

"You found her?" He whipped back around to Jorid. "Where did you pick her up?"

"She came back on her own," Jorid said. "She needs to talk to the Baliant."

Corte's eyes danced to Kitieri before he took a step toward Jorid, lowering his voice. "You're *helping* her? Are you serious with this shit?"

Kitieri cut her eyes to the side, watching Jorid square his shoulders in her peripheral vision.

"Yeah," he replied, a hard edge lacing his tone. "I'm serious with this shit. Get the Baliant, will you?"

Corte emitted a hateful hiss. "In case you forgot, Jorid, this is the bitch that—"

"I know who she is," Jorid snapped. "And, in case *you* forgot, our Commander is set to rot in prison unless we do something. This is me doing something. Now will you call the damned Baliant already?"

Even as Jorid's last word rang in the air, the double doors sprang to life with a loud creak and all of them turned to focus on the short, stout figure silhouetted by the inner chamber's light.

"Ms. Kitieri," Minna said with a soft smile in her voice. "The Baliant awaits your presence."

As Minna turned back into the chambers, Kitieri tossed a quizzical glance at Jorid, who shrugged. Corte motioned with his spear for her to stay back, peeking into the room.

"Let them in," came Catarva's smooth voice from within.

Corte pulled back, glaring at Kitieri as she and Jorid stepped through the doorway, and the heavy doors latched behind them.

As soon as Kitieri pulled her hood back, the vibrant white robes against the far right wall caught her eye. Minna stood beside the statuesque figure at the massive round window as the Baliant stared out at the Church grounds below.

"Impeccable timing, Ms. Kitieri," Catarva said, facing the glass. Her gaze seemed fixated on a specific point on the ground, and Kitieri frowned at the back of her head.

"You knew I was coming."

Catarva slowly turned her face from the window, tearing her eyes from their point of focus. Kitieri suppressed a shudder as they came to land on her, amber irises glowing yellow against Catarva's dark skin in the lamplight. Words failed her as she stared into their illuminated depths, captivated.

"I expect you've some pressing news to share," Catarva said, ignoring the earlier statement. Kitieri paused, sifting through the possibilities before realizing what she must mean.

"Inra couldn't be saved," she said. "I'm sorry."

"Unfortunate, to say the least," Catarva replied, her gaze unwavering. "Inra was a strong and loyal officer. However"—the word sent chills down Kitieri's spine as the Baliant faced her head on — "that is not what I meant."

She moved forward, flowing white robes giving the impression of a gliding specter, and Kitieri stumbled back a step. Though she'd never felt exactly comfortable around the woman, this Catarva scared her. A quiet enigma, surrounded by a coursing energy so strong that it raised the hairs on Kitieri's arms.

Under Catarva's impervious calm, something dark and angry thrashed, and Kitieri read it in her hard amber eyes as she drew closer. *She knows.*

As the Baliant reached for her, Kitieri planted her feet and lifted her chin. She would not run. If she was going to call herself an equal to this woman, she'd have to earn it — right here. Right now.

Long fingers brushed her throat as Kitieri matched the woman's glare, and her lightning stirred defensively at the touch. It rushed through her in answer to a silent call, ready to protect her from harm even as it burned her raw, mangled hands under the bandages, and Kitieri bit back the whimper in her throat.

She'd die before she showed this woman weakness.

The ghost of a smirk crossed Catarva's lips as she lowered her hand from Kitieri's throat to slide it under the flap of her cloak, revealing the brooch. Kitieri glanced to the identical pin on Catarva's breast as the woman's fingers traced the metal against her pounding heart.

The moment she'd dreaded. Would Catarva see it as a betrayal?

"Is it?" Catarva's soft voice startled her, so close that Kitieri felt her breath on her cheek.

"Is it what?"

"A betrayal." Catarva's lips were at her ear now, and chills ran up Kitieri's spine. She turned her head closer to Catarva's, their cheeks almost touching.

"You tell me," she whispered.

Catarva lingered in her proximity a moment longer before pulling back.

"I apologize for my misstep earlier," she said, her velvety voice back at full volume for the rest of the room to hear. "Impeccable timing, *Baliant* Kitieri."

She whipped around, walking back to the window to resume her fixation, and Kitieri silently released the breath she'd been holding. The burn of her lightning dissipated with Catarva's retreat, and she stood cold and breathless while Jorid and Minna gaped at her.

She followed Catarva to the window, and Minna scampered from her place to give them room.

Stepping up to the glass, Kitieri followed Catarva's line of sight down to an empty stone walkway leading out from the Church, lit with a single lamp at the garden's edge. Anticipation quivered in the air around her.

"You've come to strike an alliance, then," Catarva said.

"Possibly."

"The Churches don't exactly believe in alliances, you know."

"Mine does."

"Because you need me."

"You need me, too."

Catarva raised an eyebrow. "You are playing with a fire you don't understand, Kitieri," she said.

"Maybe so, but nothing was getting done your way."

Catarva's nostrils flared. "I'd beg to differ," she said, "but it doesn't matter. We're here now, and we can only move forward."

Kitieri regarded her for a moment, taking in her calm composure belied only by the small, darting movements of her eyes as she watched the walkway below.

"You're not going to ask about—"

"The Church of Shirasette?" Catarva finished for her. "I've known about them for quite a while. It was only a matter of time before they exploited that loophole."

"Then you're not angry about another Church?"

To Kitieri's surprise, Catarva's shoulders jumped with a small laugh.

"How can I be angry at people trying to survive?" she asked. "The Church of Shirasette arose out of necessity. They do for their people what I cannot do for mine, and what Tiernan has *never* done for his. I understand their existence, and why they chose you. But…" Catarva took a deep breath, lowering her chin. "There is more at work here than exploitable laws and petty politics."

"So tell me."

The muscle in Catarva's jaw tensed. "Everything we know, everything we are, is a balancing act," she said.

Kitieri looked away, fighting the urge to roll her eyes to the ceiling. More *stupid* riddles.

"It's not a riddle," Catarva said, and Kitieri's head snapped around. "What?"

"You're tired of the riddles, but that's not what it is. There are two gods and two Churches for a reason. That is the foundation upon which this world was built, and a disruption of that balance will have dire consequences. We are already seeing it."

"All right," Kitieri snapped, "*how* are you reading my mind?"

Catarva smirked. "You give much away without words. But... I will admit it's one of the many gifts I inherited from my dear mother."

The venom in the last two words took Kitieri by surprise.

"Still, if you prefer to say it aloud," Catarva went on, "tell me, then, Kitieri. What do you hope to gain from an alliance between our Churches?"

Kitieri glanced back at Jorid, remembering the words she'd spoken at the gate. Would Catarva be as receptive?

"Your Board is corrupt," she said quietly. "I know you can see it. Amadora is working with Stil, and thousands will die if we don't do something. You can't tell me you accept what they're doing—what they've done to Haldin. Catarva, that man would give his *life* for you. It's written all over his face every time I see you together. You can't seriously tell me you're just going to leave him dow—"

"I'm not leaving him *anywhere*," Catarva hissed with a sudden rush of anger, eyes flashing yellow again. Kitieri fell back a step, shocked by the uncharacteristic outburst.

Of course.

She'd been blind to miss it. Their closeness. Their little exchanges. Their shared glances.

"Wait," she breathed. "You... you love him, don't you?"

Catarva glared at the window, working her jaw back and forth. "My personal feelings have never and *will* never matter. But I will do what is right, and Haldin is a loyal and indispensable Commander. He was wrongly imprisoned, and I will see that wrong righted."

Kitieri nodded slowly, still processing the new information. For reasons she could not comprehend, a sinking weight pulled on her heart.

"So, what are you going to do?" she asked, pushing the unexpected emotion aside. "Call another Board meeting to reverse the sentence?"

"Something like that."

Kitieri watched her, scrutinizing her every movement. Nothing with the Board was that easy, and they both knew it.

"Impeccable timing, Ms. Kitieri…" She looked back to the window, chewing the inside of her cheek as understanding dawned.

"You're banking on Amadora making the trade. Haldin for me."

Catarva did not answer, returning to her stoic nature.

"I can't blame you." Kitieri shrugged. "It's only fair. But—"

"Kitieri."

"—I think I can do you one better."

Catarva paused, and Kitieri turned to face her.

"Trading me for Haldin will only treat a symptom of a deeper evil," she said. "Sure, you'll have your Commander back, but Amadora will still run this place into the ground, and she will destroy you the first chance she gets. She'll feed the Church of Enahris to Stil on a silver platter, and you will lose *everything*. You won't have to worry about Haldin's imprisonment, because he'll be dead."

"Kitieri," Catarva said again, louder this time.

"If you really want Haldin back, you need Amadora *gone*. And I can help with that."

Catarva raised an eyebrow, her posture shifting toward Kitieri. "Is that so?"

Kitieri swallowed, taking a deep breath. If Catarva didn't go for this, she'd have to answer for that promise she'd made to Jorid. In the back of her mind, she imagined Bat's fit upon hearing *that* news.

"Amadora's power rests with the Board, right?" she asked. "She bullies them into submission and gains a unanimous vote to override your input. I know my trial can't be the only time she's done that."

Catarva regarded her a moment before releasing a soft sigh.

"No, it wasn't," she admitted. "She's fought me since the day I took her seat as Baliant at fifteen, and she was demoted to Chief Advisor."

Kitieri jerked her head back as the statement hit her like a battering ram.

"I'm sorry, what?" she demanded. "Amadora was Baliant before you? How in the hells did you unseat her? And at *fifteen*?"

"It's a long story," Catarva muttered, "but she'd do anything to remove me if she could."

Kitieri shook her head, forcing an expedited recovery. At least it halfway explained the old woman's hells-ridden determination to bring her own Church crashing to the ground. What mattered more was that Catarva saw it, too.

"Right," she said. "So you *know* Amadora is a cancer that will destroy this Church."

"I do," Catarva replied. "But some things must be allowed to run their course."

Anger flushed Kitieri's cheeks. "Like Haldin or myself rotting in a cell until you deem it time to do something?"

Catarva's eyes flashed, but she did not look away from the window. "You wouldn't understand."

Kitieri stepped forward, incensed, coming so close to that Baliant that she brushed the long white sleeve of her robes.

"Yeah, no one could ever understand, huh?" she snarled. "Gods forbid you fucking share anything with anyone, because no one could ever be as smart as *you*."

Catarva rounded on her, taller than a giant and eyes bright as the sun. "You want to know what I know?" she hissed, lowering her face to Kitieri's. "You want to carry my weight? You think you *can*?"

Catarva's anger chilled Kitieri, and her stomach dropped to the floor even as she met the Baliant's glare. She would not back off. She *couldn't* back off. Her own Church depended on her just as much as this one did.

"Try me," she spat back, lifting onto her toes. Catarva's eyes burned golden, so close to Kitieri's that she could almost feel their fire.

"You're not ready." With those words, the Baliant whipped away, and Kitieri was left shaking in her own fury.

"Fine," she ground out through seething breaths. "Whether or not you want to trust me, you still need me. You told me so the day Haldin put the oran bands on me. You were willing to cross Amadora to bring me on and train me for a reason. Unsurprisingly, you won't tell me what that reason is, but you're not going to get it if I'm locked in a cell.

So I get that you're ready to trade me for Haldin, but there *might* be a way to get both of us."

Catarva pursed her lips. "Go on."

Kitieri studied her for a moment, assessing her body language. Catarva probably already knew what she was about to say, but she needed to say it anyway.

"Amadora is a bully," Kitieri said. "And bullies are nothing without their back-up. Turn the Board against her, and she loses her power."

Catarva snorted. "The Board. They're as bad as she is."

"I don't think so," Kitieri replied. "I know I only got a glimpse of them, but a few seemed like they could be swayed if the power dynamic shifted—like Rulka."

Catarva shook her head. "Rulka and the rest of them are complacent. They know they will benefit from a system that sacrifices the poor to allow them to continue living when the lightning grows too strong. Convincing them to relinquish that privilege just to overturn Amadora, the one who planned the entire thing, will not be an easy task."

"It's easy to be complacent when no one *knows*," Kitieri said. "But that's not the case anymore. Thousands of people know now, and there is strength in numbers. The stronger the Church of Shirasette grows, the less power the Boards have. The poor are standing up for themselves, and their entire system of tyranny will crumble. We can use that."

Catarva lifted her chin. "What are you suggesting?"

"Call the Board meeting," Kitieri said. "Let them see me. She can't touch a Baliant."

A smirk crossed Catarva's face, and Kitieri's heart skipped a beat. A good smirk?

"Not yet," Catarva said to the glass.

Kitieri frowned. "Why not?" she asked. "What are you waiting for?" When Catarva did not answer, Kitieri released an exasperated sigh. "Every minute we waste is an eternity for Haldin in that hole, so can you be straightforward with me for *once*?"

Catarva's eyes narrowed to slits as she focused on the walkway far below.

"All right, Kitieri," she said. "I'm willing to accept your offer of an alliance. I believe we can help each other, but we need to make another deal first."

Apprehension rose in Kitieri's throat. "I'm listening."

"I know there is much I have yet to tell you," Catarva said, "and I will. I promise I will answer all of your questions when the time is right, but until that time, I need you to trust me. Can you do that?"

She looked sideways at Kitieri, eyes glowing in the shadow against the dark window, and Kitieri looked away from their smoldering burn. Everything about the woman's secrets and cold demeanor raised the hair on the back of her neck, but she didn't have much choice in the matter. She nodded silently, and Catarva dipped her head in acknowledgment, glancing back to the window.

"Ah," she breathed. "There she is."

Kitieri followed her gaze down to the walkway, where a figure in a hooded, deep magenta cloak was crossing through the lamp's light. Catarva pulled away from the glass with a smug grin.

"*Now* we call the Board."

CHAPTER 18

Kitieri glanced back at the lamp, where the magenta cloak had disappeared into the darkness beyond the Church garden, as Catarva swept across the room to the oblong table.

"Who was that?" she asked.

"Minna." Catarva ignored her, beckoning to the woman as she gathered slips of paper off the table. "Please deliver these to the Board right away. Let them know it's urgent, and if you can, let them see Amadora's summons on top."

Kitieri watched her go before looking back to Catarva.

"It was Amadora," she breathed. "You waited for her to leave to call the meeting."

"Yes. For years, I've watched her sneak out after dark to run to him. After today's events, there was no doubt she would leave tonight." Catarva sniffed. "They've much to fret over."

Kitieri grinned. A Board without its bully would make for an interesting night.

"In the meantime," Catarva said, "you and I have an errand to run."

She strode for the door, and Jorid sprang forward to pull it open. Kitieri jogged a few paces to catch up before forcing herself into a more dignified walk, extending her strides past their comfortable length to close the distance. Catarva stepped out into the hall with a nod at the officers on guard.

"Officers Jorid and Corte, will you accompany Baliant Kitieri and myself to the dungeons?"

Kitieri bit back her laugh as Corte's eyes almost popped out of his skull. His mouth moved wordlessly for a moment before Catarva's gentle voice cut off any response.

"Now, please. Time is of the essence."

Jorid led the way down the stairs, beginning their long journey from the top to the bottom of the Church, and Corte fell in line behind Kitieri, leaving the one remaining officer standing dumbfounded at the doors to the Baliant's chambers.

As they descended, Kitieri felt Corte's eyes boring into the back of her head. The energy rolling off him hit her in pulsing waves, and she fought the urge to look behind her.

His whisper over her shoulder surprised her, and she jerked her head to the side. "Taking your rightful place in that cell, after all?"

Kitieri gritted her teeth, imagining a backhanded fist to his face, as Catarva spoke. "You will see your Commander freed, Corte."

Corte's hovering presence vanished as he fell back in embarrassed silence.

Kitieri's pulse quickened as they passed the last window before the stairs took them below ground. She vividly remembered the scuffle with Deep Voice and High Voice at this very spot, and the feel of Haldin's warm, calloused hand clamped around her mouth.

Haldin.

As she watched Catarva's flowing robes ripple behind her, dragging down each stair in a regal train, the twinge in Kitieri's heart returned. What had she expected? That Haldin would ever care for *her*? His trainee? The reason for his imprisonment?

She shook her head, casting off the unwelcome thoughts.

An eternity and a half later, Kitieri's boots hit the stone of the Church's lowest floor and the cold, damp air chilled her even through the cloak. The metal door at the end of the dim hallway loomed, stark and cruel in the flickering light, and Kitieri swallowed the emotions welling up within her.

A lone officer stood at the door, leaning on his spear, and his head snapped up at the sound of their approach. He squared his slumped shoulders instantly, bowing to the Baliant.

"Officer Shanid," Catarva greeted the light-haired man. "Open the door, please."

Shanid blinked, glancing between every member of the party. Kitieri knew his orders. Amadora had probably banned Catarva from seeing Haldin, just as Haldin had been banned from seeing her. But Amadora wasn't here, and if what Jorid had told her was true...

"Do it," Jorid said, probably as quietly as his gruff voice could go.

"I assure you, Officer, you will face no consequences for breach of orders," Catarva said.

With a quick nod, Shanid reached for his keys and turned for the door. The poor man had probably spent his entire shift contemplating the release of his Commander *without* permission, Kitieri thought.

The metal door screeched on its hinges, opening to a pitch-black cell. Had Amadora even bothered to have the lamp oil replaced? Kitieri looked down at her shaking hands, clenching them into fists to still their tremors.

"Haldin?" Catarva stepped past Jorid and Shanid, white robes framed by the blackness. Only silence answered her, and Kitieri closed her eyes.

Please, let him be all right. Let him be —

"Catarva?"

The soft voice crept from the shadows, and Catarva rushed forward into the cell. Two arms wrapped around her waist, interrupting the stark white of her garment, and Kitieri looked away. She caught Jorid's eye as he did the same, and they exchanged a grin.

"Well," he said, "you made good on your promise, *Baliant*."

Kitieri's grin widened, and she looked back as Haldin emerged from the cell, blinking furiously. He squinted, straining to adjust to the torchlight before his face broke into a wide smile.

"Kitieri," he said. Her heart jumped at the sound of her name, and she hoped to the gods the dim light would hide her blush. "You *did* come back."

"Did you really think I wouldn't?"

Haldin jerked a thumb over his shoulder toward the darkness behind him. "Like I said, I wouldn't have blamed you for running away and staying away. Is Inra with you?"

Kitieri's smile fell, and she bit down on the inside of her lip.

"I'm sorry," she whispered. "I couldn't save her. Stil killed her anyways."

"Damn it," Haldin cursed under his breath. "Then..." He looked between Catarva and Kitieri. "What's the occasion? Did someone push Amadora down the stairs, or is this a rogue jailbreak?"

"A bit of both," Catarva replied, to shocked silence from the group. The laugh that followed was one of the most human sounds Kitieri had ever heard from the woman, and she joined in with the echoing laughter from the others.

"There's much to explain," Catarva continued, moving for the stairway, "but we'll have to do it on the way. The Board is being called to assemble as we speak."

KITIERI BREATHED a sigh of relief as they reached the final flight of stairs—the endless climbing and descending was getting tiresome. Catarva and Haldin walked so closely together in front of her that their hands brushed repeatedly, exchanging hushed tones, and Kitieri chose to watch her feet instead.

"Baliant Catarva," Minna called from the door, "the messages have been delivered, and the Board is preparing to meet. A few of them were right behind me."

Catarva nodded her thanks before breezing through the open chamber doors, Haldin on her heels. Kitieri hurried after them at Minna's beckoning request, leaving the officers out in the hall as the door closed behind her.

"We will have one chance at this tonight," Catarva said quietly, turning to both her and Haldin. "They will expect Amadora's presence, and I predict most of them will flounder without it. Ghentrin will be the key. He's her second, and a big part of Amadora's influence over the Board, but he has one major weakness. He's—"

A loud knock made Kitieri jump, and Catarva's head snapped up.

"Follow my lead," she whispered.

Minna opened the door to three black robes; Kitieri recognized Darrow, Rulka, and the blond man whose name she didn't know. Darrow's slitted eyes burned into Kitieri before he turned to Catarva.

"There had better be a *very* good reason you went against the Board's sentence," he drawled in his slow, honey-like tone. "*Two* Board sentences, technically."

"Indeed." Catarva's voice cut like ice as she gestured for Darrow to take his seat. Rulka's eyes burned with the same curiosity as the day of Kitieri's trial as she moved to her own seat.

"You returned," she mused quietly, almost to herself.

Kitieri did not answer, but consciously softened her expression as she watched the woman sit, and Rulka surprised her with the ghost of a smile.

"You'd better have a damned good reason for this summons, Catarva!"

Ghentrin's loud, boisterous voice could be heard all the way down the hallway, and he burst through the door with his fists clenched into balls of rage. Red-faced and winded from the climb, the man stopped dead in his tracks.

"What in the two hells is this?" he thundered, chest heaving.

"An emergency meeting, as my summons indicated," Catarva replied coolly.

Ghentrin's chest heaved even harder, and he shook a meaty finger at her. "You don't have the authority to do this."

"The Baliant may call on their Board at any time, Advisor," Catarva said. "It's quite plainly written in our laws."

"I mean *this!*" Ghentrin swept his hand through the air, gesturing at Kitieri and Haldin standing to either side of her. "Criminals should rot in prison!"

"I agree," Catarva said. "*Criminals* should be imprisoned. Please take your seat, Advisor."

Ghentrin's eye twitched as he puzzled through Catarva's statement, and Kitieri tried not to grin. For all his blustering, he wasn't the brightest lamp in the Sanctuary.

Instead of moving to his chair, though, Ghentrin started to back toward the door.

"I won't have your trickery, Catarva," he grumbled. "You want to undermine the Board, and I won't have it!"

"Refusal to honor your summons is an offense punishable by your suspension from the Board," Catarva said.

Ghentrin paused, face growing redder, as the last Advisor

appeared behind him. "Well," he sputtered, "we can't have a meeting without the Chief Advisor."

"Amadora received the same summons as you," Catarva assured him. "She will be here, I'm sure. Unless, of course, you know something I do not."

Ghentrin's cheeks flushed a lovely shade of purple, and Kitieri was sure he would burst if he blew himself up anymore.

"Have a seat, Advisor." Catarva nodded to his chair, and Ghentrin's lip twisted into a hateful snarl.

"I'll meet," he said reluctantly, "but I will not sit. Not at *your* table."

Kitieri rolled her eyes inwardly. This man was desperate for any semblance of power.

"Wonderful." Catarva smiled at him, clasping her hands before her. "While we wait for the Chief Advisor, I wanted to thank you all for convening on such short notice. I do apologize for pulling you from your evenings, but recent events demand an explanation."

"You're damned right, they do," Ghentrin huffed. "I want to know why this criminal isn't back in her cell, where she belongs!"

He pointed violently at Kitieri, and a surge of anger rushed through her. Her lightning rippled in response, biting at her burns, but she pushed the pain away as her heart pounded.

Sorry, Catarva, it's my lead now.

"Because you do not have the right to imprison me," she said, loud and strong, and all eyes in the room snapped to her.

"The hells, we don't," Ghentrin sneered back. "We are the Board. We have the right to do whatever we damned well please."

Kitieri curled her lip. "You're not *my* Board. And you can't touch me."

Grabbing her Church's book from its inner pocket, she pulled the ties of her cloak loose. The heavy garment crumpled to the floor, revealing her full garb beneath. Her high-necked, long-sleeved black robe met her tall black boots at her knees and a bright blue sash cinched her waist, falling in a wide, shimmering swath of satin down her left leg.

Thank the gods Bat didn't force me into one of those all-white get-ups.

Ghentrin stared, confused, until Rulka uttered a soft gasp.

"The crest," she said, standing. "She wears the mark of a Baliant."

Ghentrin's face flushed red again, and his eyes bulged.

Just when he was starting to calm down, too, Kitieri thought. *Shame*.

"Bullshit!" he shouted. "You're no more a Baliant than I am a god!"

Kitieri tossed the book onto the table, where it landed with a sharp smack. Ghentrin stomped forward, deliberately slow and menacing as he swiped the book up into his hands. Scanning the first page, disgust blossomed across his round features as he thumbed through the following pages. At length, he looked up at Kitieri with barely controlled rage.

"This means *nothing*," he spat.

"That is objectively false," Catarva said, her voice light and musical next to Ghentrin's gravelly anger. "Our law technically allows their claim to independence."

He rounded on her, ready to spit fire. "You *support* this?"

"It is out of my hands," Catarva replied. "The Church of Shirasette is now a valid Church in our city, and the Church of Enahris will recognize them as such, whether you like it or not."

"I will not recognize some horde of pathetic, uneducated, worthless swine as a *Church*!"

Kitieri's lightning snapped with her temper, and her face screwed up momentarily to bite back the cry that tried to escape. Catarva shot her a concerned glance, and Kitieri forced in a breath.

"Well, Advisor," she ground out, "here's something you might recognize. Those pathetic, uneducated, worthless swine are no longer under your control, and our numbers are growing every day. Now that we are a legal Church—one that actually cares for its members—you can watch those numbers explode. Your apathy and Stil's tyranny are no longer the only two choices in this city, and in case basic math fails you, I'll spell it out. The more members we gain, the more you lose."

The Board members around the table swiveled their heads between Kitieri and Ghentrin, too enthralled by the exchange to interrupt. They really *were* spineless without Amadora telling them how to think and act.

Keep up the pressure.

"And here's another tidbit of information for you," Kitieri continued, leaning forward. "My Board and my entire Church know who and what you are. *All* of you."

She turned to the rest of the table, eyes sweeping over the Board, coming to rest last on Rulka. No faint smile graced her features now, and she dropped her eyes to her lap.

"Know who we are," Ghentrin mocked her, laughing. "What the hells are you on about?"

Kitieri tore her gaze from Rulka, dragging it over each Advisor more slowly this time. Finally coming back to Ghentrin, she said, "Both the Chief Advisors have made it abundantly clear that they want the people of this city dead. You have betrayed your Church and your responsibility, and *thousands* know about it. Whatever secrets you thought you were keeping are out."

"Betrayed—*tch*—I..." Ghentrin forced a laugh, but Kitieri watched his eyes dart pleadingly to the rest of the Board. None of them looked back at him. "I... I didn't..."

"You have purposefully kept the common people from the resources and help they need, treating them as nothing more than slaves fit only to die mining your cintra, *and* we know you've been manufacturing a war with the Church of Histan. The poor dying wasn't enough, right? You need the officers dead, too. The fewer left alive when the lightning takes over, the more resources will be left for you." Kitieri snorted in disgust, shaking her head. "I have to give it to you, it was a solid plan, and it might even have worked... if the whole city hadn't found out about it."

Beneath the blustery red of his cheeks, Ghentrin paled. He looked again to the Board, and started stammering as Darrow leaned in to whisper something to the man beside him.

"So tell me, Ghentrin," Kitieri went on, "what do you think will happen now when the lightning takes over? When the people didn't lie down and die like they were supposed to, and your officers won't fight for you? What do you think will become of a Board that murdered and demeaned its people for their own benefit? Do you think they'll show you mercy? Do you think you *deserve* it?"

Ghentrin stood still, save for the rise and fall of his rotund chest. He didn't bother looking to the Board this time.

"Well." He cleared his throat. "I... Well, *I* didn't betray anyone. I'm not the Chief Advisor. You're putting this on me, when it's Amadora you need to be talking to!"

"Yes, well, I don't see her here—do you?" Catarva said, furrowing her fine brows as if deeply troubled by the revelation. "At this point,

Amadora is in violation of her call to summons, and risks being suspended from duty. As her second in command, this matter *does* fall to you, unless you can speak for the Chief Advisor's whereabouts at this time."

Ghentrin's breathing quickened, and he opened his mouth to speak when Rulka stood and cut him off. "I know where she is."

"Rulka," Ghentrin growled.

"What?" she snapped. "I see no need to defend her when all she's done is drag us down into this hole with her. You know that I was against this from the start, but she doesn't make that much of an option."

"I know where she is, too," said the blond man, standing up next to Rulka with the other nameless Advisor.

"She went to the Church of Histan," Rulka said.

"Why?" Catarva tilted her head.

Rulka glanced down at her hands before responding. "To expedite the war. With the lightning—uh, Kitieri— on the loose, she said it was time to get this over with."

"Histan's Church is organizing to move officially?" Catarva asked.

"She was going to push for that."

Catarva nodded. "Then we will meet them."

Kitieri turned to stare at the Baliant, and she caught Haldin's hard glance from her other side.

"But," Catarva continued, "all of you on this Board will need to choose which side you'd prefer to be on when this happens. As Baliant Kitieri so eloquently stated, the people will *not* look kindly upon you should you stay the course; but there may be a chance for redemption yet."

Rulka nodded. "I'm with you, Baliants."

"So am I," Blondie said. "We never should have let her push us to this."

Darrow and the final Advisor exchanged the same glance as before, and Ghentrin finally found his voice before they could speak.

"Wait, wait," he said, waving a hand at the two men. "All of this doesn't change the truth about the lightning. It *will* take over. I know... I mean, I'll admit that Amadora's plan was ruthless, but what happens when no one can go outside? What happens when there are thousands of mouths to feed but no one can work? Stil's cintra hoards can only protect so many of our farms, and the numbers just don't add up. We can't—"

"Yes, people will die," Kitieri said, stepping on his words. "People are dying *now*. They die every day because they are forced to go without the protection you take for granted. The thing you never considered, though, was that everyone deserves an equal chance at life. Sending others to slaughter so you can live in comfort is sick, and if you can't see that, Ghentrin, then you don't deserve a second chance. If you want to run to Stil and Amadora, you're free to do that, but don't think they'll protect you any more than they've protected their own people. If you want to live, your best option is to join us."

Ghentrin held Kitieri's glare for only a moment before dropping his chin to his chest.

"She's right, Ghentrin," Rulka said. "Amadora would just as soon stab you to help herself, and you know it."

The man let out a rush of air, deflating his puffed-up chest at long last. "That she would," he said. "Well, it appears I've got no choice."

The triumph Kitieri felt showed in Catarva's beaming face.

"What happens next?" Rulka asked.

"First, we uninvite Amadora from the Board of Advisors," Catarva replied. "Then... we move on the Church of Histan."

CHAPTER 19

Cloak tied securely around her shoulders once more, Kitieri stole through the labyrinth of hallways within the Church of Enahris.

It's late, she thought. How long had they been in that meeting? But she grinned to herself. *Bat will understand. Everything is going just like I promised.*

She lifted her hand to rub her tired eyes, and winced at the scream of her burns. The salve was wearing off fast now, and the pain was becoming a constant distraction.

Turning a corner, Kitieri came into view of the door to her old quarters. *Finally.* She paused just outside, fist poised to knock.

Why am I so nervous?

She lowered her hand, and instead moved to press her forehead against the door. "Taff. Jera."

Shuffling sounds came from within, and Kitieri heard whispers from the other side. "Taff, did you hear that?"

Kitieri pressed her lips together, suppressing a laugh. Jera's idea of a whisper had never been quite on the same level as everyone else's.

"It's me," she said softly.

The door whooshed open with such force that it sucked the edges of Kitieri's cloak into the room, and two small bodies immediately glommed onto her.

"KIT—"

"*Shhh!*" Kitieri dropped into a half crouch, waving her hand in Jera's face. "Inside—come on."

Taff fell back into the darkness, yanking Jera with him, and Kitieri closed the door behind them. This time, she fell to her knees to accept two hugs so tight that they squeezed the air from her lungs. Emotion tore at her throat, and tears spilled down her face as she took in their familiar scents and the feeling of their arms around her. Gods, how she'd missed them.

Jera sobbed against her shoulder, antagonizing Kitieri's own tears, as Taff whispered in her other ear.

"We thought we were never going to see you again."

Kitieri squeezed her eyes closed, longing to hold them more tightly than her burns would allow. "I know," were the only words she could muster. After several more deep, shuddering breaths, she sat back on her heels.

"I'm so sorry I went away," she whispered. "I can't imagine what you two went through."

"We were worried for *you*," Taff said.

"Yeah," Jera said with a loud sniffle. "Haldin was really nice to us. He came and got us for breakfast every day."

"It's *Commander* Haldin, Jera," Taff corrected her.

"He did?" Kitieri asked, blinking her remaining tears away. Jera nodded, a small smile spreading across her wet face. "Did you thank him?"

"Every day," Jera said proudly, and Kitieri smiled back.

"Well, that was very good of him," she said. "And everyone else has been nice to you?"

Taff looked down, and Jera tossed him a quick glance before looking away. Kitieri's shoulders tensed.

"Tell me," she said gently. In the flickering light of the single candle behind him, she leaned forward to inspect Taff's face. "Is that…?"

She lifted her gloved thumb to Taff's cheek, but he jerked away. As the soft light washed over that side of his face, Kitieri could see the bruised skin around his eye.

"Taff!" She broke her own whispering rule as she leaned sideways to get a better look. "What happened? Who hurt you?"

"It's fine," he said, trying to force his voice deeper than it naturally wanted to go.

"It's *not* fine!" she hissed. "Who touched you?"

Taff's eyes turned on her in the flickering hint of light. "I started it," he said.

"Why?"

"Bronick said some shit."

"Taff, you shouldn't say that word."

"Why not? You do."

Kitieri drew back with a quick breath. "What did Bronick say?"

Taff lowered his eyes. "He called you a murderer. He said you'd kill us if you ever got out, and you should rot down there forever. So I punched him."

"But Bronick's friends are a lot bigger than Taff," Jera added, the corners of her mouth downturned. "He got really hurt."

"I'm *fine*," Taff said again. "It was almost a week ago—it doesn't hurt anymore."

Kitieri bit down on the inside of her lip, blinking back a fresh wave of tears. "Taff, I am so sorry you had to go through that because of me."

"It wasn't because of you." He lifted his head, and in his eyes, Kitieri noticed a sharp glint she'd never seen there before. "What they did to you was unfair, and I'm not going to stand around and let people who don't even know you say whatever they want. You're *not* a murderer, you were protecting Jera. I'd have killed him, too."

Taff's vehemence shocked Kitieri, and she found herself caught between crying and laughing. Taff had always been the gentle soul of the family—the quiet, introspective one with a love for books and solitude. Seeing this change in him broke a piece of Kitieri's heart, but it had only been a matter of time. This world did not reward the gentle ones.

Like Noia. Kitieri swallowed, fighting for words as Jera spoke in a sad, quiet tone.

"Are you back for real?" she asked.

Kitieri took a shuddering breath, clearing her throat.

"We're running, aren't we." Taff's hard gaze reflected the flickering candlelight.

"A lot has changed," Kitieri said.

"I knew it," Taff muttered. "You escaped, didn't you?"

"Well—"

"We have to *leave*?" Jera's face fell.

"Yes. But it's a good thing."

"Where are we supposed to go?" Taff asked. "We can't go back home; they'll look for us there."

Kitieri put her hands out to stay any further interrogation.

"I know this is a lot," she said. "You've both been through so much, and I'm sorry. But you've followed me this far because you trust me, right?"

Jera looked up at Taff, who nodded solemnly.

"Then I need you to trust me now," she said. "Get dressed, and pack up whatever you want to keep."

Without another word, Taff disappeared into his room, while Jera stood wide-eyed in the dim common space.

"What about Ashes?" Her high voice cracked under the threat of more tears.

"Oh, honey, Ashes is fine," Kitieri promised. "When this is all over, we might even be able to come see her again."

"But she was gone today, just like in my dream," Jera said. "You and then Ashes."

Kitieri bit her lip. "What if I told you that Ashes was busy being a hero?"

Jera lifted huge eyes to Kitieri's. "Taff would say you were lying to make me feel better."

"No—it's true." Kitieri smiled. "Ashes saved lives today, and she's back safe now. You should be proud of her."

Jera smiled thinly. "But... won't she miss me?"

Kitieri longed to stroke her sister's hair, to pull her into a tight embrace, but kept her charred hands at her sides. "She'll be a lot happier if you're safe. Come on, let's get your things."

Jera sniffled, but allowed Kitieri to guide her into her bedroom, where she gathered her meager possessions into a small bag. A lump formed in Kitieri's throat as she saw just how little her sister had that didn't belong to the Church.

"Can I keep these?" Jera asked her, holding up her riding breeches and boots.

Kitieri's chin trembled. "Yeah, go ahead and keep those. I don't think they'll mind."

As Jera finished packing, Kitieri slipped into her own room. The blankets were still in a crumpled heap upon her bed from the night she'd left her sister sleeping to answer the lightning's call.

She shook those thoughts from her mind, turning to the top drawer of her dresser. After grabbing the single, shining round she'd earned for her short time as an officer, Kitieri slipped the drawer's only other occupant into her cloak pocket before meeting her siblings at the front door.

"Hoods up," she whispered, "and remember to be very quiet, okay?"

She led them through the hallways and down the stairs, turning away from the exit into the training yard as they passed it. Taff frowned at the door as they moved deeper into the Church.

"Kitieri, where are we going?" he whispered. "Aren't we leaving?"

"In a minute."

She followed the hall that ended in a tall doorway, and Taff slowed his pace. "We're *stealing*?"

Kitieri turned. "I'll make up for it, I promise. But you two have a ways to go, and I won't send you out there without protection."

She pulled out her set of officer's keys and fumbled through them with her bandaged and gloved fingers, finally managing to find the right one and unlock the closet housing the Gadgets.

"Quick, put them on," she instructed, "then we'll head out through the training yard."

As her siblings complied, Kitieri eyed the walls of black leather packs. She'd left hers at the tree outside the gate on the far side of the Church, and they weren't going that direction.

She *should* take one of these, she knew... but she hesitated. Pretending that her body and element were still intact would only get her so far, but the charade was important. Catarva needed her lightning, and their alliance rested on that fact. She could keep up the act a little longer.

"Aren't you getting one, too?" Jera asked in her attempt at a whisper.

"I'll be fine," Kitieri lied, locking the closet door once more. "I'm not going as far as you."

"We're going *alone*?" Taff hissed. "You haven't even told us where."

"No, you won't be alone." Kitieri ignored the loaded glance

exchanged between her brother and sister as she headed for the training yard.

She breathed in the cool night air as they exited, relieved to step out of the Church. Something about its stone walls felt suffocating to her, like she could no longer get a full breath within their confines. Even though every second she spent outside was dangerous, she much preferred the night's embrace.

At the gate, two gray uniforms stood with their backs to Kitieri, facing the Square. One turned back at the sound of their approach and raised a startled hand.

"Orders of the Baliant," Kitieri said before he could speak. "No sign of the Chief Advisor yet?"

"Uh." The officer lowered his hand, glancing to his companion. "No. Not yet."

Kitieri nodded, passing between them as their eyes followed her. Haldin had supplied all his posted sentries with just enough information to be useful, and Amadora wouldn't come to this gate, anyways. She was bound to return to the south gate from which she'd left, but just in case...

Taff and Jera close behind her, Kitieri crossed the wide Square in the shadows of the border trees, out of range of the lamps highlighting their twisted trunks and branches from beneath. As they left the warm glow behind, Kitieri squinted into the darkness for any sign of Bat.

"Will you tell us what's going on now?" Taff demanded.

Kitieri took a deep breath. "There is a place in the city called the Church of Shirasette, and they help people. They take them in when they have nowhere else to go, and offer food and protection."

"Like Noia and Vina?" Jera asked.

Kitieri looked down at her with a sad smile. "Yeah. Just like them."

"Are they there?" Jera's eyes lit up.

Kitieri sighed. "Vina is still at the Church of Histan right now, but I promise you I am going to change that." She tensed her jaw with a silent inhale. "I promised her mother I would take care of her, and I will."

"And the Church of Shirasette is where we're going?" Taff asked.

"Yes," Kitieri replied. "The Church of Enahris isn't safe anymore. There are people that would use you against me, and I need to make sure you're in a place they can't find you."

"Do they have horses?" Jera asked.

Kitieri grinned at the memory of Ashes just standing in the open lower floor of the warehouse as she'd come down the steps. "Not yet, but they're working on it."

"Why can't you come with us?" Taff asked.

"I have things to do here first."

"When will you come, then?"

"As soon as possible."

"That doesn't tell me anything."

Kitieri cut him a hard look, and he gave it right back to her.

"I'm doing everything I can," she said. "You two will always come first, but a lot of people are depending on me right now."

"Let me help."

"Taff, no."

"Why not?" he shot back. "I've been learning to fight. I can *help*."

"I know, and I appreciate that, but Jera needs you more."

Taff growled under his breath. "That's all I'm ever good for."

"Taff," Kitieri snapped. "This isn't about that. I don't doubt your abilities—"

"Yes, you do." Taff's eyes flashed like silver. "You don't think I'm good enough or smart enough or strong enough to help, but I *am*."

Kitieri stopped walking. "Listen to me, Taff," she said. "This is not about you. This is bigger than all three of us, combined. There's more going on here than you know."

"Then tell me!" Taff ripped his hood back and glared up at her, pale hair disheveled in the faint starlight, and Kitieri's reply caught in her throat as she saw the spitting image of herself demanding the same of Catarva. His anger, his passion, his helplessness all mirrored her own, and she wanted nothing more than to grasp his shoulders and tell him everything. But that wouldn't make him ready to hear it.

Her shoulders dropped in a heavy sigh as she heard Catarva's words to her only hours before. *"You're not ready."*

Could anyone ever be ready…?

"Do you think you two could be any louder?" Kitieri spun at the sound of Bat's voice, and watched her small, cloaked frame appear from the deep shadows between two buildings. "And what in the two hells took so long? I was *this close* to busting in there after you."

"Sorry I'm late," Kitieri said, squaring her shoulders, "but I think you'll agree it was worth your time."

"Is that so?"

Kitieri grinned before beckoning her siblings forward. "This is my friend, Bat," she said. "She helps run the Church of Shirasette."

"Yes, I *help*."

Kitieri ignored the sarcastic comment. "Bat, these are my siblings, Taff and Jera."

"A pleasure," Bat said, offering her hand to both of them in turn. "Now out with it, Baliant. What's so worth my time?"

Kitieri shot a quick glance around them before stepping in close to Bat.

"Amadora is out," she whispered. "Overturned. The Board went against her, and they're ready to support us."

Bat jerked her head back, tilting it at an odd angle to look up at Kitieri from under her hood. "You're shitting me."

"I'm not. Catarva accepted the alliance, and wants to move as soon as possible."

"As in… *move* move?"

"Yeah. Amadora met with Stil tonight to speed up the war, so we don't have a lot of time. If we're going to avoid unnecessary deaths, we need to meet them first. How fast can you get your end together?"

"Oof." Bat shook her head, even as a smirk played on her thin lips. "Eriat's gonna be pissed I woke him up, but we can meet you at midday."

"That's perfect," Kitieri said. "Catarva's going to attempt the diplomatic approach and demand to see Tiernan, so I'll need to stand with her while you and Eriat split up and execute the other two parts."

Bat shook her head. "I'd feel better if I was with you. Stil's proven he's ready to play dirty, and they won't accept you as a Baliant quite as easily as Catarva did. Catarva saw a way to benefit from it, but Stil's liable to lose his actual mind. There's still a *lot* of danger here, even if you're mainly just the decoy."

While Kitieri recognized the blatant truth in Bat's words, it was nothing new. The same niggling fear had lodged itself in her own mind, too.

"You can't," she replied. "You're supposed to get Vina out of there while Eriat and his team head for the cintra."

"We *will* get Vina," Bat assured her, "and as many of the other kids as possible. Believe me, I don't like them in there any more than you do, but I have others that can handle it."

"I'd really rather you led that part." Kitieri shook her head. "You know the Church better than anyone."

"Trust me," Bat said. "It will be fine. The kids are basically invisible to those people, as long as they're wearing brown. No one looks at them, speaks to them, or cares what they're doing as long as they appear to be on a mission. The only part of the plan with a real risk of exploding is yours. You're poking a sleeping monster here."

Kitieri scoffed. "It's *hardly* sleeping."

"I mean with Tiernan." Though there was no one around, Bat lowered her voice even further. "No one knows what's going on with him. It's been so long since he's made any sort of public appearance…"

"That's kind of the point," Kitieri said. "If the Church cannot produce a *functional* Baliant, they're not a Church. Wasn't that why you needed me so badly?"

Bat rolled her eyes with an exasperated sound. "That's different."

"Catarva doesn't see it that way."

"Well, you're in more danger than she is."

"How?"

"UGH!" Bat lifted her hands, miming the act of strangulation. "You are being purposefully stubborn."

"Look, you're not going to talk me out of this," Kitieri said. "I'm standing with Catarva. I have a responsibility to be there."

Bat moved her hands from their tense stranglehold to interlock her fingers in a more gentle grip. "And I have a responsibility to stand by *you*. If neither of us are budging, we might as well come to terms with it right now."

Kitieri sighed. "All right. Fine. But if Vina doesn't make it out of there, I'm holding you personally responsible."

"Understood." Bat dipped her head. "And, just out of curiosity, how much of this plan does Catarva really know?"

"Ehh…" Kitieri squinted. "It didn't really… come up."

Bat chortled, shaking her head. "Well, this will be interesting if nothing else."

That's one word for it, Kitieri thought.

"Listen, I have to stay here and wrap up this end of things," she said. "Amadora will come back at some point and we'll need to deal with her, but now you know I'm safe. You can take Taff and Jera back and make preparations on your end, and we'll meet you in Histan's Square tomorrow at midday."

Bat nodded and Kitieri turned back to Taff, who was watching her intently.

"I really am sorry," she said, softening her tone. "I understand how you're feeling. I wish I could bring you with me, but —"

"It's too *dangerous*," Taff grumbled. "I know."

Kitieri chewed on her cheek. She hated parting with him like this, but she had no choice. Dropping into a crouch, she opened her arms to Jera, who rushed to hug her.

"Be good for Bat," she said, fighting a sudden lump in her throat. "You'll see me again before you know it, okay?"

Jera nodded against her shoulder.

"All right, kids," Bat said, about as kindly as Kitieri imagined was possible. "Time to head out."

She held out a hand to Jera, who leapt forward to take it in her own, and Kitieri forced a smile. Jera could make friends with a stray rock. It would make her life easier in some ways, but harder in others, and Kitieri ached to follow them. Jera was too accepting, and Taff was too suspicious. They needed her…

"They'll be fine," Bat said, as if reading her mind, and Kitieri made an effort to turn her forced smile more natural.

"I know."

Bat turned to walk back into the shadows, Jera still holding her hand, and Taff followed without a glance back at Kitieri. His silence hurt, but it was no more than she deserved.

She watched them go until they were long out of sight, swallowed by the shadows, and pain tore at her heart as she longed to run after them. She'd only just gotten them back, and now…

A metallic tang in the air reached her nose, and panic spiked through her. *Oh, fuck.*

She turned on her heel and sprinted for the Church, her element squirming within her. It wriggled down her arms to gnaw at her burns, and Kitieri pushed harder.

Maybe… *maybe*… if this Strike had a long build-up, she'd be able to make it to shelter.

Her lightning flared as the charge jumped, and Kitieri stumbled with a loud gasp. *Not gonna be a long one.*

The Strike was coming *fast*... and she was too far from the Church. As she strained her eyes for any hint of the Square's glowing lamps, a different light caught her eye.

Not a light. Robes.

"Catarva," Kitieri panted, running for her. "What are you doing? There's a Str—"

The first warning ripped into her, and her lightning popped through her gloves in a brilliant arc of white light. Kitieri doubled over, screaming as the element seared her bloody arms, burning up the bandages and rendering the expiring salve utterly worthless.

Catarva was at her side in an instant.

"Where is your PCR?" she demanded, pulling Kitieri back up straight. Through her violent shaking, Kitieri lifted her eyes to Catarva's hard amber gaze, brushing over the black straps that interrupted the white of her robes.

"Catarva, I can't... my hands..."

A low, angry growl came from Catarva's chest, and she ripped the glove from Kitieri's hand to reveal the bloodied and yellowed bandages.

"Fool," she hissed. "You came out here unprotected, *knowing* your lightning was useless! Do you realize what you've done?"

The second warning sent Kitieri to her knees, wrenching her from Catarva's grasp and slamming her forehead into the cold cobblestones. Her only awareness of her own scream was the raw pain in the vibrations of her throat. The screaming and writhing couldn't help her—not even the cool stones could take away the immense burn that attacked her senses, flickering to black.

A heavy weight pushed Kitieri down, and she collapsed under the pressure. A memory—Stil's boot on her back, stomping her to the floor...

The cool relief of unconsciousness came for her, and her body went limp as her lightning recoiled, the burn subsiding from her arms. Her cheek was numb with cold, pressed against the street...

Wait.

Kitieri opened her eyes. She wasn't unconscious. This was not the sweet, blissful blackness for which she'd longed...

The hem of white robes swayed at the edge of her vision, and Kitieri lifted her eyes to the woman standing over her. Catarva stood with her face to the sky, arms splayed out as if in invitation. With growing horror, Kitieri realized that the black straps were gone.

The third warning barely touched Kitieri, her lightning subdued under the influence of the Gadget now resting on her back. Catarva staggered, her strangled cry ringing in Kitieri's ears as understanding dawned.

A sacrifice.

"Catarva," she croaked. Her voice refused to speak at full volume, and she pushed up under the weight of the Gadget.

"Don't," Catarva ground out, flicking her long fingers in Kitieri's direction. Gravity overpowered her, slamming Kitieri back to the ground. With great effort, she lifted her head just enough to see Catarva back away.

Just enough to watch the blue bolt set the night sky ablaze, unstoppable in its fury.

With a blinding flash, the Blue Killer came for its victim, and the white robes disappeared.

CHAPTER 20

"*Catarva!*"

The force pulling Kitieri to the ground vanished, and she threw the Gadget from her back as she launched herself to her feet.

The white robes were gone; all that remained was a pile of black ashes, tendrils of fine smoke rising into the night. Kitieri skidded to her knees at the corpse's side, clapping one hand over her mouth in horror.

"Oh, no," she whispered. "Oh, gods, what did I do? She's dead. She's dead." She bent forward over the ashes, eyes squeezed closed as unbidden tears leaked out the corners.

Why would she do that? Why did she sacrifice herself for me? I can't do this alone. I—

A rustle in the ashes snapped Kitieri's head up, and a subsequent groan sent her scrambling backwards. Bright amber eyes opened beneath the layers of dark soot, and Catarva coughed.

"What the *fuck*?" Kitieri shrieked, the words all blurring into one high-pitched yelp. "Catarva? You're... *alive*?"

The ashes shifted, and the black, flakey remnants of the robe slid off Catarva's dark shoulders.

"May I borrow your cloak, Kitieri?"

Kitieri blinked several times, mouth open in shock, before she managed to comply. She draped the garment over Catarva's body, forcing herself to meet the unnerving gaze.

"How are you alive?" she whispered. "I *saw* the Strike take you. No one could survive that."

Catarva closed her eyes, rolling her head away from Kitieri with a sigh.

"I came out here to speak with you," she said, her voice dry and raspy, "because it was time for me to be honest." She coughed. "To come clean about who I am. But I guess a firsthand demonstration is as good as any explanation."

With a grimace, she pushed herself up to a sitting position under the cloak, and Kitieri put out her hands. "Whoa, you should probably stay down."

Catarva waved her away. "I'm fine," she said. "It just takes a moment to recover."

"You've been... struck before?"

"Unfortunately, yes." Catarva sighed. "A few times, in the early days of the Blue Killer. I found that it was so drawn to me that merely stepping foot outdoors could trigger its onset, so I took to staying inside as much as possible. That Strike just now was likely my doing, but I didn't know you would leave the Church unprotected."

She shot her a hard look, and Kitieri bowed her head as her shame wrestled with burning curiosity.

"Why do you trigger the Strikes?" she asked. "And how in the hells do you survive them?"

Catarva grinned. "Because the lightning is meant for the gods."

Kitieri stared for a moment, one cheek scrunched in confusion, before her eyes opened wide. She fell back out of her crouched position, catching herself with one gloved hand. Her burn wounds bit with a painful flare, and she sucked in a hissing breath as she pulled her hand out from under her, rolling onto her shoulder.

"You're not telling me..." She stuttered as the words caught. "You're not... a... y-you're a *god*? You're... *Enahris*?"

Catarva's grin widened, and she laughed.

"No. I'm not Enahris," she said. "I'm only half-god. Enahris is my mother."

Kitieri's air rushed from her lungs as if she'd been punched in the gut.

"This is insane," she muttered to herself. "This isn't real. Gods aren't real."

"I assure you, they are."

"That's impossible."

"Just because you don't see them, Kitieri, doesn't mean they don't exist."

"Then where *are* they?" Kitieri flung one arm out, gesturing to the still darkness around them as she got to her feet. "Do they even care what's happening here? Do they care that people are *dying*, and it's going to keep getting worse?"

Catarva's expression turned melancholy. "They don't know."

"What do you mean, they don't *know*?" Kitieri snapped. "Aren't gods supposed to know everything?"

Catarva took a deep breath. "You must understand, Kitieri, that they exist on an entirely different plane than we do. While, yes, they are meant to be responsible for the world to which they are bonded, that would demand their presence and attention. I gather that it requires great amounts of energy for them to take our form and walk among us, so they choose not to. It's more convenient for them to remain in their own realm, blissfully unaware of the troubles of mortals, even when those troubles are their doing. Would you mind helping me up?"

She reached out a hand, and Kitieri reflexively started to offer her own before the bandages caught her eye and she jerked it back. "I—uh…"

Catarva waited expectantly, hand still outstretched. "Please?"

Kitieri glanced down at the bloody bandages.

"Do you remember what I asked of you when we made our alliance?" Catarva asked.

"I will answer all your questions when the time is right, but until that time, I need you to trust me."

Biting down on her bottom lip, Kitieri braced herself for the excruciating pain and extended her hand.

She felt the pressure of Catarva's grip and tensed her body as weight pulled against her, but felt no objection from her burns. She dared to open one eye to see Catarva standing before her, taller and more intimidating than ever before draped in the black cloak instead of her signature white, their hands still locked in a tight grip.

When Catarva released her, the hand that Kitieri pulled back felt completely different from her other. She tested it, touching the soaked bandages, and felt nothing.

"What did you do?" she whispered, unsure whether to feel horrified or ecstatic. "I can't feel it. I can't feel my arm."

Catarva watched silently as Kitieri ripped off the bandages, unwrapping them from her elbow to her fingers. As the soiled strips fell to the ground, Kitieri gaped at her arm.

Where she'd expected oozing wounds, she saw new, white skin, still streaked with the blood, salve, and pus that had soaked into the bandages before their removal.

"How…" She ran her fingers from her wrist to her elbow, feeling the slight tickle where there should have been melted, mangled flesh.

"One of the better traits I inherited from my mother." Catarva smiled. "Your other is burned, too, correct?"

She offered her hand again, and Kitieri took it without hesitation this time. She closed her eyes as the incessant pain receded under the glove and wrappings, traveling up her arm to heal all of the minor burns Stil's fire had inflicted. As the heat left her body, Kitieri released a long sigh of relief and gratitude.

"Thank you."

"Well," Catarva replied, tilting her head, "what is a lightning without her element, after all? Come."

As Catarva turned for the Church, Kitieri fell into step beside her. "So, you haven't… uh… told Enahris about the lightning?"

Catarva scoffed. "If I could, I would. My mortal blood keeps me bound to this realm, and her increased absence is a direct result of my existence. She had me for one reason only—to lead the Church in her stead. I was seven years old the last time I saw her. That was the day she announced to the Board that I would take over as Baliant when I came of age at fifteen."

"Ah." That explained Amadora's unseating. Kitieri smirked at the thought of her unholy outrage at a fifteen-year-old demoting her to Chief Advisor.

"By no means was my appointment standard practice," Catarva continued. "Baliants and Chief Advisors are voted in by the Board as lifetime appointments, so you can imagine the uproar my situation caused. But all my mother told me was to keep the balance. She kept repeating it, over and over, as if it was the only worry or responsibility a Baliant should have."

Right, the riddle... "What balance?" Kitieri asked.

Catarva's features tensed in the furthest reach of the Square's light.

"The balance of the Churches," she said. "Even the gods have laws, and the law of balance rules their realm. With such a small inhabitable portion, our world only has two bonded gods, but there are worlds out there with five, ten, or even twenty gods. The rule of balance keeps them working in harmony, and prevents the wars of the past from ever happening again."

"Whoa," Kitieri said, putting out a hand to stop further explanation. "There are other *worlds*?"

Catarva chuckled. "Yes. Many of them. Mortals are restricted to the world on which they were born, but thousands are out there, and they all have bonded gods to rule and care for them. It is their divine responsibility, but gods can be... volatile beings. The law of balance was established to ensure that no one god could overthrow the others, thus taking control of an entire world for themselves, and their Churches are their mortal measurement."

Kitieri's head spun with the information. It still felt so impossible, like some big, elaborate joke. But not a shred of humor graced Catarva's features as the corners of her lips pulled down with worry.

"What if they don't keep the balance?" Kitieri asked.

"You're seeing it," Catarva replied, gesturing to the sky.

"The *lightning*?" Kitieri's eyes followed Catarva's gesture.

"Yes," Catarva said. "Like I said, the lightning was meant to affect the gods. It's a punishment for the imbalance, a warning that things have gone awry. One Church is stronger than the other." A frustrated sound emanated from her throat. "I would go to the hells and back if I thought it would help me fix it. My mother thought leaving me in her place would ensure peace and balance, but she could not have been more wrong. Amadora has fought me relentlessly since the day I took the Baliant's seat, and turned the Board against me. Every decision I made, she challenged. It broke our Church, cracked our foundation, and left us weaker than the Church of Histan. That's what triggered the lightning, but the punishment meant for them is only killing the mortals under their charge."

"Then..." Kitieri swallowed. "If you're half-god... why didn't you get rid of Amadora earlier? You could have, I don't know, used your powers or something."

"I could have," Catarva said, nodding, "but the game of politics is dark and complex. My first responsibility was always to keep the balance for fear of dire consequences, and I needed Amadora's power. Don't forget that I was only fifteen at the time, and I wanted the position no more than Amadora wanted me to have it. I was terrified that if I removed my Chief Advisor, who was still seen by many as Enahris' Baliant, I would break the balance. By the time I'd grown into my position, the damage was done and the Church was stuck with her."

Catarva released a long, shaky sigh. "I failed in the only purpose my life has ever had. I could not accomplish what my mother expected, but that does not mean this is over. I have a responsibility to my people, many of whom I have already failed to save. But if I can save them moving forward, I will do it, no matter what it takes."

Kitieri chewed the corner of her lip, taking in the information in silence. Catarva's palpable emotion tugged at her heart, and though she longed to comfort the woman, she had no idea where to start. Catarva was right; all they could do was move forward.

"How do we do that, then?" she asked.

Catarva lifted her chin, and the proud shape returned to her shoulders under the black cloak.

"That's where *you* come in," she said. "They say that the Blue Killer always takes a victim, right?"

"Yes?" Kitieri frowned.

"What happens when it doesn't?"

"You mean… when I repel it?"

"Exactly." Catarva stopped at the base of the Church stairs. "Never have I met a lightning with such an ability. The only thing that explains it is the way your lightning must have developed under lock. Where most could never regain their control once the Strikes started, yours *adapted*. It actually learned from the Blue Killer while in lock, syncing with it in some way that I never thought possible. And now, you are the *only* one capable of wielding our link to the gods."

Kitieri blinked. She'd never put much thought into *why* her lightning behaved the way it did, but Catarva's confidence in her control made her nervous. Whatever Catarva expected of her, she hoped she'd be able to deliver…

"How is it a link to the gods?" she asked, skirting the topic.

Catarva's knowing grin set Kitieri's nerves further on edge. "When the lightning does not claim a victim, it hits the gods. And it hurts. If my experience is anything like what they feel, they will have to take notice sooner or later."

"Wait, it hurts you when I repel a Strike?" Kitieri asked, suddenly conscious of every bolt she'd spurned.

"I feel all of them," Catarva replied. "It knocked me down the first time, the day you survived your Judgement. I *know* my mother feels it, too."

Kitieri nodded slowly as the pieces started to click into place.

"That's why you need me," she whispered. "I can get their attention."

"Yes." Before Catarva lowered her eyes to the ground, Kitieri caught their flash of pain. "But it's a desperate attempt. My greatest hope—and it's a long shot—is that by speaking with Tiernan, we can begin to take steps toward righting the balance. Stil has refused to let me anywhere near him, but now that he's busy warmongering and you're standing beside me, we have a chance. Until then, I need you to repel as many Strikes as you can. Maybe, in *some* convoluted way, we can pull off a miracle."

Before Kitieri could reply, a shriek sounded from the south side of the Church and she twisted to look over her shoulder.

"The south gate," Catarva said, starting for the echoing sound. As they rounded the corner, Kitieri saw Haldin physically blocking the south gate with his spear as a figure in a long magenta cloak barked, and her heart jumped into her throat.

Amadora.

"You cannot stop me!" The shrill words became audible as Kitieri and Catarva drew near. "I have a right to enter this Church! I want Ghentrin here right now!"

"He's already on his way," Haldin replied. "Until then—ah, Baliants." He dipped into a low bow at their approach, and Amadora turned with a malicious snarl.

"Catarva," she screeched. "Just *what* do you think you're doing?"

"What I should have done years ago." Catarva's low voice moved like velvet, but cut like steel.

Amadora sneered. "Your power here is a farce, and everyone knows it. *I* run this Church."

"You used to," Catarva countered.

Amadora sniffed. "That didn't change the day you usurped my seat. A child has no place in such a role." She leaned in, baring her teeth. "Not even the child of a *god*."

Catarva breathed in slowly, her chest rising.

"Lineage means nothing," she said. "A miner's daughter has proven herself a more capable leader than you could ever hope to be."

Shock and hatred flashed across Amadora's features, and her beady eyes flicked to Kitieri. Fully aware of her visible Baliant's crest and attire, Kitieri watched with satisfaction as the Chief Advisor turned bright red in the gate's lamplight.

"This is despicable," she spat. "You have no Church—how *dare* you wear that crest? You are a disgrace to the title of Baliant—you both are!"

Kitieri stepped forward, boots crunching on the loose stones scattered across the path, and her lightning skittered down her healed arms as anger flushed her neck and face. The cold darkness of her solitary confinement came rushing back, and she heard Amadora's words echo through her memory, condemning her. Condemning Haldin. Condemning her siblings to the heartbreak of another abandonment. She remembered the woman's smug, hateful smile as she'd sent her far underground, never to see the light of day again. Sparks flew from Kitieri's fingers, and she stepped in so close to Amadora's face that the woman leaned back, fear flashing in her eyes.

She could kill her. Just a single bolt. It was no more than she deserved for the destruction and havoc she'd wreaked, for those she'd already killed and those she would kill in the future, all in the name of greed.

Amadora took a step back under Kitieri's glare, clinging to her twitching snarl even as it faltered, and Kitieri closed her lightning off with a clenched fist.

Not yet.

"You measure a Church by its power," Kitieri said, for Amadora's ears alone. "I measure it by its people. Its heart. A Church should *serve*, not control and murder. So you tell me, Amadora, who's the real disgrace?"

Amadora scoffed, emboldened by the absence of sparks in Kitieri's hands.

"You know nothing about power," she hissed. "I did you a favor, sending you away. You're just an ignorant little bitch playing at godhood, and I can't *wait* to see you kill those snot-nosed little brats yourself."

Before she could take another breath, Kitieri's fist smashed directly into her smug mouth. Amadora hit the ground with a cry of shock and rage, and Kitieri stooped to her knee to lean over her face before she could recover. Behind her, neither Haldin nor Catarva moved a muscle to pull her back.

"Talk about my siblings one more time and I will end your miserable fucking life," she growled through clenched teeth.

"*Officers*," Amadora cried. "I've been assaulted! *Arrest her!*"

Kitieri stared at her, watching her wave to Haldin and Jorid. A quick glance back at Haldin's expression was enough to send Kitieri into a fit of laughter.

"You think they'll help you?" she asked through continued bursts of giggles. "The people you've undermined, bullied, and imprisoned? The people you've treated as *pawns*? Why should they come to your rescue?"

Amadora turned wide eyes on her, taking on the look of a cornered wild animal.

"You're finished, Amadora," Kitieri said.

Footfalls sounded behind her, and Kitieri glanced over her shoulder to watch Ghentrin's large frame shadow the gateway. She studied him for a moment, unable to make out his expression with the lamp at his back. As Catarva spoke to him, a metallic scrape pulled Kitieri's attention back to Amadora, and she turned just in time to see the flash of steel.

Kitieri jerked away as the dagger's blade sliced through her sleeve, cold metal biting into her arm. She rolled out of range before the blade could find more purchase, kicking the dagger from Amadora's hand, but the woman had already lost her grip. She writhed on the ground, twisting and seizing with her mouth open in a silent scream, and Kitieri whirled to find Haldin's hand outstretched. As he snapped his arm back, Amadora collapsed into a limp pile of black and magenta fabric.

"Try it again," he said, "and I will kill you."

Amadora gasped, desperate for air as her shaking body regained motion. "How…?" she wheezed.

"How dare I?" Haldin leaned forward, and Kitieri was surprised at the intensity in his pale eyes. "Is that really the question you want to ask me?"

"G-Ghentrin!" Amadora reached out her shaking hand, adorned with jeweled rings that sparkled in the light.

"You brought this on yourself, Amadora." A new voice came from behind Ghentrin, and Kitieri realized that Rulka had accompanied him. Amadora's eyes darted to her before coming back to Ghentrin, hard and angry.

"Ghentrin!" she snapped this time, regaining her strength. *"Do something!"*

The man shook his head, his dark beard dragging across his chest. "Get out of here, Amadora," he said. "They know. *Everyone* knows."

Amadora got to her feet, yanking her cloak close around her with a flourish.

"You sniveling traitor," she hissed. "Let me guess—you fell for the promise of forgiveness and some peaceful life if you turned on me. You've never had a spine. None of you have! I made this Church what it was, and I alone can promise your survival! But you want to go soft on me now. How *rich*."

She backed away, inching toward the edge of the light's circle.

"A real shame Stil's pawns never managed to kill you, Catarva," she sneered, with a cutting look at the Baliant. "The false Gadget I gave that man would've done well if this goddamned lightning hadn't been there to test it."

Kitieri's eyes widened, hot ire coursing through her veins. *I fucking knew it.*

The cool night air brought nothing but dizziness as she sucked it in.

"And you deserve to die with them," Amadora told Ghentrin. "Your little moment of conscience will cost you dearly. You want to pretend at nobility and honor now, but it's too late. You can't take back what you've done, and you can't stop the wheels you've set in motion."

She turned, sweeping her eyes over the small gathering. "You will all die, and I will relish your pain."

With that, Amadora spun on her heel and fled into the dark night. Kitieri rushed after her, intent on the billowing magenta disappearing through the border trees, but a strong grip on her arm pulled her back. She whirled, ready to fight the hand that held her until she met Catarva's golden eyes.

"Let her go," Catarva said.

"She'll run right back to Stil!" Kitieri cried, ripping her arm from Catarva's grasp to gesture after the disappearing cloak.

"Let her." Catarva looked down at her. "When can your Chief Advisor be ready?"

Kitieri snapped her mouth shut, taking several steadying breaths through her nose. "She said midday."

"Perfect."

CHAPTER 21

T he late morning sun beat down on Kitieri's back as they walked the streets of Shirasette. People scattered from their path, gaping at Catarva's striking white robes as they passed.

"I still don't understand what makes you think Tiernan will see you," Haldin said, walking on Catarva's other side with his spear cradled in one arm. Five gray officers of Catarva's personal guard trailed them, and Kitieri tried to keep Inra's image from her mind.

"He cannot refuse," Catarva replied. "He is obligated by law to respond to a fellow Baliant, and if he cannot, there will be consequences."

Kitieri stared straight ahead, only half listening as her mind turned to the parts of the plan she had neglected to share with the Baliant.

The high peak of the Church of Histan loomed over the rooftops, and Kitieri's heart fluttered as her system flushed with nerves and, though she hated to admit it, fear. Stil's long, pockmarked face flitted across her mind, and she took a steadying breath.

To deny that Stil scared the shit out of her would be a lie. The worst pain of her life had been at that man's hands, and yet here she was, walking back to him willingly. She glanced over at Catarva, still engaged in discussion with Haldin. What did *she* have to fear? She was half-fucking-god. Stil couldn't touch her.

"Kitieri?" Catarva's soft voice cut into her thoughts. "Are you all right?"

"Yeah. I just… really hate this place."

As they left the shadows, walking directly into the glaring light of Histan's Square, Kitieri braced herself. There was no turning back now.

Squinting against the sun, she scanned the Square for Bat. Two brown cloaks broke from a small group of people near the pillar, mercilessly victim-free at the moment, and Kitieri squinted harder. Admittedly, she didn't know much about the brown-cloaked children, but as she recalled her past observations of their extremely submissive, silent behavior, their interaction with a group of adults outside the Church struck her as odd.

She broke away from Catarva and her guard, heading for the petite cloaked figure at the group's center. The hooded head turned toward her as she approached, and the slight nod confirmed Bat's identity.

"You're early," Bat said.

"So are you," Kitieri replied. She could hear Catarva behind her and knew they needed to move before their arrival was heralded prematurely, but she glanced after the brown cloaks trotting toward the Church. "What was that about?"

"What?"

Kitieri turned a glare on Bat. "*That.*"

She pointed to the brown cloaks and caught the shorter one looking back at her. From under the hood, a wisp of straight, pale hair caught in the breeze as the taller one pulled them forward.

Kitieri's heart plummeted to the stone beneath her feet as she uttered the unconscious whisper. "Jera."

She launched after them, and a hand gripped her arm. As her body twisted involuntarily, Kitieri harnessed the momentum to swing a hard left hook into the side of Bat's head. The woman reeled backwards, and another set of strong hands grabbed Kitieri's arms.

"That's my *sister*!" she shouted.

"Kitieri!" Catarva's voice went in one ear and out the other.

"You were supposed to keep them *safe*!"

Bat recovered, leaning back as Kitieri attempted another swing that never reached full extension. Haldin pulled her back, holding her against him as she kicked and struggled.

"Kitieri." His soft voice in her ear dulled her rage as her breaths came hard and fast, and she looked back past Haldin to find the brown cloaks gone from sight.

"Hands are feeling better, I see," Bat said. "They'll be fine! I told you last night—"

"*Both* of them?" Kitieri shrieked.

"It was Taff's idea. He wanted to help."

Kitieri's fury spiked again, and she bucked in Haldin's grip only for the officer to spin her around away from Bat.

"I understand that you are upset, but this is not the time," Catarva said. "We need to move *now*, or Stil will be warned of our presence. We've already made too much of a scene."

Her hard tone forced sense into Kitieri's wild anger, and her breathing slowed.

"Okay. I know. I got it," she said, splaying her hands.

Haldin reluctantly released his tight hold on her as Kitieri drew deep gulps of air into her lungs. Confident she would keep her composure, Catarva turned for the Church stairs, every eye in the Square trained on her striking figure. Haldin stayed right behind Kitieri as she followed the Baliant, and Bat appeared in her peripheral vision just outside swinging range.

"They're invisible in those robes," Bat said. "I promise. They were by far the best candidates for the job."

"Don't fucking speak to me," Kitieri hissed. "I am flattening your nose the next chance I get."

"Fair enough," Bat said. "But you'll thank me when this is over and you have that baby girl in your arms."

"Keep talking and I'll upgrade you to a bolt of lightning."

"Shit, Bat, I don't think the Baliant *needs* a personal guard."

Kitieri looked back at the new voice to find the small group that had accompanied Bat pulling off their cloaks, revealing sleek blue uniforms that matched the long sash trailing down Kitieri's left side. The young woman in front flashed Bat a blindingly white smile, contrasting against skin darker than Catarva's, her black hair pulled back into a tight bun.

"Kitieri," Bat said, "meet your Commander, Lara."

"Go to hell," Kitieri snapped at Bat, before turning a kind smile on Lara. "It's a pleasure to meet you, Commander. Thank you—*all* of you —for being here."

"I assure you, Baliant, the pleasure is ours." Lara's bright smile widened.

As they approached the wide Church stairs, Kitieri picked up the pace to walk directly beside Catarva. Tears of anger and worry for her brother and sister stung her eyes, and she bit down hard on her cheek to keep them at bay. If there was ever a moment to not show weakness, it was now.

"Stop." One of the red officers at the door put out a hand. "Who—"

"You know who I am." Catarva's commanding voice bounced off the smooth Church walls, and the officer shrank back as he exchanged glances with his partner. "Baliant Catarva Tihnerin of the Church of Enahris, and…"

Kitieri started as Catarva looked to her.

"Baliant Kitieri Manon of the Church of Shirasette," she introduced herself. The words may as well have been rocks on her tongue for how awkward they felt, but the red officers' expressions changed quickly.

"We demand to speak with Histan's Baliant," Catarva said.

"Th-the Baliant is currently unavaila—"

The officer's words dried up in his throat as Catarva pulled out a tight scroll of papers bound with a silver ribbon, which she slipped off the end.

"According to the law of Shirasette," she said, eyes scanning the page, "a Church Baliant must be fully capable of carrying out *all* duties. This includes the responsibility of communication with their fellow Baliant, or Baliants, as the case may be."

As Catarva looked up, the red officer paled. "Go get Stil," he muttered to the other.

"Stil said he wanted no interruptions—"

"Any Advisor, then." The first officer spoke through clenched teeth. As the second reached for the door, it sprang open from the inside.

"What seems to be the problem here?" asked a squat man in a black robe, and Kitieri instantly recognized him as the man who'd accused her of trading the fake Gadgets with the black market. Beso.

"Advisor," Catarva said, voice level and cool, "we have come to speak with your Baliant."

"Ah, Catarva..." Beso grumbled, looking as if he wished he'd never come to the door.

"*Baliant* Catarva," she corrected him. "And this is Baliant Kitieri Manon of the Church of Shirasette."

Beso's beady eyes panned to Kitieri, growing three times their normal size. "YOU—"

"According to city law," Catarva spoke over him, "Baliant Tiernan has an obligation to reply to his fellow leaders. Written requests have been ignored and denied, and we are now demanding the Baliant's presence."

Going red in the face, Beso looked between Kitieri and Catarva. "This... *this* wretch is not a Baliant! I will not—"

"I assure you, she is," Catarva said. "And currently in much higher standing than your own, given that she is able to speak for her own Church."

Beso's red cheeks took on a purple hue, and a vein in his forehead looked ready to pop.

"You know the law, Advisor," Catarva went on. "Without leadership, your Church is invalid. A Church must have a capable Baliant, and it is our right to speak with him."

Through his sputtering, Beso managed to find a few of his words and drew himself up as tall as he could go.

"These things must be handled through the Chief Advisor," he said. "He is in close council with the Baliant, and will be able to—"

"We didn't ask for the Chief Advisor." Kitieri's own voice surprised her. "We asked to speak to the Baliant."

"You have no authority—"

"She *does*." The razor-sharp edge in Catarva's tone cut across Beso's words, sending him back a step. "Advisor, take us to your Baliant immediately, or forfeit the credentials of your Church."

Beso's eyes darted between them as panic started to set in. Though Kitieri wasn't familiar with the law Catarva had invoked, the Advisor clearly was. He huffed repeatedly, as if struggling to catch his breath, while his face changed colors.

"Before sunset, if you please," Catarva said with a cold smile.

With a rush of pent-up air, Beso whipped around to march into the Church; Kitieri exchanged a quick glance with Catarva as they followed, officers filing behind them. As they made their way through the Sanctuary, Kitieri noticed an increase in red officers around them, lining the walls to watch their procession. Though their presence set her further on edge, every red uniform she saw here was one fewer to discover Eriat or her siblings. Kitieri ground her teeth, suppressing the emotion that welled up in her chest at the thought of Taff and Jera within these walls. If Stil discovered them...

Beso stormed past Histan's towering sculpture with its sword held high, shoving a brown cloak aside on his way to the door. Kitieri sucked in a breath, sparks rushing to her fingers, but a hard glance from Catarva stilled her impulse.

The Advisor labored up the stairs at an excruciating pace, puffing with each step. Catarva followed with poise and patience, while Kitieri felt ready to rip her hair from her scalp. The sun slid further into the afternoon with each passing window until she was fighting the urge to scream. The narrow staircase made her feel itchy and sweaty, and Kitieri tugged at the tight, high-necked collar of her robe. Glancing back, she caught Lara's dark eyes, filled with the same frustration as she bobbed her head impatiently, and grinned. At least she wasn't the only one.

At long last, the marathon of stairs came to an end, and Kitieri found herself facing a set of double doors almost identical to those of Catarva's chambers. Two red officers stood to each side, watching the congregation file up the stairs with mounting concern on their faces. As Beso charged straight for the doors, the officers stepped in to block his path.

"I'm sorry, Advisor, you cannot enter," one said. "By orders of the Chief Advisor, no one is to enter these chambers under any circumstances."

Beso rolled his eyes. "Get out of my way, will you?"

"I'm sorry, Advisor. Chief—"

"Well, Stil's not here!"

"I cannot—"

"I am your superior!" Beso shouted. "Unless you want a taste of the pillar tomorrow morning, you will move."

Whatever fear of Stil the officers harbored, their fear of the pillar was clearly stronger, and Kitieri actually pitied the young men as they shuffled out of the way. Beso burst through the double doors into the Advisors' empty meeting room.

"Wait here," he growled, continuing through the next door. Though she did not dare say it aloud, Kitieri was amazed they'd gotten this far. If Stil had come to the door instead of Beso…

That's why Catarva let Amadora go last night. Kitieri smirked.

"I don't like this." Catarva's soft voice beside her grabbed Kitieri's attention, wiping the smirk from her face.

"What?" she whispered.

"Something's wrong. Tiernan isn't… here."

"What? How do you know that?"

"I should be able to feel him, sense him, from here and I can't. It's like—"

A strangled shriek from within the Baliant's chambers reached their ears, and Kitieri rushed after Catarva into the spacious dining room, where a middle-aged woman with wild brown curls stood planted in the next doorway.

"What are they doing here?" she hissed vehemently, fingers latched to either side of the doorframe like long claws. "How dare you, Beso! No one enters here!"

"Amilla, they're invoking the law," Beso said.

"I don't care! No one goes in here."

Catarva clasped her hands politely in front of her as she turned to Beso. "Need I repeat myself?"

Beso's mouth opened and closed like an ugly fish that had flopped out of the water, lying on the bank struggling for air, and Kitieri studied Amilla more closely. What kind of power did this caretaker have to make Beso consider crossing Catarva again?

While the Advisor floundered, Amilla fixed Catarva with a cutting glare.

"The Baliant is not well," she said with a threatening edge. "You will have to return at a later date."

Catarva pushed past Beso, dwarfing him with her presence.

"I have officially submitted request after request to speak with Baliant Tiernan, and all have been denied. I have my records and those of your Church to prove it. This man has been 'unavailable' for ten years. This *is* the later date."

"You can't just—"

"I can, and I will. Move aside."

Panic mounted in Amilla's eyes as Catarva approached, and she bared her teeth like a cornered animal. The woman's behavior sent chills down Kitieri's spine, and apprehension rose in her throat. She was clearly unbalanced, but insane enough to attack a Baliant...?

"Catarva," she warned, starting forward, and Amilla's crazed eyes snapped to her.

"You," she snarled. "I know who you are. The sniveling little bitch who broke my Stil's nose. He'll be delighted to see you've returned."

Kitieri's narrowed eyes widened as she understood Amilla's words. *My Stil.* The Baliant's sole caretaker. A wave of nausea accompanied the dark realization, and Kitieri sucked in a breath.

"All right, that's it," she said, summoning white sparks to her fingertips. "This is over. Get the fuck out of the way."

Amilla glanced at the popping sparks with a hiss-like laugh. "You want to kill me?"

"I want you to step aside so I don't have to."

Something flashed in the woman's eyes, and with a wild screech she rushed at Kitieri, clawed hands aiming for her throat. As Kitieri braced for the physical impact, a flash of blue darted to her side. Lara whipped around behind Amilla, throwing her arm across her throat in a stranglehold before slamming her to the ground.

"Haldin, the door," Catarva barked, and Haldin's boot slammed into the thick wood just over the handle. Amilla unleashed a bloodcurdling scream, writhing on the floor beneath Lara's knee, as Haldin's third kick splintered the wood and threw open the door.

Stagnant air wafted from the room, hitting Kitieri like a wall. Haldin motioned back for them to follow, pointing to the great curtained bed against the far wall. Dim lamps burned on either side, casting an eerie light.

Kitieri crossed slowly, gagging on the thick air.

"Baliant Tiernan?" Catarva called. "We have come to speak with you."

Silence hung in the room like a heavy blanket, threatening to smother any who walked here. Coming to the foot of the bed, Kitieri exchanged a nod with Catarva before they split to each side, pulling back the gold and crimson curtains.

Kitieri fell back with a garbled shout, letting the curtain fall closed. Clutching her stomach, she emptied its contents into a nearby decorative vase, retching until there was nothing left. Her hands shook on the edges of the vase, and she squeezed her eyes closed in an attempt to eradicate what she'd seen.

"Fucking hells," came Bat's low voice behind her.

"What?" Beso bellowed. "What is it?"

He ripped the curtain back, uttering a pathetic cry. Kitieri spat into the vase, ridding her mouth of its foul taste, and straightened.

Lying in the bed was a shriveled, blackened corpse, fingers curled into gnarled knots over its chest. Catarva reappeared from the other side, her expression a mix of horror and outrage.

"This," she said to Beso, pointing, "is an embalmed body, at *least* ten years dead."

Beso's stubby fingers trembled as he held his hands up in defense. "I... I didn't—"

"Enough of the lies!" Catarva boomed, and Beso leapt back like she'd swung a sword at him. "Your Baliant has been dead for *years*, and you have kept it a secret. Every single action, every single policy, every single person killed in the name of Histan over the past ten years is *invalid*. Your Church and its vicious ways are over."

Beso backed away, eyes darting about the room for some kind of escape, when a chilling voice stole Kitieri's breath.

"How kind of you to pay our dear Baliant a visit."

Kitieri's blood turned to ice as Stil's tall, lean form darkened the door.

"Stil," Beso stuttered, "I-I didn't know—"

"Shut up," Stil snapped at him. "Go ring the bells. We've an important announcement to make to the Square."

As Beso fled the room, Kitieri spotted the magenta cloak and caught a glimpse of Amadora's silver hair behind Stil. Past her, Amilla's shrill, crazed laugh filled the room, and flashes of red, gray, and blue uniforms caught her eye .

Shit. Her heart pounded.

"Stil." Hatred dripped from Catarva's lips as she said his name. "You hid Tiernan's death to take illegal control of this Church."

Stil smirked. "I had to, didn't I? You know Chief Advisors are ineligible for Baliant, and Tiernan was a bumbling idiot."

"You know what this means," Catarva spat. "You have no Baliant, and your Church is in collapse. Your power is gone."

The venomous grin that spread further across Stil's long features struck terror into Kitieri's heart, and she clenched her fists to stop their shaking.

"Oh, I don't think so," he said. "I *am* the power of this Church. They have followed no one but me for the past decade, and not a single Advisor, officer, or common pig will dare cross me."

He advanced into the room, eyes locked on Catarva.

"You fail because you're *weak*, Catarva. Your feeble attempts at handouts and saving people have backfired, and coming here will be the end of your reign. It's your word against mine now, and *I* witnessed something very different in this room today. Your Board will back my version of events, and confirm that you came here to murder Baliant Tiernan because you knew there was no chance at victory over our superior military force."

Kitieri's heart was in her throat, listening to Stil's words with abject horror, and she glanced to Catarva. Was that a *smile*?

"It appears you've not been updated on current events," she said softly, gaze flitting to Amadora's form as she made to slink away through the dining room. Stil's confidence flickered as he spun on the woman, stomping on the trail of her cloak.

"What is she talking about?" he demanded. Amadora froze, shoulders hunched. Stil's chest inflated with rage as he turned fully to her. "You LOST THE BOARD?"

His voice thundered through the room, rattling the narrow windows. Amadora cowered before him, trembling hands coming up over her head.

"They betrayed me—"

"You *lied* to me."

Quivering violently, Amadora turned slowly to face him. "I thought—"

"Silence." Stil's cutting tone severed Amadora's excuse, and he lifted a fiery hand. "You are beyond useless."

Amadora's screams filled the room as she went up in a giant burst of flames. She ran from the chambers, flailing like a tattered rag doll and trailing black smoke behind her as Stil whirled back to face Catarva.

"It doesn't matter," he said over Amadora's echoing screams. "They will still take my word over yours, because *I'm* the one they fear. You're finished—*both* of you."

He turned a sneer on Kitieri, his hand engulfed in flames once more. Kitieri fought her paralysis, calling her lightning to her hands, but it balked as she tried to send it to Stil.

His Gadget. FUCK.

Stil brought his hand down, and an intense blast of heat washed over Kitieri from one side. She ducked away, shielding her head and face as the entire bed caught fire. Angry flames traveled up the thick curtains to lick the ceiling, traveling at an alarming rate to the walls around them.

"Amilla, get the money and meet me in the Square," Stil snapped.

"Where are you going?" came the woman's shrill voice.

"The cintra."

The sound of the Church's bells shook the floor beneath Kitieri's feet, and she choked and coughed as the room filled with dark smoke. Peering through the haze, she found Stil gone from the doorway.

"Get out!" Haldin shouted, and Kitieri followed Catarva's white robes out of the room. Lara awaited her with a ready stance, the blood streaming from her temple turning the blue collar of her uniform a grotesque purple.

"Are you all right?" Kitieri leaned in close as the haze between them grew thicker.

"Fine, Baliant. Let's get out!"

Smoke followed them through the meeting room and out into the hallway, where Haldin and Catarva ran for the stairs. Kitieri stopped cold, spinning around as Bat nearly smashed into her. She caught the woman's arms, pulling Bat's face in close to hers.

"Taff and Jera," she said over the crackling flames. "Where are they?"

"They're probably long gone by now, safe with the officers," Bat replied. "Come on, we need to — "

"I'm *not* leaving them!"

Bat paused, then gave a curt nod. "I'll show you where they went."

They rushed down the stairs after Catarva, now long out of sight with her gray officers, and Bat hooked a left turn on one of the wide landings that branched into a new labyrinth of hallways. Even down several floors, the fire and smoke followed them, eating through the ceiling and walls like a ravenous monster, and Bat cursed under her breath.

"This fire is unnatural," she said. "Stil is accelerating it. He's determined to bring this whole thing to the ground."

Kitieri's heart raced as they sprinted through the nearly deserted network of hallways. Why weren't people running?

"Where is everybody?" she panted.

"The bells." Bat jerked her head up to the ever-present sound of their deep chiming. "They're congregating in the Square. Almost there!"

As Bat turned another corner, Kitieri spotted a huddle of dark cloaks at the far end cornered by a fallen, burning beam, some cradling swaddled, crying bundles. At their front, a shock of straight pale hair sent Kitieri's heart into her throat.

"Jera!" she cried, closing in on the group.

The girl did not look up, focused intently on the beam with her hands, and Kitieri realized she was attempting to summon enough water to put out the wide beam.

"*Jera!*" she screamed louder, and the girl snapped her head up. Beads of sweat dripped from her face, damp hair clinging to her skin as she broke her focus.

"Kitieri!" Her wide smile showed her missing tooth. "You're here!"

Another beam collapsed behind them, and a wave of searing heat filled the hallway as one of the swaddled infants screamed.

"All right!" Bat shouted. "Hold your breath, everyone!"

As soon as Kitieri could fill her lungs, fighting not to choke on the building smoke, Bat waved a hand. Kitieri frowned at her as she stood, eyes closed, with one hand clenched in a fist.

What in the hells is she...

In the next instant, the flames around them sputtered and faded, shrinking back into the walls and disappearing from the beam.

Air. Kitieri's eyes grew wide. *Fire can't breathe without air.*

Bat beckoned the children forward, directing them under the high end of the beam in silence. Kitieri grabbed Jera's hand as she crawled under, and they rushed back down the hallway to the stairs. Bat let out a loud rush of air, and the fire roared back to life behind them as they ran for the ground floor.

"Jera, where's Taff?" Kitieri asked.

"He went ahead," Jera replied, panting as she clung to Kitieri's hand. "He went first so there weren't that many of us together."

"So he's outside?"

"I think so. I was supposed to wait a while, and then the fire started... but we got baby Vina! Ani has her!"

Jera twisted even as Kitieri pulled her forward down the stairs, pointing at one of the crying babies in the arms of a brown cloak behind them.

"That's amazing, Jera! You did *incredible*," Kitieri said, squeezing her hand. "Come on, let's hurry."

The fire had not yet reached the Sanctuary as they sprinted down the red runner, bursting out into the afternoon sunlight. Kitieri pulled up short at the top of the wide stairs, jaw dropping at the massive crowd milling in the Square. Red uniforms punctuated the sea of dark clothing as they pressed into the open space, avoiding only the central pillar and its dais, where Catarva stood surrounded by her guard. Water elements, officer and commoner alike, lined up before the Church in an attempt to douse the raging flames that licked the stone façade through shattered windows.

"Good people! Members of the Church of Histan!"

Kitieri turned, searching for the source of the shout, and looked directly above her at the bottom of the balcony protruding over the Church's doors.

"I carry heavy news!" Beso's voice continued.

"Come on, kids." Bat moved forward, ushering the brown cloaks to the stairs, and Kitieri looked down at Jera's hand still entwined in her own.

"Go with Bat," she whispered, looking up to catch the woman's eye. "She *promises* to keep you safe this time."

Bat twitched an eyebrow with an easy grin, extending a hand to Jera.

"I *promise* promise," she said.

With another nod from Kitieri, Jera trotted after Bat and the other brown cloaks, winding through the clamoring crowd like unseen ghosts. Kitieri ran down the stairs, shouldering forcefully through the crowd until she reached the stone steps of the dais.

"Our Baliant has been *murdered*—" Beso cried.

"Where have you been?" Catarva hissed as Kitieri broke through the crowd to step up beside her.

"Saving my sister." Kitieri turned to survey the crowd. *But where is Taff?*

" —by these two!"

Kitieri looked up at the balcony, where Beso pointed a shaking finger at them as a roar erupted from the gathered crowd. Gray and blue officers formed a circle around the dais, weapons at the ready as the people turned toward them. As Beso opened his mouth to shout again, Kitieri felt a powerful surge of energy pull on her lightning. A warning...?

"These so-called Baliants have committed an act of war against our Church, and—"

A powerful bolt of blue lightning tore through the sky, and Kitieri gasped as her element zipped through her.

Her relief at holding it back turned to horror as little pieces pelted her head and neck. She held out her hand, catching the black, gravelly bits that fell from the sky, and looked up to see the balcony empty. Gagging, she dropped the charred pieces to the ground.

"The warnings," she rasped, hoarse. "There was barely any warn—"

"I was wrong."

Kitieri snapped around to Catarva, whose dark skin shone with sweat. Another Strike cracked on the far edge of the Square, inciting a wave of panic through the crowd.

"I was wrong," Catarva said again, voice breaking as screams erupted. "The Church of Enahris was never the weak one. *This* was the broken Church. This one, with all its power..."

Blue lightning cracked with minimal warning right beside Kitieri, charring a young woman mid-scream.

"What is happening?" Kitieri screamed over the mayhem.

"The two years we thought we had are up." Catarva's whisper cut through the chaos. "The balance is gone. The Church of Histan has fallen."

CHAPTER 22

Catarva's words ringing in her ears, Kitieri looked out over the panicking crowd with a deep, raw horror growing in her gut. Hundreds of people pushing against one another in a futile attempt to flee, her siblings somewhere among them, all ripe for the reaping as black smoke billowed up from the Church to block out the afternoon sun.

The two years are up...

Another Strike reared its head, shooting a hard, fast warning through Kitieri's body. Her lightning screeched, raking down her arms in an attempt to burst free, and Kitieri squeezed her eyes closed.

No. You can't lose control. Not now.

She clenched her fists, stilling her element even as another warning zap threatened to wrench it free. No emotion, no emotion...

After three quick warnings, the Blue Killer roared down for her. She raised her hand as the energy tore through the sky, repelling it before it could touch her. Catarva cried out beside her, doubling over with a staggering step.

"Shit!" Kitieri's hand flew to her mouth. "Catarva, I'm sorry, I—"

"No!" Catarva waved her hand. "Do it. It's the only way now."

"What does that mean?" Kitieri asked. "What happens now?"

The Baliant shook her head, amber eyes wide as she lifted them to the flames rising from the Church roof, charring the light stone where they licked from the windows. Another set of warnings came, and the repelled Strike sent Catarva to her knees this time.

"I don't know how many Strikes I can fend off," Kitieri panted, wiping the sweat that was beginning to drip from her brow into her eyes.

"Just as long as you can," Catarva ground out.

The double doors to the Church were flung open and a tall form emerged, silhouetted by the hot, sinister glow from the flames within. Face darkened with smudges of soot, Stil stepped out onto the stairs, eyes locked onto Kitieri's, and the people scrambled out of his path to the pillar. As the man stepped out of the Church's shadow, Kitieri's gaze dropped to the small form he gripped before him.

"Taff." The whimper tore from Kitieri's lips as her heart lurched into her throat.

"Stealing my cintra," Stil growled, words simmering in a boiling anger. Every trace of his former smugness was gone, replaced with a maniacal glint in his narrowed eyes and twisted snarl. "You killed our Baliant, and *stole from me*."

His fury ripped across the Square, hitting Kitieri with almost physical force as Taff flinched in the man's grip.

"Well, I've got something that belongs to you, too." His powerful thunder came down to a menacing growl as his long fingers slid up to grip Taff's jaw. Kitieri started forward off the dais before Haldin and Lara caught each of her arms, pulling her back.

"Get the *fuck* off me!" she hissed, jerking against them.

"Kitieri, don't take his bait," Catarva whispered behind her. "Don't—"

Stil's hand turned red hot, his fire searing Taff's skin, and Kitieri's brother let out a heart-wrenching scream as he fought the man's grasp.

"*Taff!*" she cried through streaming tears. "I will *fucking kill you*, Stil!"

The man released Taff's jaw with a dark laugh, leaving angry, blistered skin where his hand had rested.

"Give me back what is mine, and I may leave him partially unscarred."

"I don't have your cintra!" Kitieri shot back.

Stil planted his hand on the side of Taff's face, covering his cheek and right eye, and Kitieri barely heard her own scream as it sounded in tandem with Taff's.

She twisted hard against the officers' hands, wrenching free from Lara first. Though Haldin lurched forward to catch her, Kitieri was already flying off the dais, all of her hate and anger trained on Stil as his grin widened.

He shoved Taff to the ground as Kitieri bounded up the wide Church steps, lightning snapping in white arcs all around her. She didn't care how unruly the element got now. The stronger the better to *end* this miserable piece of shit.

A warning surged through her body, and Kitieri skidded to a stop halfway up the steps. Stil held both hands out, engulfed in flame, awaiting her with a crazed smile.

"Ahh, going to kill me?" he mocked her. "Your lightning can't overcome the cintra. You've *never* been strong enough. You're nothing but a pathetic little bitch."

"You're right." Kitieri's chest heaved, sweat pouring freely down her face and neck in the face of the roaring fire that spilled from the Church doors. The second warning came, and Kitieri let her lightning react to its charge in all its brilliant glory. It snapped and sizzled, sending Stil back a step as his confidence wavered.

"My lightning isn't strong enough to overcome a Gadget," she said, advancing slowly up the steps now. "But your time is up."

Stil emitted a hiss, lip curled. "I will *always* rule. *I* am the feared one. *I* carry the power. I have ruled this Church for *ten years* without so much as a single acknowledgement."

Despite the churning panic, Kitieri felt the crowd quiet behind her as Stil's voice cut through. His eyes widened, realizing what he'd just announced, and his snarl deepened.

Kitieri laughed, lifting her hand as the third warning came. She pushed its energy forward, knocking Stil back several more steps, and his wide eyes snapped up to her as he regained his balance.

"You can't touch me!" he shouted. "You can't breach a PCR—"

"I don't have to, Stil," Kitieri said, gaining the top of the stairs. "The two years you thought you had are up. The day the Blue Killer takes over is here—the day the lightning overpowers the Gadgets."

Stil's eyes darted back and forth as he backed closer to the intense heat of the fire, seething through his stained teeth.

Kitieri raised her hand, calling the coming Strike as she lowered her voice to a quiet growl. "And the Blue Killer answers to only one."

Stil's mouth twisted into a horrified scream as Kitieri harnessed the Blue Killer's full power. Her lightning sang within her, working in tandem with the Strike as the blue bolt came crashing down.

A deafening crack and spray of rubble pushed Kitieri back, and she lifted her arm to protect her face. Through the clearing dust, dark smoke arose from a blackened pile of ashes where Stil had stood, mingling in the breeze with the fire he'd set ablaze.

Absolute silence permeated the Square, and Kitieri wondered if the blast of the Strike had damaged her hearing. She turned to face the crowd, and watched one man lift his fist with a triumphant cry. Cheers rippled through the people, growing to a roar as Kitieri stood paralyzed by shock.

Don't cheer... Cold dread flooded her system, turning her blood to ice. *Run.*

Another warning jolted her, reigniting the desperate cries from the Square as people resumed their stunted escapes. The exits between buildings were crammed with bodies, slowing foot traffic to nearly a standstill.

"Kitieri?"

At Taff's rasping call, Kitieri rushed to her brother's side, ignoring the burn of the second warning as she lifted his shoulders from the stone in a gentle cradle. "Gods, Taff, I'm so sorry. I'm so fucking sorry. I never meant —"

"You killed him." His burned face was blistered in the shape of a handprint, one gruesome eye melted closed. Kitieri nodded, biting hard on her bottom lip.

The third warning ripped her lightning from her hands with searing pain, and she scrambled back away from her brother. As much as she longed to hold him, it was too dangerous. *She* was dangerous.

As soon as she repelled the Strike, another warning pummeled her.

"Shit," she whispered, closing her eyes. This wasn't sustainable. Her eyes stung with sweat, and her hands were shaking. Even repelling *one* was exhausting...

The warnings doubled up, one Strike's second warning colliding with another's first, and Kitieri's shoulders bent forward against the agony. Her lightning lashed out every which way, utterly uncontrollable now, and it was all she could do to keep track of the warnings. She became vaguely aware of Catarva's huddled form on the dais, suffering worse than she was. Blue, gray, and red officers alike ushered people from the Square, working to unclog the exits, but Kitieri feared it would never be enough. Even if they made it into their homes, what then? They would only be trapped there, facing the slow death of starvation...

She sank to her knees, borrowing the energy it took to stand to repel more Strikes. It was all she could do now. Hands shaking violently, she threw yet another Strike back into the atmosphere. Maybe this was it... the best way a lightning could hope to die.

The sound of clattering hooves and wooden wheels reached Kitieri's ears, and she lifted her head. Atop a giant wagon, driving four muscular draft horses out into the Square, Eriat shouted something at Bat.

"What in the *hells*..." was the only phrase Kitieri could make out.

"Eriat, you son of a bitch!" Bat's voice came from much closer to Kitieri, somewhere near the base of the stairs. "You did it!"

"You doubted me?"

"Come on, kids, to the wagon. The cintra will protect you."

Through the pain of two more double warnings, Kitieri watched the brown cloaks trot to the side of the wagon as Bat came running up the stairs.

"Kitieri," she breathed, lifting her fingers to her mouth as they locked eyes.

"Stay away from me," Kitieri managed, dropping her gaze as another bolt of white lightning lashed out to char the carved stone banister. "Just... get Taff. Help him."

Though she couldn't see Bat's nod, she knew it was there. The woman slipped past her, lifting Taff to his feet to help him down the stairs, and Kitieri closed her eyes. The Blue Killer came again, one Strike after another, and she pushed it back with every fiber of strength she still possessed.

At least Taff and Jera were safe for n —

Ice-cold air blasted in Kitieri's face, blowing her hair off her neck and freezing the sweat that drenched her skin and clothing as a blinding light beyond any Strike flashed in the Square. Kitieri blinked repeatedly in the wake of the flash, rubbing the tears from her eyes to see two vague figures at the foot of the stairs.

"Catarva." The smooth, buttery voice, registering just a hint of surprise, was unlike anything Kitieri had ever heard, and she squinted through the smoke. A dark-skinned woman in a long white dress faced the pillar, black hair falling in tight curls all the way down her back.

With a deep, slow breath, the Baliant forced herself upright, lifting her chin. "Mother."

The simple word shook Kitieri from her exhausted daze, and her eyes opened wide.

"You finally came." Despite her efforts to still her shaking, Catarva's voice still trembled.

"Would you mind telling me what's happening here?" the woman asked. Enahris. A *god*. A *real* god, standing right here—

A deep baritone voice rattled Kitieri's core as the figure beside Enahris turned. "Why the *fuck* is my Church on fire?"

A tall, broad-shouldered man stood at the base of the stairs, looking up at the all-consuming inferno raging behind Kitieri, and she was struck by his resemblance to his statue.

Histan.

Enahris turned beside him, piercing golden eyes coming to land on Kitieri. Another warning pulsed in the air, and Enahris' eyes narrowed suspiciously.

"The balance is *broken*," Catarva said. "Look around you. Your people have been dying for years, and it finally had to come to this. Our end."

Enahris tore away from Kitieri to face her daughter once more.

"And whose fault is that?" Her buttery tone laced with a subtle venom as Kitieri gritted her teeth against the second warning. "What were the last words I said to you when I left you here in my stead, Catarva?"

"You mean when you abandoned me at seven years old to do the work of a *god*?"

Even facing her back, Kitieri could see Enahris' bristling anger awaken as the third warning pulsed.

"It doesn't take a god to run a Church," Enahris said. "You should have been more than capable of balancing out *this* idiot."

As she gestured to the god beside her, Kitieri called and repelled the looming Strike. Three distinct cries rang through the Square, and Kitieri looked up again to see Enahris and Histan sprawled out on the stones, Catarva clinging to the pillar for support.

Enahris pushed herself up, golden eyes snapping to Kitieri with glowing hatred.

"You," she hissed, climbing to her feet. "*You're* the one causing this." She stalked forward, hateful gaze locked on Kitieri.

"She did not cause this," Catarva said. "You did. Your negligence has destroyed this world."

"*My* negligence!" Enahris spun back to her daughter.

"Enahris," Histan barked. "Enough. We have to fix this."

"*I* don't have to fix anything," the god hissed. "You're the one with the Church on fire, Histan."

Histan opened his mouth to retort, glanced up at the fire, and snapped his mouth shut with a click of his teeth.

"I did my part," Enahris continued. "I left an heir to keep the balance while you"—Enahris emitted a low, terrifying laugh—"you were too busy living it up, chasing tail and getting drunk in any realm but this one. You never cared about this place or your duty, while I did everything in my power to—"

"You never gave a shit, either!" Histan fired back. "Leaving a half-mortal child in charge of your work is *hardly* responsible. If I'd known this place was falling apart, I would have been here, but neither of us knew until those shocks started coming full force. Now that we know, we have a responsibility to fix it."

"No, Histan. This is not my fault! I won't—"

"The High Council won't give a flying fuck whose fault it is," Histan thundered. "Our job was to keep balance and we failed, which means we will *both* go down for this."

"No." Enahris stepped toward her counterpart. "We won't. You want to fix this so badly? You suddenly have such a bleeding heart for these people? Then break your bond to this world and give me your crest."

Histan's hand flew to the half-circle brooch pinned to his chest, glinting gold against his black shirt, and Kitieri noticed its mirror image in silver against Enahris' white dress. Just like the Baliants' crests...

Histan shook his head. "There must be two. Our laws—"

"Break your bond and bear the consequences of your own failure, Histan," Enahris cried.

No... Kitieri watched Histan lower his bright blue eyes to the golden crest. She met Catarva's eyes and saw her racing thoughts reflected in the Baliant's face.

Horrified and enthralled by the gods' argument, Kitieri had almost missed the next set of warnings. She felt the Strike's surge of energy at the last instant as it moved to claim a young girl gaping in utter awe at the gods. As Kitieri reached out to call the lightning, Enahris whipped around.

"Don't you *dare*!"

A strong force knocked Kitieri back, pushing her dangerously close to the raging fire behind her and breaking her connection with the Blue Killer. In the wake of the loud crack and blue flash that followed, Kitieri twisted to find the little girl's blackened body crumbling into a pile of ash, and felt a hoarse scream leave her throat.

"*Enahris*!"

The god ignored Histan's cry, advancing up the stairs toward Kitieri now. "As a matter of fact," Enahris growled, fiery eyes locked on Kitieri's, "I've had just about enough of you. Your element's usefulness has run its course."

The white-clad god loomed larger than life as she ascended the stairs, towering over Kitieri with a menacing grin. Kitieri curled her fingers, summoning her lightning, and Enahris' dark laugh sent chills down her spine. With a swat of her hand, even from ten paces away, the god knocked the white sparks from Kitieri's hands.

"Idiot," Enahris sneered. "Only a god can kill a god."

Enahris lifted her hand, the air shimmering like a trick of the light over her fingers, and Kitieri braced herself for the pain. For death.

I told you, I'm not a god.

"Mother."

Catarva's silky voice cut through Kitieri's thoughts, and she lifted her head to find the Baliant standing only one step behind Enahris.

"Stay out of this, Catarva," Enahris snapped, looking over her shoulder. "You're as much a failure as *that* poor excuse of a god. My biggest mistake was trusting you to lead my Church."

Catarva stood as still as the pillar, her expression that perfect picture of calm that Kitieri had come to so deeply respect.

"But don't worry." Enahris tilted her head with a patronizing smile. "When this creature is gone and Histan breaks his bond, I doubt even *you* can screw it up from there."

Enahris turned back to Kitieri, still wearing that sickly sweet grin as Catarva spoke.

"I am twice the leader you'll ever be."

The god's grin morphed into a snarl, but she did not look back.

"And if you want Kitieri dead, you'll have to go through me."

Enahris rolled her eyes, throwing her head back. "Oh, spare me the theatrics, Catarva. I'm not in the mood, and you're not god enough to stop me."

"I am."

Catarva lifted her hand to the back of Enahris' neck, long fingers curling around her throat from behind. Enahris went completely still, save cutting her eyes to the side.

"Only a god can kill a god. Isn't that right, Mother?" Catarva's sneer was unsettlingly identical to Enahris'.

"You're not a god," Enahris hissed. "You're a disgusting half-breed. A necessary evil. Try to kill me, and you'll find out just how weak you really are."

Catarva leaned in close to her mother's ear. "But I *can* kill you."

"You will die."

Catarva's snarl widened into a smile, and her amber eyes flicked to Kitieri. "Gladly."

"Catarva, *no!*" Kitieri had barely managed the words before Enahris' golden eyes shot open wide, tongue lolling from her mouth in rasping gags under Catarva's vice-grip.

They toppled to the stone, Catarva's hands locked around her mother's throat, with a deafening scream. Enahris clawed at her as they began to emanate a bright aura, heat rolling off their bodies in palpable waves until Kitieri could no longer watch. She shielded her eyes from the horrific brilliance until a hot wave of energy rushed over her.

Enahris' human form erupted into a shower of blinding golden sparks, burning Kitieri where they touched her skin, and Catarva collapsed into a still heap.

"*CATARVA*!" Kitieri shrieked, scrambling to her. Gently, she rolled the Baliant over to pull her head into her lap, and weary dark brown eyes looked up at her.

"Kitieri," Catarva whispered, fighting for each shallow, ragged breath. "Shirasette… will look to you."

"No." Kitieri's throat closed off as two tears splashed onto Catarva's dark skin, and a hard sob cut off further speech. Haldin bounded up the stairs, falling to his knees beside Kitieri and Catarva's eyes, now devoid of their amber glow, drifted to him as a soft smile touched her lips.

"I love you, Haldin." Her whisper grew fainter. "I always have."

Tears streaming down his face, Haldin scooped up Catarva's hand and pressed it to his lips. "I love you, too."

Her eyelids flickering open and closed, Catarva slowly dragged her gaze back to Kitieri. Barely audible, she said, "Lead them."

"I can't," Kitieri whispered, swallowing against the sobs that shook her shoulders.

Catarva's faint smile twitched again. "You must."

Smile still on her lips, Catarva's breath left her body, and she went limp in Kitieri's arms. Haldin bent forward, shaking with silent sobs as he held her hand in his, and Kitieri turned away with one fist pressed to her mouth. All the air had fled from her lungs, and she could not seem to replace it as the unbearable pain blocked off her throat.

"She was right."

Kitieri gasped and started at Histan's voice just behind her, twisting to look up at him. As gently as possible, she transferred Catarva's limp body into Haldin's arms, standing shakily on untrustworthy legs. The god's blue eyes registered nothing but pain and remorse as he bowed his head.

"I am sorry," he said. "The gods were meant to guide and teach the people of their bonded worlds, and protect them from harm. In these pursuits, I could not have failed more spectacularly. I see the pain and destruction here, and I know it is our fault. *My* fault."

Kitieri blinked the tears from her eyes, watching Histan carefully.

"I won't ask forgiveness," he continued. "But I see now that gods have only ever harmed this place. With only one god, the destruction and death will continue…" Histan drew in a deep breath, lifting his head. "I will accept the consequences of my failure, and take my leave."

He pulled the golden brooch from his chest, offering it out to Kitieri in the palm of his hand.

"I relinquish my bond to this world, and accept my banishment from the mortal realms."

He pressed the warm metal into Kitieri's hand, lingering only an instant before stepping away. Before Histan's foot could hit the stone, his human form was gone.

A cool, clean breeze stirred across the Square, and Kitieri lifted her head to breathe it in. The relentless heat and pain bled from her body, her element receding until she could feel no trace of the pulsing she'd always carried with her like a second heartbeat. She curled her fingers, calling her lightning back to no answer.

"Haldin," she whispered. "Can you use your element?" She waited for his answer, staring down at her hands.

"N... no," he said.

Kitieri released her pent-up air in a loud rush, tears springing once again to her eyes.

"It's over," she said, curling a fist around Histan's crest. "The elements are gone. The gods' power is gone. It's... *really* over."

A tear streaked down her cheek as Kitieri turned to the Square below. Hundreds of people stared up at her, wide-eyed and uncertain, and stark realization dawned. Thousands more would look to her in that same way in the days, months, and years to come. They would look for a leader.

Catarva's final words sounded in her mind.

You must.

Kitieri nodded, summoning her strength as Haldin stepped up beside her. Her gaze moved from his soft, pale eyes to Lara and the officers at the pillar, to Bat and Eriat at the wagon, to Taff and Jera with little Vina in her arms, and Kitieri smiled through her tears.

She would do what she must, but she didn't have to do it alone. With the Blue Killer gone and the Churches destroyed, the city of Shirasette would finally taste freedom.

And, for the first time since she'd discovered her element, Kitieri found the will to look forward to tomorrow.

EPILOGUE

Kitieri stood at the great window on the top floor of the Council Hall, overlooking the wide courtyard below. A large crowd was beginning to congregate around a veiled central monument, murmuring in hushed, excited tones.

Footsteps on the stairs behind her pulled Kitieri from the window, and she turned to see Bat reach the top of the stairs.

"Oh, don't tell me that's what you're wearing," Bat said, scanning Kitieri's appearance with a dubious look. The past ten years had deepened her wrinkles and brought the wisps of gray in her hair to the forefront, covering almost her entire head in silver.

Kitieri grinned, looking down at her mother's black leather jacket, marred and stitched with repairs. Kitieri found it a miracle the thing had survived at all. It didn't see near the use it once had, but on this particular day, she longed for the closeness of those long gone. The soft, worn leather felt like their touch on her shoulders, guiding her.

"I like it." Kitieri shrugged.

"It's a special occasion," Bat whined.

"Exactly."

Kitieri walked past Bat, running her hand along the wide, smooth banister as she descended the stairs, and the woman followed with a quiet sigh.

"Loosen up," Kitieri laughed, nudging her arm. "It's not like everyone's eyes are on me, alone, anymore."

Bat shot her a quick side smile. "You know that's not true," she said. "Today may be our *official* fresh start, but you're the one who got us here."

"That's completely unfair. I didn't do any of this alone."

"'Tear down the pillar! Level the Churches! Shut down the mines!'" Bat raised a fist with her mock shouting. "Sound familiar?"

Kitieri raised an annoyed eyebrow.

"Point is," Bat said, "they will follow you until you die, equal Council or not."

"I'm still wearing my jacket."

Bat chuckled through her nose. "I know."

Eriat awaited them at the foot of the stairs, dressed in a smart tailored doublet. He twitched a white eyebrow at her attire, and Kitieri held up a hand.

"I don't want to hear it," she said, and felt the two exchange a look behind her back.

"All right, Eriat, can you tell me *now*?" Bat begged for the fortieth time.

"No, woman," Eriat barked good-naturedly. "What would be the point of enduring all your nagging on the subject if I told you ten minutes before the unveiling?"

"It's bullshit that Kitieri knows and I don't."

"Well, it was Kitieri's idea," Eriat said. "I'm just the artist."

Kitieri grinned as Bat released a huffy sigh. Kitieri pulled open the Council Hall's front door, and the sea of smiling faces turned to her with a swell of murmurs. As they resumed their conversations, Kitieri paused at the top of the Hall steps.

"What's wrong?" Bat asked.

"Nothing." Kitieri smiled. "I'm just... proud of them."

Bat nodded, looking out over the crowd. "Took them a long time to stop the cheering thing, didn't it?"

"Way longer than I expected."

A tall figure in a sleek gray jacket approached the base of the stairs, and Kitieri descended at a quick trot. "Well, Taff, don't you clean up nice?"

Though Kitieri stood on the bottom step, her brother still towered over her. Despite the burn scars down the side of his face and the milky white eye where Stil's fire had forever taken his vision, Taff was a dashing young man. Brilliant beyond his twenty-one years, he had easily secured a seat among the twenty Councilors in Shirasette's first city-wide election.

"I figured at least one of us should look the part," Taff said, laughing at the dark grin Kitieri gave him.

"Where's Jera?" she asked, scanning the crowd. She could pick out the other Councilors and their families, and watched Haldin gently stop a child from tugging on the veil that covered Eriat's mysterious creation. His co-chief of the Civil Force, Lara, stood nearby in her matching blue uniform, and flashed Kitieri a bright smile as their eyes met.

"Late, as usual," Taff replied.

"Come on," Bat said, "it's almost time."

As Kitieri followed Bat into the crowd, a high squeak caught her attention. "Councilor Kitieri!"

Kitieri turned to see Tira pushing through the masses, followed by a line of giggling children.

"Tira, you came!" Kitieri stooped to hug the squat woman.

"Well," Tira panted, fanning herself, "rounding up the young ones can be quite a chore some days, but I wouldn't have missed this for the world!"

She turned, smiling fondly at the group as Minna waved emphatically from the rear of the line.

"Wow, they've all grown so much," Kitieri muttered, mostly to herself.

"Ten years now." Tira nodded, planting her hands on her hips. "Can you believe it? I remember when every one of them was just a tiny little baby, all wrapped in brown." A shudder shook Tira's shoulders, and she waved her hand. "Thank goodness those days are over."

Kitieri squeezed her arm with a warm smile. She could not agree more with that sentiment.

The sound of clattering hooves cut off Kitieri's response, and she turned to find herself face to face with a dappled gray horse. Ashes stuck her dark muzzle out, velvety nostrils flaring as she demanded the standard piece of carrot Kitieri always brought with her to the stables.

"Sorry, Ashes!" she laughed, running a hand down the mare's face. "I don't have anything this time. I didn't realize you'd be *coming*."

With the last word, Kitieri threw Ashes' rider an irritated look.

Jera grinned down at her, her long, windswept ponytail catching the late morning sun as she jumped from the saddle.

"Sorry we're late," she said, "there was a situation at the stable."

Coming around the horse, Kitieri saw the mud splattered across her sister's loose white shirt, even flecking her face and unruly bits of hair.

"I can see that." Kitieri folded her arms.

"It's not like you have room to judge appearances here, Kitieri," Taff said from beside her.

Before Kitieri could fire back at her brother, a short bay gelding stopped on Ashes' other side, and a mop of wild dark curls came bouncing around the horse.

"Vina!" Kitieri dropped to one knee as Vina ran to her, and she was met with the scents of mud and horse manure as the girl's body hit hers. "*Oof*, you smell."

Vina stepped back with a huge grin.

"One of the studs got out of his stall, and he was trying to get in with the mares," she announced. "Me and Jera had to round them all up, and—"

"'Jera and I,'" Taff mumbled.

"Oh, leave her alone, Taff," Jera said, waving a hand at him as she crossed to stand beside Vina. "She's turning into a badass little rider, Kitieri, you should see her!"

Kitieri shifted her weight to one leg, planting a hand on her hip. "I'm starting to think you're a bad influence on her, Jera."

Jera slapped a hand to her chest, feigning offense.

"She's not!" Vina piped up. "I love the stable. And the cats. I want to have a shelter for sad, homeless animals when I grow up, too!"

Kitieri smiled down at her.

"You'd be great at that," she said, smoothing the windswept curls atop her head. "But you know what every good shelter owner needs?"

"What?"

"A good education. Starting tomorrow, you're going to spend more time at school than you do at the stable, okay?"

Vina moaned, throwing her head back.

"And Jera is going to make *sure* you do that. Aren't you, Jera?"

Jera rolled her eyes, flipping her hand up in the air. "Yeah, yeah, all right. Hi, Haldin!"

Kitieri looked over her shoulder to see Haldin approaching with Lara behind him, and smiled.

"Are we about ready?" he asked, glancing to the cloth cover billowing in the breeze.

"Yes, yes, it's time!" Eriat clapped his hands with a loud pop. "Kitieri? The honors?"

Hands suddenly tingling with nerves, Kitieri drew in a deep breath. She allowed Haldin to help her up onto the big stone dais surrounding the veiled monument, and a hush fell over the crowd. Kitieri's heart pounded as she looked out over the people, every eye turned to her. She'd practiced this. She could do this... but unexpected emotion clogged her airway as she was struck with the parallels to that day on the steps of the Church of Histan ten years ago. The same expectant people watched her now, craving leadership. Craving stability. And at long last, that was something she finally felt prepared to give.

She swallowed the lump, clearing her throat.

"People of Shirasette," she called, voice echoing back off the Council Hall. "This is the day we've long awaited—the day our loved ones gave their very lives for us to see. This is the day we've worked for, cried for, *bled* for. This is the day we finally take our government and our lives into our own hands, and the Councilors elected by our *own* people take their official seats in office."

Cheering broke out, and Kitieri took the brief pause to swallow another wave of fresh emotion.

"In honor of this day," she continued, quieting the people once more, "Councilor Eriat has created something truly marvelous. To represent the fallen—all those who lost their lives to the lightning, and those who sacrificed for the ones they loved —we honor the woman who truly made this day possible. The woman who made the ultimate sacrifice to free our world of its bonded gods."

Clenching her jaw against the rising emotion, Kitieri grasped a handful of the heavy cloth and pulled down hard. The veil slipped from the top, fluttering to the ground as a collective gasp rose up from the people.

Pale cintra glinted in the sunlight, sparkling in thousands of little crystals brought together to form the tall, proud sculpture.

Kitieri uttered the name, unable to tear her eyes from the beautiful, elegant face. "Catarva Tihnerin."

The roaring cheer that erupted throughout the wide courtyard shook the ground, and Kitieri stepped back off the dais.

"Great job," Bat whispered in her ear, squeezing her shoulder. "Eriat, it's fucking brilliant. I love the cintra."

"Well, it *is* my specialty…"

As the two continued, Kitieri turned to Haldin. The man's jaw worked back and forth, tears shining in his blue eyes as he stared up at Catarva's immortalized form.

"She was… really something," he managed.

Kitieri nodded, moving to stand closer. "She really was."

Haldin lowered his gaze, turning a sad smile on Kitieri. "You're really something, too," he said. "I'm proud of you, Kitieri."

With that, he turned and disappeared into the crowd, leaving Kitieri with a sad smile of her own.

"It's beautiful, isn't it?"

Kitieri turned around, finding Lara on her other side, and her smile widened. In the ten years she'd gotten to know her former Commander, they'd become close friends. Lara's easy smile and genuine nature made her a joy to be around.

"Yeah. It is," she agreed.

"Hey, uh…" Lara looked down at her feet. "I don't want to be too forward, but… there's something I've been wanting to ask you."

"What's that?"

After a short hesitation, Lara leaned closer to Kitieri. "How inappropriate would it be for a civil chief to ask a Councilor on a date?"

Warmth rushed to Kitieri's cheeks, and an unexpected laugh burst from her lips.

"I don't think there's any law against it," she replied. "Yet."

Lara's white smile was blinding as she laughed, eyes crinkling at the corners. "All right, good," she said. "Tomorrow?"

Kitieri nodded, smiling back. "I'd like that."

With a tiny bow of her head, Lara turned away as Jera threw a long, lanky arm around Kitieri's shoulders.

"All right, can we go get something to eat now?" she asked. "I'm *starving*."

Kitieri and Taff exchanged glances, and Vina giggled.

"What?" Jera demanded, throwing out her upturned palms, and Kitieri laughed—fully, genuinely laughed.

"Yeah, let's get something to eat," she replied, turning from the shimmering statue with a final glance.

"You know what I just thought of?" Jera asked with a grin.

"What?"

Jera's eyes sparkled as she looked at Kitieri. "The Manons survived, after all."

ABOUT THE AUTHOR

K. M. Fahy is an American author with a deep love of all things creative. When she's not lost in her fantasy worlds, Fahy performs professionally on the clarinet, teaches a private woodwind studio, and has had the honor of hanging multiple art shows featuring her original acrylic paintings.

Fahy grew up in the rolling hills of southern Illinois, running her horse through the deep woods, learning archery on her dad's recurve bow, and cultivating a love of adventure that would later find its way into the unique worlds of her fantasy novels. Now an avid backpacker in the Rocky Mountains, Fahy draws inspiration from real-life experience to create the deep and relatable characters she always loved to read about as a girl.

"The Lightning's Claim" is Fahy's debut novel, and she is thrilled to embark on this journey with much more to come! Follow her on social media or her website for frequent updates.

https://www.kmfahyauthor.com

facebook.com/kmfahyauthor

instagram.com/k.m.fahy_author